Store Up the Anger

By Wessel Ebersohn

STORE UP THE ANGER
A LONELY PLACE TO DIE

Store Up
THE
ANGER

Wessel Ebersohn

DOUBLEDAY & COMPANY, INC.
GARDEN CITY, NEW YORK
1981

Sam Bhengu is fictitious, as are all the other people in this story, the only
exceptions being historical figures like Nelson Mandela and Beyers Naude.
Their personal characteristics and circumstances, together with the events described, apart from historical events such as the Cato Manor riot, are all
products of the writer's imagination. This story is not derived from a knowledge of actual incidents or real people. The dialogue also is wholly fictitious.

Library of Congress Cataloging in Publication Data:
Ebersohn, Wessel.
    Store up the anger.
    I. Title.
PR9369.3.E24S78   823
ISBN 0-385-17406-3
Library of Congress Catalog Card Number 80-2076

This story is dedicated to the memory of the people of Sophiatown and old Cato Manor. It is also dedicated to those who passed through pain and humiliation at the hands of the security police and were willing to talk about it.

It is true . . . that in the end each man kills himself in his own selected way, fast or slow, soon or late.

—Karl A. Menninger

Store Up the Anger

Sam Bhengu knew that he was dying. Ever since the pain had stopped he had known it. But the reality was not yet upon him. They had killed him and now it was only a matter of waiting, but in his mind it was no more than a vague, almost theoretical realization.

Warrant Officer Fourie was seated at the table near the door, just as he had been for most of the night. In front of him a paperback novel lay open, his right hand pressing the pages flat to make reading easier, but he was not reading. His face was turned toward the darkened window so that he would not be looking at Bhengu or the other policeman. His hair, normally fixed primly into position, was hanging loose over his forehead, the only mark Bhengu could see on him of the night's struggle.

If Bhengu had turned his head a few degrees more he could have seen the second policeman. In the corner of his field of vision he was aware of the indistinct image of the man where he sat rocking slowly back and forth on a steel office chair, his shoulders coming to rest on the wall behind him on each backward cycle. Bhengu was unable to look directly at him. The way he had seen the man's face a few hours before came strongly back to him, but he shut it out of his thinking.

He was surprised at how clear his vision was. Every line and shadow in Fourie's face was clearly delineated. The table at which he was sitting, the window beyond and the desk near the door, were all new, their outlines sharper and their colors more vivid. He tried lifting his shackled hands to be able to see them too, but there was no reaction at all from his arms. They remained unmoving, hanging limply across his stomach, held together by the link of the handcuffs.

How long had it been, he wondered. That part was gone. He remembered what had happened, but the details even of that were uncertain. The wall clock above the door indicated that it was five. He reckoned that meant Brown had been away for seven hours, five hours longer than he had intended. He looked toward the window where Fourie was sitting and thought he saw a softening in the darkness that was more than just the glow of the city lights. Bhengu wondered why the pain had stopped. Everything had become so clear and easily understandable, yet he was going to die and there was no pain. They must have broken whatever it is that feels the pain, he thought. Perhaps a nerve had been severed, cutting off the damaged part from the part that feels the pain.

The small sack, no larger than a man's fist, lay on the floor next to the bed. If his hands had been free and if he had been able to move them, he could have reached out and picked it up. It had toppled over onto its side, spilling some of the beach sand onto the floor. It looked innocent now, like a child's toy, used and discarded. He turned his head away. It was not possible to look at the bag, just as it was not possible to look at the policeman. The two were one in his mind. The policeman was the bag and the bag was the policeman. He could not separate them.

He tried to move, to roll over onto his side. This time there was a faint reaction from the muscles of his body, a small tremor of effort, but the movement was weak and the manacles were holding his feet fast. In order to see his feet he lifted his head slightly. Around each ankle he could see the broadening where his feet must have jerked against the steel cuffs. On the outside of one ankle the skin was torn for perhaps two or three centimeters. The blood had coagulated there forming a dark scarlet line, with a thinner line trailing forward to his toes where the blood had run. His feet were held in place by a steel bar, fitting behind his legs, with a cuff locked into position over each ankle. The feet seemed broad and flat at the end of a foreshortened body, his legs limp and shrunken. His wrists where the cuffs had fitted more closely than around his ankles had swollen so that the bright steel rings now pressed tight against the skin. His chest and stomach were broad and flabby, heaving deeply with each breath. Lifting his head a little further, he could see his penis, little more than a contracted vestige, retaining no interest in life.

Holding up his head was an effort, and he allowed it to drop back onto the mattress. His body looked tired, but it was still a body. His breathing was strong, and all the penis needed was a little of the right inspiration and everything would be all right. And yet he was dying. It was not important. Later it might become so, but for the moment it was of no importance. What was important was the terrible clarity of his senses.

He closed his eyes and listened to the sounds in the office. The chair, rocking slowly back and forth, the steel frame tapping against the wall, and the soft sound of feet moving on the carpet with the movement of the chair, immediately dominated his senses. The sound of breathing was strong, labored but even, and for a moment he imagined that this was also coming from the man on the chair. Then he realized that the sound was synchronized with the movement of his own chest. From beyond the office walls the sounds of the early-morning traffic, the sporadic beat of a steam engine and the crash of metal on metal from the shunting yards in the docks all reached him muffled by the buildings and the closed windows. He thought that he even heard a shouted order coming from the dock area. The coach successfully coupled, the engine's beat became slow and regular, gradually fading as it moved away down the track that passes the small-boat harbor and runs on toward Maydon Wharf. In the silence left by its departure he heard only the muted sounds of the traffic, his own breathing and the movement of the chair, still regular, as it had been when he first became aware of it.

A new sound joined the others. Bhengu distinguished the humming of the elevator. When it stopped he heard the doors open and the sound of Lieutenant Brown's rubber-soled shoes on the tiled floor of the passage.

Brown unlocked the door to let himself in and locked it again from the inside. Bhengu opened his eyes to look at him. He was a man of about thirty with an unlined face, a small rosebud-shaped mouth and a full head of wavy black hair that was always carefully combed. Like Fourie, he wore a light-gray suit. He had come in quickly, smiled briefly and apologetically at the two other policemen and paused for a moment in the center of the office. "How's it going?" he asked.

Fourie had not looked around when he entered, but was still staring at the window. The book he had been reading lay closed on the table. His jacket hung over the chair. Bhengu noticed for the first time how tired he looked. The lines of his face were deeper, more clearly defined, and his skin seemed to be a yellow color. He did not react to Brown's question.

Bhengu could still not look at the other one, but he could almost feel the studiously blank facial expression and the habitual shrug. "In and out," the man's voice said.

Brown's eyes focused consciously on Bhengu for the first time since he had come in. Bhengu saw him come closer and saw the amused good humor in the lieutenant's eyes. Obviously the night had treated him well. Bhengu felt a playful slap against his naked thigh. "How we doing, Sam?"

He looked up at the smiling face. There was no possibility of his answering the question.

Brown raised his eyebrows quizzically and went to sit down at the desk halfway between the bed where Bhengu was manacled and the door. "Not your night for talking, Sam? Well, you're going to do some talking sooner or later. We can keep you here for a long time, you know."

"How was it?" It was the voice of the one who was rocking on the chair.

Brown looked at him uncomprehendingly for a moment, then he grinned, a warm knowing expression. "Not bad. She's one of those that can't ever get enough. She would have kept me in bed forever, but I said to her, Christ, your husband's coming home. Do you want me to sit here until he walks in and finds me? Not a damn. I'm getting out of here."

"Are you going back?"

"Sometime maybe. But not for a while. Too much of a good thing stops being a good thing. Somebody starts to notice you leaving the apartment every morning, and then where the hell are you?"

"Did you put a pillow under her?" Bhengu could hear the eagerness in his voice. The sound of the chair's movement had stopped. "She's got a flat ass."

"Bugger off," Brown said. "Everything quiet here? No trouble with Sam?"

Fourie's eyes took in Brown's face, moved to the one on the chair and then back to Brown. The one on the chair spoke. "No trouble. What trouble could he give us?"

"Did he say anything?"

Fourie's eyes again examined the face of the other policeman. "Nothing," the one on the chair said.

"You question him?"

"You said we mustn't."

"How about some coffee? Whose turn is it?" Fourie got an electric kettle out of a steel cabinet next to the window and left the office to fill it. "Why's Len so quiet?" Brown asked.

"Doesn't feel like saying anything, I suppose."

"Fuck it, that woman," Brown said, trying to revive the other man's interest. This time he got no reply. Fourie came back and plugged in the kettle. "Sorry we can't give you any coffee, Sam. But they said nothing to eat or drink. You'll get something during the day."

Bhengu looked curiously at the lieutenant's good-humored face. He had never seen Brown looking more pleased with himself. It was strange that they should be addressing him at all, though. They were among those that were planning for the next day, the next week or the next year, even the next cup of coffee. To them a cup of coffee was still a matter of importance.

For the first time since his arrest, Bhengu's nakedness did not bother him. That he was naked and they were clothed now only emphasized the distance between them. He knew that in their terms Brown was close to him, no more than two or three paces away, and yet he had the sensation of a wide empty space separating them, making it impossible for them to reach him, or touch him in any way. The policeman's face was puzzled. "All right, Sam. This is one of your quiet days, huh? You aren't going to talk to us today?" The puzzlement changed to chagrin and the policeman looked away. "All right, Sam," he said.

From outside the sound of the morning traffic had become louder and more consistent. Through the window Bhengu could see the rooftop silhouettes of the old shop buildings at the bottom of West Street, the sky behind them a soft gray. In another hour or so the day staff would come in and it would start again. The difference was that now their questions

no longer mattered. They could ask him what they liked and do
what they liked to him. They would not be able to harm him
anymore. Bhengu knew that he had no further reason to fear
them. He closed his eyes again and listened to the sound of a
teaspoon clinking in the bottom of a cup as Fourie stirred the
coffee. The mild early-morning chill of the tropical night lay
lightly on his skin, drawing it taut across his chest and raising
his nipples like those of a woman who had been aroused.
That's all that is aroused, he thought. Will I ever have another
woman? No. This was it. There would be no more women, as
there would be no more of anything else. He tried to remember the last woman, but something in his mind impeded
the thought. As clear as his thinking was about the present, so
impossible was it for him to remember. But there were images,
flickering disjointed pictures—thighs rubbing warmly against
each other; a stomach twitching convulsively in orgasm; the
curve of a back, shoulders moving and stretching with
pleasure . . .

At once Sam Bhengu did not want to die. He wanted a
woman, once more. Just to hold and be held, to be warm
around and inside her once more; just once more would be
enough. Was there a particular woman? He tried to remember, but could not. He tried to imagine a woman on the
bed with him. He tried to imagine her skin against his, pressing smoothly against him from his shoulder down to his feet,
but he was unable to. There was not the slightest stirring in his
genitals.

The medium through which Bhengu's thoughts traveled became perfect so that each mental process was set apart, isolated from the others. Even the air in the room seemed
clearer, the objects and people standing out in sharp relief,
somehow intensified, seeming to reveal some part of themselves to him that previously had been hidden.

The day staff was coming in. The elevator was moving almost continuously as the building filled up. The door had already opened twice to let in new arrivals. Bhengu listened to the sounds of the conversation as the interrogation team took over. He knew them all by their voices. He picked out that of Major George Engelbrecht, the officer in charge of the interrogation. "That bloke who got Taylor could shoot straight, hey?" Some of his juniors laughed dutifully at the remark, the laughter tailing off into other sorties on the same subject.

"That man knew how to use a rifle."

"I would've given what to see that kaffir-brother's face at that moment."

"He was the most surprised dead Communist in Africa."

Bhengu had known Taylor for five years before the white man's banning order had been imposed. The order had restricted him to the municipal limits of Durban, prevented him from being in the company of more than one person at a time, prescribed that he report to the local police station weekly and spend every night in his own home. That way banned people were always sitting targets. When the killer called they would always be at home, as Taylor had been. The shot that had killed him had been fired through a glass panel in his front door late at night when he had gone to investigate a noise on the front porch. It had happened three months before the banning order was due to expire.

With his eyes closed the room was full of the sounds of their voices and the sounds they made moving around the room: chairs being shifted, a drawer opening and being closed again, the door . . . His ears, like his other senses, seemed to have increased their scope, magnifying the sounds until they pressed in upon him, crowding the air all around.

He opened his eyes and seeing them seemed to bring them back into perspective. They were again a small group of men, not the overpowering presence he felt when he could not see them. Engelbrecht was at the desk where Brown had been sitting earlier. He was reading the night shift's entry in the diary. Brown was next to him, standing carefully erect in the presence of his superior officer. A small group, all in civilian clothes, were gathered around the table where Fourie was still seated. They were all members of the interrogation team, excepting the one who had been rocking on the chair and now stood nearest to Bhengu with his back to him, his broad fleshy torso cutting out Bhengu's view of Fourie. Among all the voices he could not hear Fourie's. What had taken place during the night seemed to have removed the small dark-haired policeman's desire for socializing. "All quiet during the night?" Engelbrecht was asking.

"Altogether quiet, Major," Brown replied.

"Nothing to eat or drink?"

"Nothing, Major."

"Did he pee?"

"Just once."

"Have you got it?"

"In the jar."

"Away you go then. Go get some sleep. You'll have to stay on nights until we've got what we want. You may have to do more than just watch him."

Fourie left first, waving his right hand in a halfhearted gesture and glancing quickly at Engelbrecht. "Good-bye, Major." Brown left straight after him, still in good spirits, aiming a playful punch at one of the warrant officers in the interrogation team. The other one stayed longer, talking to the men around the table, keeping his back to Bhengu as if he did not want to look at him either. Eventually he left, pausing for a moment in the doorway, still facing the group at the table. He was carrying his jacket over one shoulder and the back of his shirt was crinkled and marked with dried sweat. There was something about his sweat. Bhengu could not remember what it was. He knew there was something . . .

Four policemen remained in the office. Major Engelbrecht sat, sprawling, at the desk, his right knee protruding above its surface, resting against it, the fingers of his left hand trailing loose on the carpet. He was a tall, lean man, his face also lean except for a broad fleshy nose. His lips were thin, almost non-existent, and above the upper lip he wore a pencil-line mustache. No one ever saw him without the sunglasses except when he was cleaning them, and at such times he looked only at what he was doing. Bhengu wondered if he wore the sunglasses when he was in bed with his wife. A woman had once told him that his eyes were wild during intercourse. She had said that the pupils dilated when he entered her. He imagined that Engelbrecht's wife saw nothing but her own reflection in the sunglasses.

The other three policemen were all still at the table. Engelbrecht was not a man who encouraged familiarity. Captain Gerrit Strydom, the senior among them, was wearing a dark pin-striped suit and had not yet removed his jacket. He was pale, freckled, red-haired and solemn-looking. In appearance he could have been a dominie of the Dutch Reformed Church, of which he was a member. Warrant Officers Piet Kleynhans and André de Jager were both young policemen, eager to do well, whose faces did not yet display the marks of their trade: the flat inscrutable eyes that give nothing away, tell nothing of the men to whom they belong.

Bhengu turned his head to take in the floor, but the little bag of sand was gone. While his eyes had been closed, the one who was so partial to it must have taken it away. He saw Engelbrecht turn and nod to one of the warrant officers. The young man came forward and bent over him. He could smell his aftershave lotion, the sharp musk perfume tickling the insides of his nostrils. The light from the window reflected from the chromed key. He felt the cuffs yield on his wrists and a moment later on his ankles. The warrant officer went back to the table.

"Come and sit over here, Sam," Engelbrecht said. They had brought up a chair so that he could sit opposite Engelbrecht.

The security policeman was far away from him. Bhengu knew that the few paces that seemed to separate them were an illusion. For him to get up and walk to the table would not have brought them any closer together. He looked at Engelbrecht, but he could not see the man, only the reflected image of the fluorescent lights in the sunglasses. "Come and sit here, Sam."

There's no point, Bhengu thought. We had little to say to each other previously. Now there is nothing.

"Don't play games with me, Sam. Come and sit over here. You don't want to be shackled again, do you?"

He looked at the chair they had moved into position for him. It was a tubular-steel office chair, a very ordinary chair to sit on, especially when you considered the unusual nature of their business. The other three policemen, just behind Engelbrecht, all had their attention concentrated on Bhengu. Strydom looked composed and severe, his arms rigid at his sides and his fists tightly clenched. The two young warrant officers looked stern and determined.

"All right, Sam. You want us to drag you to the chair, then we'll drag you." He half-turned his head and nodded in the direction of the two warrant officers. The two young men were next to Bhengu in a moment and lifting him to his feet, then they were dragging him to the chair, his legs reacting lethargically to the forced motion, his penis flapping against his thighs like a piece of old leather.

From close by, Engelbrecht was as anonymous as he had been from across the room, his sunglasses hiding his eyes and everything behind them. Strydom was seated at the corner of the desk next to him, taking off his jacket carefully and removing a spot of fluff from one of the shoulders before hanging it over the back of the chair. Looking down, Bhengu could see the feet of the two warrant officers, close behind him, one on either side.

"You are a man of violence, Sam," Engelbrecht said. His voice was soft and neutral. In common with his face, it betrayed nothing. "You parade as a man of peace, but you are nothing of the sort. You seek to overthrow the State by violent means. I have proof of it . . ." The smooth soft voice moved on from word to word, accusingly, without emphasis or excitement. Bhengu had heard it all before, during seven previous detentions. "You pretend to espouse nonviolence, but that is only a front. You deliberately further the aims of communism. We know that . . ." The major's thin lips barely moved as he spoke, the words little more than a murmur. This was the introduction. Engelbrecht always started an interrogation slowly, very often with a sermon, working himself gradually into a condition of righteous self-justification. Bhengu wondered if the security policemen of any other country preached to their prisoners. Jason Gumede, who had been a theology student before his banning, had once told Bhengu that during interrogations he spent hours arguing theology with them. In their own way Engelbrecht and his colleagues saw their role in life as making the republic safe for Christianity. "The Bible speaks against violence," Engelbrecht was saying. "The commandment says, 'Thou shalt not kill.'"

Bhengu thought about the youngsters of Soweto who had been killed in the rebellion. He thought about those who had been removed from their homes in the early-morning hours and had never come back. He thought about himself and the one whose name and face he must still shut out of his conscious thinking. No, he thought. I'm going to make it. I'm going to make it, if only to be there when you bastards get yours.

He was leaning forward in the chair, his shoulders rounded. His arms hung between his thighs, shielding his genitals. His head was very heavy. Someone had fastened a weight to the base of his skull, forcing it forward and down. In order to see Engelbrecht's face at all he had to concentrate on lifting his head, struggling against the weight. He tried to pull back his shoulders, but they stayed in the same position.

"You said you went to Johannesburg to patch up trouble in Convention?" Engelbrecht paused for confirmation. At the angle he was holding his head, Bhengu could again see the fluorescent lights reflected in his sunglasses. He wished that the glasses could be removed so that he could see into the man's eyes. He wondered if he would see a soul within them or if the other man was not a man at all, but some sort of single-minded question-asking machine. "That's what you said yesterday. You said that you went to Johannesburg to patch up trouble within Convention." Again Engelbrecht waited for a reply. "Is that right, Sam? Is that why you went to Johannesburg?" The voice was still calm and even. "Are you going to answer me?" Bhengu wondered at the mental impediment that would result in such a manner of speaking without moving the lips. "You'll have to answer sooner or later. I can keep you here for as long as I like. I can keep you here and I can keep you naked, until you tell me what I want to know."

No, you can't, Bhengu thought. You can't keep me here. You can keep me for the moment, but you can't keep me for as long as you like. You can keep me until it's time, but you can't keep me any longer than that.

Angered by his thoughts, he resisted them, telling himself again that it was not so, that everything was going to be all right. He had the will to live, and that was all that mattered . . .

"You admitted that you drew up the pamphlet. It was the August eighteenth pamphlet, wasn't it? It was all about bodies lying dead in the street, wasn't it?" The voice had risen fractionally, something of the detached coolness having gone. "You don't have to answer me, Sam. You can hold out a while longer. But you will answer. Smith heard you talk to Jele about it. We have Smith's confession, signed and witnessed."

Smith's confession? Bhengu wondered how it had been obtained, if they did have it. If it had been after something like last night, then it was all right. The little yellow man would have signed anything and not known what he was doing. Willie Smith would have held out as long as any man. Bhengu wondered if he might have held out too long. Willie might also be dying. Govender had held out too long and had been found hanging in his cell.

"Do you think we're going to allow you to endanger our women and children?" Strydom was speaking for the first time, his words neat and precise, his eyes looking straight into Bhengu's. He was the Special Branch man who, more than any of the others, really believed that what he was doing was his Christian duty and had to be done well. "What sort of men would we be if we allowed you to bring violence and destruction to our country and endanger the lives of our women and children? Think about that. That's why we aren't going to let you out of here until you tell us what we want to know."

"You didn't stop in Johannesburg." Engelbrecht had reimposed the detached note on his voice. "You drove through the Free State to Kimberley. You went to see Winnie Mandela. You went to see Sobukwe. Why? Why did you go to see them? What were you up to, Sam?"

Sobukwe, Mandela—the names held an echo in his mind.

Somewhere far away in his experience the two names had had a meaning. The sounds of them, lingering in his consciousness, were familiar. Exactly how he had heard of them or what they meant to him he could not remember.

"You are going to tell me, Sam. You are going to tell me today. You've been wasting enough of my time. You went there to form a United Revolutionary Front, isn't it? Isn't it, Sam?" The coolness of the voice was only part of a thin and fragile layer that covered what was inside. In the man's voice Bhengu could hear the layer cracking. His eyes were held by the lips, moving fractionally more now. Bhengu wondered if, when the control went and the major went over to shouting, he would be able to shout without moving his lips. "Isn't it, Sam?" The voice was louder and more bitter and the lips were moving more. For him to have shouted through closed lips would have been too much to expect, Bhengu reckoned. "Isn't it, Sam?"

Strydom's eyes were gray points of steel in the artificial light. Bhengu felt that here, at least, he could see the man. The look in Strydom's eyes troubled him. It was not hatred. He had looked for hatred, expecting to find it there. It was rather an unyielding severity, like the eyes of an overly harsh schoolmaster. Bhengu had sinned and had to be punished. It was not a matter for hatred.

Engelbrecht had a sheet of paper in one hand and was holding it out to him. Only the little smile on his thin lips showed his triumph. "You want to read it, Sam?" The voice was light, almost playful. "Smith's confession? You want to see what he told us?" Engelbrecht held it out until it was only a few centimeters from his face. The statement was on a foolscap sheet, filled with double-spaced typing, and at the bottom was what appeared to be a shaky version of Willie Smith's signature. "You want to read it, Sam? Read it, Sam." The words and letters ran into each other, back and forth across the page until they became a row of blurred gray lines, the letters pushing along from left to right until they tumbled off the edge, spilling onto the floor. Eventually Engelbrecht withdrew it. The smile on his mouth had grown wider. It was the closest to an expression of real pleasure Bhengu had ever seen on his face. He could see the security policeman's teeth for the first time since he had known him. "Well, Sam? You've read it, now what do you say? There's no use shutting up now. We've got you, Sam. Make it easy on yourself. Admit what you did in Johannesburg." The way Bhengu's shoulders were hanging forward had started to worry him. He tried again to pull them back, but again nothing happened. Perhaps if I concentrate, he thought. He tried his left shoulder alone, concentrating on the back muscles that would normally control it. But it seemed to be disconnected, like the part of his brain that normally experienced pain. "You aren't getting away with this," Engelbrecht was shouting and he had to open his mouth wide to do it. One of his hands was raised to partially cover his mouth, as if he was ashamed of opening it so wide.

"There was a second reason you went to Johannesburg," Strydom said softly. The soft unemotional voice was far more menacing than the major's shouting had been. Engelbrecht might enjoy the power he exercised over prisoners, but Strydom would take little pleasure in it. Despite that, he would do whatever he felt was necessary, and possibly more than was necessary. "You had to get away from her, didn't you? You can't sustain a relationship with a woman, can you? You had to go to Johannesburg to get away from her."

✠ ✠

"Here comes your lovely brother," Sam heard his father say.
"Look at him," Winifred said. "I'm so embarrassed I can die."

"Bam, bam, bam," Sam said, punching at his father's knees with a succession of right swings. He was unable to use his left hand because he had his shorts clamped tightly under that arm.

"Why didn't you put on your pants before you came out?"

"Bam, bam," Sam said, getting past his father's guard and landing a right hook on his kneecap.

"He's so tribal," Winifred said.

Sam's shorts fell to the ground as he forgot them for a moment to try a left cross. Leaving them on the ground, he scrambled onto the bus bench, working his way in between his father and sister. "No," Winifred said. "First put on your pants."

"Sam, get your pants on," his father said.

"Bam, bam," Sam said, working to his father's stomach with both hands. Then, knowing how far he could afford to push things, he slid to the ground and started struggling into his shorts.

"Look at him showing everybody, just like the children who don't go to school," Winifred said. "You wouldn't think he's a Christian."

"Come on, Winifred," his father said. "You bathed with him the other night."

"There was no light in the kitchen and the water was black."

The motor bus turned the corner and came down the narrow road toward them, its engine roaring, the sound amplified by the buildings on either side. The large crowd of people, who had been waiting for it, started shuffling forward in preparation for boarding. Some had been sitting on boxes or suitcases filled with their belongings. A group of old women, wearing blankets around their shoulders, had been sitting on the edge of the pavement and were now struggling to their feet, their broad buttocks waddling like the tails of a flock of ducks going for a walk. Sam's father helped him into his shorts and then picked up the suitcase. Herding the children before him, he started edging his way into the crowd to get a good position when the bus stopped.

"Abednego told a lie so that he wouldn't have to go to jail," Sam confided to his father.

"What's that, Sam?"

"Abednego was caught by the police. So he told a lie so he wouldn't have to go to jail."

Sam's father was a tall, broad-shouldered man with even African features. His looks were spoiled by a lower lip over which he seemed to have little control. It drooped open much of the time and quivered nervously when he was under any sort of strain. Sam was looking at his face and he saw the lip quiver. He was not sure what it meant this time, but he knew that normally it meant that something unpleasant was happening or about to happen. "All right, Sam," his father said.

They got onto the bus and struggled down the aisle between pushing travelers and hand-held suitcases. Winifred, who was two years older than Sam and who he thought looked very pretty today in her red dress, had taken his hand. She saw herself as her brother's protector. "Abednego told a lie." Sam was determined to discuss the matter fully. "If you were going to jail, would you tell a lie, if you knew one?"

"You must never tell lies, Sam."

"But, if you were going to jail, would you tell a lie if you knew one?"

"Everybody knows a lie," Winifred said.

"*I* don't," Sam said.

The bus was moving and Sam's father had a seat, but he and Winifred had to stand between his father's knees. A very fat woman was standing just in front of him, his face coming level with her huge buttocks. From inside her clothing the smell of layer upon layer of unwashed sweat reached into his nostrils. "Does this mama wash?" Sam asked his father.

"Quiet," his father whispered.

"But does she?"

"Keep quiet, Sam."

"I don't think she does."

"I can die," Winifred said.

Inside the bus the people were packed close together, all the standing room having been taken. Everyone seemed to be talking. Dense waves of sound surrounded the children: loud voices speaking Zulu, Sotho, Tswana, Xhosa and English competing with each other for a very limited range of intelligibility. In the seat behind them an old man was smoking a pipe, filling the air with a dense fog of tobacco smoke. No part of the scene was new to them. Having always lived in townships, they had been part of crowded gatherings at weddings, funerals, parties, football matches, on public transport, and in the house they shared with three other families. They had both been born in crowded rooms, had lived their short lives under those circumstances, and had come to see being crowded as the normal human condition.

"I want something to eat," Sam whispered to his sister. "Eggs."

"Where will Papa get money for eggs?" Winifred's voice was contemptuous of her brother's lack of consideration.

"Do eggs cost a lot?"

"Yes. And they make me want to vomit."

"Eggs?" Sam could not believe it.

"Yes."

"Not eggs," Sam said with conviction.

Winifred brought her earnest brown face right up to her brother's. "It was terrible what you did at the bus stop, taking off your pants. I nearly died."

"What about you?" Sam asked, his eyes sparkling with six-year-old malevolence.

"I don't do that."

"You and Joyce got dressed in the room together and you could see each other."

"It was just me and Joyce."

"You looked at each other."

"We did not."

"You looked at her."

"I did not."

"She saw your titties and you saw her titties."

"Keep quiet, Sam. You don't know what you're talking about."

"Stop annoying your sister, Sam," his father said. "She hasn't got titties yet."

"When she's thirteen she'll have small ones," Sam said.

"Shut up, Sam. What do you know? Oh, Papa, if anyone hears him I'll die."

"Be quiet now, Sam," his father said. "Remember your sister's a lady."

Sam waited until his father's attention had found some other point on which to focus and he was staring straight in front of him. Then he pressed his lips against Winifred's ear. "You're not a lady. You're a big fat pest," he whispered. Winifred drew away from him, her mouth hanging wide open, scandalized. "And also you don't know what you talking about self."

"I know all about those things." Winifred's tone of voice was outraged.

"From Lord Jesus made me I know everything," Sam said.

"That shows what you know. Lord Jesus didn't make you. Mama and Papa did. And I know how they made you."

"Swear."

"I swear by my cross and my Bible."

"Swear by your kiss to God."

"I swear by my kiss to God."

"You know nothing." Sam was certain of it.

"I know more than you'll ever know."

"I know this bus is going slow."

"Anyone knows that."

Leaning past the buttocks that were blocking his field of vision, Sam could see down into the road. The bus was struggling up a long incline in low gear and a line of cars was coming quickly and effortlessly past on the outside. He looked at the succession of white faces at the steering wheels of the cars. He knew that life was wonderful for white people; just about perfect, in fact. There was no bitterness in Sam's thought. It was a simple fact of life, like the fact that Winifred was his sister. "Look at them all coming past," he said to Winifred.

"Cars go faster than buses," Winifred said.

"Anyone knows that," Sam said. "If they try to pass us the driver must go to the one side, then if the cars go to the other side, we must go to the other side, then if they go back to the one side, we must go back to the one side. Then they can't get past us."

"The driver will get into trouble."

"But the cars will have to stay at the back."

The bus had stopped and everyone was getting off. Sam's father was herding Sam and his sister along the aisle until they hopped off the boarding platform into the roadside dust and ran clear of the crowd. He came up to them, looking hot in his green tweed jacket and his wide spotted tie. Winifred had told Sam that their father's tie was the most beautiful thing she had ever seen. He had the suitcase in one hand and took Sam's hand in the other. "Take Sam's other hand, Winifred," he said.

Sam held his free hand behind his back. "It doesn't matter," he said.

"Give her your hand, Sam."

"It doesn't matter, Papa."

"Sam, give her your hand or get a hiding."

Sam glanced at his father's face and saw the lower lip quiver for a moment. He gave Winifred his free hand and they waited on the edge of the pavement for a car to pass. Ahead of them and stretching up a gradual slope on either side of the road was Sophiatown. Sam could see the corrugated-iron rooftops where they crested the hill and disappeared from sight into the valley beyond. A very old, barely legible sign at the street corner told him that they were in Meyer Street. For as far as he could see the road was tarred, not at all like Alexandra, where a cloud of yellow dust almost always hung over the township, stirred up by passing cars and the crowds of people, most of whom were children. In Alexandra, at Sam's eye level, you were always breathing dust.

Most of the houses bordered the road directly, without gardens, and were neat brick buildings, recently painted and topped with corrugated-iron roofs. Others were no more than shanties, unpainted, the plaster coming away, some of the walls made of rusting iron sheets. Nowhere at all could Sam see anything growing. At a tap next to the road a string of children between the ages of five and fifteen were waiting to fill all sorts of containers. Some of the older ones had buckets, or steel drums from which the tops had been cut away to turn them into buckets. One small boy whose nose and mouth were connected by two gray streams of mucus held a used jam tin in both hands. Sam had visited Mama Mabaso with his parents previously, so he knew that the children at the tap did not live in the houses on either side. They were the children of the tenants who lived in the rooms behind the houses.

Sam walked a few steps behind his father and sister. He watched his father's long-legged walk, seeming to go up on the balls of his feet at each stride, and tried to imitate it. But then he remembered that Winifred had laughed at him when at other times he had tried to walk like his father, so he stopped doing it and concentrated on taking long strides instead. He wondered what she would say if she saw him taking long strides. He knew that she would laugh, so he stopped doing that as well. Despite his attempts to hide it, Sam thought very highly of Winifred and her opinions. She was walking directly in front of him, the sides of her skirt flapping and the tight little plaits that stood away from her head in all directions vibrating stiffly with each step. Far ahead he could see the shelf of rock, yellow with dust from its own weathered surface, against which Meyer Street ended. He remembered that Mama Mabaso lived with her son, Robert, and also Little-Mama Zibi and Papa Phineas, who were poor and would have been tenants if they had not lived with Mama Mabaso. Her house was the last one before the rock shelf. Sam could see the front of the house, neatly painted white, its roof red and overhanging more than the other houses.

Sam ran a few steps to catch up to his sister. "I can see the house where Mama Mabaso stays," he said.

"You can't," Winifred said. "It's too far."

"I can see it. There it is with the white in front."

"Papa, Sam can't see the house yet, can he?"

"Right at the end," Sam said, "with the white in front and the red roof sticking out."

"That's right," his father said.

"Who saw it first?" Sam asked his sister. When she made no reply he asked, "Who's the best at seeing things first?"

"Not you."

"I saw it first. Who thought best which house it is?"

"Oh, shut up, Sam."

"Who's the champion at seeing things far away? Who's the best leader for seeing things?"

"Keep quiet, Sam," his father said. "It's not important."

"I'm the best," Sam whispered in his sister's ear.

Winifred pulled her head away and looked up at her father. "Sam gave me a dirty look on the bus," she said. "He looked up and down me, then he looked away. That's how you give a person a dirty look." Her father did not react in any way. His attention seemed to be with the white house at the end of the road, his eyebrows drawn together in a frown. "Is Mama dead or what?" Winifred asked suddenly. It was a question she had been wanting to ask her father for a long time. Sam watched his father's face. He and Winifred had often talked about their mother, but neither had ever had the courage to approach their father about it. Without having a rational reason for it, each felt that discussing their mother would anger him. Their father glanced down at Winifred, the frown around his eyes unchanged. "She never visits us anymore. Is she dead or what?" Winifred continued. Sam only remembered his mother as a large, rather distant presence who had never been with them for very long at a time, but Winifred had told him about her. All the things she had told him were about how sweet and kind their mother was and how beautiful, and Sam was too young to realize that they were all his sister's inventions. "We never visit her either," Winifred was saying.

"We will," their father said without looking down.

"Where is she?"

"In Zululand."

"Why does she always stay in Zululand? Why doesn't she stay with us?"

"She likes it there. She's lived all her life in Zululand."

"I will like it there too. I wish I could live all my life in Zululand. Sam too. We would like to live all our life in Zululand—where Mama is."

"Yes," Sam said.

"Be quiet now," their father said.

"But will she visit us again?"

"Be quiet now."

"Can you write her address for us, Papa? Then we'll write her a letter," Winifred persisted.

"Be quiet. I don't want to talk about this."

"You don't want to get in trouble with Mama—I'm wrong or right?" Sam asked.

"Be quiet both of you. It doesn't help to talk about some things."

"Papa . . ." Winifred's voice was uncertain, the word only half formed.

"Yes. What do you want now?" her father shouted. Winifred's face immediately became blank of expression as she withdrew beyond the range of his anger. "What do you want? Speak, child. What do you want now?" Winifred withdrew further from her father, her face an expressionless front behind which she could hide in safety. She had slowed down and was walking further from him. Sam was walking so close to his sister that their arms touched. "Speak, child. Tell me what you want." Their father's voice was loud and insistent, but Winifred could no more have answered than she could have arranged getting her mother back. At once his voice changed and he spoke more gently. "All right, tell me what you want. Tell me, girl." But Winifred looked straight ahead, showing no sign that she had heard him. "Winifred, what is it? You can tell me." He was pleading with her. "Tell me, girl. What is it? All right, we'll soon be at Mama Mabaso's place."

The walls of Mama Mabaso's house were so white that Sam was sure his eyes would hurt if he looked at them long enough. He and Winifred climbed the broad steps and waited behind their father while he knocked on the door. The door was opened by a small, very thin woman who held her mouth pinched primly together as if she was always sucking up liquid through a straw. She was dressed in a broad-pleated brown skirt and a bright-yellow blouse. Diagonally across the blouse from shoulder to hip a blue sash with black embroidery advertised the name BETHANIE WOMEN'S CLUB. She opened her eyes wide and cocked her head to one side. "Well, if it isn't Mobiki and the children," she said, stepping aside for them to enter.

"Hello, Little-Mama," Sam's father said.

As they entered, Little-Mama bent forward, bringing her face close to those of the children without touching them. "And how are you two?"

Winifred dropped her head slightly and looked at Sam out of the corner of her eyes. "We are well, Little-Mama," she said.

"That's good," Little-Mama Zibi said, straightening up. "I suppose you've come to see Mama Mabaso. Nobody ever comes to see me." Sam looked up at his father's face and saw his embarrassed frown. Before his father could reply Little-Mama Zibi continued, "It's all right. You don't have to say it. Mama Mabaso is out in the back with the tenants." She led the way down the passage to the back of the house. As she walked she swayed to the rhythm of a melody only she could hear, the full skirt swinging to and fro around her little stick-like body.

"Are you going to a club meeting today, Little-Mama?" Sam's father asked.

"I'm just trying on my new uniform. We're having a parade on Saturday. You and the children should come." Sam's father looked quickly down at his feet without answering. "We're starting at Freedom Square and going up Meyer Street to Gerty Street and then down to Freedom Square again. We've got a nice band, with saxophones, the lot. You must bring the children."

Sam looked into the open doors of each room as they passed. He saw carpets on the floors, a bright green-and-yellow coverlet on a bed, a painting of moonlight on water, highly polished straight-back wooden chairs around a long dining-room table, and a radio-phonograph with a roll-up top and a place for records underneath. To his eyes it was all wonderful. It was even better than his father's other house had been, the one where they had stayed for a short time while his mother had been with them, before they went to stay in the room again.

At the back of the house the kitchen was part of a long glass-enclosed stoep. On the far side of the stoep a lean teen-age boy, wearing a white sweater and faded denim jeans, was stretched out full-length on a narrow bed, looking up at the ceiling. He got quickly to his feet when they came in. "Hello, Robert," Sam heard his father say.

Robert responded by shrugging and grinning shamefacedly down at his feet as Sam's father nodded toward him and passed out of the door into the backyard behind Little-Mama Zibi. As soon as Sam's father had gone his face became stern, looking suspiciously at Sam and his sister with one eye closed, possibly appraising them. To Sam it was a very superior way of looking at people. He resolved to practice looking out of one eye every time he got the chance. "You see this?" Robert said, pointing to the kitchen cupboards. "American kitchen." Sam and Winifred looked at the cupboards and then back at Robert. "You see this?" Robert took hold of the denim material of his jeans between the thumb and forefinger of one hand. "American blue jeans."

Sam was admiring Robert's American blue jeans when Winifred pulled him out of the back door. They stopped at the top of the back stairs. In the yard below, a long, narrow red-brick building like a barracks held six or seven separate rooms around which a sketchy lawn grew. The only other vegetation was a smallish oak tree right at the back, up against the fence. In front of the rooms three middle-aged women were bending over tin tubs, washing the clothing which, if they were without a man, was probably their only source of income. Nearby eight or nine near-naked children were amusing themselves with simple games not requiring more complicated toys than a piece of plank or a smooth stone. Next to one of the doorways an old man in tattered unwashed clothing sat smoking a pipe.

From out of one of the rooms came another woman, taller and broader than the washerwomen. As soon as she saw Sam's father she started toward him, threading her way nimbly between the playing children and drying damp hands on the back of her dress. At the sight of her, Sam and his sister went down the steps after their father.

Mama Mabaso could have been any age between thirty and sixty. To Sam she was large, invulnerable, all-knowing and possibly eternal. When he had heard the name "Mother of God" at school he had always thought of her. Her face was broad, the cheekbones so high and prominent that they seemed to force her eyes to slant upward on either side, her nose wide, the nostrils large and flaring. She was shouting before she was halfway across the yard. "Lucy, Mina, look who's here." The washerwomen stopped working to look in the direction of the newcomers. A few heads appeared in doorways and the old man looked up with sleepy drugged interest. The children swarmed after Mama Mabaso, eager to be part of any new thing. Sam slipped in behind Winifred for protection and took her hand. He saw Little-Mama Zibi go back into the house, looking grieved at not receiving any attention herself. Mama Mabaso stopped in front of them, her huge face alight with pleasure. She shouted over her shoulder. "It's my sister's child." The children of the yard stood in a circle around Winifred and Sam, ragged clothing that had not been intended to fit the wearers fastened in place by safety pins, makeshift rope belts or buttons that had been moved to positions where they would be more effective. Sam felt ashamed of his well-fitting shirt, shorts, shoes and socks.

Mama Mabaso was talking to his father. "What are you doing here, Mobiki?"

"What am I doing here? I have come to see you, Mama."

"That's good. I hope there is not trouble, Mobiki."

Sam looked at his father's face. He saw the lower lip quiver again and he was sure that Mama Mabaso had looked straight into his father's thoughts. Sam hated the way his father's lip quivered. He wished it would stop.

"I would like to speak with you, Mama," his father said.

"Of course you can speak with me, my child." Mama Mabaso's attention turned to Winifred and Sam. "And who is this?"

Winifred bit her lip, half-smiled and looked down at her feet. "Winifred, Mama."

"It can't be Winifred. You're so big. When I last saw Winifred she was a little girl. Tell me your name."

Winifred's smile grew slightly, she glanced quickly up at Mama Mabaso's face and then down at her feet again. "It is Winifred, Mama."

"It is Winifred. How did you get so big, Winifred?" She reached out a huge brown hand and laid it on Winifred's head.

Winifred said nothing. The sidelong glance she gave Sam said, I can die.

Mama Mabaso seemed to notice Sam for the first time. "This big man can't be Sam." Sam looked at Winifred and sucked in his cheeks to stop himself from smiling. "Where have you been, Sam? Why haven't you come to visit me?"

"I'm here, Mama," Sam said.

Mama Mabaso laughed loudly, her broad mouth opening generously. "I'm here, Mama," she repeated. "I see you, Sam. I'm glad you're here."

"Mama, if I can speak with you . . ." Sam's father's voice was anxious.

"You can speak with me, Mobiki." She turned to lead them into the house. For the first time she noticed the suitcase Sam's father was carrying and she looked quickly at his face, her expression becoming troubled. Then she walked ahead of them up the stairs and into the back doorway where Robert was sitting on the bed again, still surveying the children critically out of one eye. "Robert, did you see who's come to visit us?" Mama Mabaso asked him. Robert got to his feet again and this time greeted Sam's father formally, then looked sternly at the children. Sam stayed close to Winifred, who was looking straight ahead of her as if she had never been afraid of anything in all her life. Mama Mabaso crouched before the children, bringing her face down to their level, her large soft breasts heaving at the effort. "Children, you go and play outside while I talk to your father. Sam, look after your sister." Sam sucked in his cheeks again. He knew Winifred would be angry at the idea. "Robert will also be outside." She gave Robert a look that held an instruction in it. "If you need anything, you can ask him."

Outside, Robert sat down against the wall of the rooms just like the old man. He closed both his eyes as if he was going to sleep and had forgotten about Sam and his sister. The two children came to a stop close together near the back door of the house, but everyone else seemed to have forgotten about them. The children of the yard had gone back to their games, the women to their washing, and the old man to his dagga or alcohol-inspired dreams. Sam looked up at the house. He could see his father and Mama Mabaso still standing where they had left them in the kitchen. His father was talking very quickly and looking down at his hands. Mama Mabaso was looking intently at his face, and the troubled look that Sam had seen on her face when she first noticed the suitcase was still there. "Sam, I want to vomit," Winifred said.

"Why?" Sam asked.

"I don't know why. I just want to vomit. Where's a place?"

Sam went up to Robert, who still had his eyes closed. "Where's the lavatory, please?" he asked. Robert's eyes remained closed as if he had heard nothing. "Could you tell me where the lavatory is, please?" Robert opened one eye and looked at Sam through it. Sam knew that he had to learn to do that in just the same way. Then Robert raised an arm and pointed to a far corner of the yard. "Thank you," Sam said. Taking Winifred by the hand, he led her in the direction Robert had pointed. "It's over there," he told her. "Try to hold it inside until we get there."

"I don't know if I can."

"Well, try."

They found the lavatory at the end of the row of rooms. Sam held the door open for Winifred to enter, then he waited outside for her. From inside he could hear the choking, gargling noises interspersed with sobbing that always went with Winifred's vomiting. She stayed inside a long time with Sam standing guard at the door, worrying in case someone else might want to use the lavatory, knowing that he would have to stop them from entering while Winifred was inside and not feeling sure of his ability to do so.

Eventually Winifred came out, looking gray and with little splashes of vomit on her clothing and a streak of it at one corner of her mouth. "It smells so bad in there I vomited extra. Where's a tap, Sam? Can you see a tap?"

"I saw one tap next to the house across the road," Sam said to her. Taking her hand again, he led her toward the side of the house.

"You mustn't use that lavatory." It was Robert's voice. "That's the tenants' lavatory. Our lavatory is in the house."

Sam looked in his direction, but he was still sitting with his back resting against the wall and his eyes closed as if someone else had spoken. Sam and Winifred went down the side of the house and across the road, seemingly even more alive with children than before, and into a cemented alley next to the house opposite. The house itself was as imposing to Sam as Mama Mabaso's had been, but the alley and the yard at the back to which it led were completely different. The tap was at the back of the alley where it entered the yard, and a jagged channel had been chopped into the cement to drain excess water and any other liquid waste from the yard into the road. Around the tap the channel was choked with bits of cardboard and newspaper and had formed a slimy stinking dam that the children had to jump over. From the yard they could hear the sounds of life, the same sounds of life with which the bus and the yard behind Mama Mabaso's place had been filled: the shouting, crying, laughter and cursing made by too many people living in a space far too small to house them.

Opening the tap a little way so that the water trickled out slowly, Sam captured it in his cupped hands and washed Winifred's face. Then he splashed water on her dress to wash off the vomit. "All right, Sam. I'll do it," she said.

While Winifred washed herself and without actually coming out from behind her, Sam looked into the courtyard. It was a large rectangle surrounded by thirty or forty corrugated-iron rooms, all of which emptied into it. Some of the rooms seemed no larger than a coal shed, while the larger rooms might have been about the size of a small room in Mama Mabaso's house. Most of the doorways to the rooms stood open. In some of them there were no doors, and pieces of sacking or canvas hung across them in place of the wooden door that had probably long since been used for firewood. In the center of the cement courtyard there were also washerwomen at work, but this time there were a dozen or more with the washing in bundles on the ground. As Sam watched, two girls about the same age as Winifred carried a huge bundle of wet washing to a place out of sight behind the rooms. All over the courtyard groups of small children were playing. One group, whose members were all completely naked, were damming up the overflow from the washerwomen by lying down in front of it on the cement before it could drain away into the alley. Around the perimeter against the corrugated-iron sheds a number of old men and a few younger ones sat smoking pipes or cigarettes they had rolled themselves with newspaper or drinking home-brew liquor out of jam tins.

"This is not a nice place like Mama Mabaso's. I'm wrong or right?" Sam asked.

"It's a horrible place."

"Mama Mabaso's place is nice."

"I don't want to be there either. I wish Papa would finish talking to Mama Mabaso so we can go now."

Suddenly Winifred's face stiffened and she made a little involuntary grunting sound. She ran past Sam down the alley toward the road, splashing through the dammed water in the channel, carrying her hands wide on either side of her as if balancing, her little plaits shaking stiffly. The gasped word "Papa" that Sam had heard as she came past him was left hanging in the air like the insubstantial ghost of what she was feeling. He followed as she turned at the entrance to the alley and was lost to his sight. Up ahead, the green-painted body of a car moved slowly past the opening between the houses and stopped. Sam thought he heard Mama Mabaso's voice and his father's intermixed, the two speaking at the same time.

When he came out of the alley Winifred was lying face downward on the tarred surface of the road screaming, her hands beating the ground, and he could see by her face how frightened she was. He heard his father's voice again. It was saying, "Go on. Go on. Don't stop." His father was in the back seat of the car that he had seen come past the entrance to the alley. It had come to a stop in the middle of the road with its engine still running. Sam saw his father's lower lip quiver as he looked at Winifred. Then his father's eyes found his and Sam saw something of the fear in Winifred's eyes in his as well. "Go on," his father told the driver again.

The car's engine roared once and it jerked into motion. Without thinking Sam sprinted forward, drawing momentarily closer until, gathering speed, the car moved quickly away from him. Through the back window he could vaguely see the outline of his father's head. From down the road behind him he heard Mama Mabaso's voice calling.

Sam stopped in the middle of the road, looking after the car until it rounded the corner at the bottom of Meyer Street. He was aware of other children running up to and stopping around him. They had thought that chasing the car was a game and they were joining it. Sam could hear their voices and the sounds of their feet on the road, but he could see nothing except the corner at the bottom of the street where a moment before the car had paused before turning. Now there was only its lingering image in his memory. He turned and saw that Robert had followed him and was standing a few paces behind, his face concerned and looking at him out of both eyes. Mama Mabaso, in her black dress, was a large dark form in the middle of the road, kneeling next to Winifred and lifting her into her arms.

✠　✠

Bhengu was back on the bed, but he was free of the shackles. The security policemen were all gathered around the table near the door. Lategan had joined them. Bhengu had his eyes closed, but he recognized the colonel's voice. "I called Roberts. He said he'll come straight over."

"He's shamming." It was Engelbrecht who had spoken.

"I know it. All I want is a certificate from Roberts."

"Will he give it?"

"Roberts is all right."

The soothing warmth started in Bhengu's testicles and spread smoothly to his buttocks. It felt as if something with its own warmth had been spread over that part of him. He tried to lift his head to see, but the weight was still attached to the base of his skull and was now holding it down to the mattress. He wished that the warm feeling would spread further and cover all of him.

"All I want is a certificate," Lategan repeated. "Oliver Mthembu always has strokes when he's detained, and afterward there is nothing wrong. What did he say when you showed him Smith's confession?"

"Nothing. He said not a word all the time."

"That's all right. We've got plenty of time. Just let Roberts come. We can't afford to take any chances with him."

The warmth around his testicles and buttocks had faded and had been replaced by a clinging, penetrating cold. He could feel his testicles shrink into tight little knots and the enfolding mattress cold against the skin of his buttocks. It felt as if a barely perceptible breeze, a soft stirring of the air, was taking place under him and between his legs; a cold winter movement, steady and patient.

Bhengu could see them out of the corners of his eyes, his head partly turned toward the table. He saw Strydom nod in his direction to draw Lategan's attention, and he saw the colonel turn to look at him. "You awake, Sam?" They had been talking Afrikaans among themselves and he changed to English for Bhengu's benefit. He walked the few steps across the room and stopped at the foot of the bed. "You going to talk to us now?" He paused for a reply, unhurried, patient and sure, like the stirring of the air beneath Bhengu's buttocks. "I can wait."

Colonel De Wet Lategan was short and sturdily built. His face was square, the nose flattened at the bridge as if it had been broken at some time. He held his chin tucked in like a boxer afraid of taking a punch on it, perhaps to reinforce himself against shocks from outside. His normal expression was a wary smile. It was a confident face, one that reflected the power he knew to be his. The eyes were the same as those of all the older men among them, hooded, the inner life hidden, giving nothing away.

But would you look that way if you were here and I was standing over you? Bhengu's mind asked. Would you still be wearing that smile? How confident would you be then? Would you still stand so square, your shoulders held so straight, if my men had just done it to you? Will you have that much control when it's your turn?

"I know you're shamming. I know you, Sam. We've gone a long road together."

We've gone a long road, Bhengu's mind told him, but not together. You were going your way and I was going my way. The ways crossed a few times, but we were never going together.

Outside it was daylight, turning the policemen at the table into little more than silhouettes. He could see the tops of the double-storied buildings on the far side of the park and the bobbing, coasting, white-winged flight of a myna against the sky. The light from the window fell on Lategan from the side, lighting half of his face and leaving the other half in shadow, seeming to divide the security policeman in two.

But then there are two parts to you, Bhengu thought. I've seen the human side and I've seen the business side. He knew that the human side of Lategan and his men faced inwardly only, toward their own little community, excluding all else. And he knew the other side intimately, the closed side, where no arguments are valid, where everything unfamiliar is a cause for suspicion.

"Roberts is going to tell us anyway, Sam. It'll be easier for you if you cooperate. If Roberts says there's nothing wrong with you . . ."

He had heard it all many times before. Cooperate with us. It'll be easier on you. Your friends are all confessing. What's the point? You don't think you can beat us, do you? We can keep you here . . . we can make sure that no one ever quotes you again . . . you'll stay in solitary . . . we've been watching your wife, and would you like to know who she's been going with . . . you know you can't beat us, Sam . . . you can't beat us . . .

"Dr. Roberts."

"Good morning, Colonel. Good morning, gentlemen."

Roberts was a small, innocent-looking man in his early thirties. The top of his head was completely bald and shone as if polished. His eyes were worried, but the worry was hidden behind a brisk and businesslike manner and a rapid-fire way of speaking. "Is that the one, Colonel?" he asked, nodding in Bhengu's direction.

"He's the one, Doctor."

Roberts opened his bag, but left it on the desk without taking anything from it. He sat down on the bed next to Bhengu and then got up again. "This man has urinated all over himself."

"He's done that before," Lategan said. "That proves nothing. He could have done that on purpose."

"I suppose he could," Roberts said to him. "Sit up, old chap," he said to Bhengu.

He wondered how to sit up, how to bring into play the muscles that would have moved him into a sitting position. Roberts was speaking again, "How do you feel, old chap?"

He heard his own voice, disembodied, apparently controlled by something outside of his will. ". . . feel, old chap."

"There's nothing wrong with him. He can speak. What did I tell you?" Lategan's voice sounded pleased at his discovery.

STORE UP THE ANGER

"There was never anything wrong," Engelbrecht said.

"Do you feel all right?"

". . . all right," Bhengu's disembodied voice said.

"Sit up, old chap," the quick-sounding voice of the doctor said. Bhengu pressed down on his elbows, but the weight at the base of his skull held him fast. "Help me with him," he heard Roberts' voice say.

"He can do it if he wants to," Lategan said.

"Help me with him."

The doctor leaned across him to take hold of the arm on the side against the wall. A wave of bad breath from his mouth was blown up into Bhengu's nostrils. He saw Lategan move toward him and felt his hands take hold of the other arm, then they were lifting him into a sitting position on the edge of the bed.

Roberts took a stethoscope from his bag and Bhengu felt the cold circle of the sensor against his chest and back as it was moved from point to point. The little doctor's face was close to his own and he looked at his eyes, but they were detached and impersonal, interested only in doing the job for which he was being paid.

The stethoscope was gone and Bhengu found himself looking into a needlepoint of light, coming from something in the doctor's hand. The light disappeared and then shone into his other eye. "Let him lie down again," Roberts said.

On his back, he watched the top of Roberts' bald head moving quickly back and forth as the doctor's hands probed purposefully into his stomach. The points of the fingers were massaging in little circles, starting just below the rib cage and moving down, exploring his internal organs. "Does this hurt?"

Nothing hurts, Bhengu's mind tried to tell the doctor. The part that hurts is broken. Now nothing hurts.

The fingers plunged deep into him. "This? Does this hurt now?"

No, not now, not at any time.

He could feel the hard points of the doctor's fingers, searching for any swelling, any irregularity, working into his gut just inside the hips, then low, along the bottom of the pelvis, but the feeling was distant like soft raindrops through a plastic raincoat. The doctor's fingers transferred to his genitals. He felt them pushing his penis aside as they scrutinized his testicles, running the membrane of the sac between thumb and forefinger. The doctor paused, fingering the skin gently in one small area. "Some enlarged veins here," he said.

There was no reaction from the security policemen and finally the doctor's hand withdrew. A moment later the same fingers were stroking the skin of one of his ankles lightly. "What could have caused this?" he heard the doctor ask.

"It must have been the manacles."

"This bad?" The doctor's worry was not as well hidden as it had been earlier.

"It was the manacles." Lategan's tone was flat and noncommittal.

Bhengu could see the unasked question in the doctor's face. Roberts was looking at Lategan but the colonel was looking past him, the expression of his face bored and faintly irritated. The doctor dropped his eyes. Bhengu felt his fingers on one of his wrists, then on the other. He watched the little man's innocent face and he saw the eyes flash quickly toward Lategan and away again. Again the question remained unasked. Bhengu knew, and he imagined the doctor knew, that if the question had been asked the answer would have been the same. "It was the manacles." How could it happen, Bhengu wondered, that, if you were lying down quietly and the manacles were lying quietly, they could do that to your hands?

The doctor's hands were on his face, lifting the eyelids to look underneath them, then investigating his mouth, turning over the lips. He held the upper lip, rolled over, for longer than the others. Bhengu felt the doctor's fingers touch the damp skin on the inside of the lip. They tasted like sweat and tobacco. The worry on the doctor's face and the unasked question were unchanged. He allowed the lip to fall back into place. "I want him over on his stomach," he said.

Lategan was close to him and Bhengu felt the grip of the policeman's fingers on his left arm. Roberts had his hands under him and one of the warrant officers had hold of his left thigh. Bhengu felt himself lifted and rolled over onto his stomach, his face pressing against the mattress, its stale body-and-rubber odor all around him. He felt hands take hold of his head on either side and felt it turned toward the window. Then the doctor's fingers were probing the area of his kidneys. The skin of his back where the doctor was working felt tight-stretched, like the skin of a drum, the fingers seeming to make little impression on it.

"We haven't been able to communicate at all with him today," Lategan was saying. "He was a medical student for four years. He knows all the symptoms. I think that has something to do with it."

"I want you to try and walk now," the doctor said. "Get him into a sitting position," he told the warrant officer. "I want him to try walking."

"If he wants to, he can do it." Lategan moved in next to him, and the warrant officer stepped back to allow room for the colonel.

Bhengu felt himself lifted to his feet by the security policeman and the doctor, one having hold of each arm. He saw the doctor release his grip and step slowly back, his hands still raised, the fingers spread wide as if he might have to step in to prevent Bhengu from falling. "Let him go now," he said to Lategan. Bhengu felt the policeman's grip released and saw him step back as well. To his own surprise he was still standing.

The faces of the two white men were very close to his, the doctor's frowning uncertainly and Lategan's grinning, looking well-satisfied with himself. "There's nothing wrong with him."

"I want you to walk," Bhengu heard the doctor say. He was still looking at Lategan. "I want you to try to walk. I'll stay close to you so that you don't fall."

"He won't fall."

The two faces were close and then drawing away from him, coming close again, and again drawing away from him, moving smoothly like ripples on the surface of a lake. Looking down, the floor seemed far below him, his legs brown and naked tapering down till his feet flattened out, broad and shapeless on the floor.

"Try to walk," the doctor's voice said.

Bhengu felt his legs moving. He was walking across the room, past Lategan and Roberts, his stride choppy and uneven, as if one leg was shorter than the other. He looked down. The floor was still just as far away. His legs were moving in jerky spasms, causing his penis to bob back and forth like a ball at the end of a rubber band. He passed the desk where Engelbrecht was seated and saw the blank stare of the sunglasses turned toward him. Strydom was walking backward, retreating before him. "Watch the window," he heard Lategan say. "We don't want a Timol affair here." One of the warrant officers ran past him and around the table to reach the window, turning his back on it when he got there. Strydom had stopped before the closed door, his hands raised to waist level.

As he reached the table in front of the door, Bhengu felt himself turn. He saw the images of Strydom and the warrant officer whirl away as his eyes turned and he felt himself moving back toward the bed. The white faces of the second warrant officer, Lategan and the doctor, seeming even more than usually pale in the light from the window, waited for him in front of the bed. The walking was worse than lying down on the bed. Lying down, his nakedness was more a private matter, as if he was a patient in a hospital; but walking, he was exhibiting it. It was not the nakedness in itself, but the fact that they were not naked that made the difference between them. Only the blurred pallor of their faces at his eye level and the occasional quick movement of a hand, were visible outside of the expensive suits they wore. They also had genitals that protruded obscenely in front of their bodies like those of no other animal alive, but theirs were hidden away, while his were on display. The eyes of the second warrant officer (Bhengu had heard him called André) were on his genitals, as if he had never previously seen anything of the sort.

The worried eyes of the doctor, the confident eyes of the colonel, and the transfixed eyes of the warrant officer whirled away as he turned again. Engelbrecht's sunglasses passed in front of him, the glasses turning to follow his movement. He moved toward the window again, his jerky stride carrying him forward unevenly, his eyes fixing on the face of Strydom, white against the door, and then the warrant officer, darkly silhouetted in front of the window. He was turning and turning, his legs carrying him on without conscious instruction. The walls and furnishings in the room had become a whirling band, his eyes not focusing on any object for more than a moment, and set into it were the white faces of those who were watching him, also blurred, but standing out sharp and clear on the screen of his mind.

"There's nothing wrong." It was Lategan's voice, sure and without emphasis.

"I must say, there doesn't seem to be anything organic," Bhengu heard the doctor say.

He was turning and jerking forward, and turning and jerking forward, and turning, and turning, and turning, and the only reality was the sight of the faces, now absent of expression, to his eyes, and the sad spasmodic dance of his genitals.

Behind and above the whirling of the room was the sound of voices, and Lategan's was dominant. "I want a certificate," he was saying.

"What sort of certificate?"

"I want a certificate to say I can go on interrogating him."

"He should be examined again. He should be watched."

"There's nothing wrong with him. The certificate doesn't have to say that he's a hundred percent. It only has to say that he's all right to be interrogated."

The room had stopped turning and Bhengu was back on the bed. Someone had replaced the blanket with a dry one that felt warm under the skin of his back and buttocks. The portion of the ceiling that he could see was in shadow, interrupted by a bright narrow reflection from the window. Roberts was folding the stethoscope neatly and replacing it in his bag. His face looked more worried than before and he was careful not to look at either Bhengu or any of the policemen. He said something very quickly. Bhengu deciphered the words, ". . . more thorough tests."

"You said yourself there's nothing organic."

"No . . ." The word was left hanging as Roberts searched for an answer.

A few paces away from him on the other side of the room the colonel's eyes watched every shade of expression on his face. Lategan was no taller than the doctor but broad and muscular where he was narrow-shouldered, Roberts' arms and legs feeble, carrying only the muscular development necessary for his chosen profession. The latent violence in the security policeman was a tangible part of the air in the room, and Bhengu could see that the doctor sensed it.

"If there's nothing organic, what's the problem?" The voice was calm and undramatic, but insistent.

"His speech sounded a bit slurred." Roberts was closing his

bag and examining its clasp as if it was something new to him.
"It was coherent."
"Why did he pass urine in bed?"
"That could have been deliberate. He knows all the right
symptoms. He studied medicine for three years, four years,
I'm not sure. I just want a certificate to say he can be interrogated, to say what you found, in fact." Roberts looked quickly
at his face and then around at the other security policemen.
He still avoided looking at Bhengu. He was one small weak
man who doubted his own authority among five strong ones
who were sure of theirs. "Would you like to sit at the table
over there?" Lategan asked. There was no indication in his
voice that he might accept anything less than the certificate for
which he was asking.

Engelbrecht made way for Roberts at the desk, the slightest
unpleasant indication of a smile threading its way along the
edges of his mouth. Strydom was still in front of the door.
Roberts sat down at the desk and reopened his bag. From it
he took a pen and pad. He wrote in silence, tore the sheet
loose and lay it down on the table. Then, without looking up,
he replaced the writing materials in his bag and went quickly
out of the room. The warrant officer at the window chuckled
briefly, but Lategan looked curiously at him, his expression
devoid of humor, and the chuckle died as quickly as it had
started. The colonel walked slowly to the door, his expression
thoughtful, absentmindedly beckoning to Engelbrecht to come
with him. He stopped before the closed door with Engelbrecht
on one side of him and Strydom on the other. "I want results,"
he said. He spoke very softly, obviously not intending that
Bhengu should hear. But Bhengu's senses seemed to have ex-
panded until they reached to every corner of the room, making him aware of every sound or movement, hearing the
breathing of the warrant officer nearest him, even picking up
the mood and intentions of each of the five men in the room

with him. "I want some progress," Lategan said softly. "Write
a report in the log. Say he attacked you this morning and
there was a struggle. He may have hit his head."

Engelbrecht's nod of acceptance of the idea was barely perceptible. Lategan glanced over his shoulder at Bhengu. The
self-satisfied smile had left his face. As he went out of the
room there was only the single-minded purposefulness Bhengu
had come to expect there.

Bhengu watched Engelbrecht sit down at the desk and
bring a sheet of paper out of a drawer. He looked at it as if he
was reading the printing on it. Then he raised his head.
Bhengu was not sure that the policeman was looking at him,
the sunglasses making it impossible to be certain. For a moment the sunglasses were stationary, the eyes hidden, but certainly busy, weighing, deciding; then Engelbrecht gestured
quickly, a brief turning of his head and a quick nod in
Bhengu's direction. The two warrant officers came silently
across the room and lifted him from the bed. The hands of
one of them lost their grip on his arm and he went down on
one knee. He felt the hands close around his bicep again and
he was dragged forward without being lifted to his feet, both
legs trailing on the ground, his knees sliding smoothly over the
floor. They lifted him onto the chair and unconsciously he
raised his arms and dropped them between his thighs.

"Covering up, Sam?" Engelbrecht asked. Again his mouth
held the beginnings of an unpleasant smile. "You can't cover
up from us, Sam. Sooner or later we learn everything about
you. There's nothing we don't know about you. We know
about every part of your body and every part of your life. And
what we don't know we are going to find out. We've got time
on our side."

There it was again. They have time, they said. No, Sam
Bhengu thought, now time is on my side. You've only got a
little time, a very little time. It's all gone now. I've got no time

and you've got no time to work on me. Not that you would
have gotten anything from me. You never did in the past. You
sure as hell never will now. You've got no time. Now time is
my friend.

"We've got time on our side," Engelbrecht said again. "I'll
keep you as long as I like and I'll keep you naked as long as I
like. You know what the law says about section-six detainees.
The law says no access may be had to section-six detainees,
not even by a court of law. You're ours now, Sam." The soft
expressionless voice went through it all as if it was rehearsed.
The blank lenses of the sunglasses filled impersonally the
places where his eyes should have been. "You'll get no visitors, no clothing, no food, no reading matter, nothing to drink
—until I have what I want. There's only you left, Sam. All
your friends have confessed. All your old leaders have gone.
We've dealt with them. Where are they now? Where are your
old leaders? Where is Sobukwe now? Where is Mandela
now?"

✠   ✠

"It's the Mandela plan," Robert said wisely. "I thought you
knew."

"The Mandela plan?" Sam asked.

"Nelson Mandela worked it out. That's why it's called the
Mandela plan. The M plan."

"The M plan," Sam said, his voice sounding awed. "What
is it? What will happen?"

✠   ✠

The other policemen, the warrant officers and Strydom, had
taken up the attack as if on cue. From all around him Bhengu
heard the questions shouted at him, repeating themselves over

and over . . . "Where are they now? Where are they now?
Where is Sobukwe? Where is Mandela? Where are they?
Aren't they your leaders? Why aren't they leading? Where are
they now? Where is Mandela?" Only Engelbrecht was silent,
letting the others do the shouting for him, the blank impersonal lenses of his sunglasses staring fixedly at Bhengu. The
unpleasant little smile was now fastened immovably to his lips.
It asked the same questions: "Where is Sobukwe? Where is
Mandela?"

⌘   ⌘

"They will pay only four hundred pounds," Mama Mabaso
said.

"Four hundred pounds is nothing," the schoolteacher said.

"Then we have to live in one of their little pondoks. We
can't even be allowed to buy our own house."

"What did you pay for your house in the first place?"

"Joseph paid seven hundred pounds," Mama Mabaso said.
"That was twenty years ago. They say the house has devalued
in the meantime. They say only four hundred pounds of the
value is left."

"You must not take it."

Mama Mabaso shrugged. She was buttering the rolls for
dozens of hotdogs, spread in rows across the kitchen table.
The space under the table was filled with cases of liquor, all of
it illicit. This was the "Prohibition Era" when the people were
not allowed white man's liquor. Sam knew that it was for this
reason that the shebeen moved to a different house every Saturday night, tonight being Mama Mabaso's turn. The cops
could not raid a shebeen if they did not know where to look
for it. The shebeen belonged to Shakes Moloi, and he provided the money for the refreshments which would be sold at
increasingly high prices as the evening progressed. Mama Ma-

baso had told Sam that she was satisfied with the 20 percent of the profits she would get. It was a lot better than the 10 percent Alex Mkela used to pay when he ran the shebeen.

The schoolteacher was dressed in a brown suit and tie. He was a neat, ineffective-looking little man who walked with the toes of his feet pointing outward. Even now, sitting on a straight-back chair looking seriously at Mama Mabaso, his toes pointed toward opposite walls of the room. Sam, sitting on the bed on the other side of the stoep and scribbling spasmodically at his homework with a ballpen, wondered how it had happened that the bones in the schoolteacher's legs had set in that unlikely position. His curiosity about the matter had led him to look at the pictures in books on anatomy in the Priory Library and he had come to the conclusion that the little man's femurs were twisted outward.

"You must not take the money," the man with the twisted femurs was saying. "I don't believe the electorate will ever allow them to move us by force. I'll tell you how I see the situation. If you tell them you are not moving, they have to go to the Resettlement Board. The board has to go to a magistrate. The magistrate issues the order. Then ten cops come to move one family. If they want to move fifty thousand people, they will need five hundred thousand cops. Resha explained it to us. He said the electorate will never stand for it."

"Resha said that?" Mama Mabaso asked.

"Yes. He said that at Freedom Square last Saturday. You should have been there. The people should attend so that they can hear what our leaders have to say." Sam knew that the schoolteacher saw himself as a member of the Sophiatown intelligentsia and, as such, automatically an envoy of the Congress leadership. He also knew that the little man's only qualification for filling the position of schoolteacher was his having completed high school himself. It was a fact that often seemed to escape him. "The situation is that the whites are

Christians," he said. "They will never stand for force being used against so many people."

Sam looked wonderingly at the adults. He could not understand what they were worrying about. He knew that the cops would never be able to move the people out of Sophiatown. It was impossible. We have the M plan, he thought. As soon as it starts working everything will be all right. Everyone will work together and the Nats will be powerless. Mandela. He turned the name over in his mind. What a great man he must be. Nelson Mandela, he whispered. The name felt good in his mouth. He had brains to work out a plan like that. He was a real leader. The M plan, he whispered to himself, savoring the thought, the M plan.

"At least we will get something," Mama Mabaso said. "A lot of people will get nothing. The Indian lawyers have the deeds. They will get everything."

"You must not even think of taking the money," the schoolteacher said.

Mama Mabaso looked at him for a moment out of her wide-open impassive eyes, but she said nothing. There was a hesitant knock on the back door and Sam slid off the bed to open it. A boy of his own age came into the room. He was coatless, wearing neatly pressed black trousers that were shiny at the seat, a spotlessly white shirt, the collar of which was frayed all around the edges, and a broad red tie with a picture of a Hawaiian dancer. He looked embarrassed in Mama Mabaso's presence and almost frantic at seeing the schoolteacher. He bobbed his head up and down as if looking for an opening through which to escape.

"Good evening, Johnson," Mama Mabaso said.

"Good evening, Mama," the boy said.

"Don't tell me you are coming to the shebeen, Johnson?" the schoolteacher asked.

"No, sir," Johnson said, bobbing his head more quickly than before. "I came to visit Sam."

"You are so smartly dressed. I thought you must be coming to the shebeen."

"No, sir." Sam sat down on the bed again and Johnson came to sit next to him. "What are you doing?" Johnson asked.

"Math. I want to finish so I don't have to do it tomorrow."

The schoolteacher started saying something to Mama Mabaso about the situation and the necessity of appealing to the electorate's Christian conscience.

"Why do you always keep the cap on your pen?" Johnson asked softly. "I always throw mine away."

"I don't want it to write in my pocket."

"Is that why they have them?"

"Yes."

"A Parker's better because it just sucks it in."

"Who can afford a Parker?" Sam asked.

Johnson dropped his voice still lower. "Sir has got one," he said.

The front door banged open and Winifred's hurried stride was heard in the passage. Sam heard her voice clearly through the closed door as she passed the room he shared with Robert. "Hello, stupid." Robert's muffled rejoinder was lost through the intervening walls, and a moment later the kitchen door banged open as loudly as the front door had and Winifred threw a brown canvas kit bag so hard across the room that it thudded against the wall on the far side. "Hello, Mama. Hello, Mr. Sibisi. Hello, stupid."

"Stupid yourself," Sam said.

"Child, you should have been here long ago to help me," Mama Mabaso said.

"I'm sorry, Mama. The practice lasted longer than I expected. You should have heard Joyce. She was beautiful, especially in the Handel."

"The viennas are over there. The mustard is on the shelf."

"I still have to dress," Winifred said. She was wearing her black school tunic, with white shirt and black tie and stockings; a shapeless conception designed to bury as deeply as possible whatever sexual attractions the wearer might possess. "If the people start coming and see me like this, I'll die."

"Help first, dress afterwards," Mama Mabaso said.

Winifred started spearing the viennas with a fork and laying them on the rolls. "The prize-giving today at the Priory was terrible," she said. "Did you see Sam, Mama?"

"Of course I saw Sam." Mama Mabaso smiled at Sam, her huge old face softening perceptibly.

"Everybody else looked so serious when they got their prizes, but Sam looked so pleased with himself. He had such a big grin. I was so embarrassed I nearly died. Then he held out his hand to shake hands with Father Stephens, but before Father Stephens could shake hands with him he took it back again, then he held it out again, and before Father Stephens could take it again he took it back. Afterwards I just couldn't look. All my friends turned around and looked at me. It was terrible."

Sam grinned helplessly. He never had any answer to Winifred's attacks, especially when they were so well researched.

"Sam won the prize and Sam deserved the prize," Mama Mabaso said. "That is what's important."

Sam's grin took on a bolder tone. It was an expression that was always guaranteed to infuriate Winifred and most others at whom it was directed. It held within it the suggestion that he somehow had the better of them.

"All right, Sam. We all know you won the prize," Winifred said, turning to look at Mama Mabaso so that she would not have to look at Sam's grin. "Mama, these American hotdogs are beautiful," she said.

"Everything will be ready," Mama Mabaso said. "I've got hamburgers as well. And curry and rice. And the drinks. Everything Shakes said. I've got a big can of sour milk too."

"Sour milk, Mama?" Winifred was appalled.

"What's wrong? Everybody loves sour milk."

"But at a shebeen? I'll die if you bring out the sour milk, Mama."

"They'll love it," Mama Mabaso said defensively.

"Oh, Mama, you're so old-fashioned. You can't have sour milk at a shebeen. What will the people say? How can you be so old-fashioned? With American hotdogs and Louis Armstrong and Mahalia Jackson records and everything? I'll die."

Mama Mabaso looked around at the faces of the other people in the room. "I'm not old-fashioned. You're just a stupid kid and you've still got a lot to learn. They all love sour milk."

"But at a shebeen?"

The longer Winifred belabored the point the more Mama Mabaso doubted that the sour milk was a good idea. "Go then," she said. "Go and get changed. That's what you want to do."

Winifred dropped the fork on the table, scooped up her bag and, flashing her own triumphant grin at Sam, fled down the passage to the room she shared with Mama Mabaso. "Will she go on studying after this year?" the schoolteacher asked.

Mama Mabaso shook her head. "She wants to go to the Fort, but I told her that I can't send everyone. So the boys must go. She is a clever girl, but she has enough education now. I'm not against a girl getting education, but Winifred has enough. Are you staying for the shebeen?"

The teacher's face became thoughtful, as if this was a weighty matter for a man in his position to consider. He started explaining to Mama Mabaso about how busy he was.

Johnson leaned close to Sam and said, "Winifred's beautiful."

"What?" Sam asked. His mind had been unable to accept the accuracy of what his ears had heard.

"Winifred is beautiful."

"Who?"

"Winifred."

"My sister?" Sam looked straight at him and Johnson nodded seriously. Sam could hear Winifred's voice in the passage, where it sounded as if she was talking to Robert. He got up thoughtfully and walked to the other side of the kitchen where Mama Mabaso was working. He stopped in the doorway and looked at his sister where she was leaning against the doorpost of Robert's room. The light from the room was falling on her face and on the front of her tunic. Even through the unflattering insulation of the tunic the size and firmness of her breasts was obvious. In her face, and most of all in her eyes, there was a zeal for living such as he had never seen in the face of anyone else. To his surprise, and for the first time in his life, Sam realized that his sister was beautiful.

"Is that girl still not getting dressed?" Mama Mabaso asked. "Excuse me, Mr. Sibisi, I must go and have a look at what is going on there."

"I must go myself," the schoolteacher said. "As I explained . . ."

"Are you sure you won't stay? Shakes won't charge you entrance."

"No. No, thank you." The schoolteacher bowed slightly to Mama Mabaso and retreated toward the back door. As he reached it he said, "Good-night," to Mama Mabaso, and then separately to the two boys. "I'll just go out this way . . ."

Sam watched Mama Mabaso move determinedly down the passage toward Winifred. Seeing her coming, Winifred lifted her hands for protection. "I'm going. I'm going. I was just talking to Robert."

"What about the rest of the food?" To Sam even Mama Mabaso's back looked angry. "What about the curry and rice?"

"I'll dress very fast," Winifred said, still retreating and finally getting cornered against her own bedroom door. As she reached for the doorknob Mama Mabaso got hold of one of her arms and, jerking her away from the door, aimed a blow at her sturdy buttocks. "Stop, stop. I'll be fast," Winifred yelled. Then, moving in close to Mama Mabaso with all the skill of a professional boxer clinching to avoid punishment, she wrapped her arms around the older woman and hugged her. "Oh, this mama of mine is so beautiful. I love her," she said.

Mama Mabaso held the girl against her body for a moment and then disentangled herself. Holding Winifred at arm's length she shook her head helplessly. She knew that she was being handled, but she also knew that there was nothing she would be able to do about it. "I need you in the kitchen," she said at last.

"Oh, Mama, Bloke was at the choir practice. He said I'm so mature I must be much more than sixteen. He said I look at least twenty. Do I look at least twenty, Mama?"

From where he was standing it seemed to Sam that Mama Mabaso's eyes were shining more than usual when she answered. "My child, to me you look no older than you did when you first came to me."

"Oh, Mama," Winifred said, and the two women hugged each other again. Sam was sure that they were both crying. He retreated from the door, not anxious to be seen watching them.

"Sam Bhengu, waar's jy? Waar's jy? Vandag gaan jy praat?" It was Strydom speaking. Engelbrecht had moved away to the table, where he was sitting on its edge, more anonymous than ever against the light from the window, his face no more than a shadow and the eyes with the sunglasses two deeper shadows. Strydom repeated the same words, still in Afrikaans: "Sam Bhengu, where are you? Where are you? Today you are going to talk." Bhengu had been through this so many times in the past, them questioning, accusing in Afrikaans and himself answering in English. Almost all of them were Afrikaners and using Afrikaans to deal with someone whom they thought did not understand it well was part of their stock-in-trade. Answering in English always infuriated them, driving them to greater efforts. "Where are you, Sam Bhengu? Where are you? Look around you. Tell me where you are."

In hell, and you are Satan, Bhengu's mind said. He tried to bring the thought through to his tongue, his will driving it, trying to compel it outward into the air. But there was nothing. Inside his mouth he could feel the presence of his tongue, like a piece of sticky dead meat, unmoving.

The gray steel points of Strydom's eyes were looking straight into his, penetrating his brain, the security policeman leaning forward on the desk, bringing his face close to Bhengu's as if they shared some frightful intimacy. "This man is still not coming out with the truth," he said, the Afrikaans words a taunt and a warning, telling Bhengu again, although it would be impossible for him to forget it even for a moment, that he was not among his own people, that he should remember where he was. "This man is still not coming out with the truth. He is not cooperating."

Not cooperating, Bhengu wondered. Not cooperating? In which way did you expect me to cooperate?

"Jy sal weet," Strydom said. "You will know." He said it as

surely as if he had read Bhengu's thoughts. "You will know where you are. You will know in whose hands you are."

I know, Bhengu's mind said. I know where I am.

Strydom was holding the sheet of paper from which Engelbrecht had been reading earlier and rattling it up and down, the expression on his face telling Bhengu that he might as well come out with it; the paper told them everything anyway. The fingers, holding the sheet of paper, were clean, smoothly rounded at the ends and pink, the fingernails immaculate, filed to even lengths. He had put on his jacket again and Bhengu could see the perfect whiteness of the cuffs protruding from either sleeve and the gold cufflinks with black stones set into them. He wondered if Strydom chose the cufflinks himself and, if he did, how much time he had spent choosing them. "This is not a statement," the security policeman was saying. "Four sentences is not a statement. Did you think we would accept four sentences as a statement?" He looked around the room as if playing to an audience. "This man is still not cooperating," he told the imaginary audience. "Why is this man not cooperating?"

❇   ❇

The room was full of cigarette smoke, dancing couples and the recorded ecstasy of Louis Armstrong's trumpet. Bloke Chamane, the man who had told Winifred how adult she looked, tipped the ash from his cigarette in a studied, carefully elegant movement. He was wearing black trousers with a silver stripe down the leg and a pink sports coat, and everyone knew that he was a member of the Congress working committee. It was even said that he was a personal friend of Mandela.

"Just wait," Bloke was saying. "Just wait and see. The situation is that we have got everything under control."

"And when the cops come to move us—will everything be

under control then?" The questioner was a man in his early forties, light-skinned and sturdy, his nose wide and flat.

"Everything will be under control. The M plan . . ."

"The M plan," another voice interrupted him. "We hear about this M plan, but no one tells us what it is, this M plan."

Bloke slowly filled his lungs with smoke from his cigarette and looked pityingly at the speaker. "You want the Nats to learn our plans?" he asked.

"God, no." The man was startled at the suggestion.

"You don't think," Bloke said. "That's why we have to keep it top secret."

"When will it happen, the plan? What day?"

Bloke looked past the questioner. He might have been expecting to be called away on more important business. "The M plan comes into play on the day before the removals begin, not a moment sooner."

"We must know what to do. We want to follow the M plan, but how will we know what we must do?"

Bloke looked quickly down at his watch and started to move away from the little group that had gathered around him. It was his way of telling them that the time of a member of the Congress working committee was precious, even if he was spending the evening at the shebeen. "The situation is that everything is under control and you will all be told what to do. The M plan caters for everything the Nats can do."

Someone took Bloke by the arm to stop him from leaving. "Come on, Bloke. You know us all. Tell us about it."

Bloke looked at the offending hand with a pained expression on his face. "This is top secret, my friend," he said. "Only the committee knows. And Nelson himself, of course."

"Nelson Mandela?" Sam asked. He had been determined not to draw attention to himself by saying anything, but the great man's name had slipped out before it could be stopped.

Bloke grinned at him and went through the motions of

knocking a little more ash from the tip of his cigarette. "That's right, son," he said. "Nelson Mandela." It was a lordly acknowledgment of him, and Sam glowed warm all over with pride.

Before he could enjoy any more of his new glory, Winifred had moved smoothly into the room carrying a tray of curry and rice, miraculously avoiding collisions as she wove her way in and out among the dancers. Sam's eyes met hers and she came straight toward him. "Mama wants you in the kitchen, Sam," she said.

But Sam had too recently been treated almost as an equal by a member of the Congress working committee. He glanced at Bloke's back, retreating across the room, having finally escaped the attention of the others. "I'm too busy at the moment," he said, "much too busy."

"Well, don't say I didn't tell you. You better go."

Winifred disappeared among the dancers to deliver her curry and rice, pausing for a moment to whisper something to Robert, who was dancing cheek to cheek with a plump girl in a cheap cotton dress. None of the men who had been gathered around Bloke had heard the exchange between Sam and Winifred, and Mama was waiting in the kitchen and she could get very unreasonable if he did not come as soon as he was called. He considered the alternatives for a moment, then slipped through the doorway and headed for the kitchen.

In the kitchen Mama Mabaso was buttering the rolls for still more hotdogs, while Little-Mama Zibi, swollen up with her first pregnancy at the age of nearly forty, was stirring a pot of curry on the stove. With the back of a hand that already held the butter knife Mama Mabaso involuntarily wiped the sweat from her forehead and continued buttering almost without interruption. "Yes, Mama," Sam said.

She glanced quickly up at the source of his voice. "Oh, Sam, I want you to take Johnson and go to his mama . . ."

"Johnson's gone home, Mama."

Mama Mabaso stopped long enough to get a good look at Sam. "Why did he do that?"

"He asked someone to dance and she laughed."

"Silly boy," Little-Mama Zibi said. Since the start of her pregnancy she had become very wise and motherly, the look on her face suggesting that she had achieved something unique in all human experience. "He should have come to me. I would have had something to say to that girl." She was narrow-hipped, and as a result the child rode out hugely in front of her, while underneath her thin little legs seemed to have shrunken until only the bones remained. "I don't know what's got into that child," she said of Johnson.

A passing look of amusement toyed with the corners of Mama Mabaso's mouth. "So he went home?" she asked. Sam nodded. "Boys." She shook her head, the amusement flickering in her eyes. "Then you run to Johnson's mama and ask her if Thombina can't come to help me. Tell her I can't manage all the work with just Winifred and Little-Mama Zibi." Sam started slowly for the door. "Run, Sam. I want her now, not tomorrow morning."

Sam took the back steps in one stride and then dashed down the side of the house, keeping close to the wall to avoid Mama Mabaso's flowerbeds, picking his steps faultlessly in the darkness. In the alley on the other side of the road he saw the figure of a girl, briefly outlined against the glow of the braziers inside the yard. Sam hurdled the front wall without slowing, but stopped in the middle of the road. From within the yard he could hear male voices intoning a sad rhythmical tribal melody, the lead singer's hoarse baritone voice telling the story, the others joining him in the chorus, harmonizing effortlessly. Sam went the rest of the way across the road and down the alley, being careful to keep to the side so that he would not run into the tap in the center. It was the same alley where he had washed the vomit off Winifred on the day their father had brought them to Mama Mabaso. The inspired thought flashed through his mind that perhaps Johnson's mother was in the yard and he could give her the message there. Almost immediately the neutralizing knowledge that Johnson's mother would never be found among all those tenants registered in his mind and he suppressed the whole matter entirely.

He stopped at the end of the alley, next to the tap. On the concrete surface of the yard, between the corrugated-iron shacks, a large crowd of tenants were having their own party. A number of wood-burning braziers, made of large cylindrical tins with holes punched all over to allow free movement of the air, were glowing red and providing the only light. Steam was rising from black cast-iron pots on top of some of the braziers. Sam braced himself against the smell of cooking ox lung. The group of about ten men, who were providing the show, were squatting on their haunches on one side of the yard, making little shuffling, foot-stamping movements to the rhythm of their singing. The lead singer was on his feet, walking up and down in front of them, miming one of the Zulu legends that were still lovingly preserved by the simple people of whom Sophiatown's backyard tenants largely consisted. Occasionally he sang a stanza or a few lines solo, then the other voices would join his, filling out the drama. The children of the yard sat close to them, their skinny brown legs crossed, forming a half-moon that completely surrounded the performers, their eyes and faces alight with the excitement of the story. At the back the adults sat on old packing cases, unsprung steel divans with coir mattresses, wooden kitchen chairs, or simply blankets spread out on the cement. Standing close to the entrance and listening carefully to grasp the meaning of the Zulu words, Sam picked up a few sentences of the story. It was about a great hunter who had the power to turn himself into whatever sort of animal he chose. It was exactly the sort of tribal legend at which life in the Sophiatown owner class had taught him to sneer. Sam had often been told that that sort of thing amused the tenants, but someone who was educated would hardly be interested.

The lead singer, a thin wiry man in frayed flannel trousers and a torn shirt, was dancing about in front of the chorus, rocking back and forth with one arm extended above his head in imitation of an ostrich. Sam moved closer, working his way in among a group of boys his own age. A hard adult hand smacked him sharply across the buttocks and he sat down on the cement, wedging himself into a small space between two other boys. He looked around to see who had slapped him, and a buxom woman with a bright red scarf around her head waved a warning finger at him. The momentary fear that his relatively fine clothes would be noticed and prove an embarrassment to him passed through his mind, then the story seized his imagination and neither his clothing nor the message for Johnson's mother existed as matters of any importance at all.

The little storyteller was a master of his art. He became an elephant, trumpeting before charging, feeling the air with the sensitive tip of his trunk to discover the presence of the lion. He became a crocodile, lying in wait for the innocent and unsuspecting. To the children's great amusement, he became a hippopotamus, waddling awkwardly from one mud puddle to the next. Sam listened carefully to every word, watching attentively every gesture. The storyteller had created a different world and everyone in the yard was pleased to escape into it for a while, leaving Sophiatown and its troubles behind.

When the story ended it seemed to Sam that it had lasted just a few minutes. The smaller children sighed and smiled sleepily at each other, very sorry that it was over, but too tired to try to avoid their mothers, who were already looking for them to send them to bed. The men gathered into small groups to continue discussions that had probably been interrupted by the storytelling. Sam started back toward the alley, bothered slightly by the dim awareness of an errand he should be running for Mama Mabaso. Near the entrance to the alley a small group of middle-aged men were sitting in a circle on straight-back chairs with a packing case in the middle for a table. They were smoking and drinking home-brew liquor from jars. They had paid no attention to the storyteller, having probably heard the same story many times before. "It's all right for the situations," he heard one of them say in English. "They own the house. We own nothing." Sam was immediately interested. He was one of the "situations" the man was talking about. The people who lived in the houses were called "situations" by the tenants because of their great love of discussing the situation. Many sentences opened with the words, "The situation is . . ." Sam stood completely still, flattening himself against the cool iron wall of the shed, having again stored his errand for possible later attention. "The situations say we must resist, but they don't drop the rent."

"It will be bad to give Sophiatown to the Nats," a second voice said.

"In Orlando you get a house for three pounds. Here I get one room for two pounds two shillings and six cents—one room for me, my wife and the kids."

"But it will be bad to let the Nats steal Sophiatown." This was a third and younger voice. "Father Huddlestone says we must resist."

"Father Huddlestone does not live in one room with the family. If I was a situation I would also resist. Father Huddlestone does not pay the rent."

"What will you do?"

"What will I do? I will go to Orlando in the truck and take the house."

"And if you come to Orlando and there are no houses?"

"There are houses. I have been there. I have seen them."

"And if there are ten thousand families and two thousand houses, then it's still one family in a room."

"If there are five families in a house, the rent is only twelve bob."

"And the bus fare? Orlando is far."

"The house is better than the zinc pondok."

"It's all right for the situations . . ."

"The situations live like whites. They want us to fight so that they can go on living like whites."

"Sophiatown is better than Orlando. Orlando is nothing."

"Where is the swimming pool in Orlando? Where is the bioscope?"

"You cannot live in the swimming pool or the bioscope. I will take the house."

"The M plan . . ."

"The M plan is for the situations."

"What is in the M plan?"

"Nobody knows. Even the situations don't know. We must resist, but nobody says how."

"No plan is good when the police come with guns. I will take the house in Orlando."

Sam worked his way free of the crowd. Once he reached the alley he broke into a run, again keeping close to the side to avoid the tap. Moving with the supple effortlessness of the young, he turned into the road and ran smoothly down its center. The cool night air, buzzing at his ears and through his curly African hair, was heavy with the smoke of hundreds of braziers like those in the yard he had just left. Normally he loved running at night with the cool air all around him, his clothes blowing and billowing, but now he was barely aware of it. What he had just heard had driven even the story out of his mind. He had never heard the people of Sophiatown talking that way. He had thought that everyone loved Sophiatown as he did and would rather die than leave it. Of course most of his dealings had been with situations like himself. For months now he had heard only what his own class had to say about the impending removals. What he had heard on the subject from the people who visited Mama Mabaso's home filled his thoughts continually. "The situation is very bad. The electorate don't know . . . I can't sell. They offer me two hundred but I paid four hundred . . . We were here before the whites in Westdene. We came from Prospect when they didn't want us there. They said Prospect was too close to town . . . My papa bought this place. We built the tenants' rooms ourselves . . . I've been a Congress supporter for fifteen years. Now they've got to do something. We are looking to Nelson . . . I bought thirty years ago. They say I've had half the value now. So I only get half price . . . We've had our place ten years. We pay eleven pounds every month. Now they want to buy it from us and there are no title deeds. The Indian attorney has the title deeds. They say it was never our house. My papa paid the deposit . . . This is a Christian country. The electorate won't allow . . . The situation is very, very bad . . . But the M plan . . . Mandela worked out everything himself. Nelson is a clever man. He had some of those white Communist lawyers helping him. They know all the tricks . . . The M plan . . . The M plan . . ."

Sam had rarely heard what the tenants had to say. Occasionally at Freedom Square he had heard them try to put over their point of view, but their English was always so clumsy and long-winded that even the other tenants lost interest. He had never thought that there could be anyone in Sophiatown who was not even interested in hearing the details of the M plan.

Running with the freedom and imperviousness to physical strain of the truly preoccupied, Sam swung out of Meyer Street and down Good Street, past the cinema, now in darkness, its doors closed, and into the street where Johnson lived.

He reached the house, a broad red-brick structure that Johnson's family shared with another family. Clearing the low brick wall by doing little more than kicking his feet up high as he went over, Sam dashed around to the back, down the passage between the first row of tenants' rooms and the house, and knocked on the back door.

It was a while before Johnson's mother answered. She was a big-bosomed woman, rather stern-faced, but she had always been kind to Sam. Now she looked sleepy and irritable, her eyes red-lined. She screwed them up as she squinted in Sam's direction. He was standing in the shadow, the light from the door not quite reaching him. "Sam, is it you?"

"Hello, Mama," Sam said. "My mama asks if Thombina can't come to help her?"

Johnson's mother's face looked puzzled at Sam's request. She glanced into the kitchen. From the direction in which she was looking, Sam could tell that she was reading the time on the kitchen clock. "Your mama wants Thombina to come now?" she asked.

"Yes, Mama."

"To do what?"

"To help her, Mama—with the shebeen."

"With the shebeen, Sam? It's past two o'clock. The shebeen will be finished."

Sam thought about this for a moment, but he knew Johnson's mother had to be wrong. "It was still going when I left there," he said. "My mama said I must ask if Thombina can't come to help. The work is too much."

A little knowing smile formed around the corners of Johnson's mother's mouth and around her eyes. "Did you come straight here, Sam?"

"Yes, Mama," Sam said truly. "I . . ." But then he remembered the story and the conversation he had heard in the yard.

Johnson's mother's eyes were wide, holding an amused expression, her head cocked slightly to one side. Sam looked away from her eyes to a spot on the wall of the house and back at her again. "I think you should run home quickly, Sam," she said. "I don't think your mother wants Thombina anymore."

Sam backed slowly away from her, continually glancing down at his feet or at the spot on the wall, his feet impatient to be running again. He was halfway to the corner of the house and Johnson's mother was still in the doorway, looking after him with the same amusement in her face, when he stopped and looked straight at her somewhat uncertainly. "Mama, what are you going to do when the removals come?"

She looked surprised at the question. "I don't know, Sam. Why do you ask?"

"Nobody seems to know."

"I think we will go to Orlando." She must have seen the shock on Sam's face because she continued quickly, "The house does not belong to us."

"But don't you want to stay here, Mama?"

"Of course we do, child, but what can we do when they come to move us?"

"What about the M plan?"

Johnson's mother shrugged. "Perhaps it will work." The manner in which it was said did not indicate much confidence in the idea.

Sam turned and ran, leaving her standing in the open doorway. What he had learned in the past few hours had combined to make him uncertain of many things. But of one thing he was sure. They should resist. Sophiatown was theirs. They had bought it and built it and now it was theirs. It was not just that it belonged to them. It was part of them, and, for their part, they were Sophiatown. To just give it up and go away was more than his thinking could accommodate.

Coming around the corner at the end of the block, he was

startled to see that Mama Mabaso's house was in darkness, the shebeen closed and Shakes and his customers all gone home. Sam went quietly down the side of the house, hoping that he would be able to get in without knocking and waking the household. At the back the kitchen light was burning and the door was slightly ajar. For a moment Sam feared that something might be wrong and he leaped up the stairs, throwing the door wide open.

Mama Mabaso was sitting on the floor in front of an open cupboard. On the floor next to her were two cardboard boxes. One was already filled with old pots and pans and pieces of material, and she was busy filling the second. At his sudden entry she turned angrily toward the door without rising. "Where have you been, child?" But Sam's attention was occupied by the two cardboard boxes on the floor and he did not answer immediately. "Child, where have you been?" Mama Mabaso's broad old face was truly angry.

Only the fact that she was very tired saved Sam from a hiding. Her question had still not penetrated beyond his preoccupation with the cardboard boxes. "Mama, the boxes?"

Mama Mabaso allowed her attention to be diverted to the boxes for no more than an instant. "Where were you, Sam?"

"Mama, what are the boxes for?"

Mama Mabaso lunged at a broom which was leaning against the wall not far from her, got hold of it at the base of the handle and swung it at Sam all in one movement. The blow caught him on the right kneecap, momentarily crippling him. "Eina." He held onto the affected kneecap with both hands, hopping painfully up and down on his remaining good leg. "Eina, Mama."

"What were you doing, Sam?" Mama Mabaso shouted.

"Johnson's mama," Sam yelped.

"And where's Thombina?"

"In bed. Johnson's mama said it's too late."

"And what did you do before you went there?"

Sam hesitated before answering, and once again the broom was lifted up in businesslike fashion. "I heard a story."

"You heard a story? Where?"

"With the tenants in Mama Mkela's place."

Mama Mabaso dropped the broom against the wall. "Sam, Sam," she said sadly. "When are you going to learn to be a good boy?"

Sam thought briefly about the question. He could find no answer for it. No one else knew how hard he tried to be good and how impossible it was. In the back of his consciousness he heard Mama Mabaso speak again, also something about being good, but he was not listening to her. "What are the boxes for, Mama?"

She turned away from him and continued packing the boxes. "The boxes are for packing. I am packing the things I use little," she grumbled. "Everything is cleaned up after the shebeen. Winifred helped me and we did it very quickly, but I didn't want to go to bed until you came home. So I started doing this."

"Why? Why are you packing?"

"The removals, child. Where do you live that you haven't heard of removals?"

"I live here, Mama. I know about the removals."

"Good. That is why I am packing. To make it esaier when the time comes."

"But we must resist," Sam said.

Mama Mabaso turned to look at him again. Her big old face was soft with tenderness. "Who is going to resist?" she asked. "The police will come with guns. Will I resist? Will you resist?"

"But what about the M plan, Mama?"

Mama Mabaso's chuckle was short and humorless. "There is no M plan, child."

"But Bloke says . . ."

"Bloke and the others play games for children. I don't believe Nelson ever made a plan to stop the removals. He would know that no plan would work." Mama Mabaso was looking at his face, and there must have been something in its expression that she seldom saw there. She stopped speaking for a moment to look at him. When she continued it was very gently. "We will live in Orlando. It will be all right. They will give us a pondok."

"Perhaps they will not come with guns," Sam said.

"They will come with guns. But even if they didn't the tenants would go. They are very poor and afraid. They would not resist. We cannot blame them."

"But we can resist."

"If the tenants go, who pays the bond?" Sam was staring at her uncomprehendingly. "Child, we cannot live like this without the money from the tenants. If the tenants go, we will have to go too. You want to go to the Fort. It costs money. If we have to leave, I will take the money for the house and you can go to the Fort with that."

"Mama . . ." Sam's voice was suddenly very young and uncertain. He did not want to believe what she had been telling him, but he knew that of all people she never lied to him.

"I speak truly, child. There is no M plan."

⌘   ⌘

The window was in darkness and Fourie was drawing the curtains. Brown was seated at the desk looking disconsolate, possibly having second thoughts about his decision of that morning to stay away from the young lady with whom he had spent the previous night. Without looking directly at him, Bhengu was aware of the third policeman, sitting on the table near the door. His head seemed to be bent forward, as if he was looking down at the floor. It was still impossible for Bhengu to look at him.

He did not remember the day duty leaving or the night shift coming in to replace them. Seeing them there, he was afraid again. He closed his eyes. He hated it all with the frightened ineffectual hatred of all political prisoners everywhere. He hated being there against his will. He had never learned to handle it the way some of the brothers had. He hated being in the presence of these people, looking into their empty eyes.

"What about some coffee, Len?" The voice was Brown's, bored and irritable. Bhengu heard no answer from Fourie, but the door opened and closed and he imagined Fourie on his way down the passage with the kettle. Brown always treated him as his personal servant.

With his eyes still closed and still trying to shut out his fear, Bhengu heard a movement from the desk, and then the soft sound of feet moving across the carpeted floor. The door opened and closed a second time. He opened his eyes and looked straight up at the ceiling. In the corner of his field of vision he could see that the desk was now empty. The only policeman who remained in the room was the man sitting on the table, and he seemed to have turned his head to look at Bhengu. He remained in that position for only a few seconds more, then he moved, slowly, lethargically, getting to his feet. With his eyes directed at the ceiling, Sam Bhengu watched the policeman coming across the room toward him. Bhengu's bladder contracted violently, and for the second time that day he felt the warm flood of urine between his thighs and over his testicles, damming up briefly under his buttocks before being absorbed by the mattress. He hated this more than anything else; the thought that it was fear that squeezed the pee out of him. He wished there was some way he could mop it up or at least hide it.

The shadow of the policeman fell over his face and he

closed his eyes so that he would not be able to see him. The only important thing was to control his bladder so that he did not pee again.

✠ ✠

The knocking was very soft and in the early morning twilight it was some time before Sam realized that there were men in the yard. They were in the shadow of the rooms and, with the growing light of the sky beyond, he saw them for the first time when one of the doors opened. In the deeper darkness of the open doorway he could see a movement of figures. He could not yet see what they were doing. Without switching on the kitchen light Sam moved closer, going down to the end of the stoep until he was directly above them. Almost pressing his face against the window, he looked down into the yard. The two men closest to the doorway, one standing on either side, were wearing overcoats and flat-topped police caps. As he watched, Sam saw one of them turn to speak to the other, his white face clear and ghostly against the near darkness of the room. Through the closed windows Sam could hear the sound of the policeman's voice, apparently calm and unemotional, the words blurred and indistinguishable from each other. At the corner of the house he could see two black policemen dressed the same as the two whites. They were waiting patiently with their hands in the pockets of their overcoats, facing the open doorway and the backs of the other two. The policeman who had spoken switched on a flashlight and entered the room, keeping the flashlight beam pointed straight down at the floor. The second white policeman motioned to the two blacks with a wave of his hand. They came away from the corner and passed him to stop at the second room. One of them knocked on the door, again very softly. Inside the first room Sam could see the light of the flashlight flitting back and forth as the policeman moved around inside the room. A moment later he came out followed by Mama Nunu, the old tenant who lived there with her sister. Mama Nunu's eyes were wide with fright and uncertainty and in her arms she carried a large bundle, like a pile of washing, wrapped in a blanket. She had dressed hurriedly and was wearing her old black coat and slippers without the scarf she normally wore around her head. A moment later her sister followed, glancing nervously at the policemen as she passed them, carrying a wooden kitchen chair by the backrest in one hand and a small tin trunk in the other. Mama Nunu lifted the bundle of clothing onto her head and set off for the side of the house with her sister following.

The two policemen came away from Mama Nunu's room, moving deeper into the yard. They passed close by the window from which Sam was watching, and for a moment Sam could see the face of the one with the flashlight clearly. He was very young and his expression was serious, possibly even concerned. It was only a moment and then the two policemen were moving on, passing the second door, which was now open, the frightened face of a tenant visible in the doorway, and on to the third door. Sam heard the soft knocking and saw the door open almost immediately. The policeman's flashlight flashed on again and Sam heard him speak, followed by a startled exclamation from someone inside the room. From within the second room there were also voices now, and already one of the children, a little boy of about six, was standing outside, dressed in a shirt and shorts with a polo-neck jersey, five or six sizes too big for him, hanging loosely down to midthigh, his feet bare. Mama Nunu and her sister came back around the corner without their luggage and reentered the room. A moment later they came out, carrying a narrow steel divan.

Sam turned and ran through the kitchen and down the passage, moving quietly so as not to wake the others, until he reached Mama Mabaso's room. He opened the door and entered without knocking—something he had never done before and would normally never have done at all. Mama Mabaso was lying on her back and snoring softly through her wideopen mouth, her broad face like a dark shadow on the white pillow slip. One fleshy arm protruded from her nightdress and lay outside on the coverlet. Sam took hold of it and shook her gently. "Mama, Mama," he called softly.

With a brief stirring of her head on the pillow she woke and sat upright, her eyes taking a moment to pick out Sam in the darkness of the room. "What is it, Sam?"

"Mama, they're here. They're stealing the tenants." The words came out quickly, breathlessly.

"Stealing the tenants? What do you mean, child?"

"They're stealing the tenants. The police are stealing the tenants."

"Go. Go out of the room. I'll get dressed." She waved a hand brusquely at him and he scurried out of the room, pulling the door closed behind him.

Sam went quietly down the passage to the front of the house, moving on the balls of his feet, and into the living room. The debris of the shebeen—cigarette ends, used matches, empty liquor bottles and pieces of colored paper streamers—had been swept into a neat pile next to the door. Sam picked his way between Shakes's linoleum-covered tables and slipped in behind the curtains so that he could see out into the street without disturbing them.

From the window he could see three big open trucks, parked one behind the other. From the backyards up and down the road streams of tenants were coming, carrying their few belongings in their arms or on their heads and loading them into the trucks. Some of the people were already sitting on the trucks with their goods, ready to be taken to Orlando. There were policemen, both black and white, wearing overcoats and carrying rifles, guarding the trucks and the entrances to a score of backyards and patrolling up and down the road on both sides.

From the passage Sam heard the door of Mama Mabaso's room open, and he left the window to go to her. As he reached the passage he saw her enter the kitchen. He caught up with her at the place from which he had been watching earlier. She was standing still, leaning her weight on the window frame and looking down into the yard. The policemen were no longer in sight, having moved on to the rooms at the back, from which a steady stream of people, all hurriedly dressed, coats and jerseys pulled on over unbuttoned shirts, shoelaces untied, hair standing awry and carrying their possessions in boxes or bundles, flowed through to the street and the waiting trucks.

Sam looked at Mama Mabaso. The light of the sky was brighter now and he could see every line and wrinkle in her brave old face. Something about the way the light reflected from her eyes gave them an almost unreal look, such as you might see in the painting of an angel by an old master. He could see no expression at all. It was as if what was happening was beyond emotional reaction. She had known all along that it was coming, but now that it was upon them it was too much to accept as real. With the tenants gone their monthly rent was gone, and there was no longer any possibility of meeting the bond repayments. It was all over. Mama Mabaso knew that for hundreds of her people the Sophiatown dream was about to end in a sudden awakening to reality. Sam stood next to her until the last few of the tenants had come back for the last time and carried away an unpainted wooden table and the two white policemen, coming behind them, had walked slowly past the window and around the corner at the side of the house. At length she spoke, and her voice, like the expression of her face, was flat and without emphasis. "What were you doing up, Sam?"

"I woke up and couldn't go to sleep again, so I got out of bed to see the sun come up."

"To see the sun come up?"

"It always looks so beautiful here. At Alexandra the houses were in the way, and when it came up past the top of the houses it wasn't even beautiful anymore. Here it is beautiful."

As they stood at the window the sun rose, shining through the branches of the small oak at the back of the yard, its yellow shafts penetrating the long kitchen windows and throwing sharp irregular patterns of shade over their faces. Sam turned away from the sunrise to look at Mama Mabaso again. Outside a breeze moved through the little oak tree, disturbing the network of light and shade on her face. He wished that he could have done something that would have made everything right for her.

✠ ✠

The traffic sounds from the street had all but subsided and it had been some time since any of the three policemen had moved except to turn the pages of the books and magazines they were reading. Brown was again sitting at the desk and he was reading a book that belonged to the third policeman, whose name Bhengu had not been able to remember. Perhaps he could have remembered it if he had been able to approach the fact of the man's presence, but so far it had been impossible. He had had to face it too soon. Perhaps if he had been given a little time to prepare himself he would have been able to do it.

Bhengu could read the title of the book Brown was reading. It was called *Lesbian Love*. He had watched the third policeman, the one whose name he was still avoiding, unpack a handful of paperbacks from his briefcase. He had done it shortly after he had come in, bringing them out ceremoniously one by one, and holding each one up so that the others could see the titles. All the time that he had been doing it Bhengu had watched his hands and the books and the briefcase, but he had avoided the man's face the same way he avoided his name. He could remember the titles—*Twilight Woman, Secret Techniques of Erotic Delight, Kama Sutra, The Artist and his Model;* these, together with a collection of old *Playboys*, all begged from members of the vice squad who had collected them during raids, were the third policeman's most precious possessions. Bhengu had listened to him explain how he rarely brought them out, hinting that when he did he expected them to be handled with appropriate reverence. The proud proprietor himself was seated at the table opposite Fourie, paging through one of the *Playboys*, the corners of its pages worn and gray from much handling. Fourie was reading a Western. Apart from the time when he had made coffee at Brown's instructions, he had been concentrating on his book. He had said very little since coming on duty, seeming to avoid speaking as far as he could.

Inside his mouth Bhengu's tongue was thick, lifeless and sticky where it touched the roof or sides of his mouth. He tried to move it and he felt the edges twitch feebly, heavy, like flypaper against the insides of his cheeks. On the desk between Fourie and the third policeman a one-liter plastic container of orange juice waited to be finished. Through the milky translucent material of the container he could see the deep-orange color of the liquid more than half filling it. He could imagine the smooth soft liquid flowing around his tongue and into the dryness of his throat, healing wherever it touched.

"Yissis, look at this one," Van Rooyen was saying. Bhengu found himself acknowledging the policeman's name, momentarily overcoming his fear enough to allow it into his conscious thinking. He could still not look at the face, but the name drove strongly into his mind until it filled every corner, pervading all of his consciousness, an instrument of torture that allowed no area of relief. "Yissis. She looks so innocent, but look at her." He held up the magazine so that Brown and Fourie could both get a good view of the picture. It showed a naked teenage girl crawling on hands and knees across the ruffled sheets of an unmade bed. Her full dome-shaped breasts hung straight down, the pink of her nipples exactly the same color as the flush on her cheeks. "Yissis," Van Rooyen repeated.

Fourie glanced at the picture and went back to his reading. Brown lay down the book he was reading on the desk. "You know how many times you've shown me that picture?" he asked. "About a hundred."

"Look at her. Look how innocent she looks."

"It's like Du Toit's wife," Brown said. "She always makes such a show about what a good woman she is. In the meantime she's so randy her eyes just about tip over every time a bloke looks at her."

Van Rooyen chuckled. In the corner of his field of vision Bhengu could see the policeman's fleshy stomach shaking. "Poor Du Toit," he said. "He's something else again."

"You know what the rookies call her?" Brown paused a moment for an answer, but Van Rooyen was eagerly waiting for him to answer his own question. "Spunk bubbles," Brown said. "They call her spunk bubbles. You must hear what she says about Du Toit." Brown paused again to center attention upon his impending revelations. Fourie looked up from his book, although still holding it open at the place where he had been reading. "She told my wife how she forces him to use the pull-out method. She wants nothing to do with any other method. She says the pills disagree with her and she doesn't like skins. So she holds one hand above his ass and when she reckons he's going to come she slaps him. Then he's got to pull out and pinch it closed and run for the shithouse. He's got a helluva fat ass, and she even puts on a show for the other women of how it shakes as he runs for the shithouse. And if he doesn't pull out in time, he gets nothing for a month."

Van Rooyen was laughing, shaking his head and slapping his thigh. Even Fourie was amused, a sad rather thoughtful smile around his mouth and at the corners of his eyes. "Poor bugger," Van Rooyen was saying over and over, between the laughter, "poor bugger. I dunno how a bloke can be like that."

"When André had her she told him he was a twenty-five percent doodle. She says he did fifty percent of the right things and he did them fifty percent right. She says Du Toit is a two percent doodle. All he does right is to shove it in."

Van Rooyen no longer had any control over his laughter. He was leaning forward on the desk with one arm and holding his stomach with the other. Bhengu could see the broad flabby torso shaking inside the expensive sculptured shirt and tailored trousers he was wearing.

"She says she can't take Du Toit when he's drunk, and he can't take her when he's sober. So poor Du Toit hardly ever gets anything. And when he does it's the pull-out method." Brown was feeding Van Rooyen's laughter, scratching through his memory for any other stories about Du Toit's problems with his wife.

"I'm buggered if I know," Van Rooyen was saying through his laughter. "I'm buggered if I know how a bloke can be like that."

Bhengu looked at Fourie's face. The security policeman's expression, only slightly amused, was unchanged. Bhengu's stare seemed to draw his eyes until they were looking directly at each other. It was only a moment, during which the little amusement in the policeman's eyes drained away like water being run out of a bath, leaving only the troubled thought-fulness that had been there before. Fourie turned to look in Brown's direction, his eyes vague, not focusing on anything.

The orange juice had not been moved from its position on the desk, the still-damp tumblers that they had been using standing around the container. Bhengu was glad that he was unable to ask for it. If he had been able to ask, he probably would have and he did not want to degrade himself by giving them the chance to refuse him. He could imagine the reaction. "Come on, Sam. That's our orange juice, not yours. What makes you think you can have some of our orange juice?" The faces would all be friendly and smiling. It would be a game and there would be no way that he could be anything but the loser. "I'm surprised at you, asking a thing like that. I thought you knew better than that, Sam." Bhengu had heard Lategan's order that he was to get no food and drink. They would have loved him to ask.

But the orange juice was there. Like Van Rooyen's name, it was an instrument of torture. All it needed was for one of them to pick up the plastic bottle, take the few steps across the room and pour a cupful into his mouth. It would be so easy for them to do. If they chose to do it, it would be no problem at all. While they had been drinking he had watched every mouthful, the movements of the cheeks as the liquid was drawn in by the tongue, until he had not been able to look at it any longer and had closed his eyes. Beneath him the mattress was unpleasantly clammy from the urine, still cold and clinging where his buttocks touched it, but not as bad as it had been. Compared to the swollen, sticky feeling of his tongue, it was nothing.

The conversation had moved away from Du Toit's wife. Van Rooyen was speaking, his voice thick with suppressed laughter. "At least Du Toit knows that, although his might not be the longest or the thickest, it is the dirtiest." He was being incredibly witty, and the laughter burst out of him again with Brown joining in dutifully. Fourie, his face troubled but neutral, had gone back to his book. Bhengu was sure that he was not reading, doing no more than staring at the place at which the book was opened. Van Rooyen controlled himself enough to continue. "Once he told me a long story about some girls he and another bloke took out, and he kept on about how pretty the girls were and how pretty the girls were. In the end I shouted at him, We aren't interested in how pretty the girls are. We want to know—did you put it in?" This was even funnier than the previous sortie, and Van Rooyen was laughing before he had properly completed the sentence.

Brown chuckled shortly in acknowledgment of the warrant officer's story. "What did Du Toit say?" He wanted to know.

"He said nothing." Van Rooyen got the words out between waves of laughter. "I'm sure he didn't put it in, though."

"Yes," Brown said, rocking contentedly back on his chair, "all anyone needs is a beer and a piece. If you've got that, you've got everything."

"It's the same with everybody." Van Rooyen's laughter had spluttered into sudden extinction.

"Even old Sam over there. All he wants to make him happy is a beer and a piece. Don't you, Sam?" Brown had changed ostentatiously to English for Bhengu's benefit. He looked into the stupid grinning face, the lips unusually red, the eyes shining with coarse merriment. It was an expression that would normally signal pleasure to the spectator, but to Bhengu there seemed to be a measure of hysteria in it, a wild desperation to find enjoyment somewhere. "Hey, Sam? All you want is a beer and a piece, hey? Just like us, hey?" Bhengu's attention was held by the grinning mouth, the carefully combed black hair, each lock lovingly positioned, and the hysterical eyes. All of life had been reduced to a beer and a piece; all of love and hate, dominance and submission, fear and security, pleasure and pain, calm and fury; all had been condensed to that ultimate formula—a beer and a piece. No, you bastard, Bhengu thought, that isn't what I want. I'll never have a beer again and I'll sure as hell never have a piece again. The knowledge of what he would never have was suddenly painful within him. Bhengu was not a man for regrets, but he regretted that it had come to this. He regretted all the good things that there could have been, but now would never be. What I want is to take you with me, you bastard. That's all I want.

"Everybody's got to get it somewhere," Brown said. He was maintaining the conversation at a lofty philosophical level, the same level as his a-beer-and-a-piece theory. "If you don't get it from your wife, you have to go and get it somewhere else. You can't sit around without it. You'll go off your head." Bhengu could sense a change of mood in Van Rooyen. The brutal mirthfulness had gone. He was still not looking at the policeman's face but there was a difference in the way Van Rooyen sat, more upright and less relaxed than had been the case a few seconds before. "Everybody's got to get it somewhere," Brown said again. "That's why women who sit on it and don't use it have got to watch out. They can't expect us to sit around with our hands folded. That's why some blokes get caught screwing their maids."

"Mine wasn't too bad when we first got married," Van Rooyen said. Bhengu could hear the bitterness in his voice. "She liked it then. Now she says the smell makes her want to vomit." Brown did not react to this new bit of information, waiting for Van Rooyen to expand on it. Fourie looked up quickly from his book, taking in Van Rooyen's face, his eyes betraying his interest. They only rested on the other man's face for a moment. When Van Rooyen glanced in his direction he looked down at his book again. "I tell her to block her fucking nose if it's so bad. I even hold a sheet tight around us so she can't smell anything. I know it's not her fault, but

Yissis . . . it puts you clean off, if you're just getting on the job and she turns her head nearly right around and pulls the pillow over her face to cut out the smell."

"Mine again is always sick." Brown commiserated with him. "I also know it's not her fault, but you get a bit tired of the same story all the time. You've got to get it somewhere." The thought was central to Brown's philosophy of life. "If you don't get it at home, you got to go get it somewhere else."

⌘   ⌘

"Did you?"

"Yes."

"Are you sure?"

"Yes, I did." She was lying on her back, broad-hipped and full-breasted, breathing deeply; fertile substantial womanhood. She was looking straight up toward the ceiling, not at him. In the next room he could hear the boy playing, making the engine sounds of an imaginary motor vehicle.

"You didn't really, did you?"

"No. I did."

"It didn't seem like you did. I can normally feel if you do."

"You mustn't expect me to be like a volcano every time. Sometimes it happens more quietly."

"It just didn't feel as if you did."

"I did, truly."

"Not very satisfactorily, though."

"No, it was fine, really fine."

"Normally I can feel it, but I didn't feel it this time."

"Sometimes it rattles all up and down my spine. Sometimes it happens more quietly. This time it was more quiet. But it was fine."

"I hope so."

"It was, truly, truly."

"If there's anything wrong you must tell me so that I can fix it. If I'm doing something wrong, I want to know."

"Everything is fine. There's nothing wrong."

"I believe you. But if there is anything wrong you must tell me."

"Is it so important to you?"

"Yes."

"Why? Why is it so important?"

"I want it to happen every time. If anything I'm doing stops it from happening, then I won't do it."

"You're doing nothing wrong. Everything is fine. I don't understand why you're so worried."

"I just want everything to be right. That's all."

"Everything is right. I enjoy it. Really, I do."

"It's just that since the girl it doesn't seem . . ."

"No, it's all right. I don't even think about her."

"Are you sure?"

"Yes. I only think about her when you talk about her. If you stop talking about her, I'll forget her."

"I'll stop talking about her then."

"Then I'll forget her."

"Good."

"But I don't want you to think that there is anything wrong. I enjoy it."

H   H

"Let me tell you," Brown said. "The best doodles are stupid girls. Clever women like my wife are always busy with the church things and so on. A woman doesn't need brains to doodle. She can have gone to a special school, it doesn't matter. The stupider they are, the randier they are."

"You're right," Van Rooyen said. He was still sitting rigidly upright and the bitterness was still present in his voice. "What does a woman need brains for anyway?"

"It's better for the job if your wife makes a good impression. She has to sound intelligent in conversation and so on."

"Yes, but fuck it. It's rather a lot to ask of a man to put up with it when she can't even take the smell." Brown rocked far back on his chair, his head tilted upward, and made a sympathetic little clucking noise against the roof of his mouth. Fourie had closed his book and was looking absently at its cover. "So I sent her to the doctor. Yissis, man, I thought there must be something wrong with her." Fourie's eyes moved from the cover of his book and fixed skeptically on Van Rooyen's face.

"What did the doctor do?" Brown's face and voice were neutral, not committing himself, possibly disguising his interest.

"He gave her some pills." Bhengu looked straight at Van Rooyen for the first time since the previous night. He saw the broad shapeless face, with the tiny eyes and mouth and the round almost bridgeless nose, drawn into a frown of self-pity. It was not as he remembered it. The previous night it had been nothing like it was now, but he could not remember just how it had been. That part of his memory was gone. And now the fear was also gone. Looking at the smooth, pathetic face of the policeman, he could not understand his earlier fear. To be frightened of a man with a face like that was more than he could grasp.

"How did the pills work?" Brown was keeping very careful control over himself, looking up at the ceiling as he asked the question.

"I dunno." Moving on his chair as if its surface was hard and uncomfortable, Van Rooyen looked from Brown to Fourie, and then back to Brown.

"I mean, did they work?" Brown's concentration was fixed on a point on the ceiling.

"I dunno." The chair's surface had deteriorated still further and Van Rooyen squirmed in agony.

"I mean, how did they affect her?" There was a growing tightness in Brown's voice as he strove to maintain control.

"She said . . . ah, fuck it . . . I don't wanna talk about it."

"Come on. We all have these sort of problems." Something in Brown was about to snap. He carefully avoided looking anywhere near Van Rooyen.

"Fuck it. She says the pills don't make her like me any better, but since she started taking them she looks at our neighbor a lot more often."

Brown's control finally gave and the laughter burst out of him without any resistance. His knees pulled upward convulsively, causing his feet to slip off the surface of the desk and bringing his chair upright. He brought the palms of his hands and then his head down on the surface of the desk and lay in that position, his body shaking with laughter. Fourie looked from him back to Van Rooyen, and Bhengu could see that he consciously tried to discipline his face, but it was impossible. The way Brown was laughing was irresistible. Fourie's laughter started slowly, from deep in his chest, and built up into a hoarse braying like the sound of a donkey until he was hanging onto the edge of the table, rocking helplessly back and forth. He laughed with even greater abandon than Brown, as if some part of him that had been harshly suppressed, was now suddenly freed.

Van Rooyen's tiny eyes darted back and forth from one to the other, an animal trapped in a cage and looking for a way to escape. His mouth opened as he tried to say something, but closed again without a sound. He half-rose on the chair, his face both puzzled and confused, but, realizing that there was no object in the movement, sank slowly back again. Brown, holding the edge of the desk with one hand and with the other arm wrapped around his stomach, turned to look at Fourie. As they looked at each other the laughter grew to an even greater intensity. Van Rooyen finally got to his feet, still looking back and forth between the two. "Fuck it, you blokes, hey," he stuttered. "Fuck it, hey." That was too much for Brown and Fourie. Their laughter grew to a level of near hysteria, all the time looking at each other, each feeding the other's amusement, both unable to look at Van Rooyen. "A bloke tells you something, then you carry on like this, hey?" The words came out of Van Rooyen as if he was being strangled. "Fuck it, you blokes, hey. Yissis, hey." He was shifting his weight from one foot to the other. The eyes were wild and undisciplined and now Bhengu understood his earlier fear. Van Rooyen's head turned and he looked straight into Bhengu's eyes. The panic and desperation in the policeman immediately found the point on which they could focus. "You kaffir, are you laughing at me too? Have you forgotten about last night already?" He moved quickly across the room toward Bhengu, his face fearful and crazy. Bhengu's fear returned with the force of a physical shock. Looking at the policeman's face, other things too were returning. He felt uneasy tremors of his consciousness, shiftings in his store of memory, unwelcome images registering their momentary appearance and then disappearing. They were all connected with the face of the man moving furiously toward him. He had thought that he remembered the previous night, but now there were stirrings in his conscious record of what had happened that were altering and adding to it. He tried to close his mind to them. Van Rooyen was above him, leaning over him. The laughter of the other two policemen roared loudly, filling the room, Brown snorting helplessly through his nose and Fourie braying nervously like a demented jackass, driving Van Rooyen on . . . "You kaffir, are you also laughing? You forget fast, hey?" The muscles of Bhengu's stomach drew together convulsively, but this time there was no urine left to squeeze out of him. "You kaffir . . ."

H H

The road was a baked mud track between the shacks. Higher up the hill, near its end, it was filled with goats and the little boys who were bringing them in for the night. The sounds of the goats and the shouts of the boys were absorbed into the general racket that always hung over the Manor. The walls of almost all the shacks were of corrugated iron, so the squealing of the children, the arguing of their parents, the cackling of the poultry and the cries of the goats, all reached out into the street to intermingle with the creaking of mule carts, the soulless reverberations of motorcar engines, sporadic interludes of violence, a scream—the Manor was never silent.

Sam Bhengu turned into a side street that was no more than a footpath, twisting in and out between shacks of infinite design and no design at all, all of them standing at irregular angles. He knew the path and the shacks well, avoiding the washing lines strung between them without consciously looking for them. The path turned to the right, leading him to the edge of an open hillside that dropped steeply to the valley below. Down in the bottom he could see the road, the gravel surface white between the dark green of the hills. He could see the bridge where the road crossed the river and the bus depot with a single-decker bus moving off toward town, its taillights momentarily glowing bright red as the driver braked to avoid the milk truck on its way up to Kwa Teekey. To his left, over the river, the valley was filled with smoke from the cooking fires on the far side, gathering like a dense mist on the water.

The girl was already outside the shack, waiting for him. She was dressed in a thin cotton frock and had a large imitation-leather handbag hanging by a cord from one hand. On her feet she was wearing shoes with very high, tapering heels. Bhengu was immediately amused by the shoes. He knew that it would have been impossible to walk the Manor's muddy summer roads wearing such shoes, and that she must have come barefoot, carrying the shoes in her bag, and only put them on to wait for him. As soon as he saw her he slowed his stride, wanting to look at her, to absorb everything about her in the last few moments before they were together. She was tall, far taller than most Zulu girls, her legs long and slender, her neat small calf muscles more pronounced with the high-heeled shoes; her arms like her legs long and lean, the bones small, her elbows, wrists and hands narrow. Her head was tilted back to rest against the corrugated iron of the shack, her close-cropped hair woven into a few tight plaits across the top. She was looking across the valley toward Berea Ridge, out-lined against the still-bright sky. Then she turned and saw him. She moved away from the wall, looking straight at him, the bag hanging from her fingers, but her posture had become embarrassed as if he knew something about her of which she was ashamed or that she would rather have kept secret. As he reached her she stepped back, making way for him to get to the door, her eyes on his, and when he drew too close, his eyes only an arm's length from hers, she looked down at her feet. "Hello, girl," Bhengu said.

"Hello, Sam."

He unlocked the door and let her into the shack. The door opened into a single room where the only furniture was a nar-row bed, a chest of drawers with a mirror hanging on the wall above it, and a single straight-back chair. On either side nar-row windows with drawn curtains let only a small part of the daylight into the room. He locked the door behind them and turned to face her. Her face, the eyes large, pupils dilated in the faint light, was very close to his. The smallest wrinkle had formed between her eyebrows.

"Are you afraid?" he asked.

"I don't know what to expect."

Without her shoes she was much smaller, the top of her head coming level with his nose. What she had said the first time they met passed uninvited through his thoughts. "I'm not afraid of big guys. I can stretch." He undressed her with their lips together, his tongue exploring the inside of her mouth, her eyes closed all the time, until he picked her up in his arms and lay her down on the bed.

Since the age of seventeen when he had unexpectedly lost his virginity to another seventeen-year-old in a mutual seduction on the back seat of a nearly empty bus on the way back from town, he had made love to many girls—in the brush around the Manor, in unguarded moments in shacks, or in quiet spots after dark on the unlit streets. Now he was experiencing something new. The strange mixture of fear, vulnerability, uncertainty and excitement in the girl, the way she clung to him with her eyes closed and her head hanging forward when he lifted her into his arms, the way she threw back her head and held onto the railing at the top of the bed as he aroused her, her brief convulsive orgasm before he entered her; no other woman had ever been anything like this. More than anything else, it was her eyes that he would remember afterward: half-closed and slightly squint, misty with passion and the desire to draw him right inside her and hold him there always. When he did enter her he was unprepared for the frantic pumping of her hips, as if the moment was too terrible to endure any longer than necessary and had to be ended as soon as possible, or that the coming climax had been too desperately sought to postpone it any longer. He plunged himself deeper and deeper into her, but the movements were all hers.

The light of the late afternoon reached through the closed curtains, revealing her dark nakedness, her head resting in the crook of his arm, her eyes still half-closed and holding within them the promise of further wonders. "Where are you going after this?" he asked. For reply she shrugged, making the smallest movement of her shoulders, and allowed her eyes to close. Examining her eyelids in the dim filtered light, he was not sure whether they were truly closed or whether she had left little cracks through which she could see him. "When we leave here where will you go?" Again the little shrug came almost automatically, seeming to suggest that it was of no importance anyway. "Tell me. You must know what you are going to do."

"There's a party. I'll go to the party."

"Where?"

"Khumalo's."

"With whom?"

"Philemon."

He withdrew his arm from underneath her head and lifted himself up so that he was leaning over her, resting on one elbow. "Why?"

"What do you expect me to do?" She was avoiding his eyes. He had no reply to her question. "Do you expect me to go home? I hate it there."

"Why Philemon?"

"He asked me to go."

"Just because he asked you . . ."

"Will you come with me?" It was not said challengingly. It was closer to being a request that had some chance of being granted.

"You know I can't."

"Well, then?"

His anger was a pain within him. "After this, you can just go with him?"

"Will you come with me?"

"You know I can't. Don't ask me."

"I would rather be with you. If you'll come I'll go with you."

"Stop asking me that. You know I'd rather be with you than anywhere else. But I can't . . ." The sentence was unfinished, there being no need to complete it. "Will you let him make love to you?" Her face broke into a broad grin, her teeth shining in the dim light. A stream of little giggles came bubbling up from her throat and she turned her head to his chest, pressing her forehead against it. "Will you?"

"Maybe. I'll think about it."

Bhengu took hold of both her shoulders and shook her brutally. "How can you even think about it?"

She turned her head away from him. "You're hurting me. I'm not going to stay here if you hurt me."

"Are you going to let him make love to you?"

She giggled again, dropping her head and trying to reach his chest with it, to hide her face there, but he held her at arm's length. "You're hurting me." The words came out plaintively between the giggles.

Bhengu let her go, swung his feet off the bed and sat upright on its edge with his back to her. In a moment she was up against him, pressing her naked breasts against his back, clinging tightly to him with her arms around his neck. Her voice was pleading and childlike in tone, so soft that he barely heard her. "Come with me. Please come with me."

♈ ♈

He was alone with Brown. The lieutenant had pulled up a chair and was sitting next to the bed. His unlined immature face was arranged in an expression of sanctimonious disapproval, the neat rosebud mouth drawn in tightly, appearing even smaller and neater than usual. He looked to Bhengu like the poor man's imitation of Strydom, trying to appear as incontrovertibly certain of the justice of his position as was always the case with the captain. "You know why you're shackled, Sam?" he asked in English. "You know why?" Bhengu imagined that he was about to have the knowledge inflicted upon him whether he was interested or not. He doubted that it would be of any value to him. "You know why you're shackled? You are shackled to prevent you attempting suicide. We aren't going to allow any more of you bastards to commit suicide and give us a bad name overseas. You can forget that. That's why you're shackled and that's why you're going to stay shackled." Bhengu was no longer listening to him. His thoughts were occupied by the images of friends who had been taken in for questioning, who had not come out and who would never come out again, thereby deceitfully giving the security police a bad name overseas. There had always been the press release that explained everything. A prisoner had committed suicide . . . he had incriminated himself during an earlier interrogation and wanted to avoid further questioning . . . had been depressed for some time . . . tore the cell blanket into strips . . . hanged himself from a fitting in the cell . . .

It had been very cold the morning they buried Ambrose, the Lamont Cemetery bare, as desolate-looking as the photographs of the moon's surface, piles of rocks marking the graves, the gathering small and depressed in the rain, their singing mournful, the black power salutes a sad empty gesture. He had never felt so powerless.

There was Timol. Bhengu had spoken to him a month before he went through the plate-glass window on the tenth floor of John Vorster Square. He had never heard if the Indian had been cut by the glass before he fell the long way down to the pavement.

And Lushozi. The day before he was arrested the fat man had been worried, saying that perhaps he should go underground, but Bhengu had persuaded him not to. He had said that they would never liberate themselves by going underground. They would be playing into the government's hands, bringing themselves down to the level of criminals. Bhengu had told Lushozi that there was nothing the government would have enjoyed more than hunting them down.

The statement had said that Lushozi had hanged himself from a fitting. Bhengu knew those same cells and he knew that the fitting in question was fixed to the wall so low down that Lushozi's buttocks must have almost rested on the ground when hanging from it. Bhengu had been with the family when they went to fetch his personal effects: a little neatly folded pile of clothing and one rand twenty-five in change.

Yenana's sister had come to see him a few hours after her brother had been picked up. She had pleaded with him, certain that there must have been something they could do . . . Bhengu tore himself away from his recollections. He could see everything that had happened in such detail now. The faces of the people he remembered were more real to him than the face of the policeman sitting in the chair next to him.

"You're all ballsed up, Sam. Look at you. You're all confused. You're totally ballsed up."

You're wrong, Lieutenant, Bhengu's brain reacted. I see everything more clearly than I ever did before. I see you far more clearly; a little man pretending to be something that you aren't, imitating your masters. I see Van Rooyen clearly too, an inferior swine who will have to compensate for his inferiority all his life, damaging and killing wherever he has the chance. I see Fourie, timid and pathetic, no match for the rest of you. In some other line of work he would have been a decent man. I see you all so damned clearly and I hate you more than ever before, because you'll always be blind to what you do not want to see and you'll only understand as far as your fears allow you. You'll go on brutalizing and killing until we stop you. And we will stop you. We will come for the Browns and the Van Rooyens and the Fouries . . . I'm not the last in the line. We'll come for all of you bastards.

"You want food?" Brown was asking. "You want some food?" Bhengu's tongue filled his mouth completely, pressing against the insides of his cheeks and the back of his lips, scraping against his teeth when any part of his mouth moved. To have eaten anything would have been impossible. "Of course you don't. You want something to drink. How about some of that orange juice?" The policeman gestured in the direction of the desk. The plastic container was still a quarter full, the yellow liquid glowing through the milky-white container. "You want some orange juice, Sam? I'm sure you want some. All I want is a statement from you and I'll give you all the rest of the orange juice. How's that? Is it a deal?" The edges of his tongue were serrated, scratching painfully against the insides of his lips and cheeks at any movement. One mouthful of the orange juice would change everything. He could already feel it, smooth against the delicate membrane inside his mouth. "You want some orange juice, Sam?"

A voice that Bhengu now recognized as his own answered. "Yes." It was no more than a croak and he had not meant to speak.

A smile of pleasure settled on Brown's face. "That's better. That's much better. It's about time you came out with the truth. You've been wasting everyone's time."

Time? Bhengu asked himself. Wasting everyone's time? His mind grappled briefly with the meaning of the word, but it had no meaning. He had all the time there had ever been, and he had no time.

Brown glanced down at his watch. "Sam, I'm going away for fifteen minutes. When I come back I'll take your statement. Okay?" The policeman's eyes were wide open, questioning, the pleasurable smile making his face unusually benevolent. "Okay, Sam? I'll be back in fifteen minutes." As he waited for an answer the eyes gradually narrowed and the smile was replaced by a look of troubled suspicion. "You spoke just now, Sam," he said. "I heard you. So don't bugger me around." His voice had risen uncertainly. His eyes were moving continually, seemingly without a point on which to focus. "I heard you, Sam. It's no use playing dumb now." He looked quickly at his watch again and got to his feet. "I'll be back in fifteen minutes. You see that you have your story ready." The lieutenant backed toward the door, picking up his jacket from the chair as he went, only turning his back on Bhengu as he went out. Bhengu saw the door close and heard the sound of the key in the lock. Then he was alone in the interrogation room for the first time.

Fourie had drawn the curtains of the windows on the far side, leaving a small opening about the width of a man's hand in the center. Bhengu tried to see through the opening, to gain some view of the world outside where men came and went freely. His eyes probed every corner of it for something, any form or outline, anything on the outside. Even the corner of a building or the gaunt structure of a crane, seen dimly in outline, would have been welcome. But the darkness was total.

He closed his eyes and listened, hoping that his ears would have greater success. Almost immediately he heard a high raucous cry. He was sure it was a gull . . .

But it may have been something else, perhaps only a mechanical sound, the scream of unlubricated metal on metal. Down in the shunting yards two coaches crashed together as they were coupled, followed by a second crash as loud, and a third softer one. Bhengu thought he heard the squealing of the train's brakes. From the street below, the cacophony of a motorcycle engine penetrated the walls and windows to reach him. No other sounds did. There was a final crash from the shunting yard and that was all.

He was aware of his feet. On the outside of one of his ankles there was a chafed place that was worse than the rest. He tried to move it, but it was held fast. He tried again, pushing the leg down to force the manacle up toward the calf. Again there was no movement. He pulled hard to lift his head off the mattress, and it lifted just enough for him to see down the length of his body. His feet were suspended above the mattress, resting on the steel crossbar of the manacles and held in place by the cuffs. Just above the right ankle he could see a place where the skin was broken and rumpled into little ridges, revealing pink layers of tissue beneath. He could also see that the cuff was loose around his ankle, so he should have been able to move his foot. He tried a third time, again concentrating on driving it deeper into the cuff, but again there was no movement. He had not even seen a reaction in the leg muscles. Both legs were dangling limply from the manacles, the knees hanging outward and the flesh drooping down away from the bone, making them look thinner than they were. His penis, limp and redundant, had disappeared between his legs so that only the little bush of pubic hair was visible beyond his sagging belly. He allowed his head to drop back to the springy surface of the mattress. From the passage he heard the sound of approaching footsteps. He closed his eyes. Brown would wait a long time for his statement. Bhengu would try not to think about the orange juice.

❉   ❉

"Perhaps the opposition . . ." Robert started to say.

"They are all part of the ruling elite," Bhengu said, "and their interests and the interests of the oppressed will always be in sharp conflict."

"Maybe things will change," Robert said unhappily.

"Do you see anything changing?"

Robert shrugged. "You're too political for me, Sam. I just want to be left alone to live."

"Do you call this being left alone?" Bhengu waved a hand in the direction of Shumville and the valley. "They'll be up here again tonight, searching the shacks, scratching through our things, knocking holes in the stills."

Robert turned down the corners of his mouth. "I haven't got a still," he said.

Bhengu shook his head briefly in disgust and turned to look at Winifred where she was standing at the coal stove, the sweat running down her face. It was midsummer and the corrugated-iron-walled room would have been hot in the damp tropical heat even without the fire. Winifred dropped to her haunches and swung open the door without using a cloth, snatching quickly at the handle to avoid burning her hands. She put a few more cut pieces of wood into the fire and straightened up again to stir the big cast-iron pot on the stove. She was wearing a cotton dress with a bright sunflower design on the material, the skirt hanging to below her knees and flaring in a way that made her look broader than she really was. In the years since they had left Sophiatown she had matured into a tall buxom young woman, not unlike Mama Mabaso in build. When they were seen together she was always spoken of as Mama Mabaso's daughter, something that pleased both of them very much. Now her face was distressed. Bhengu could see the worry in her eyes and the little wrinkles around them, but something in the way she was looking at him prevented him from approaching it while Robert was with them. He and Robert were seated on either side of the long wooden kitchen table that had come with them from Sophiatown, the same one on which Mama Mabaso had made the hotdogs for Shakes Moloi's shebeen. The light in the room was coming from the fire and from the open door where the late-afternoon sun threw a yellow patch onto the opposite wall. The surface of the floor was a mud-and-dung mixture, plastered almost perfectly smooth by Winifred's practiced hands, with a small sheet of linoleum in front of the stove. The room had two doors: the back door of the shack through which the sunlight was coming in and through which, if he turned his head, Bhengu could see the corrugated-iron wall of the next shack, only ten or twenty paces away; and a door that was closed, leading into the next room. "Where's Mama?" Bhengu asked Winifred.

His sister nodded in the direction of the closed door. He leaned forward in his chair, intending to get to his feet, but she held up a hand to stop him. The movement was quick and nervous, and the hand was as quickly withdrawn as it had been raised.

"Still a long time to supper?" He was trying not to look at Robert or even acknowledge him. The mood would pass, but occasionally Robert's attitude to the rights of his people became a little too much for Bhengu.

"Not long," Winifred said, her worried eyes examining Bhengu's face as if she would uncover some secret there.

"All I want is to be left to go my own way," Robert said. Bhengu turned his head right away from him, his eyes directed absently at the flames he could see through the slots in the stove door. "I just want to live my own life."

"Good Christ, Robert, didn't you once live in a place called Sophiatown? Do you remember what happened there?" Bhengu's voice was harsh to his own ears. He was still angry because the girl was going to the Khumalo's party, but Petronella would be back and he would not be able to be there. The thought of the girl possibly drinking too much and going outside with Philemon . . . And then to have to discuss politics with Robert.

"Sam, please," Winifred said.

The distressed note in her voice was chastening and Bhengu was immediately sorry for his outburst. He turned his chair so that he would not be facing Robert, but not before he saw Robert's shoulders hunch up in his habitually helpless shrug. Bhengu glanced toward the door and the low angle at which the sunlight was coming in. The girl would probably be arrived at the Khumalo's already. Christ, how he hated it.

Without warning, a tall slender young man in a dusty white suit came in at the door, casting a momentary shadow on the opposite wall. He threw his arms wide and snapped the fingers of both hands. "Hey, hey, hey," he shouted, looking from one face to the other of the three people in the room. Then, looking at Winifred out of the corners of his eyes with what was intended to be a lecherous expression, he flapped his hands together in a crude representation of sexual intercourse. "Hey, hey, hey," he repeated.

"Watch yourself," Bhengu said to him, his head partly turned toward the boy, but his position on the chair unchanged.

"Hey, baby," Msima Mzolo said to Winifred, but this time he kept his hands still. Bhengu took in the excitement in the young face, the eyes set far apart and so wide open that he could see the whites all around the irises. The suit jacket was hanging open and he was not wearing a shirt underneath it, his brown chest glistening with perspiration. On one lapel he wore a homemade cardboard badge with the legend AWAY WITH PASSES. "Hey, Sam," he said. "When can I bhepa your sister?"

"I told you to watch yourself," Bhengu said.

"Come on, Sam. A man should always be willing to give his sister to a brother in the liberation struggle." His mouth opened wide, revealing gaps in his teeth, as he forced out a loud mirthless laugh. He reached out and took Winifred by the arm, but let it drop again as his eyes looked into hers and he saw the contempt there. "How about it, baby?" he said, wearing his lecherous expression, but now not looking directly at Winifred's face.

Bhengu was on his feet and facing Mzolo. The white-suited boy made what appeared to be a few quick loose-limbed dance steps, moving his right hand to the inside of his jacket at the same time. Almost immediately a broad-bladed sheath knife appeared in the hand. "The knife will speak, Sam," he said. He jiggled the knife blade quickly up and down, causing it to flash momentary golden reflections around the room. His mouth was stretched wide in a grin, displaying the irregular arrangement of his teeth, but the large eyes with the whites all around the irises were nervous, possibly even hunted. Bhengu was looking straight into his eyes from little more than an arm's length, standing completely still. Mzolo made a few more dance steps and the knife was put away as quickly and neatly as it had appeared. Robert, who had remained seated, drew a deep breath and shook his head. Mzolo glanced at Bhengu again, an uncertain grin flitting across his face, and then sat down at the table next to Robert. Bhengu waited a moment, looking at his sister, before he too sat down. Winifred's contempt for Mzolo had left her face and the obvious distress had returned. Bhengu turned away from her and looked at Mzolo, seated on the far side of the table. The boy spread his arms wide in the same gesture he had used when he had come in. "I am the son of my father," he said, "and tonight I will kill the son of Maketa."

"You talk like a fool," Bhengu said.

"Tonight I will kill the son of Maketa and I will bring back his mtondo and his amesende for proof."

Winifred averted her face, concentrating her attention on stirring the pot that was bubbling steadily on the stove. Bhengu could see how sickened she was at the thought of the severed genitals. "This is the talk of a fool," he said harshly.

"This is the talk of a man who knows," Mzolo said. "I saw them tonight and I saw the son of Maketa and tonight I will kill him. I am the son of my father." He waited for a reaction, but this time Bhengu was silent, watching his face. Robert was leaning his elbows on the edge of the table and looking down at the floor. Winifred, at the stove, was dishing up helpings of mealie-meal porridge and gravy for the three men at the table and for herself. "Twenty-two cops raiding in Jeep Coat tonight. I saw them break six tanks and a still. The son of Maketa is among them. When they find my still I will kill the son of Maketa."

"They will kill you."

"They will see nothing." Mzolo reached inside his jacket and the knife came out again. From out of a trouser pocket he brought a rumpled much-used white handkerchief. Theatrically, like a stage magician before an enthralled audience, he hung the handkerchief around the knife, holding both handkerchief and knife in the same hand. Then he moved his hand forward, handkerchief and knife together, striking the blade into the table between Robert's elbows. No one who had not seen him wrap the handkerchief around the knife, seeing his hand move, would have guessed that it held anything besides the handkerchief.

"Will you pay for the table?" Bhengu asked.

Robert had jerked away from the table and was now sitting upright. Mzolo pulled the knife loose and returned it to the inside of his jacket. "That is what I will do with the son of Maketa. And I will cut off his mtondo. I am the son of my father."

"Your father's mtondo," Bhengu said tiredly.

"The knife will speak," Mzolo said. "One of the white cops asks, what am I doing watching them? I keep quiet. He asks again. Again I keep quiet. He says, what language do you speak? I point to my badge. I say, this language."

"You will bring us trouble," Robert said.

"The son of Maketa will have the trouble. I have got two forty-four-gallon drums, gaveen, in Jeep Coat, buried under my brother's house. One drum korrêr in Shumville in Mama Zuma's yard, and four drums gaveen in Two Steeks. If they find one, the son of Maketa will have trouble." Winifred put the plates before the men, giving each a spoon with which to eat. Then she sat down with them.

"Msima." Bhengu said his name thoughtfully.

"I am Msima, the son of my father," he mumbled through a half-filled mouth.

"Msima, I am talking to you," Bhengu said. "Do you hear me?"

"I hear."

"You want to fight. That is not bad. But to fight for the stills is foolishness."

"They are searching. If they find my GV or my korrêr, the son of Maketa dies."

"Do you hear me, Msima?"

Mzolo's eyes rested on Bhengu's face for an instant before they flitted away to drift around the room. "I hear."

"Good. We must choose our battleground ourselves. We must fight where it is best for us to fight. The gaveen is not the right thing to fight for. If we fight for the gaveen, then we let them decide where the battleground will be."

"For what will we fight?"

"Many things. We can fight to stay in the Manor or we can fight to get rid of the passes or we can fight for equal pay, but let us not fight for gaveen. The country will see us as drunkards. We must choose our own battleground."

"Seven drums good stuff, three months old. I can get four, five hundred pound. I will fight for the gaveen and the korrêr."

"Have you not got ears?" Bhengu asked. "Do you not hear what I am saying?"

"Go bhepa a dog," Mzolo said dispassionately.

❡   ❡

The loudest sound in the room was the sound of Van Rooyen's breathing, even and relaxed, but with a hoarse whistle as if the air from his lungs was being driven past an obstruction. He had his feet on the table and, with his chair rocked back and leaning against the wall, he had been asleep for more than an hour. Brown was also asleep, resting forward on the desk, his head on his arms. Fourie had opened the curtains halfway and was standing at the window, looking down into the street, his hands folded tightly behind his back. As Bhengu watched, he started walking slowly back and forth in front of it. Bhengu looked at his face. It was pale yellow in the electric light, and the lines on his forehead and at the corners of his mouth were more sharply delineated than they had been twenty-four hours before. He walked slowly, pausing often, his feet almost silent on the carpet, covering the narrow width of the room in no more than five or six paces. Occasionally he stopped before the window to look out into the night. Bhengu wondered what he saw. He wondered what the time was. The wall clock above the door had stopped at ten past nine. He could hear no sounds at all from outside, so it was likely that it was very early morning, perhaps three or four o'clock. In that case the policeman would be looking down into empty streets, lit by the streetlamps and the windows of the shops down on Point Road. He might see the occasional man on foot, walking quickly, possibly glancing fearfully into the shadows; or a car, stopping needlessly for traffic lights to change, its headlights penetrating the windows of shops and sweeping through the park on the corner. Looking at Fourie's face, though, it was more likely that he saw nothing. The warrant officer's consciousness was absorbed by things inside him, not by what he was seeing.

He stopped halfway across the window, still facing the direction in which he had been walking. Turning his head slowly, he looked straight into Bhengu's eyes. It was a short time before his attention fastened onto the image of the other man. When it did he drew back as if startled. For a few seconds Fourie looked straight at him, the expression of his face an amalgamation of shock and concern, then he turned again to the window. For a long time he kept his back to Bhengu. From where he was lying Bhengu could see the white bloodless blotches on the security policeman's hands where he gripped them tightly together.

⌘ ⌘

Bhengu waited in the doorway until Robert and Mzolo, following the vagaries of the path, the younger man's white suit like a beacon in the gathering dusk, were lost to his sight behind the lowest row of shacks. Winifred was still seated at the table, having started her supper after the others. "What's the trouble?" he asked her. She turned her face away from him, shaking her head, and he could see that she was crying.

Bhengu went across the room and opened the other door. There was no lamp in the room, but in the light from the tiny curtained windows and from the open doorway he could see Mama Mabaso kneeling at the side of her bed. The room was small and contained a cupboard, two beds and a washstand with a basin. Mama Mabaso's head was resting face downward on the coverlet, her arms stretched out before her in an attitude of supplication. Bhengu glanced back at his sister, but her face was still averted. The old woman's body was so still that she may have been asleep. Bhengu could see her face and that too was still, the lips unmoving. He regretted having come in and possibly having disturbed her, so he remained motionless in the open doorway, not wanting even to back away and close the door in case the sound he made might disturb her. Eventually the old woman's chest heaved in what seemed to be a sigh and she turned her head toward him. She remained in that position for a while, her face obscured by his shadow. Knowing that he had the light behind him and not knowing if she could see his face, he let her hear his voice. "It is I, Mama."

"I see you, my child."

She raised one hand from the bed, the movement slow and tired, and beckoned to him with it. He moved toward the bed and the light from the kitchen fell on her face. Bhengu's eyes fixed onto a thin black line, running straight from just below her hairline to the tip of her nose. At first he thought that it had been no more than a trick of the shadow, but he bent quickly forward to see more clearly and the line was still there. Then he saw the sorrow in her eyes. "Who is it, Mama?" he asked. She shook her head and motioned for him to close the door. Bhengu pushed it closed; then, with his hands flat on the coverlet, he knelt next to the old woman. "Who is it, Mama?" he asked again. "Can you tell me?"

It was a moment before she spoke and her voice sounded calm and peaceful, very soft in the darkness. She might not have heard his question. "When will Petronella be here?"

"She should be on the next bus. Robert went down to the depot to fetch her."

"Why did you not go, my child?"

"I wanted to talk to you, Mama. I asked Robert to go."

She seemed to think about his answer before speaking again. The dull reflection of a fire from the corrugated-iron wall of the shack next door built up slowly, adding to the fading daylight. Mama Mabaso's form was large and dark at the side of the bed. She had dropped her head again. "You should have gone to meet her yourself, Sam. The child is very unsure of you. Will the little one be with her?"

"Yes, Mama."

"Ah." And he heard her sigh, deep and sad, as if something in what he had said had given her cause for regret. "Sam, you must look after the little one."

"I will, Mama."

"There is nothing more that you can do for the little one than to care for his mother." Bhengu thought about the girl. He thought about the way she lay on top of him after love-making, her hips between his legs, her hands massaging his biceps, running over his shoulders, his own hands stroking her back, trailing smoothly over her small neat buttocks; the way eventually she would wriggle up onto him, her breasts against his chest, until her lips reached his, her tongue probing quickly into his mouth, suggesting other more delicious prob-ings; the way her lips pressed into the base of his neck, again and again, warm and soft, clinging, moving, until he felt his erection strong against her stomach. "You must care for Pe-tronella, Sam," Mama Mabaso said.

"I will, Mama."

"It's not good to go with another woman, my child."

"It means nothing, Mama."

"That's not true, Sam. I can see its meaning in your face, my child. And it's a sin."

"All right, Mama."

"Will you not go with her again?"

"I will think about what you said."

"It's a sin, Sam."

"Yes."

Mama Mabaso knew him better than anyone did, excepting only Winifred, and she knew that there was no sense in press-ing him further. "And will you still go to Johannesburg?"

"Yes, Mama."

"Will they not be waiting for you?"

"I don't think so."

"There are many informers."

"I don't think they will be waiting for me, Mama."

"Consider carefully before you go, my child."

"I have considered. It is a matter of self-respect."

"Self-respect is nothing. Consider the little one. And the woman."

"I have considered them. My son must not be ashamed of his father."

"Sam, Sam." Her voice was tired with the weariness of a very long struggle. It was the weariness of Sophiatown and now Cato Manor. "A man's life is not his own. A man's life is a link between his father and his sons. You may not use your life as though it is yours to trifle with. Your life is not your own."

"I know. It is because my life is not my own that we came to Durban. We only left Johannesburg because I was needed here for the struggle. The work sent me. The struggle is more important than my life."

"Perhaps it is, Sam. But your life is a link between your father and your sons. If a link is broken the chain is broken."

"I will be careful, Mama." The old woman sighed again and, even in the half-light, her body seemed to sag, as if some of the spirit that held it upright had left it. "Mama?" Bhengu asked, his lips searching for ways to phrase his question, afraid to ask it and even more afraid of hearing the answer. "Mama, for whom are you mourning? Are you mourning for me?" She said nothing, and in the feeble light he could no longer see the line on her face. He could see how she was shaking her head slowly from side to side.

✠ ✠

Fourie had not moved from the window, his hands still tightly clasped behind his back, his feet a little way apart, his head tilted forward, directing his gaze downward to the street. Van Rooyen's breathing was still strong, noisy and regular, but his face was twitching, his lips forming silent words, as he struggled through a bad dream. On the desk the plastic container of orange juice had been emptied. Bhengu could see the last traces of the liquid in the glass tumblers. Handling his thirst was easier now that the orange juice was gone. His tongue was still overlarge and rough around the edges, still sticking to the insides of his cheeks, but at least he did not have the orange juice where he could see it. It would be easier now to keep his attention diverted to other channels.

The policeman came away from the window, being careful not to look in Bhengu's direction, and switched off the office lights. Then he sat down at the table opposite Van Rooyen. With the lights off the window was no longer dark, the glow of the street lights throwing shadows of the window frames onto the ceiling, while the spasmodic flickering of a red neon sign glowed brightly in the dense sea air. Above the buildings the sky was black with the blackness of night, but also yellow with the absorbed light of the city.

Fourie had moved the chair until he was facing the window with his back to Bhengu, his shoulders hunched forward and his hands clasped together between his thighs. He was careful not to look around.

✠ ✠

He left Mama Mabaso's shack, running quickly, picking his way effortlessly down the path. From the moment when he had heard the first of the women's cries, a full-throated high-pitched oo-loo-loo-loo-loo sound, he had been running. The voice of a second woman joined the first, her tone more shrill than the other. The first voice stopped but the second continued, rising high above the Manor as if it had its source somewhere in the smoke-laden sky, growing in intensity as he drew near to the area where the police raiding party had been operating. The sound continued for so long without an interruption in which to draw a breath that it seemed impossible that it could have been made by a human being, then its form was changing and becoming something intelligible. Other women's voices had joined it, adding to the insistent hysteria of the sound, but the words, shrill and blurred, reached through to Bhengu's mind. "Africa! Africa! come back Africa!"

He ducked under a clothesline, avoided a row of refuse bins that almost blocked a narrow opening between two shacks, and entered a broad dirt road running across the slope of the hill, the shacks set well back on either side. There were already people on the road hurrying in the direction from which the women's cries were coming. Immediately in front of Bhengu a man in torn flannels and a dirty vest was carrying a broom handle, sharpened to a point, and making little practice jabs at the air on all sides. To his right, moving at a stumbling jog, a fat man had a heavy ax hanging straight down from his left hand, its vague metallic presence gleaming gray in the last remnant of daylight. Ahead, a group of women, sturdy Zulu matrons, scattered off the road onto a vacant piece of ground. As he passed the place Bhengu saw that a few of them were already coming back at a hurried leaning-forward waddling trot, weighed down by rocks they had been picking up. Some were still kneeling or bending over. Others had a number of stones, each larger than a man's fist, cradled in their arms or the front of their skirts, and a few had one in either hand, their arms hanging down at their sides. On either side Bhengu could see the movement of people leaving their shacks or coming back to fetch some sort of weapon: a cane knife with a curved blade, a homemade panga or a length of rusted-steel pipe; whatever they had.

The women's voices were a loud chorus now, not far ahead, apparently coming from the place where the street Bhengu was on crossed one coming up the hill. The crowd was denser there and moving forward slowly, youngsters darting in and out among them, bobbing from side to side, looking for openings that would enable them to get closer, but being held back by those in front. The shrill voices of the women were insistent, high above the other voices and the noise of the crowd. "Kill the Dutchmen. Come back, Africa. Kill the Dutchmen." He reached the edge of the crowd and forced his way in, leading with his right shoulder, shoving and wriggling through gaps between others who were also pushing forward. Ahead he heard a voice that he recognized as Mzolo's, shouting, "Do not retreat. The bullets will be finished. Do not retreat." He broke through between two middle-aged women, stout, barefooted, wearing shapeless cotton dresses, and cradling rocks in their arms. In a gap to his left he saw Mzolo, crouching low as if for shelter, his white suit smeared dust-brown around the back. Bhengu immediately noticed the handkerchief, hanging innocently down from his right hand. As the boy moved, hopping forward into an opening caused by a movement of the crowd, still crouching low, there was a moment in which Bhengu could see the unyielding form of the knife blade within the folds of the cloth. Then the crowd closed between them and Mzolo was lost to his sight. Loud, above the noise of the shouting and the scuffling of feet, the report of a revolver caused a shock wave, running back from the front rows of the crowd. For the first time the pressure was coming back at Bhengu as those at the front pressed away from the police.

Second and third shots, as loud as the first, followed immediately with Mzolo's hoarse voice still shouting, "Do not retreat. Do not retreat. The bullets will be finished." The cries of the women had become a piercing blur, only the one word, "Africa," being at all intelligible.

From the moment he had joined the hurrying crowd on the road something had been happening inside Bhengu. It had to do with the cries of the women. It also had to do with the police invading their homes and destroying the stills. It had to do with a memory of Mama Mpanza's liquor being tipped out onto the ground and the way it had run away in muddy streams until it sank into the dust. And it had to do with older pressures, partially suppressed memories of past insults and indignities, earlier invasions of their territory, removals from their homes, recollections of places like Sophiatown, the rough handling of Mama Mabaso and Winifred during a pass raid while he had watched helplessly; and it had to do with what was happening inside everyone in the crowd. The growing excitement, the strange wild elation, was transmitted through the air from person to person until it had reached everyone, infecting them all. Finally, for those close enough to see it, it had to do with the fear they could see in the eyes of the policemen.

There was a choking tightness at the top of Bhengu's chest, constricting his breathing. The soles of his feet and the palms of his hands were damp with perspiration. The eyes of those closest to him were stretched wide open, seemingly enlarged. He heard his voice join the wild shouting of the mob as if he had no control over it. Two more gunshots sounded, again sending ripples of fear through the front rows of people, causing them to thrust backward against those behind. Bhengu pushed hard and broke through the front out into the open.

The policemen, about twenty of them, had formed an untidy ellipse and were edging slowly up the hill, the faces of the

closer ones clearly visible in the twilight. Two of the policemen on Bhengu's side were white, both very young and frightened and both carrying their revolvers in their hands. On the
inside of the ellipse a small group of people—some only partly
dressed, without shoes or shirts, some with clothing dirtied
during the day's work, one thin old man in a torn denim overall that had long since lost its sleeves—moved reluctantly with
the policemen, their faces showing almost the same strain and
fear as those of their captors. The black policemen were
armed only with batons, and these were also out and being
held in front of them and shaken at the crowd as if the shakers
believed they possessed magical powers.

The crowd behind him pushed hard again and Bhengu dug
his heels into the ground and leaned backward, his arms outstretched on either side, trying to hold back its weight. On either side of him there were others doing the same, also reluctant to get any closer to the line of policemen. The resistance
held for a moment, and then they were thrown violently forward, Bhengu stumbling and almost falling. But immediately
the force went out of the push and the people seemed to hesi-
tate, perhaps surprised at their own audacity. He could see the
face of the nearer of the two white policemen clearly. The
mouth was compressed into a hard, tight little line, but a tuft
of straight brown hair was protruding across the forehead
from beneath the peaked cap, giving an incongruously boyish
look to the grim expression of his face. "Stand back," Bhengu
heard him shout, the fear in his voice apparent to those close
enough to hear him. The second word had ended in a high-
pitched quaver. Someone behind Bhengu had started laughing, a coarse brutal sound without any pleasure in it. "Stand
back. I'll shoot. Stand back." On the uphill side the crowd had
thinned, moving out of the way of the policemen and their
captives. Bhengu saw a few young boys on that side, who had
been slow getting away, scatter under a wave of baton blows.

"Stand back. Stand . . ." The white policeman's voice failed completely at the same moment as he collided with the policeman to his left. His cap fell forward over his face, eluded the hand thrust out to catch it and landed at his feet. The crowd was pressing forward again and the line of policemen retreated further, almost by reflex. One of them tramped on the cap, crushing it. The young policeman moved forward, for a moment out of line, his eyes searching the ground. At that moment a rock the size of a tennis ball, thrown from just behind the front row of the crowd, hit him hard above the left ear. Bhengu saw the pain and surprise on his face as he lifted his hand to the spot. From beyond the policemen a woman's voice was repeating, "Come back, Africa. Come back, Africa," with monotonous intensity. A second rock hit the policeman on his right shoulder. The arm seemed to collapse, paralyzed by the blow, the revolver falling straight down into the dust. He bent forward immediately and picked it up in his left hand, but an incoherent roar of triumph had issued from the crowd, and the people were throwing stones all along the line of police. Inside the line, which was no longer an ellipse or any regular shape, the captives shielded their heads with their arms. One of them was shouting, "No. Don't throw. No."

Then the policemen were running up the hill, still trying hopelessly to maintain their line. A rock caught one of the black policemen in the small of the back and he went down on his hands and knees, his body arching painfully backward, and was immediately overrun by the mob. In the corner of his field of vision Bhengu saw the khaki-uniformed figure try to rise, but then he disappeared behind a screen of running figures. A few more gunshots punctuated the noise of the crowd, but the sounds were flat, diminished by the fever flowing like a river over them all. The constriction around Bhengu's chest had become painful. The hinges of his jaw on either side ached and he could feel his breath being driven back and forth through his mouth in quick shallow bursts, but above all other sensations was the fierce vengeful joy that he felt and could see in the eyes and hear in the voices of all around him.

The policeman closest to him, one of the blacks, had turned his back on them and was running hard, his baton still tightly held in his right hand, his broad pith helmet bobbing with the movement of his head. Concentrating on the retreating back, Bhengu sprinted hard. He heard another revolver shot, but again it was a matter of no consequence. On either side in front of him he was aware of policemen running, having surrendered any sort of order. The policeman's back was close in front of him and he punched hard for the area of the kidneys. He saw the man stumble and slow. His shoulder caught the khaki-coated back, spinning him off to the left. One of the policeman's legs splayed outward and Bhengu felt the foot catch his ankle. As he fell he saw the blade of a panga swing downward, a flash of reflected firelight indicating momentarily its passage. Bhengu went down on his chest, turning his head to keep his face away from the ground. He had half risen, his hand still on the ground, when someone ran into him, tumbling full-length and rolling over his back and head. A heavy boot tramped hard on the fingers of his right hand, then a second and third body, pushed by the weight of the crowd, came down on top of him. He crawled to his right to get clear of the sprawling bodies. Again he tried to rise. This time he was unaware of the charging figure. He felt only the blow above his right temple.

They were throwing rocks against his skull, one after the other. He could hear the bones cracking like an eggshell. He wondered why it took so many rocks to do it. They were falling like hail, and as each one landed his skull cracked a little further. He was surprised that there was anything left of it. A

woman's voice reached his ears, the high shrill notes cracking
with the cracking of his skull. "Come back, Africa. Hit the police. Come back, Africa. Hit the police." Mzolo's voice joined
hers. "I am the son of my father," the boy was shouting.

Bhengu's skull stopped cracking. They must have stopped
throwing rocks at him. Winifred's face was before him, silent,
but its expression imploring, "Be careful, Sam. Take care.
Please, take care." She was doing something to his head. Possibly she was mending the cracks.

A pair of naked brown feet attached to two thin youthful legs
trotted past Sam Bhengu's face, hesitated and returned the
way they had come. Mixed with the noise of the mob were
new sounds. A drumming like the sound of hail on a tin roof,
but more jarring and metallic, the splintering of wood and the
sound of revolver shots, still muted, almost muffled, were superimposed on the shouting voices; hoarse and shrill, male
and female, young and old, together an incoherent roar of
murderous ecstasy. The moment of unconsciousness had
changed something in Bhengu and he was no longer a part of
it. He got to his feet and turned in the direction from which
the noise was coming. The mob, with newcomers joining it,
many of them carrying stones, was swarming around the front
part of the long corrugated-iron shed they called Kwa Teekey.
On all sides the streets were full of people, hurrying to become
part of the action or hanging back to watch.

The sound of the voices changed, a breathless "ooo" sound
issuing from the center. At the same time there was a sudden
turbulence in the crowd against the shed, and the young white
policeman who had lost his cap burst through the close-
packed mass of people and came running straight at Bhengu.
He was bleeding from the side of the head where the stone had
caught him and also from a clean cut starting near the eye and
ending at his chin. His shirt had been torn down the front and

he had lost his revolver. A part of the crowd was only a few paces behind, led by a young man in a striped sweater. The young man was carrying a heavy wooden club, held at shoulder level, ready for use. The policeman's eyes, wild and terrified, fixed on Bhengu for a moment, then he veered hard to his right to avoid him. His feet slipped on the loose dust of the road surface and he went down. The club swung once and bounced off his back. Bhengu heard his grunt of pain, but he was immediately on his feet and running again, cutting off the road toward an opening between two shacks.

He may not have seen the shallow ditch ahead of him or he may have been weakened by the blow on his back, but he fell a second time as he went into it. Bhengu saw his fear-filled face looking back over his shoulder in the moment before the club descended again. Two quick blows were struck, then the policeman was crawling out of the ditch on the far side, his limbs working in jerky staccato fashion. The others too were on him now. A tall man in a polo-neck sweater raised a rock the size of a football above his head and brought it down hard.

Bhengu turned away. What he had just seen had not happened. Such things did not happen. Many times in the past he had spoken to the people of the Manor, telling them to fight the apathy that infected them, to act before the will to act disappeared completely. Now they were taking his advice. Their apathy was being swept away like driftwood before a tidal wave. They were killing the police.

A second policeman, one of the blacks, broke his way through the crowd and set off hard down the hill, running as fast as he could and keeping to the center of Booth Road. Farther up and moving away from him another group was gathered around something on the ground and beating at it with sticks, clubs and pieces of water piping, the blows falling so fast and with such intensity that Bhengu was sure that no one could survive them.

In the near-darkness Mzolo's white suit, although dust-covered, stood out sharply against the dark bodies and the more subdued colors worn by most of the others. Bhengu saw him bounding past the back of the crowd, his knife in hand, the handkerchief no longer in evidence. He thought he saw blood on the blade, but it was being swung through the air too fast as Mzolo waved it above his head and the light was too bad. The boy's head was turning continually from side to side as he looked out for any killing in which he might be able to participate. Something in the gap at the side of the shed drew his attention. Bhengu saw him running in that direction, the knife now held low in the stabbing position. Then he had disappeared down the side of the shed into the darkness of the alley.

Bhengu took a few aimless steps in the direction in which Mzolo had gone. He stopped and, looking around, saw the small group of men coming away from the ditch where they had caught up to the policeman. The one with the club, his chest heaving after the recent exertion, was walking in front. Bhengu could not see the policeman. The tall man who had dropped the rock onto the policeman was walking at the back, grinning and talking to one of the others. He had long arms that hung loosely from his shoulders, swinging freely as he walked. The fat man with the ax whom Bhengu had passed along the road was also with them. He was looking very stern, even sullen, like the father about to tell his son that "this is going to hurt me more than it hurts you." The ax was still hanging heavily from his right hand. Behind them in the ditch Bhengu saw a movement. Then the policeman was sitting upright, the expression of his face bewildered, the eyes wide and vague, unable to focus. The only marks on his face were the wound on the side of his head and the cut down his cheek.

One of those at the back of the group coming away from the ditch also noticed him. He grabbed hold of the sleeve of the fat man's pullover. "He lives. The cop lives."

The fat man turned back to the ditch, the sternness on his face becoming indignation. "I'll finish the dog," Bhengu heard him say.

The one who had alerted him continued to hold onto his sleeve. He seemed to be trying to hold him back. Bhengu could see that he was speaking, but he was facing the wrong way and his voice was swamped by the noise of the mob. The others had also stopped and were looking back toward the ditch. The one with the club shouted and his voice carried clearly to Bhengu. "Leave him alone. Let him hit the dog."

The fat man went down the easy slope into the ditch. He took the ax handle in both hands. The policeman started to turn his head toward the approaching figure, his eyes glazed. Bhengu had the impression that somewhere in that consciousness was a shadowy foreboding of what was coming. He saw the ax lifted and swung down hard. One of the others moved into his line of vision so that he did not see the blow fall.

Bhengu turned and ran into the crowd, unconsciously following the path that Mzolo had taken. He tried to force his way to the alley, but he had pushed himself too far into the struggling mass of people and he was being pressured from behind, impelled toward the shed. Just in front of him someone threw a rock that hit the corrugated-iron wall above a shattered wooden window frame. From the front voices were shouting, "Stop throwing. Stop throwing . . . The police are dead. Stop throwing . . . stop at the back . . . stop throwing." Over the heads of those in front of him Bhengu saw the hunched-up back of someone climbing through the window, being pushed by those behind. Immediately others were following, scrambling over the corrugated-iron ledge, brushing past the shattered remnants of a wardrobe, still partially blocking the opening. To his right through a momentary gap in the crowd Bhengu saw that the door was also broken, the bottom and outside torn away, and those closest to it were pressing past the splintered ends into the shed.

More and more people were climbing through the window. The momentum of the crowd was all in that direction, carrying him toward the shed. Through the window he could now vaguely see people crowded close together, jostling each other, but without direction, moving purposelessly back and forth. If the policemen were dead there was nothing left for them to do. A sense of disgust for the shed, the dark opening where the window had been and what lay beyond it, gripped Bhengu. The eagerness of the crowd, like an external force driving everyone onward, had become repellent to him. He ducked down and drove hard to his left, leading with his head. Someone grunted as his head drove into a chest. He was thrown toward the wall of the shed, losing his footing and almost falling, but steadying himself against the backs of others in the dense-packed mob. He dropped his head and drove forward again. A man's voice swore short and sharp next to his ear. "Christ!" Then he broke through the tangle of bodies and struggling limbs and he was out in the open. The alley was to his right, and in the darkness he could see the light color of Mzolo's suit. One of his arms was pumping back and forth in a series of swift underarm blows. Bhengu moved forward into the darkness, stumbled over the yielding mass of a body on the ground and steadied himself against the wall of the shed. Mzolo was coming to meet him. The boy stopped close in front of him. What light there was was falling on his face. His eyes were screwed up as he struggled in the darkness to discern Bhengu's features. The excitement in him was a tangible reality, reaching out to Bhengu, but now revolting him by its wild oppressive insistence. "You are still standing here? There is fighting to be done." His chest was heaving in short shallow breaths. The knife was in his right hand, but Bhengu could not look at it.

"What did you do, Msima?"

"It looks like you don't want these dogs to die. I will fix you the same way."

"What did you do?" Bhengu repeated.

"I have killed the son of Maketa and I have killed the grandson of Maketa."

"You mad bastard," Bhengu said.

"There he lies."

Bhengu pushed past him, feeling his way to the place in the alley where he had first seen Mzolo. The body of the child was lying face upward. Bhengu knelt next to it. He got his hand in under the oversize shirt he was wearing. Feeling for the heart, his hand ran across the skin of the child's stomach. All over the stomach area were little oblong places where the flesh or intestines, warm and sticky, seemed to be erupting through the skin. His hand jerked back involuntarily at the touch, then he plunged it forward all the way to the chest, pressing it, palm down, over the area of the heart. For a moment he imagined that he felt the boy's heart beat against the tips of his fingers, but then he was sure that there was nothing. The smooth skin of the young chest was as warm as in life. Pressing his hand against it, feeling its warmth, it seemed impossible that the heart should be still. He brought his ear down to the child's mouth, but the noise of the mob was too great for him to be sure of anything. Again part of his consciousness told him that he was hearing the boy's breathing and feeling it against the side of his face, but the chest under his hand was unmoving, the lungs inactive.

Lifting the boy into his arms, Bhengu carried him down the alley toward the front of the shed. The young body, still soft with the suppleness of life, bent backward around his arms, the slender limbs hanging almost straight down. The sounds of the mob bore in upon him, the screams of anger and bloodlust intermingling with the groans of pain and anguish. Now he hated it all. He felt enclosed in an envelope of noise: the movement of bodies, the few occasional rocks still crashing against the wall of the shed, but more than anything else the sound of human voices that had lost all natural inhibition.

He emerged from the alley into the fringes of the mob, looking around for Mzolo, but the throng of bodies, now drifting aimlessly without an object against which to exercise its remaining anger, had swallowed him up without a trace. He carried the boy's body across the road, skirting the denser part of the crowd, and laid it down in the dust before a burning brazier in the yard of one of the shacks. The child's face was smooth and expressionless, the eyes closed and the mouth slightly open. It reminded Bhengu of the look of ecstasy on the face of a woman making love. The boy could not have been more than seven or eight years old. Bhengu lifted his shirt. The stab wounds were surprisingly free of blood. The flesh beneath, pressing through the openings where the skin was broken, looked like a whole series of pouting lips waiting to be kissed.

Bhengu straightened up. The little figure on the ground looked so fragile and innocent, so wholly a victim, that he shuddered.

On the other side of the brazier up against the wall of the shack his eyes picked up a movement. A man and woman were full length in the dust copulating, illuminated by the light from the brazier. Bhengu could hear the man's grunts of pleasure.

⌘ ⌘

Fourie had the light on again and he was trying to read. Every few minutes Bhengu heard a page crackle as it was turned.

The policeman was still seated at the table opposite his colleague and he was still facing the window. Bhengu could see the slow regular movement of his shoulders as he breathed. At the back of his head the hair was trimmed short, standing stiffly away in little straight bristles. Through the bristles he could see the white skin of the back of the policeman's neck and the lower part of his head. The white skin and the straight close-cropped hair, together, were the key to all things: power, opportunity, security; they were the symbols of the inner group. It was their absolute hegemony that had made Sam Bhengu an outsider. And it was because he had challenged them that he was here now and this thing was happening to him. His eyes were held by the back of Fourie's head and he stared for a long time, his attention consumed by the color of the skin on the back of the policeman's neck and the way his hair was cut.

Bhengu knew that Fourie was troubled. He also knew that the policeman would get over it, somehow suppressing the unwelcome emotion, tucking it away into some already cluttered recess of his subconscious. Then he would be free to be again part of similar actions. And always, regardless of his mistakes or crimes, he would have his sure passport to the inner circles of power and security. The white skin and the short straight hair would carry him through.

Bhengu's eyes took in his own body. He could see only the deep-brown chest, rising regularly with the movement of his breathing, and his arms, hanging loose, cuffed over his stomach. There was no way you could be part of the establishment with natural assets like those. It was impossible.

He looked at Fourie again and watched him turn a page of the novel, obviously working hard to maintain his concentration. Bhengu hated him more than the others. To him the Fouries were worse than the Van Rooyens and the Browns, because those like Fourie felt within themselves that what they

were doing was evil. But they covered it up, driving it deep
into the unconscious corners of their minds, and they went on
doing it. They would always.

🙰 🙰

The bullets must have entered a lung. The man was sitting on
the ground, one of his legs tucked underneath him, being held
upright by a friend on either side. He was coughing and holding one of his hands in front of his mouth. Every time there
was a pause in his coughing he would lift his hand to his eyes
and stare fascinated, in the semidarkness, at the little bits of
froth, blood and pink membrane scattered over the palm.

On the road the men were setting up a roadblock. They had
collected refuse bins from shacks in the streets round about
and were filling them with rocks and builders' rubble from a
site near the shed where the policeman had died, rolling them
into position across the road. The Saracens would have to
come up the road to enter the Manor, and the talk among the
men constructing the roadblock was that the Saracens would
never get past the row of refuse bins. They did not have the
power to push them out of the way. "And, if the cops get out
to move the drums, they will get the same as the others,"
Bhengu heard a voice from the road say. His attention was
drawn to two of them struggling to roll a drum, already filled
with rocks and pieces of brick, into the middle of the road.
One of them was Mzolo, who had lost the jacket of his suit
and was dressed only in the trousers, the original color of
which had changed to the same red-brown as that of the
Manor's paths and tracks. The other was the fat man who had
finished the cop with the ax. A man Bhengu recognized as old
Johannes Chamane was standing at the side of the road with a
blanket wrapped around his shoulders, shouting instructions
to the workers, his thin old-man's voice trying to assert an au-

thority that had been lost many years before. "Move it. Move it along. Block off the road. Don't let the cops come in and steal the people. Move it. Move it."

Bhengu turned away from the men working on the road-block and the man with the bullet in his lung. It had all become so futile. The man with the bullet in his lung was going to die. The policeman had died. The boy had died. The road-block was just going to be pushed over by the police Saracens when they came. And who was going to try to stop them with the Browning machine guns mounted in their gun turrets? God only knew how many more were going to die.

They were fools. They were all fools; an army in faded overalls, dirty flannel trousers, discolored vests, torn shirts and cracking faded shoes; a bobtail regiment, optimistically arming themselves with pangas and cane knives, even the branches of trees; the gaveen in their collective bloodstream telling them that they would be able to keep the cops out, that the Saracens were weak and clumsy and would never get past the barricade, that the Browning machine guns never hit anything . . .

Even in the near-darkness and at some distance he recognized the sunflower pattern of the material. It was hanging down in a wide loop, the body wearing it suspended in a horizontal position, being carried. The crowd closed around it, cutting it from his view. Bhengu started toward the point in the crowd where he had seen it. The steps he took were slow and wooden, as if he was suffering from a partial paralysis. The fear of what he thought he had seen was slowing his movements, weakening something in his legs. He stumbled once, then his will took control and he was moving faster, weaving and pushing his way through the crowd. People were blocking his path, still coming from all sides, pressing toward the shed where the policeman had died. The air around him was filled with the joyous drunken shouts of "Africa! Come back, Africa!" He bumped hard into a short, broad, bare-footed woman, spinning her around so that she was sent stumbling away backward, facing him. He heard her shouted insult, "Asshole," as he pushed on, glancing once at her, troubled by her anger despite the far greater fear within him.

Thinking that he had reached the place where he had seen the sunflower-patterned material, Bhengu came to almost a complete stop, his eyes searching the crowd in the direction in which it had seemed to be moving. His steps were now small and hesitant, without conscious direction, carrying him along uncertainly. A flutter of cloth in the darkness among the moving arms and legs, the dense mass of bodies, was somehow distinguishable to Bhengu. For a moment it stood out clearly from the movements made by flanneled legs, the waving of cotton dresses, and the swinging of blankets that were secured at the neck and swaying with each stride of the wearer.

It was gone again, cut off by the newcomers to the ranks of the rioters: bored teaboys, messengers, laborers, washerwomen, servants; all recruited by their curiosity and the promise of excitement. He was running now, his eyes fixed in the direction where he had last seen it. He was going directly against the stream of people, twice bumping hard into those who were slow getting out of the way. This time he did not look back. He saw it again, the sunflower pattern clearly visible. The body of a man got in the way for a moment, and then he could see the whole length of the skirt. She was being carried. The man carrying her feet was obscuring his view of her, but he could see the skirt hanging straight down and dragging on the ground. He was drawing closer quickly and he could see that it was Robert who had her by the shoulders. He seemed to have his face partially averted so that he would not have to look at Winifred.

Her head was hanging back so that Bhengu saw it last. As he caught up to them his eyes went over her body, looking for the wound. The top of her throat and the lower part of her jaw seemed to have been destroyed, leaving a bleeding crater where they once had been.

⌘   ⌘

"That Van Rooyen." Brown shook his head, speaking softly so as not to wake the subject of his gossiping. "I don't know about him."

Fourie had turned his chair so that he had his back to the window and was facing Brown and Bhengu. He kept his attention on Brown, being careful not to look directly at Bhengu. His face was yellow and lifeless, the cheeks hollower than usual and his mouth drawn thin and turned down at the corners. He made no reaction to what Brown had said.

"Let's face it, he's a crazy bastard." His voice held a friendly intonation. The meaning of the words seemed to be that Van Rooyen was a good old crazy bastard. "He's a crazy bastard. If my wife said something like that, I would never tell anyone else." He shook his head again. "She doesn't like him any better, but she looks at the neighbor more often." He laughed softly, looking to Fourie for support, but the warrant officer's laughter was all used up. The tension he had held inside himself had been released by the earlier laughter and now there was nothing. Fourie met Brown's eyes momentarily, then looked down at the floor. There was no sign of amusement in his face. "I'm bloody glad my wife is not like that," Brown said. "A woman like that is all right for a bit of fun, but to marry . . ." He snorted loudly. The idea of any sane man marrying such a woman was ridiculous. Brown chuckled again, but again Fourie's face remained expressionless, and the chuckle, existing in isolation, dried up humorlessly.

Bhengu studied the look on Fourie's face. The only trace of expression was the faint fold of a frown between his eyebrows and the down-turned corners of his mouth, but there was an element in his expression that might have been troubling even to a casual observer. To some extent it was the strange unhealthy color of his skin, but more definitely than that it was something in his eyes, or perhaps something that was absent from his eyes. They had become neutral, withdrawn from life. To Bhengu, Fourie's eyes seemed to say that he was surrendering all involvement in human affairs. From now on he would be no more than a spectator. Involvement brought problems and responsibility, and Fourie seemed to be retreating from both.

Cowardly bastard, Bhengu thought. You run away. You pretend to yourself that you aren't as guilty as the rest. You sit there with your blank face, but you'll be going home to screw your wife and play with your kids and you'll be coming back to guard me tomorrow night and after me somebody else. But I'll be facing it. And I'll be alone.

Brown was looking at Fourie, an expression of feigned severity on his face. He possibly felt that the warrant officer had wounded his dignity by not laughing with him. "How about some coffee, Len?" There was a challenge in his request, suggesting that Fourie had better not show any reluctance this time.

He did show no reluctance, getting up, unplugging the kettle and going straight out into the passage to fill it without saying anything. The expression of his face was unchanged, passive, following orders.

Brown watched him go; then, with the expression of severity and suspicion still on his face, the little rosebud mouth pursed tightly, he turned his attention to Bhengu. "So, Sam, you're awake again, hey? You ready to give me that statement now?" He had not moved from the desk, but he waved the file that he intended to use for the statement at Bhengu. His manner was too exactly that of the confident competent security policeman, never doubting his authority, or the justification for his actions, to be real. Play-acting, Bhengu thought. The whole thing is nothing more than a game to him. Bhengu could see how he had modeled himself on the others, succeeding in being no more than a cheap imitation of what they were. "What about it, Sam?" The eyebrows were raised but still contriving to frown, the mouth pinched even more tightly. Come on, Sam, the expression of his face was intended to say. You know that you can't resist us. Sooner or later you're going to tell us, so tell us now.

Bhengu wondered what the right kind of confession from himself would mean to Brown's career. Promotion to the rank of captain within a year? Acceptance to the inner circles of the Special Branch? Even Brown was an outsider to some extent in that very exclusive group. His English surname, home language, and accent when speaking Afrikaans would always be problems to him. Down the years he had learned to imitate most Afrikaner ways of speech and behavior. Among his colleagues he was a good Englishman, but he was still an Englishman. To overcome such a disadvantage he would have to do something that few of them ever managed in a career, if in fact it was possible to overcome such a disadvantage. The Lategans, Strydoms, Engelbrechts and Van Rooyens never really trusted anyone who had not grown to adulthood within the same mental isolation, subject to the same fears and prejudices, did not have the same in-bred ideals and, of course, the same complexion as they had. The Browns would always be suspect, the Bhengus excluded.

Van Rooyen snorted loudly, his face twitching nervously, without waking. Brown looked at him and laughed shortly, shaking his head. "Fuck it," he said. Then he looked back at Bhengu, imposing the former severity on his face, indicating to the black man that the joke, whatever it was, was not for his entertainment. "Don't think we'll let you get away with it, Sam. Just don't think that."

⌘ ⌘

"We must bury her now, right away," Bhengu said.

The face of the old woman was blank with grief, as it had been when he had come to her in her bedroom, but there was no weeping. She had been mourning Winifred since the previous day and had already accepted it as one of the many unchangeable conditions of her life. She did not seem to have grasped the meaning of what he had said. She looked into his face curiously, perhaps waiting for him to clarify his statement.

"Why?" Robert asked.

"All the people will be burying their dead before the police come. If they know that Winifred was shot they'll take us all in for questioning. We'll all be suspects. They'll be searching for the dead and wounded tomorrow."

"But what about the funeral, Sam?" Mama Mabaso asked.

"I sent Alfred to Father Victor to ask him to meet us at Little-Mama Zibi's place. We'll have to bury her in the veld."

Mama Mabaso shook her big old head slowly from side to side, trying to come to terms with what Bhengu was telling her. "Why not in the churchyard?"

"They'll be looking for new graves. It's the only way. Everyone will have to do it. We don't want them digging up the body."

"What will we tell about her? What will we say happened?"

"We'll say she went away. We have to hurry, Mama."

"I don't know, Sam. I don't know." Her voice sounded uneven and bewildered.

"Father Victor will be taking the service. Everything will be all right."

"I don't know, Sam."

"It will be all right, Mama. Father Victor would not do it if it was not all right."

"No. No, he won't. Are you sure he won't, Sam?"

"Of course, he won't."

"What about a coffin?" She looked absently around the room, as if expecting to see one.

"There won't be a coffin."

Winifred's body lay on the table. Petronella and Bhengu had dressed it in a white nightgown and had bandaged her chin, throat and mouth with a sheet torn into thin strips. The blood from the wound had congealed before quite oozing through the wrappings, only darkening them slightly on the outside. Folded neatly next to the body was the blanket in which it was going to be wrapped. What remained of the girl's face seemed at peace, the eyes closed.

Bhengu looked directly at his wife for the first time since they had brought Winifred's body home. Even while they had prepared the body for burial they had been absorbed in what they had to do, recognizing each other as little more than associates in a task. Petronella was standing against the wall of the shack, her eyes still wide with fear and unbelief, holding the child in her arms and rocking up and down on the balls of her feet to keep him quiet.

"When must we go?" It was Mama Mabaso who asked the question.

"We'll have to go right now," Bhengu said. "The police will be coming soon. And Father Victor will be waiting for us."

❁   ❁

"Coffee, Sam?" Brown looked relaxed and friendly. He might have been issuing a social invitation to a fellow policeman. "Would you like some?" He held the cup close and Bhengu

got the smell of the coffee, but there was no answering mois-
ture in his mouth. "You sure you won't have some?" Brown
started drinking it himself, standing above Bhengu and sip-
ping the warm drink slowly. Involuntarily Bhengu's mouth
opened and closed a few times in imitation of Brown. The policeman's neat little mouth burst open in a single short laugh,
spraying him with droplets of coffee. "Oh, you would like
some? How about that?" He crouched next to Bhengu and
held the cup next to his face. Bhengu's saliva glands were
straining unproductively to produce a little relief for his
tongue and the membrane on the inside of his mouth. "You
can have some, Sam. You want some—you can have some. It's
right here, Sam. You can have some. You only have to say.
You can have anything you want."

⧖ ⧖

Bhengu and Robert went up the path slowly, with Robert
leading. They were carrying Winifred's body, wrapped in a
blanket, on a stretcher made from two wooden poles and a
second blanket. Mama Mabaso, Little-Mama Zibi, her husband Phineas, little Alfred, who was wearing only a vest, and
Father Victor, almost invisible in his black toga, only the cler-
ical collar showing up at all in the darkness, came up the path
in single file behind them. Petronella had stayed at home with
the child to keep him out of the night air. Bhengu could hear
the crunch of the spade Father Victor was carrying when he
used it as a walking stick on the steep places in the path.
Ahead, against the relative brightness of the sky, he could see
the outline of the last row of shacks, skirting the path on both
sides till near the crest of the hill.

From close in front of them at the side of the path there
was a sudden scrambling sound and two very thin dogs
bounded up the incline, stopping once to look back, then

sneaking down a narrow alley between two shacks when they saw that the party was still coming toward them. Behind them they left a metal refuse bin, tipped over onto its side, spilling its contents onto the grass fringe and across the path.

The sound of metal crashing heavily against metal, the roar of truck engines and the screams of the mob were distant now, far behind them. The shacks they were passing all seemed to be deserted. Possibly the occupants were all down at Kwa Teekey, taking part in the evening's entertainment. Joining the other sounds the hammering of one of the Brownings was short, but the little column on the path stopped to listen. It was the first time that any of them had heard the sound made by the machine guns. The note of the crowd changed immediately. The sound of anger in the voices immediately changed to one of fear. The hammering of the Browning reached Bhengu's ears again, equally short the second time, but equally authoritative. Even at that distance Bhengu could hear that the mob was in a state of panic. The second salvo was followed by more heavy metal-against-metal crashes as the Saracens forced the barricade. Bhengu could imagine the rubble-filled refuse bins, which would have been too heavy for the weak engines of the Saracens, being pushed over effortlessly and sent rolling down the hillside or into the walls of shacks.

Winifred's body swung heavily from side to side on the makeshift stretcher as Robert, concentrating on the ground in front of him, followed the twists and unevenness of the path, sometimes almost coming to a stop as he felt ahead in the darkness with one of his feet. Wrapped in a blanket the girl's body was broad and featureless, the feet protruding on Bhengu's side. Occasionally it would start slipping toward him and he had to ask Robert to stop so that they could move it forward again.

They stopped on the crest of the hill, just beyond the last line of shacks. Across the valley on the far side of Berea

Ridge the moist sea air glowed yellow with the absorbed light of the city. Immediately below them, unlit except for scattered flickering oil lamps, candles and braziers, Cato Manor was a dark, barely perceptible presence. The sharp geometric shapes and angles of the shacks were dimly visible in places, indicating that there was more than just a hillside between them and the valley. Far away to the right the darkness was broken along Denis Shepstone Road by the beams of headlights sweeping through the alleys and openings between the shacks, momentarily casting long shafts of light across an erratic series of corrugated-iron rooftops. The machine gun had been quiet since the second burst, and the noise of the mob had stopped almost completely. Only a few scattered shouts, more fearful than defiant, still reached Bhengu's ears. All that remained were the sounds made by the trucks' engines and the headlights, now stationary, lighting a narrow patch in the broad darkness.

⚜ ⚜

The coffee was finished, the unwashed cups scattered on the table between Fourie and Van Rooyen. Fourie had returned to reading his book, avoiding Brown's sporadic attempts to start a conversation. Van Rooyen was awake again. His jacket, which had been hanging over the back of his chair, now lay in a heap on the carpet. Somehow his shirt had become crinkled even though he had been sleeping in an upright position. His eyes moved restlessly between the faces of the other three men in the room, the expression of his face sullen and wounded, almost hunted, Bhengu thought. Most of the time Van Rooyen's attention was with Brown, watching the lieutenant's face carefully to see if everything was still as it had been before, or if the revelations about his wife had changed anything.

With his feet up on the desk again Brown seemed bored and disgruntled, not looking at either of his subordinates. Fourie had not been directly insolent, but the way he showed no interest in what Brown had to say was a new experience for his senior officer. In any branch of the police, and especially in the one in which they were employed, you were always interested, amused or impressed, as the occasion required, by whatever your senior officer said, and on whatever subject he was discoursing. But Fourie had been indifferent. Not hostile or even bored, he had just not been interested, the pale tired face passive and remote, leaving the other man with the feeling that all was not as it should be. His authority was somehow being brought into question. It was true that Fourie had made the coffee without any hesitation and that, as soon as he was asked or possibly before, he would go quietly, passively and without argument to wash the cups, but when Brown had spoken about the rugby season that had just ended he had looked at him politely while he was speaking, and as soon as the lieutenant finished, without reacting to it in any way, Fourie had gone back to his reading. This had happened three times and, while it could not be seen as insubordination, it was not the accepted thing. Brown had never seen any of his senior officers treated that way. He had certainly never treated one of them that way himself. What was worse was that on the last occasion Van Rooyen had been awake and Brown had seen the momentary surprise in the bloated face.

Bhengu had watched and listened to them night after night. He knew their views on sport, politics, departmental promotions, sex, himself, the orange juice sold by the café down on the corner, Colonel Lategan, Warrant Officer Du Toit's wife, Black Label beer, and all the other important issues of their lives. He had watched the petty struggles for dominance among them and had seen Fourie gradually accept the omega position and Brown hang onto the alpha spot by the magic of

his rank. Then tonight he had seen Van Rooyen's status de-
cline as can only happen to a man whose friends know that his
wife regularly refuses him. He had known them more intimately than that, though. He had felt their hands upon his
body and had struggled with them, his body making brutal,
merciless contact with theirs. He had felt their punches, wild
and hard to his body, and he had fought back, knowing that he
had no hope of winning, that there would always be too many
of them. And he had felt those other blows, not hard, but insistent, continuous, seemingly never-ending, until his brain
was like a Ping-Pong ball inside his skull.

It lasted only a moment, but in that time the conscious part
of Sam Bhengu slipped effortlessly away from his body. It was
against the ceiling and looking down on the men in the room.
He saw the policemen, still sitting in the same positions:
Fourie reading, withdrawn from the struggle, surrendered;
Brown insecure, uncertain of his authority; and Van Rooyen
actually fearful, his manhood called into question. And he
could see the body of the black man on the bed, leaner than
he remembered it, or thought it would be, the flesh drooping
and the eyes closed, the legs hanging limply from the bar to
which they were chained, his genitalia drooping shrunken between them as if looking for a place to hide. Then he was
being drawn back, reluctantly and not knowing how to resist
it, the moment of freedom ended. The large dark body, now
only barely alive, seemed to be altogether motionless. It was
no more than a prison.

✶ ✶

"I know that my redeemer liveth, and that he shall stand at
the latter day upon the earth: whom I shall see . . ." Father
Victor's soft cultured voice sounded more like that of an English university don than that of an African priest. He was

standing at the head of the grave, holding his closed Bible in both hands and reciting the words from memory. On his right were Little-Mama Zibi sobbing loudly, her voice breaking into an occasional plaintive wail that had to be stifled before they could continue, her husband, patient and stoical, his hands folded in front of him, and Mama Mabaso, silent and leaning heavily on Robert. They were all featureless shadows in the little clearing between the trees, their faces hidden by the almost complete darkness. Little Alfred had been sent home by Father Victor while they were digging the grave. The priest had taken hold of the little boy's shoulder and whispered to him, "You are cold, my child. Can he not go home, little-mother?" The mother's reply had been lost to Bhengu's ears in the sound of the spade striking into the hard-packed ground of the veld. Bhengu and Robert had taken turns in digging, working their way slowly deeper into the ground, twice having to stop and all of them sitting down in the long grass as police foot patrols passed along the edge of the Manor a few hundred paces away, the beams of their flashlights flashing on and off between the shacks. It had been a sure sign that all resistance down at Kwa Teekey had ended. The rebellion had lasted perhaps two hours; no more than that. The only sounds from the Manor were the occasional humming of a truck's engine, and during the last hour even this had stopped. "O Lord Jesus Christ, who wast laid in the new tomb of Joseph, and didst thereby sanctify the grave to be a bed of hope to thy people . . ." A bed of hope to thy people? The words stuck in Bhengu's mind. A bed of hope? He could see no hope in the formless mound that had once been his sister. What sort of hope was that? The images of what she had been like to him all his life came pouring through his consciousness: a little girl in shining patent-leather shoes and a short skirt, taking him by the hand on the day he went to school for the first time; a big girl, buxom and confident, singing in the choir in Sophiatown,

himself sitting in the congregation admiring her; in recent
years in the Manor, coming home from her office job in town
by bus every day to cook supper on the coal stove, her face
streaming with sweat . . . She had been his protector. Even
Mama Mabaso could never be as important to him as Winifred had been. He could not see her grave as a bed of hope.
". . . the body of thy servant which we are about to commit
to thy gracious keeping; who art the resurrection and the life,
and who livest and reignest . . ." Despite the need for quiet
Father Victor's voice managed to retain all the required
priestly intonations, the saintly note, carefully cultivated over
years of practice, the slow measured rhythm of the words, the
accustomed pauses; all the devices that had become necessary to convince the believer that he was in the presence of the
Lord. The gentle dispassionate voice went on and on, leaving
nothing unsaid, apparently determined that despite the circumstances Winifred would have a proper burial. To Bhengu
the words meant nothing. Winifred had been the reality. And
he no longer had her. She would not be there when he came
home, to listen to his confessions, to make his supper, to scold
him . . . no matter what the priest recited or how saintly the
sound of his voice, nothing could change that. He was glad for
Mama Mabaso, though. He knew how highly she thought of
Father Victor and that what he was saying would be of comfort to her.

"In the midst of life we are in death; of whom may we seek
for succor, but of thee, O Lord, who for our sins are justly
displeased? Yet, O Lord most holy, O Lord most mighty, O
holy and most merciful . . ." Behind him Bhengu heard a
rustling sound in the grass, heard it stop, and then start again
closer to him. Father Victor stopped speaking and the only
remaining sound was the rustling. Bhengu turned to look in
the direction from which it was coming. Then he heard the
dog's snuffling as its nose led it toward the dead body. He

clapped his hands together once hard and the dog dashed away through the grass, coming to a stop at a distance that he felt was beyond the range of their anger. "Forasmuch as it hath pleased Almighty God of his great mercy to receive unto himself the soul of our dear sister here departed, we therefore commit her body to the ground . . ." Father Victor's voice continued, quiet and untroubled, as if there had been no interruption and everything was normal.

Bhengu knew, as they all did, that as soon as they left, the Manor's underfed dogs would come out to try to dig up the body. For that reason he and Robert had collected a pile of large stones that they would pack into the grave to form a barrier that the dogs would not be able to penetrate. "Lord, have mercy upon us," Father Victor chanted, the last two words dragged out lingeringly in plaintive supplication.

"Christ, have mercy upon us," the small congregation replied, imitating the tone and rhythm of the priest's chanting.

"Lord, have mercy upon us," Father Victor repeated. "O Almighty God, with whom do live the spirits of just men . . ."

The stall provided him with shelter for a moment. He looked across the road to the far side and the burned-out remains of a clinic, destroyed in the '49 riots, its crumbling brick walls still blackened in places. Bhengu crossed the road in a crouching run, slipped through the empty doorway and squatted low inside among the bushes that were now growing through the floor.

It was just light enough for him to make out the outlines of the refuse bins. They were strung out across Denis Shepstone Road again in a final hopeless gesture of defiance. On the way back from the place where they had buried Winifred to Mama Mabaso's place, and from there to Kwa Teekey, he had seen no signs of police patrols or the previous evening's mob. Except for the refuse bins barring the road, Cato Manor looked just as it did before dawn on any other morning. There was something that was different, though. The streets had been completely empty, excepting a few dogs who were still occupied with the perpetual search for food. Normally at this time of the morning there would be people on the streets making their way to work. The whole township seemed to be suffering from a hangover in the wake of the previous night's orgy.

The deep rumble of a heavy vehicle's engine reached Bhengu from beyond the rise, growing gradually in volume as it came up the hill. The sky to the east above Berea Ridge was now a deep gray, but light enough for him to be able to see the silhouette of the vehicle as soon as it came over the top. He looked up the road in the direction away from the sound, but nothing moved. Whoever had replaced the barricade had probably decided against defending it and had gone home to bed.

From his position he could see into the shallow ditch where the young white policeman had died. The place was still in darkness, but he was sure that the body was gone. He wondered about the boy that Mzolo had killed, and, for the first time since the riot, he thought about the girl, suddenly afraid for her safety, wondering where she had been at the time. The Khumalo's place where she was going to a party was a long way from Kwa Teekey, and she was a fearful kid who always stayed far from any threatening violence. She would be all right.

The Saracen's gun turret, flat and ugly, with the long barrel of the Browning outlined against the sky for a moment before it leveled off, came into view first. In a moment it was over the crest, its headlights glowing bright in the still-deep dusk. The dual beams of the headlights picked out the row of refuse bins and Bhengu heard the engine note change as the driver eased off the accelerator. He brought the armored car to an easy stop thirty or forty paces away from the row of drums. The hatch in the top of the turret opened and a head wearing a peaked cap appeared. Bhengu could see the man's head turning as he examined both sides of the road. After a few minutes he seemed to be satisfied that everything was safe and he moved further into the open until Bhengu could see the top half of his body. He was holding a rifle in his hands and he rested it across the front of the turret.

The man was outlined against the sky, no more than a poorly defined silhouette, and yet there was something about the lean body and the way he moved that made Bhengu sure that he was very young. Without any conscious reason for it he wished that he could see the policeman's face. But as suddenly as his head had appeared he withdrew into the armored truck and the driver moved it slowly forward, the engine revving unhappily in low gear.

Bhengu watched for a while as the driver moved the Saracen back and forth between the drums, bumping them over and rolling them clear, opening a path in the center of the road. In the slowly gathering light its broad squat shape, scrabbling awkwardly among the refuse bins, was like a pig rooting around in a swamp.

⚕   ⚕

"I have my doubts," Lategan said. He was standing in the center of the room, his hands loosely clasped behind his back. "I have my doubts about it, but he's important to us. That's why I called you."

The two doctors were close together at the foot of the bed. The older of the two, a dark thickset man, short neck broadening into his shoulders, a face with unmistakably Jewish characteristics, was looking at Bhengu, his expression serious and concerned. The other was Dr. Roberts, his wide-open eyes moving back and forth between Lategan and the other doctor.

The older doctor put down his bag on the desk and shrugged off his jacket. "Let's have a look," he said.

Bhengu could feel his hands lying at his sides and that his feet were no longer suspended from the bar at the foot of the bed. He tried to raise his head to see what they had done with the shackles, but the effort required was too great. He was very tired.

"We tried to feed him milk this morning, but he spits it out," Lategan was saying. "I have my doubts about the whole thing." The interrogation team was spread in an arc behind him as if to provide support, Engelbrecht and Strydom on either side and the two warrant officers near the door.

The older doctor came toward Bhengu and bent over the bed. He was wearing small steel-rimmed spectacles and he moved his head backward and forward, trying to bring Bhengu into focus. "What did you find yesterday, Frank?"

"Nothing organic," the quick light voice of the younger doctor said.

"Nothing?" The question was put absentmindedly, not expecting a reply.

"Nothing definite."

"Dr. Sibul," Lategan said, waiting for the doctor's attention before continuing. Only after the doctor had turned his head to look at him, did Lategan go on. "Dr. Roberts gave him a very thorough examination yesterday. We really only asked you here to check, to corroborate, you might say."

Dr. Sibul turned his attention back to Bhengu. "I see," he said. "It sounds like you have already decided what my diagnosis is to be." It was said quietly, without any hostile intonation.

The tone of Lategan's voice hardened without increasing in volume at all. "Dr. Roberts did a thorough examination yesterday."

"Do you object to my doing one today?" Sibul was looking

down at Bhengu, but Bhengu could see that no part of his attention was with him. It was all centered on the security policeman.

"Of course not." Lategan's voice was scandalized. "It might be that you're wasting your time, though."

Sibul nodded slowly. "It's *my* time," he said. Bhengu looked at the faces of the policemen. All of Lategan's men were looking at him expectantly, awaiting his reaction. But there was no reaction as Sibul leaned close to Bhengu and tapped him on the chest with the tips of his fingers. Roberts moved up to assist in the examination, his eyes continually flickering in the direction of Lategan's face.

Bhengu felt Sibul's hands on his body, probing, examining, as Roberts had done on the previous day. He saw the eyes, grotesquely enlarged by the spectacle lenses, fixed on his face, searching for any sign of pain. He saw the doctor's head turn and was fascinated by the roll of fat across the top of his neck. He heard Lategan's voice again, the tone unwavering, altogether certain that what he wanted was necessary and could not be denied him. "He wouldn't eat. He wouldn't react to questions. He wouldn't talk. He uses no toilet facilities. He doesn't pass urine at all. I'm telling you I have my doubts about it." Sibul went on working as if he had not heard him, but Roberts had turned to look at Lategan and only redirected his attention to Bhengu after the policeman had stopped speaking.

Outside the window the sky was a deep translucent blue, of a shade Bhengu had never seen before. Lategan was speaking again. "I'm very concerned for his health. He's important to us. We offer him cigarettes and cold drinks, but he accepts nothing."

Roberts' hands were under his head and lifting it, turning it toward the window. "Can't he lift his head himself?" Sibul asked.

"I think he could be malingering," Roberts said, this time looking at Lategan, seeking confirmation.

The security policeman's eyes were on Sibul. He could afford to ignore Roberts. He knew his man and Roberts was going to be no problem to him. "He was a medical student for years," he said. "I think that explains something." On either side of Lategan, Engelbrecht and Strydom stood erect, tense, possibly expectant.

Despite himself Bhengu feared them all. He feared Engelbrecht because of the part of him that was missing, the absence that had to be hidden by the sunglasses. He feared Strydom because of his blind conviction that what he was doing was right and good and Christian. He feared Brown and Fourie because they would obey orders no matter what the orders were, and they would always find some way of justifying their actions to themselves. He feared Van Rooyen because he was a truly inferior man in a position of great power, and because of what had happened. And he feared Lategan more than any of them, because there was something in the detached resoluteness of the colonel that seemed to indicate that, at least to some small extent, he understood, and despite that, he was the most ruthless of them all. Lategan knew what Bhengu's people suffered as a result of their powerlessness, but to the Lategans, and there were other Lategans, it was simply a matter of either Bhengu's people or his own people being without power. To the thinking of people like the Special Branch colonel, if they once yielded in anything, they would be yielding in all things: to torture and death, and eventually genocide.

"Do you feel that?" It was Sibul's voice. "Do you feel that?" The question was repeated. "He doesn't react at all." Bhengu was looking past him and the ring of security policemen to the open window again. "Did you do an extensor plantar?" Roberts must have nodded or shaken his head in reply because

Bhengu heard no reaction from him. He felt Sibul's damp palms and the inside of his fingers on his left calf and then on his ankle. "His ankles are swollen."

"It's the manacles." Lategan said it calmly, as a matter of fact.

"But how did they get this badly swollen?"

"He struggled. He did the damage himself."

"Can you sit up?" Sibul asked. To Bhengu the question was vague, not directed at anyone. Their dealings were with each other. They had no dealings with him. It seemed impossible that the doctor could be talking to him. "Help me with him," he heard Sibul say to Roberts.

Roberts took hold of him by the shoulders and lifted him into a sitting position. Behind Lategan one of the warrant officers took a step forward, as if coming to assist the doctors, but the colonel raised a hand and he stopped immediately. Bhengu could feel that Sibul was doing something to his right foot and he felt the momentary spasm of a muscle, then the doctor had hold of the other foot and again the muscle spasm followed. Roberts supported first one of his thighs with both hands and then the other, each time followed by sharp little blows to the hollow below the kneecaps. "Hold tight." Sibul took one of Bhengu's hands in his and pulled, trying to withdraw his hand. "Hold tight," he repeated. The doctor pulled a few times and then tried the other hand. "Hold tight," he said again. Bhengu felt the doctor's fingers slip through his grip. "Hold tight." Sibul tried again, and again with the other hand, going back and forth from one hand to the other, each time accompanied by the command, "Hold tight."

Lategan laughed low and humorlessly. "Look at that. First it's one arm that's weak, then it's the other." Engelbrecht was shaking his head slowly from side to side.

Bhengu's eyes focused on the face of Dr. Sibul, close in front of him. The doctor did not appear to have heard Lategan. "Let's get him on his feet," he said to Roberts. With one of them holding him by either arm they lifted him until he was standing erect. He could feel the coarse surface of the carpet far away beneath the bare soles of his feet, and the weight of his body pressing down on it, as the doctors released his arms. The whole of his body was numb as if it had been anesthetized. The only feeling was in his mouth, where his tongue seemed to fill it completely, pressing tightly against its roof and the back of his teeth; and his feet, which were remote, barely connected to his brain, possibly belonging to someone else with him somehow being able to monitor their sensations. "I want you to walk," he heard Sibul say. "I want you to walk across the room to the table and come back." The doctors were standing on either side of him. Lategan and Engelbrecht had stepped aside to allow him free passage.

"Come on, old chap," he heard Roberts say, "you walked for us yesterday."

"He walked fine yesterday," Lategan said. "There was nothing wrong with the way he walked yesterday."

"Come on, old chap. If you don't walk now, we'll really think you're malingering."

"Can you walk?" Sibul asked. He was watching Bhengu's face closely. Bhengu considered the question. His feet were so far away that it seemed doubtful that they would react to any order he gave them. He wondered whether it was worth trying and why they were so interested anyway. "Try to walk," Sibul said. "Can you walk?" He took Bhengu by the hand and moved a step in front of him, to lead him forward. "Come on then. Try to walk."

Lategan had his hands on his hips, his whole posture reflecting his skepticism. "We've seen these maneuvers to avoid interrogation before today. Oliver Mthembu always claims to be suffering from strokes when we take him into custody. He'll live to be ninety, I swear."

Sibul was at the limit of his and Bhengu's outstretched arms. Bhengu could feel the damp insides of the doctor's fingers, clinging tightly to his own. His hand felt as remote as his feet, barely a part of him. "Come on, then." The doctor's voice was coaxing, his attention fixed unwaveringly on Bhengu's face. On the other side of him Roberts kept glancing toward Lategan. "Come on. Take a step. Just one step."

The ceiling was bright with the reflected light of the day, both fluorescent fittings moving barely perceptibly in a gentle current of air coming in at the open window. Sibul was folding up the tubes of the stethoscope to return it to his bag. "He'll have to go to the hospital," he said without looking at anyone.

"Jesus." Lategan turned around to face the window, waggling his head theatrically from side to side.

Sibul finished folding up the stethoscope and put it into his bag. He took his jacket from the desk where he had left it. "Look, Dr. Sibul," Strydom said, his earnest face even more than usually pale in the bright daylight entering the room, "you know that he could be acting. He knows about medical things . . ."

Lategan turned back to face Sibul, his head still waggling from side to side, indicating to all that he had now finally given up all hope for the medical profession. He held up a hand to silence Strydom. "All right, Gerrie, all right." He gave all his attention to the doctor. "You know what this is going to do to our interrogation? This is going to put us months behind. It could be that he will have to be detained for longer as a result of the interrogation being interrupted. You aren't doing him a favor."

Sibul was holding his jacket in one hand, resting the other on his bag. He was looking down at the floor. "I'm sorry. I'm not willing to take the chance. I must have a specialist look at him."

"Yesterday he walked and he spoke to us. And look at the tests you did this morning. Sometimes the one arm is weak, sometimes the other. Dr. Roberts found nothing wrong with him. I've got his certificate in my office." Lategan looked at Roberts. "What do you say, Dr. Roberts?"

Roberts' eyes met Lategan's momentarily, but he spoke to Sibul. "He could be malingering." The statement seemed to contain a question.

It was the first time Sibul had heard of Roberts' certificate of the previous day. "Are you willing to take the chance?" he asked.

Roberts shrugged, a weak helpless gesture.

"I've got Dr. Roberts' certificate from yesterday," Lategan repeated. "It says there's nothing organically wrong with him. Isn't that right, Dr. Roberts?"

Sibul carefully avoided looking at the face of his colleague. "I think he's malingering," Roberts said. There was little conviction in his voice.

"There you are," Lategan said. "He stays."

Sibul put on his jacket and took his bag from the desk. He looked down at his free hand, seeming to be examining the fingernails. "As far as I am concerned he should be in the hospital. And that's what I'll say in my report."

"Jesus Christ. I don't understand this. I just don't understand this. What about Dr. Roberts' examination?"

"Dr. Roberts is entitled to his own opinion. In any event, that was yesterday. The patient's condition may have changed in the meantime."

"Patient? He's not a patient. He's my prisoner, not your patient." The puzzlement on Lategan's face suggested a total inability to understand the doctor's point of view.

Sibul started for the door, his face flushed under the vehemence of Lategan's argument. "Good morning," he said. The tone of his voice was definite and final.

Lategan moved in front of him to stop him going, both his hands raised. "Wait a minute. Wait a minute. All right." Sibul came to an enforced stop before the security policeman, his head still turned toward the floor and to the side so that he would not have to look at him. "If you insist, we'll move him to a hospital. We'll let Central know he's coming."

"He should go to Addington."

"He can't go to Addington. We can't have him in a provincial hospital."

"Central is not a hospital. It's a poorly equipped ward."

"It is a hospital. It's a prison hospital."

"They haven't got the equipment. He should go to a provincial hospital. They haven't got properly trained nursing staff either."

Sibul was still in the same position, his face averted. Bhengu could see the red color of his face, seeming to center around his temples, and the working of his jaw muscles. Between him and the door the five security policemen were an impenetrable wall. Of them only Lategan appeared at all relaxed. Bhengu knew that they would follow any order the colonel gave them. He could see that Sibul knew it too. Lategan lifted his hands in a gesture of resignation, the palms facing upward. "We can't have him mixing with other people, Dr. Sibul. For security reasons it's impossible. We'd have to clear a whole ward in Addington. And we can't stop the hospital staff from coming into contact with him. In no time there'll be a story out that he's suffering from brain damage because of something we did to him. We can't have that."

For the first time Sibul looked directly at Lategan. "It looks like brain damage," he said.

"I can't see it. Not from one little struggle. I can't see it."

Bhengu saw a sudden movement in Roberts' head and shoulders, a contraction of muscles, at Lategan's words. "What sort of struggle?" Sibul asked.

"There was a bit of a struggle yesterday morning, nothing to speak of. He may have hit his head against the ground or he may have hit it against the wall. I can't see brain damage resulting from it." He turned to Engelbrecht. "Here, George, bring us the diary. We've got an entry about it." One of the warrant officers took the logbook from the desk, opened it to the correct place and passed it to Engelbrecht. He glanced at the open page and then handed it to Lategan. "Here. It's all here." Lategan read the entry. After he had finished he gave it to Sibul. "It's all here, but I don't see brain damage resulting from this."

Sibul read the entry in the logbook and handed it back to the warrant officer. "Who wrote this?" he asked.

"Major Engelbrecht." Lategan waved an arm in his direction to identify him.

Sibul looked at Engelbrecht's anonymous face for only a moment. "Were you here when it happened?"

"Yes." Engelbrecht nodded toward his staff. "We were all here." His lips barely moved as he spoke.

"How hard did he hit his head against the floor or the wall or whatever it was?"

"I'm not saying he hit his head. There was a struggle. He may have hit his head. I'm not saying he did." Engelbrecht stopped speaking, apparently feeling that he had told the doctor enough. Sibul looked from him back to Lategan, his face showing that he expected more than just that.

"He attacked you, George. Isn't that right?"

"That's right. And he's strong. It took all of us to get him down. I don't know if he hit his head or not. He may have hit it on the floor or on the wall."

"And this happened yesterday morning?"

"That's right, early yesterday morning." His voice was expressionless and he looked at Lategan, not the doctor, as he spoke. "We were taking off his shackles when he charged me.

We pinned him on the floor. It's possible he may have hit his head."

"He was all right when I examined him." Roberts sounded defensive. He knew that he was being left out on a limb. The police were covering their tracks and they had his certificate. "There was nothing wrong with him yesterday morning."

"I'm not so sure there's anything wrong with him now." Lategan was being magnanimous, but Roberts knew that he was being told that he was on his own. It was his signature that was on the certificate.

"You said he could sham symptoms," Roberts said to Lategan. The words came out quickly before they could be inhibited, his helpless accusation directed ineffectively against the policeman. Bhengu was watching Sibul's face and he saw that the older doctor suddenly looked tired.

"He can. He can." Lategan's voice was sure and confident. He was in control of the situation again. "He was a medical student for three years, four years, I'm not sure." He shrugged. "But what do I know about medicine?"

"You never said anything about a struggle." Roberts' voice tone had become thin and complaining.

"It's not important, is it? It doesn't make any difference to your examination, does it?"

Roberts studied Sibul's face, searching for reassurance, but not finding it.

"In any case we aren't even sure that he hit his head. Hey, George?"

"He may have or he may not have," Engelbrecht said. "In a struggle like that you can never be sure. We had to put him down hard on the ground. He may have hit his head. I can't say for sure."

Suddenly everything had been said. Lategan was looking at Sibul with a little smile around his lips that did nothing to disguise the inflexible nature of his will. Sibul still had his eyes averted, still unwilling to look directly at any of them. Roberts was looking at Lategan's face now, still in the frantic hope that he was not going to be the scapegoat if anything went wrong. The other security policemen seemed all to have relaxed. Everything had been taken care of. It was Lategan who was the first to speak. "I must have him in isolation. I can't have proper isolation in a provincial hospital. It has to be a prison hospital."

Sibul inhaled deeply once. "Take him to Central," he said.

Lategan stepped aside for the doctors to leave. One of the warrant officers opened the door for them. He was grinning happily. Sibul went straight out, not looking at any of them. Roberts remained a moment longer, his eyes still on Lategan's face, but Lategan's attention was no longer with him. He seemed to have forgotten the little doctor's existence. Roberts turned to Engelbrecht, but the face with the hidden eyes was expressionless as always. Engelbrecht shrugged vaguely. Roberts picked up his own bag from the desk and followed Sibul out of the office. Only the warrant officer at the door watched him go.

After the door had closed Lategan went to the desk and picked up the logbook. He opened it at the place where Engelbrecht had made the entry and read it again. He pushed it away, sliding it across the surface of the desk, and turned to look at Bhengu without speaking.

"This stinks like a plan to discredit us," Engelbrecht said. With the doctors gone he had reverted to Afrikaans.

Lategan's attention was directed at him only briefly before turning back to Bhengu. He had become thoughtful, almost introspective. Bhengu had seen such sudden changes take place in him on previous occasions. He knew that they often preceded a change of tactics on Lategan's part. "Who's on night shift?" he asked.

"Brown." It was Engelbrecht who answered.

"Last night and the night before?"

"Yes. All week."

"Who's with him?"

"Van Rooyen and Fourie."

Lategan's eyes showed an added interest at the names of the two warrant officers. "I want you to phone Malcolm Brown at home. Tell him I want him in my office immediately." The tone of his voice did not suggest that any questioning of his orders would be dealt with sympathetically.

"Yes, Colonel." Engelbrecht's voice had immediately become more formal. Adapting his behavior to the needs of his senior officers was his special talent. It probably had much to do with the series of regular promotions that had resulted in his present rank. Lategan was still looking doubtfully, thoughtfully, at Bhengu. There was almost a point of contact between them, a moment of real knowledge of each other. Bhengu was aware of it in the other man. He could see it in his eyes and he could feel it in the air between them. Then Engelbrecht spoke again, and immediately it was gone. "What about him?" the major asked.

"Interrogate him. That's what you're here for. I'll phone Central. In the meantime you carry on."

"I can't understand it. I just can't understand it," the warrant officer he had heard them call André was saying. "The man is an Afrikaner like us. I just can't understand it. Born here in South Africa and brought up here like us. I don't know what you can do with people like that."

"I'll tell you something," Strydom said. "When people have got to that stage they're lost to our country. There's nothing you can do about it."

"But why, Captain? What goes wrong with a person like that?"

"It's the way they're brought up. That's why we've got to

get the young people. Every schoolteacher has a duty to our country, and every parent has a duty to our country. When a man gets to the stage Beyers Naudé is at he's lost to his people."

⌘   ⌘

All the venetian blinds in the house of the Christian Institute's director were closed against the possibility of someone shooting at them through an open window. It was shortly after Taylor had been shot through a glass panel in the front door of his home and most of the banned community were taking whatever precautions they could.

They sat close together in Beyers Naudé's study, the music from his portable radio turned up loud as a protection against listening devices. Beyers was leaning forward, his face earnest, gesticulating with both hands. "You know, Sam," he said. "Ours is not the only country in which the police use torture. They do in many countries."

"Yes, but we don't live in them."

"I know." His face was patient with the patience of a long struggle, ready to acknowledge, if not accept, any conflicting point of view. "What I am trying to say is that our police are not exceptions and that we are not alone in our struggle against this sort of brutality."

Bhengu was amused. "Is that supposed to comfort me?"

Beyers' face became even more earnest. He leaned further forward in his chair, determined to make the point clearly. Then he saw the amusement in his friend's face and he also smiled. "What's wrong with Joshua?" he asked.

"Double vision, ever since they used the head-shrinker on him last year. He can't afford a specialist."

"He should have spoken long ago. I'll arrange it. Tell Willie to come and see me on the weekend."

"Thanks."

Beyers acknowledged his thanks with a quick impatient gesture and went back to the point he had been making. "It's important to see torture in perspective."

"It's a little difficult when you're the one who's being tortured."

Beyers smiled uncertainly. He was not sure if he was being teased and, if he was, how he should react. Bhengu found it strange in a man who had offended his own people so sorely how careful he was to avoid giving unnecessary offense.

Bhengu heard the footsteps in the passage a moment before Beyers' wife knocked softly on the door. Beyers got quickly to his feet and paused a moment, his face preoccupied, still troubled by what they had been discussing. He opened the door and Bhengu saw Ilse take a step backward. She was holding a tea tray, a small pale woman, and she looked very tired. Down the years Bhengu had seen the same sort of tiredness on the faces of many of his friends. He knew it to be the result of years spent waiting for the visit that might never come or that might already be on your doorstep. Beyers followed his wife into the passage. Bhengu heard a brief murmured exchange of words between them, then the other man was coming back with the tray and putting it down on his desk.

"Can't Ilse come in?" Bhengu asked.

"In terms of the banning order I may only see one person at a time. Ilse is included in that."

Bhengu shrugged. "But in here with the blinds closed?"

"I know plenty of people disregard this sort of thing when they're at home, but then they have to be prepared to take the consequences if they are discovered. I'm not prepared for that."

He poured the tea before taking his seat again. Bhengu watched him with a kind of wonder. The other man always surprised him. "You are the strangest Afrikaner," he told him.

"Don't underestimate the Afrikaner, Sam."

"I never do."

"You misunderstand me. I believe that in due course the Afrikaner will adjust more easily to the black man than English-speaking whites will." He must have seen the skepticism in Bhengu's face because he went on hurriedly. "He is closer to the earth and the black man. He is more involved . . ."

From some other part of the house Bhengu could hear the sounds of Ilse moving around, carrying out her household duties behind the permanently drawn blinds. He drew his chair closer to the other man and spoke softly. "The people are asking what they must do. It becomes almost impossible to advise them correctly. Every day the rebellion continues more people die, but to just give up . . ."

"The children?"

"The children can't be reasoned with at the moment."

"I think you should advise the parents to support their children in what they are trying to do."

"But how far?"

"Try to keep them away from violence, but support them. You must support them."

"Of course, Beyers, but we are between the fat and the frying pan . . ."

"I know."

They spoke for a long time, trying to devise a method of dealing with a situation in which they both knew no method would be adequate. By the time Bhengu was ready to leave, his friend was tired. Even after all the years, the subject was too much for him. Like Bhengu, there were things he had difficulty in seeing objectively.

When Bhengu left, Beyers came outside with him. Bhengu saw him for the last time, standing on the drive next to the house, waving good-bye, a frail sixty-year-old man with sharp, rather badger-like features, a cold highveld wind disturbing his straight gray hair. It seemed inconceivable that he could have done all that he had or resisted as far as he had. Bhengu could have wept for the greatness he saw in him.

✠   ✠

"There's nothing you can do when they reach that stage," Strydom said. "You have to lock them up or shoot them. It shows how humanitarian our government is that all we do is place them under a banning order. That's what it means to be a Christian country."

"Yes. I don't know how people get to be like that."

The voice of the policeman, coming from the table behind Bhengu, faded out of his attention until it became no more than an obscure murmur somewhere at the back of his consciousness. They had put him on a chair at the window, looking down into the street. The second warrant officer was standing next to him, leaning against the steel frame of the window, apparently an insurance against him attempting suicide. Bhengu's forehead and left cheekbone were pressing hard against the pane, taking the weight of the upper part of his body. He tried to lift himself away from it, but his head was hopelessly too heavy, dragging him forward. He wondered if the weight of his head might not break the glass, cutting him on the sharp edges or even pulling him headfirst onto the pavement below. He could feel the bones of his cheek and forehead being flattened against the unyielding surface of the windowpane. Something had happened that was causing him to grow heavier and his bones to become softer. He felt the pressure of a hand on the back of his neck, further increasing the weight of his head. A voice that he recognized to be Engelbrecht's spoke softly near his ear. "Have a look down there, Sam. Those people are all free. They can come into town or go home, just as they like. They can be with their kids

tonight. And you can be like them. All you have to do is cooperate with us. Look at them. Wouldn't it be nice to be like
them, instead of being stuck inside for the rest of your life?
And, if you don't cooperate with us, you're never going to be
free again. If we can't get the courts to convict you, we'll just
detain you. There's only one way you're ever going to be a
free man again. You'll have to cooperate with us. That's the
only way. Look at the people down there, Sam. Have a good
look at them. They're all going home tonight." Bhengu felt the
hand release its pressure on his neck, and he felt rather than
heard the policeman move away from him.

He looked down at the people in the streets below. The
street that passed beneath the window was a relatively quiet
city street of old two- and three-story buildings, occupied by
small shops, cheap apartments and tired-looking businesses.
On the far side of the street a young white man, wearing
shorts and a sweater, was unlocking the door of an Alfa
Romeo coupé. Bhengu watched him slip in behind the steering wheel, move the car out of the parking place, and accelerate smoothly down to the stop sign at the corner.

Near the corner a large crowd of the people were waiting at
a bus stop. Already far too many for the bus, they would be
filling the aisles and boarding platforms, using every available
space. To get home in discomfort would be better than not
getting there at all. It was true what Engelbrecht had said,
that they were going home tonight, but it was not true that
they were free. Bhengu had been one of them all his life and
he knew that they had no authority over their own destinies.
They drifted aimlessly across the void in which they lived,
kept afloat only by that least happy of African characteristics;
their wretched capacity to endure.

On the far side of Point Road a narrow lane separated two
blocks of holiday apartments, its shadows sharp and dark in
contrast to the white African sunlight. Deep in the shadow and

leaning against one of the buildings, Bhengu could see the figure of a man, slender and of average height. He seemed to be wearing slacks and an open-neck shirt. The dark skin of his face blended perfectly with the shadow of the building so that it was impossible to see anything of his features, but Bhengu was sure that he recognized the posture. It was the way he leaned against the wall, one hand in his trouser pocket, the other hanging loosely by his side, that was familiar.

Bhengu's attention was distracted by a movement immediately below him. A uniformed policeman, a black man, was patrolling the pavement in front of the building. He seemed also to have noticed the man in the shadow of the alley because he was looking intently in that direction. He turned suddenly and walked down the pavement in the opposite direction until he passed out of Bhengu's sight. Bhengu tried to turn his head to look in the direction the policeman had taken, but it was impossible. The weight of his head pressing against the windowpane was too great. The man in the alley had not moved. Looking at him carefully, Bhengu was sure that the man was facing him and, if not watching the building he was in, then certainly one of those on either side of it.

At the edge of his field of vision Bhengu could see the policeman coming back, walking slowly this time, creating the impression that he was patrolling the front of the building, but, in fact, giving himself more time to face the alley and watch the man waiting there. The man in the alley pushed himself away from the wall and stood erect. Then he was coming down the hill, his stride loose and relaxed, stopping when he reached the pavement of Point Road. Bhengu recognized him as soon as he came out of the shadow into the sunlight. It was Jele.

Go back, go back, Bhengu's mind said to his friend. Go back. There's nothing you can do. For Jesus' sake, go back. Please, go back.

He tried to lift an arm to wave, to make any movement that might alert the other man; but his arms were as heavy as his head, dragging his shoulders forward and down toward the floor. Go back. He tried to send the message by the waves of the mind, concentrating on the slim figure on the street corner. What could he be intending? Whatever it was, it was crazy. Go back, Jele. Please go back.

✠ ✠

"Stand dead still. Nobody may move. Nobody may move at all. Those of you at your desks may sit down. The others remain standing where you are." It was the first time Bhengu had seen Lategan. The Special Branch colonel had been the first one through the door of the Convention headquarters, seven of his men following close behind and fanning out through the doors into the inner offices to cut off retreat to the fire escape, as though they knew exactly what to expect and where everything was situated. "That's right. Stand dead still. You may not move at all." Lategan's voice and manner were quick, impersonal and businesslike. The hostility born of a national guilt complex, which was clearly apparent in his men, was either well disguised or it did not exist in him. To external appearances there was no emotion in his approach to the job he had to do. They were not people to be knocked into line. They were simply a task to be completed as quickly and efficiently as he knew how. And, in Lategan's case, that was very efficiently indeed.

Jele had been washing his hands at the basin in the corner and he had frozen in that position, bending over the basin with the soap in his hands and both hands immersed in the running water. "Permission to move, sir," Jele requested, his voice light and friendly. He could have been a schoolboy requesting permission to go to the lavatory.

Lategan was watching his men move into position and watching the other Convention workers to see that no one moved. He looked at Bhengu. "You're Sam Bhengu," he told him.

"Yes."

"We are going to search your offices. I want a statement of your organization's finances immediately. You know who we are?"

They were all wearing civilian clothes, but Bhengu knew who they were. "I'll see your identification," he said.

"Sir, if you don't mind, Convention can't afford all this water we're wasting. Also I'm burning my hands. It's the hot-water tap that's running." Jele's voice had risen slightly in feigned panic.

Lategan took his wallet out of the inside pocket of his jacket and, flipping it open, held it out to Bhengu so that he could examine the identification card that it held. Bhengu examined it carefully, reading every word and comparing the face in the photograph to the face of the man holding it. All the time he was examining it Lategan held it at arm's length and held it completely still, without the slightest tremor in his arm.

"Sir, is this a torture method or what?" Jele yelled from the washbasin.

"What the hell's going on with you?" Lategan shouted at him, Jele's complaints finally having drawn his attention.

"My hands are burning."

"Then take them out of the water."

"Thank you, sir." The sense of relief in Jele's voice was so exaggerated that Bhengu and the other Convention workers all laughed.

The laughter drew Lategan's irritation toward Jele again. "What are you trying there? Why didn't you move your hands long ago?"

"I'm sorry, sir. I hate to be any trouble, but you said not to move." He paused to blow on his hands. "Anybody got anything for burned hands?" he asked.

⌘   ⌘

Go back, Jele, go back. There's no point now. There's nothing you can do and there's nothing they can do. For me there's nothing left and there's nothing they can do to me anymore. Go back. Go back and continue the work. It's the work that's important. That they've broken Convention is nothing. Organizations are nothing. Only the work is important. Go back.

Glancing up at the sky, as if the sunlight interested him very much, both hands in his trouser pockets, Jele turned and walked south down Point Road, in a few strides leaving Bhengu's field of vision. Immediately the policeman walked to the corner of the building and turned into the side street that ran parallel to Point Road. A moment later Bhengu could not see him either. At the end of the block the two men would come out opposite each other in the next street, the policeman making a show of not looking directly at Jele, and Jele pretending not to be interested in the building the policeman was guarding. In the meantime the policeman would be studying his face whenever he felt that Jele's attention was somewhere else, trying to memorize every feature. And, if he managed to get a message upstairs, the game would really be on.

Go back, Jele. For God's sake, go back.

He knew where Jele had come from and whom he represented, and he probably even knew why he had come. Bhengu could not think that Jele would have come for any other reason than to see him by chance through an open window or come upon anything that would be news in what remained of the Convention network. Bhengu had warned Jele in the past against this sort of thing, but the people wanted news and Jele was trying to get it for them. He had probably been wandering from one of the possible places of detention to another all day, watching from a distance, hoping for something that he knew would almost certainly not come. Jele knew all the prisons, police stations and Special Branch offices in the city. Every one of the Convention executives had been in more than one of them, and together they knew them all. Whatever Jele saw would spread from cell to cell, township to township, one city to the next, through the Convention structure and beyond to the simple people who had heard his name but knew no more than that he was fighting for them.

Go back, Jele. Go back.

In the month that he had been inside he had seen none of them, had had no contact at all with Jele or Mama Mabaso or any part of the world outside. Every day they would be asking themselves how long he would still be held or how long before his family would be told to come and fetch his possessions, the body . . .

Go back. Please go back.

Bhengu knew the people who would be waiting for news of himself and he knew the route the news would travel. He knew the byways, the beerhalls, the same buildings through every black township all over the country, the same dusty streets, the same little matchbox houses to the same plan, or to a plan so similar that you would never notice the difference, the same overladen buses and trains, the same empty gardens and barren cemeteries, the underfed dogs and wrongly fed children, the playing fields that had never seen grass, the old and dented cars; and always the people, crowding trains before the sun was up, surging out of them after dark, filling the streets with weary trudging figures, walking, walking, always walking, following the paths that took them closest to the few streetlights where they might be safer than in the darkness, weighted down by their apathy and the belief that nothing could ever be done to change things, going to the beerhalls to get drunk and forget the day's insults. Bhengu had lived all his life on these streets and among these people. He knew them well. And he knew the adamant face of the police that was always turned toward them, to keep them where they were, forming a lethal impenetrable barricade between city and township . . .

Go away, Jele, go, go quickly.

He knew them and he knew the resignation with which the news of his death would be received. He had grown to manhood, part of the great anonymous congregation of black faces that traveled daily between township and city to fill all the lowest positions in the structure of things. He knew how they clung to the little they had, afraid of any disturbance that might result in losing the radio, for which twenty-four payments had been made, or having the bedroom furniture damaged, which had taken thirty-six payments, or losing the job, for how then could the kids' schoolbooks be bought or the monthly train tickets to work or the rent be paid and food be kept in the pot? Bhengu knew them as individuals, not as the faceless black tide of white nightmares, and he was aware of how carefully they went through each day desperate to give no cause for offense, knowing that no lapse on their part would be tolerated. They may be abused. They might be allowed to protest respectfully. They dare not return the abuse. And always there was the police, the militant arm of an alien domination, the barrier between themselves and any pretense to power, the sure confirmation of their place in society.

No, Jele, it's not worth it. Go back.

And he knew the young that had not yet spent their lives being conditioned to becoming part of the system, that were still rebellious, still hopeful and despairing. He knew the young that had the previous year come to realize that the education they had been pursuing so eagerly would be of no value to many of them, and that the doors would always be closed unless they opened them themselves. He knew how they sought a consciousness that was not fraught with the inferiorities of the past, an inner awareness that there is no need to be ashamed of what I am. And he had seen them march until they reached the impenetrable barricade of police trucks and repeating rifles, and he had seen them die there.

No, Jele, there's no point. Please go back. Go back immediately. What good would a glimpse do? Go back.

Bhengu knew them all. He had known them drunk and sober, brave and cowardly, apathetic and alive to the possibilities of the future. He knew that it was in the unbowed hearts of the young that an anger was stirring, storing up against the day of reckoning . . .

He saw the policeman first coming out of the side street at a trot and stopping as soon as he reached the corner, then adopting an attitude of careless indifference and facing the corner of Point Road where he obviously expected that Jele would come into view again. He was careful not to look directly at it, his head turned slightly to the side.

Jele sauntered into view, his hands still in his pockets. It was clear to Bhengu that he had walked a block to the next intersection, where the policeman had seen him again, and then come back. He went as far as the crowd at the bus stop, leaning against a lamppost on the edge of the crowd and looking straight at the building. Perhaps Jele could see him. Bhengu's head was still pressed hard against the window. It must have been visible from outside. He tried again to lift a hand to wave to his friend, but again it was impossible.

The policeman was backing away from the corner toward the entrance to the building. Go, Jele. In Jesus' name, go.

Without prior indication and for no reason that Bhengu could see, Jele turned and ran for the alley. A moment later

the policeman had dashed into the front entrance of the building, the top of his cap disappearing below the windowsill
against which Bhengu's chest was pressing. Jele sprinted into
the alley, his stride long and springy up the incline. Halfway
up he vaulted a low brick wall and swung in behind an apartment building. By the time the guard, accompanied by two
white uniformed policemen, appeared on the pavement below
Bhengu, the alley was empty except for an old white woman
with two small children in beach robes and carrying towels
over their arms.

The force with which he was spun around sent him rolling off
the chair, his body swaying heavily to one side. He tried to lift
an arm to cushion the fall, but his arms felt as if they were
strapped to his sides. He was falling, tipping until his head
was swinging over like a stone in a sling. The warrant officer
caught him before his head hit the ground and lifted him into
an upright position.

"You should have let him fall." Strydom was speaking Afrikaans and his voice was outraged. "You should have let him
hit his head on the ground. That's what he wants to do. You
should have let him." The two warrant officers were close on
either side of Bhengu. He could see them out of the corners of
his eyes. They were no longer holding him and he was leaning
forward again, now with his back to the window. He tried
straightening up, but his head was a lead weight, holding his
body in its hunched-over position. All he succeeded in doing
was hardening the muscles of his neck so that he would not
appear to be hanging his head before them. "Do you think
you are beating us, kaffir? Do you think we don't know your
tricks?" Behind Strydom, seated on the edge of the desk, Engelbrecht watched him impassively, the bright sky reflected in
the lenses of his sunglasses. "So you don't want to be free?
You don't want to walk around outside like your friends?

They've all confessed and they're walking around outside now. Don't you want to be free like them? What do you want, kaffir? Do you want us to let you go without anything in return? You can't be that stupid. Do you think I'm going to let you free to start riots and revolutions and murder my wife and kids and my parents? Come on, kaffir, you can't be that stupid." The security policeman's face was angry, the eyes wild, the whites showing all around the irises. Bhengu had never seen Strydom so close to losing control. He felt a tight contraction in his stomach. He had known them to lose control before.

Bhengu hated his fear. The muscles of his stomach were a ball of sinew, bunched hard together, and there was no way that he could ease them. He hated even more that they might see the fear on his face. And he hated it because he knew it to be unnecessary. Rationally Bhengu knew that he had nothing to fear. Everything that they could do to him had already been done. But, in spite of what he knew to be true, he still feared them. He feared the loss of control he could see in Strydom's eyes and the traces of pleasure he could see in Engelbrecht's otherwise expressionless face. They held absolute power over their prisoners . . . No, it was not true. Their power over him was no longer absolute. He had no reason to fear them.

"You must be thirsty now, Sam." Strydom had changed to English and the tone of his voice had also changed, suddenly becoming friendly, the wildness in his face gone, leaving in his eyes only the faintest trace of its passing. "When last did you have something to drink? I'm sure you're thirsty now." Bhengu's tongue was raw and lifeless inside his mouth, filling it in every dimension. Yes, he was thirsty. His tongue seemed to be stuck to the sides of his cheeks as if they were all the same organ, the point of contact between tongue and cheeks feeling like the place where a wound was healing. Once the healing process was over, his tongue and cheeks would all be joined together. The cavity that was now in his mouth would be closed permanently. Perhaps then he would never be thirsty again. "We are going to let you drink now, Sam. We are taking mercy on you." Strydom nodded at the warrant officer called André and the young man went to the steel cabinet in the corner. Bhengu saw him come back across the room carrying a glass jug and a tumbler. He saw the yellow liquid, swilling back and forth in the jug, and immediately knew what it was. The warrant officer put the jug and the tumbler down on the table next to Strydom and took up his position next to Bhengu. Strydom glanced down at the liquid in the jug. "Do you recognize it, Sam. You should. You definitely should." Strydom picked up the jug and filled the tumbler slowly, the yellow liquid frothing and bubbling lightly on the surface. Then he took the tumbler in his right hand and held it close to Bhengu's face. "Here you are, Sam. I know you need it." Strydom leaned forward quickly and wove the fingers of his free hand into Bhengu's hair and pulled his head upright. At the same moment the two warrant officers clamped his arms on either side. "Drink, kaffir." He had changed to Afrikaans again, seeming to save his own language for the unpleasantnesses. The glass was lifted up and pressed against his lips. Bhengu tried to turn his head away, but there was no response from the muscles that should have done it for him. The urine poured, frothing, through his lips and into his mouth, spilling over at the corners, down his chin and onto his chest. The liquid was full in his mouth, slightly sweet, the fumes rising into the nasal passages. For a moment his tongue fought it involuntarily, then he was swallowing it eagerly as it cooled and softened the membrane on the inside of his mouth.

Strydom held up the empty tumbler. He looked at the jug again. "I think we can get another four or five out of that." He filled the tumbler a second time, smiling benignly at Bhengu. "Come on, Sam. Drink up." This time Bhengu did not fight it at all. His throat reacted convulsively, swallowing it down in long draughts, the urine healing the insides of his mouth, the fumes rising and filling the cavities in the back of his nose.

✠   ✠

"You must go. They were here two hours ago. You must go straightaway." She had been crying and the little hollows below her eyes were still damp. Behind her the child was standing in the doorway, holding onto the doorpost, his arms wrapped around it in the way he had often held onto his mother's leg when he was smaller. "You must go, Sam."

"Sit down," Bhengu said. "Sit down and tell me what happened."

"They were here, looking for you. You must go."

"Sit down," Bhengu said again. "Sit down first, then we'll talk." It was early morning and in the twilight outside men, wearing coats and jackets against the midwinter cold, were passing the window on their way to the bus depot. The child's eyes were large and frightened. Bhengu only glanced at him. His attention was with the mother. He watched her sit down on the bed, her face puzzled at his insistence. "That's better," he said. "Now relax, and tell me what happened." He sat down next to her.

She was unable to relax, sitting on the edge of the bed, her back held straight upright and looking in front of her, not at him. "They were here two hours ago—police in uniforms and others without uniforms. I think they were security police."

"Did they say what they wanted?"

"They wanted you."

"Yes, but why did they want me?"

"I don't know. They asked me where you were, and I said I didn't know."

"Which was true."

"Sam, they'll come back. You'd better go away. You'd better go right now. They want you."

"Woman, I'm not a criminal. I would not go underground. And I will not run."

"And if they torture you?"

"Then they torture me." Bhengu said it harshly and with finality, and the woman could see that the idea of his running was closed for discussion. "Now, tell me . . ." he said more gently, ". . . tell me exactly what happened."

She noticed the boy in the doorway and held out an arm to him. He ran the few short steps across the room and stood close up against his mother. "We were asleep," she said. "I heard the boy cry, but before I was properly awake there was a flashlight shining in my face. It was so bright, I didn't know what was happening. Through my sleep it was like it had suddenly become daylight. They were all around my bed and one of them was shouting questions at me. He kept asking me where you were and when I'd last seen you. They said they'd lock me up if I didn't tell. Then they took the child away. I tried to get up to go after him, but two of them held me down in the bed."

"Did they do anything to you?"

"No, they did nothing."

"If they did anything I want you to tell me."

"They did nothing. One held me by the shoulders and another pressed down on my stomach with his hand, but they did nothing. All the time I could hear the child crying in the other room."

Bhengu took the child from the woman and held him against his chest. Momentarily and for one of the few times in his life, Bhengu understood to what extent the woman and the child were part of himself and how they were affected by all that affected him. "Did they stay long?" he asked.

"I don't know how long."

"Didn't you have the house locked? How did they get in?"

"The door was locked. They must have had their own key."

"You don't know how long they stayed?"

"It seemed very long. I don't know how long. They kept asking the same questions and I kept giving them the same answers. After they went away I looked at my watch. It was four o'clock then."

"Petronella," Bhengu said. He did not often use her name. "I'm sorry you had to go through this alone."

"It doesn't matter."

"I'm sorry it had to happen like this, though."

"I'm often alone," she said simply.

"Yes." His voice was harsh again. "Did you see how many of them there were?"

"I don't know, but when they left, the boy and I went to the window and there were five cars."

"And were the cars full?"

"I don't know. I think so. Sam, you must go away."

"Where to?"

"Go to Little-Mama Zibi's place. They won't think of looking for you there."

"Wherever I go I'll attract their suspicion to that area. I can't deliver Little-Mama Zibi into the hands of the security police. I can't go anywhere." Bhengu shook his head to rid it of the thought. "In any event I'm no criminal."

⌘   ⌘

Engelbrecht produced the photograph like a magician pulling a rabbit from a hat. "You recognize him?" he asked. "You should recognize him." The policeman's face was leaden, the bright sky still reflected in the sunglasses, an aerial telephone cable silhouetted sharply against it. Every time he moved, the cable seemed to be raised or lowered with the movement of his head, until he leaned forward and it shot off the top of the lenses. "Don't you recognize him?" Bhengu looked at the photograph. It showed a lean teenage boy in shorts and a dirty vest standing in front of a tribal hut. His face had a sullen fearful expression and the long almost fleshless arms and legs were covered with round sores. Bhengu recognized him. "You must know him, Sam. I'm sure you do. He's not doing very well. That's kwashkiorker he's got. There's nothing much wrong with him that proper food won't put right. It's just malnutrition, nothing else. And those people we put him with haven't got much money to spend on food for him, I'm afraid. You haven't been much of a father, have you, Sam? He didn't get that way in the time you've been detained. When last did you see him, Sam? How much time did you spend with him in recent years?" Engelbrecht paused, holding the photograph so that Bhengu could see it clearly in the light from the window. "I took the photograph. Those sores look even worse when you get close to them. They stink too. It made me sick, I can tell you. All he needs is someone to look after him. You got to get him decent food, you know. If he gets the right food he'll be fine in a few months' time. Where've you been while he's been getting like this, Sam? Haven't you got any feeling left for him?" Engelbrecht leaned far forward, bringing his face and the photograph closer. Bhengu's eyes were fixed unwaveringly on the pitiful figure in the picture but he could not be unaware of the image of the policeman, blurred and unfocused, behind it. Without seeing them he could feel the presence of the tight lipless mouth and the hidden eyes. Engelbrecht's voice was a seductive murmur. "If you cooperate we'll let you go. You'll be able to go and look after him. You'll be able to make up for what a lousy father you've been. It's something to think about. He's in a bad way, Sam. I don't know how long a boy of his age can live like that—maybe one year, maybe two years."

✠ ✠

"Is John coming? Is there a boy my age, walking?"

From his position at the window Bhengu could see the whole length of the road down to the gravel playing field where a crowd of barefoot boys were playing soccer with a tennis ball. The road itself was more quiet than usual, a few groups of children playing their simple games, while down near the soccer field three men were drinking kaffir beer from cardboard cartons and laughing at something one of them had said. Nearer him an old woman was walking slowly homeward, a bulging brown-paper carrier bag in each hand. "No, I don't see him," Bhengu said.

"But if it's Stevie, don't call me. Because then you know it isn't John." The child was lying down on his back, pulling a wooden toy train toward himself by a piece of string. "If there's a boy walking, can I go and look outside?"

"I think you'd better, just to be sure."

Leaving the train on the floor Bhengu's son scrambled to his feet and ran out of the house, stopping against the bare wire fence and hanging from the top strand, his head between it and the one immediately below so that he could see down the length of the road. From the kitchen Bhengu could hear the sounds of the child's mother preparing lunch, the door of the stove opening and the poker scratching around among the coals. The child left the fence and ran toward him, stopping outside the open window. "There's just a girl and she's going out. The others are small, not big like me. I mean, getting big like me."

"You keep a lookout for him," Bhengu said. "I'm sure he'll come."

"If I watch all the time I'll see him. Hey, Papa?"

"Of course you will."

The boy went back to the fence. If they came they would almost certainly come up past the playing field, possibly leaving men on the side roads and along the edge of the veld behind the houses in case he tried to get away. He would be able to see the cars on the far side of the field, losing sight of them when they circled it, and seeing them again when they turned the corner at the bottom of the road. Damn them, he thought. If they wanted me they could have come at any time. I've never run away from them. They could have written me a letter and I would have come to them. There was no need to come at two in the morning.

He had done nothing that he regretted or of which he felt ashamed. But it was true that there was much he would not tell them no matter how they raided his home or at what hour. Their early-morning raid was not going to help them in any way, but this was the way they wanted it. It was all part of the treatment.

The boy was back at the window. "There's just a lady and a big white man," he said.

Bhengu started to his feet. "Where's the white man?"

The boy stepped back from the window. He looked startled at his father's reaction. "I think it's Mr. Rogers," he said.

Bhengu was out of the front door in time to see Rogers enter one of the houses on his side of the road. He had met the social worker on several occasions in the past and liked him. He was the only white man in any sort of official position Bhengu had met who behaved naturally in his company. "Is it Mr. Rogers?" the boy asked.

"Yes."

Back inside, he sat down on the chair at the window again. He hated the way he had jumped up when his son told him about the white man. This was not what he had intended. He wanted to be in control of himself when they came. To give them the satisfaction of seeing him afraid or even startled was unthinkable.

"Can I go outside in the street and wait for him? Can I?"

"I don't think your mother wants you out in the street."

"Why? Because I might get knocked over?"

"Something like that."

"That's true what I said—all those words, hey?"

"She also said something about it being too cold."

"Then I can get my jersey. Hey, Papa?"

"Yes."

He came back inside and Bhengu heard him run to his bedroom and scratch in the bottom of a chest of drawers. There were no doors in the doorways of the little house, so that by turning his head he could see the boy down on his knees, the upper sides of his feet flattened against the floor, and leaning forward, his head almost inside the drawer. "This is a nice cupboard you bought me, hey, Papa?" he heard the boy say, speaking more to himself than to Bhengu, not expecting a reply.

Outside, the street was as innocent as it had been all morning. Down on the soccer field a thin boy in a striped jersey had found an opening and was trying to thread his way past the last few defenders while keeping control of the little ball on the fickle grassless surface of the pitch. The sounds from the kitchen had stopped and he could hear the child's mother singing a hymn in the backyard, her hoarse rather tuneless voice dragging out the notes, giving the song a funereal quality.

When the boy came back from the bedroom he had the jersey on halfway and he was struggling to get his head through the opening intended for it. "I know it's the front because it's got this," he said, his voice coming from within the woolen folds, one of his hands patting the vee shape in the front of the jersey's neck. He wriggled himself into it. "My head's too big

—that's why I struggle," he said. "Now I won't be cold, Papa. I'm going outside to look for cars."

"Be careful, son."

"Yes." He pointed out of the window. "Look at that beautiful cat, Papa." Bhengu looked in the direction he was pointing. A large gray cat was sitting on the cement path of the house directly opposite, fastidiously grooming itself. "I'm going now," his son said. "I just want to see if there's a boy my age." He went out and came straight to the window. "John might come from this side or the other."

"Yes. You run along and watch out for him."

"I'll go in the road. I won't be cold with my jersey." He went quickly down the path and out of the gate, skipping, but stopped as soon as he was outside, as if he suddenly felt threatened, and leaned against the fence.

Bhengu looked at his watch. The time was eleven o'clock. He had come home five hours previously and for most of that time he had been seated at the window, watching for them. If it was going to happen, he was anxious for it to happen soon. It would be impossible for him to continue with his usual business, knowing that they were coming. No matter how tight your mental discipline you would not be able to concentrate on anything else. He wondered if this was part of a big sweep or if he was being singled out for special treatment. And was it something they wanted from him or was it just a warning?

The child had come back and was standing outside the window. "If John doesn't come, then he's a liar."

"Perhaps his mother wouldn't let him come."

"But he promised."

"He wouldn't be able to help it if his mother wouldn't let him come."

"But then he's a liar."

"He might still come."

"Look which color his tail's shining. Is he the most beautiful cat?" The boy's attention had been attracted by the cat again and for a moment he seemed to have forgotten John. "Is he the most beautiful cat, Papa?"

"Sure."

"I'll see if John's coming." He ran to the fence again, this time staying on the inside and leaning through between the strands. From his position there, hanging by his hands from the top strand, he called back, "No. There's a big white man. A big white man can't be John."

Bhengu held tight control over himself. He did not want to startle the child a second time and he had to appear to be in control when they came. "Is the white man Mr. Rogers?" he asked.

"Yes, I think it is." He leaned further out, his supple young shoulders pulled right back till the shoulder blades were pressed against each other. "Yes, it is. It's Mr. Rogers because Mr. Rogers has got a yellow jacket and he's getting into Mr. Rogers' car. That's how I know it's Mr. Rogers." The boy came back from the fence and stood close to him on the other side of the window. "You aren't scared of Mr. Rogers, hey?"

Bhengu looked at his son for a while before answering him. Perhaps he had underestimated the child. He remembered how, as a small child, his parents had tried to keep the collapse of their marriage from him and Winifred. One night years afterward in Sophiatown he had spoken to her about it. "I think we knew before they did," she had said. The brief memory of his sister twisted itself through his soul, tearing at old wounds. The men who had come looking for him—were they not responsible for that too? They were all part of the same system, elements in a common formula.

His son was looking at him questioningly, the smooth young face serious and troubled. "No," Bhengu said. "I'm not scared of Mr. Rogers."

"Because he's not a policeman, hey?"

"No. He's not a policeman."

"You wouldn't call me John, hey? Then there would be two Johns in our class. We've got two Isaacs in our class. One is Isaac Khumalo. That's not a nice surname, hey? If there's two Johns and the teacher says, John, then we don't know if it's him or me." The boy looked down the road toward the soccer game. "If he doesn't come, he's a liar."

A car came up the road on the far side of the soccer field. It left his field of vision as it circumvented the field, coming back into view at the bottom of the street and then coming to a stop almost immediately. It was an old Valiant that had been crashed and was not looking too good after a backyard panel-beating job. A man and four women got out and went into one of the houses.

"Maybe he's got to do his homework first," the boy was saying. "His mother says, You can go, but first you must do your homework. Or maybe his mother said, No you can't go." The boy was looking intently down the road, obviously studying everything that moved. "He promised he would come. What if he doesn't come?"

"I don't know," Bhengu said.

"Then he's a liar," the boy said.

⌘ ⌘

The faces of the two warrant officers were close to his, holding his attention and dominating his view of the room. Behind them Strydom was sitting on the edge of the table, his prim sanctimonious face showing signs of tiredness. Engelbrecht was at the desk, leaning heavily back, his arms hanging loosely down, the tips of his fingers almost touching the carpet. It was a position in which Bhengu had often seen him. His face was obscured by the warrant officer called Piet Kleynhans. The questions were the same ones that he had been hearing over

and over for days now. "Why did you go to Johannesburg? . . . Why did you visit Winnie Mandela? . . . What
were you doing with your secretary in Pietermaritzburg? . . .
And Sobukwe? Why did you visit him? . . . Who drew up
the 18 August pamphlet? . . . Where is Jele now?" The in-
sinuations were also the same. "Do you know that Smith has
been confessing? Do you know what he's been saying? . . . It
won't help to keep quiet. We know the answers. . . . Do you
know who your wife's been going with? . . . And your girl?
Do you know how many of your friends have had her since
you last did? . . . Do you know what she told us about you?"

Piet Kleynhans was perspiring, the sweat running down his
face from his forehead and temples to combine at the point of
his chin. Every few minutes the droplet at the point of his chin
would grow too large to cling there and would fall to the carpet. Bhengu watched it with fascination, becoming quite dis-
appointed if something happened to interrupt one of the
streams of sweat so that it did not reach his chin. Every time
he wiped one away from his forehead or cheeks, cutting it off
from his chin, Bhengu mourned it inwardly. It was most
distressing of all when the gathering flood at the point of the
warrant officer's chin was, itself, wiped away. At times,
though, the droplet would be allowed to grow too large to
cling there any longer and Bhengu would have the satisfaction
of seeing it break loose and splash softly onto the absorbent
surface of the carpet.

He examined the faces of the two young men closely, taking
in each feature: an undistinguished mouth, woolly irregular
eyebrows, an early tendency toward baldness; both faces
unlined and immature, still believing in what they were doing,
not yet realizing that there would be no glamor, only the un-
ceasing pursuit of a security that could never be achieved by
such methods; and no pleasure, excepting the pleasure of
causing pain and seeing it suffered. What they had been

taught so far would eventually become an inescapable mental necessity, exercising an almost total dominance over their lives. Bhengu could escape neither the hostility nor the sense of purpose in their faces.

He knew that they were at least as aware of the eyes of their senior officers on them as they were of the need to get information out of him. Every successful interrogation, every satisfactory confession, every enemy of the system left broken and helpless, was a victory; a step toward the next promotion, provided that your senior officers were present to see it happen. With their officers watching them, Kleynhans and De Jager had to be successful. They were the cream, the very best the police had to offer. No one could apply to join the security police. They were selected. They were the elite into whose care the State was given for safekeeping. For such duties only the best would be good enough. All their lives they would never be allowed to forget that they were the best and that they were the last line of defense against the ambitions of Bhengu's people. If they failed, all would have failed and the flood gates would be opened to anarchy and the numberless black hordes. Every security policeman, and the two young warrant officers were in no way extraordinary, knew that he stood between his people and extinction.

To Bhengu the two young faces were incongruous with the angry expressions and the hostile questions. He did not want to look at them. He had grown accustomed to the Lategans, Engelbrechts and Strydoms, but by all reasonable standards there should still have been a chance for these two young men. But perhaps, like the others, they were already past the point where they had been able to turn back.

There'll be no room for you in the new Africa, Bhengu thought. You're young and you'll live to see it, but there'll be no room for you.

The door swung open suddenly, hitting against the wall.

Lategan came quickly into the room. The skin of his face was drawn tight, the jaw hard. Lieutenant Brown was trotting behind, his eyes alert in the way a hare's might be when the dogs are after it. Lategan's eyes took in the two warrant officers and seemed to flash with the intensity of what he was feeling. "Leave him alone," he said. The two warrant officers leaped away from Bhengu as if he was the carrier of a contagious disease. Lategan had stopped next to the desk and Brown came to a halt well short of him, his eyes held by the expression on the colonel's face. Strydom had got to his feet as soon as the door opened and Engelbrecht was scrambling erect, holding onto the back of his chair for support. Everyone in the room knew that Lategan had wanted Brown brought in to see him, and the eyes of all the policemen traveled questioningly between the colonel and the lieutenant.

Lategan walked to the far side of the room, stopping before the window and nodding to Engelbrecht in a signal for the other man to join him. Engelbrecht complied with the gesture automatically, taking up a position close to the colonel with his back to Bhengu. Lategan spoke very softly. To Bhengu the sound of his voice was an indistinct mumble. He could distinguish only the words, ". . . wait first . . ." in what the colonel said.

Engelbrecht nodded once, then again, and finally shook his head. When he spoke he turned his head to look at Brown, and Bhengu could hear what he was saying. "And tonight?"

Lategan answered without looking around. "Come here, Malcolm." The sound of his voice was rasping and dry. Brown hurried across the room, stopping close to him, but unconsciously holding his head away, like a man who expected that he was going to be punched and wanted as much room as possible in which to avoid the blow. Lategan dropped his voice again, but this time Bhengu could hear what he was saying.

"If you ever walk out on a night shift again it'll be the end of your police career. Do you understand?"

Brown came to attention involuntarily. "Yes, sir."

"The others?" Engelbrecht asked the question.

The words reached Bhengu, fell away, and then reached him again, as Lategan either dropped his voice or raised it slightly in making a point. ". . . got to stay on . . . move them and we admit . . . would be a catastrophe . . . just as they are . . . it's in the log . . . a struggle . . ."

When he had finished, Brown tried to speak. "I thought they would be more . . ."

Lategan looked quickly at him, his eyes still hard with the intensity Bhengu had seen there when he came into the room. The lieutenant's explanation dried up immediately. "Do you know what I'm getting you out of?"

"Yes, Colonel." Brown was holding up his head in parade-ground fashion, looking straight in front of him.

"You stay so close to that man from now on that nothing can happen to him that you don't know about."

"Yes, Colonel."

Strydom spoke, his voice cold and clear, his habitual control having long since been reasserted. "Colonel, isn't it possible that he's just acting?"

Lategan looked at Bhengu for a moment, and during that short time Bhengu again felt near to some sort of contact with him. It would have far overstated what Lategan felt to have called it pity. It was closer to being some sort of understanding, possibly no more than the understanding a hunter feels for his quarry, now dying, but nevertheless an understanding. He averted his eyes and Bhengu sensed how difficult it was for the security policeman to look directly at him. For the first time in his dealings with Lategan, Bhengu felt a true moral superiority, a sense that matters were now in his control, not in the control of his adversary. Bhengu knew that

there was nothing Lategan could do now. And he sensed that
Lategan shared the knowledge. His men had played all his
cards and they had played them too fast. Whereas he still had
his last card and he was busy playing it. His death would give
him the game.

Lategan had not answered Strydom. He half-turned toward
Engelbrecht but spoke past him. "Now we will have to ban
him for life," he said. "He's not like the others."

Bhengu was on his feet and leaning against the wall, the
smoothly painted cement surface cold against his naked shoulder. His hands were shackled in front of him, held close together by the short steel link between the cuffs. At least that
meant that they hid his genitals. It would have been much
worse if they had cuffed his hands behind him. At the desk
Brown was making an entry in the log. Bhengu was aware of
Fourie behind him doing something to the bed. Van Rooyen
had positioned himself right in front of him, the bloated
shapeless face only a handbreadth from his, its determined
grin intended to emphasize to Bhengu that he was still helpless
in their hands, that nothing had changed. But Bhengu had
never expected that Lategan's disciplining of the night shift
might work to his advantage. He knew the nature of his relationship with Lategan and that of Lategan with his men too
well to have expected that.

Bhengu saw Van Rooyen's right shoulder move toward him
and he felt the warrant officer grab hold of his genitals, brushing his hands out of the way. He squeezed them for only a moment, releasing his grip almost immediately. The stupid grinning face moved off to the side and out of his range of vision.
He tried consciously to analyze his feelings, but there was nothing. All emotion seemed to have been drained away. Forty-
eight hours previously he would have been angered by what
Van Rooyen had done, but now it seemed hardly to concern

him. Neither the warrant officer's victorious grin, nor the remote sensation of fingers closing around testicles, could touch him in any way.

"We'll have to let him get dressed, I suppose," Fourie said, his voice uncertain, trying to anticipate Brown's wishes and possibly not eager to take the treatment of Bhengu any further.

"No. We take him just like that."

"And if somebody sees him?"

"Put a blanket around him. A man wearing only a blanket is not going to try to escape. And nobody gave us orders to let him get dressed." He looked at Fourie, anticipating his line of thinking. "I know what Colonel Lategan thinks, but I'm not so sure. This bastard is clever. And if he gets away, then we're really buggered."

"He's fuckin' acting," Van Rooyen said. "There's nothing wrong with him. We were here the whole time and we did fuck-all to him. What we did couldn't have done anything to him. I know his type. The colonel will still find out."

Bhengu felt a hand take hold of the arm that was clear of the wall and pull him gently upright. Fourie had a blanket in his other hand. He shook it open and swung it around Bhengu's shoulders. "Can you hold it?" he asked, looking down at Bhengu's cuffed hands as he waited for a reply. Bhengu felt his hands close around the edges of the blanket and hold on. Then Fourie lifted his hands to the point at Bhengu's neck where the corners overlapped. "I think we need a few safety pins," he heard Fourie say to Brown.

"He can hold onto it," Brown said. "If his big black cock sticks out, it's just too bad."

Van Rooyen leaned on the desk next to Brown and whispered something to him, his voice so low that Bhengu could hear only the sibilance of the whispered words. Brown laughed shortly and glanced up at Bhengu. Van Rooyen also looked around at him, but it was a longer look, his face still wearing the same knowing grin. To Bhengu it said, I've had you by the balls and I can have you that way again anytime I choose.

Brown closed the logbook and went to the door. "You two will have to take him on either side. He won't walk by himself."

Walking down the passage to the elevator with Brown ahead, supported on either side by the two warrant officers, Bhengu again had the sense of the remoteness of his feet, the feeling that they were not a part of him. They were moving and carrying his weight, but it did not seem to be at any instruction that he had given them. He found that he could bring his head forward to look down the front of the blanket. Brown's words, "If his big black cock sticks out . . ." bothered him. The thought of walking down the passage and into the elevator with his penis on display had become very troubling. It was more troubling than any other part of what was happening to him. A man could die with dignity. He could even be tortured with dignity, but you could not walk down the passage of a Special Branch office with your cock hanging out and do it with dignity. He managed to bring his head far enough forward to see right down to his feet. There had been no need for concern. The two ends of the blanket overlapped in front, hiding his body completely. All that was visible were his naked feet and calves, the left foot seeming to drag with each stride. The thought came to Bhengu that there was no way it could have stuck out in any event. It would never again be in a condition where that would be possible. It was now no more than a limp skin, an empty vestige to remind him of past glory.

The doors of the offices on either side were all closed, the fanlights above them in darkness. Only the fluorescent light on the landing was burning. The passage itself was in darkness.

Ahead of Bhengu, Brown was a shadow against the light, walking with a springy step in which he went up on the balls of his feet at every stride. Once the lieutenant looked back to make sure that they were following. Halfway along the passage he took a comb out of an inside pocket and ran it through his dense wavy black hair. No matter what the circumstances, his appearance would always be very important to Lieutenant Brown. In sober moments he might have been aware that the resources at his disposal for making his way in life were very limited and it would always be wisest to make the most of each one.

Inside the elevator the four of them were pressed close together, invading each other's little personal space and no man looking directly at another because of it. Brown was facing Bhengu, but looking past him. Without the use of a mirror, he had even managed to arrange the little curl that always fell across his forehead. Bhengu reckoned that such dexterity could only be the result of intensive practice over a long period, probably most of the lieutenant's life. Brown was holding his head up very straight and his eyes were narrowed. Bhengu had come to recognize it as his Strydom imitation. "I think you're trying to fuck up my career, Sam," he said, looking at the closed door of the elevator. "Warrant Officer Van Rooyen is right. He's got your number. There's nothing wrong with you, but you're trying to make it seem like we did something to you. I want to tell you it won't work. You can't keep it up forever. We're going to keep you until you crack. You can forget about getting us into trouble."

The elevator opened into the parking garage in the basement of the building. Now Brown took the arm that Fourie had been holding and the warrant officer went to open the padlocked wire gate at the vehicle entrance. Van Rooyen got into the back seat of the car first, dragging Bhengu after him. The seat took Bhengu behind the knees and he fell heavily backward, his head hitting the top of the door frame and the blanket falling open. He felt the blow as a jolting impact and his vision blurred instantaneously, but there was no pain. Bhengu's vision returned to normal with Brown bending over him, his face in shadow, trying to lift him into a sitting position on the seat. He had lost his grip on the blanket and it was lying spread across the edge of the seat and the garage floor. He tried to move his cuffed hands toward it and got hold of a corner, but his hands would not bring it right over his body. He succeeded in covering his right leg, but that was all. Again his nakedness was very important to Bhengu. He tried a second time to get the blanket over him, but this time his arms would not respond at all.

"For Christ's sake, Sam," Brown was saying, the words coming between gasps for breath, "stop worrying about your prick and help me get you into the car."

Bhengu felt Van Rooyen's hands under his armpits, and with Brown lifting him around the waist he was pulled into the back seat. Brown scooped up the half of the blanket that was lying on the floor and threw it into Bhengu's lap. His hands immediately fastened onto it, holding it in place over his genitals. Van Rooyen tried to spread it more evenly, but Bhengu had it bunched up and was holding onto it tightly. "A kaffir remains a kaffir," Van Rooyen said, shaking his head, his voice sounding surprisingly bitter, the grin removed from his face. "You're just the same, no difference."

Brown had got into the driver's seat, started the engine and was moving the car up the ramp to the entrance where Fourie was holding the gate wide open. "I can't say I'll be sorry to get off this night shift for a while," he said. "After this someone else can take a turn. I've had enough of it. So help me, I don't want any more."

Fourie closed the gate after the car had passed through it and also got into the back seat so that Bhengu would be wedged between him and Van Rooyen. As Van Rooyen had done, he made an attempt to cover Bhengu more effectively with the blanket. "Forget it," Van Rooyen said. "He's only interested in keeping his cock covered."

The car moved smoothly away into the early-evening traffic. Brown drove steadily, a man in no hurry. His only job for the night was to deliver Bhengu safely to the prison, and as he was being paid overtime there was no reason to rush.

"Colonel Lategan will still see his mistake with this kaffir," Van Rooyen said.

Brown half-turned his head as he answered. "The colonel's all right," he said. "He's a white man."

"I agree, but he'll still see his mistake with this kaffir."

"Do you know how much shit he's saved us? Making out reports and all that? I've seen the sort of shit a bloke can get into with this kind of thing—please explain what happened, please explain why it could not have been avoided, kindly give a full report . . . I've seen this kind of report go back and forth for months—then Pretoria's not satisfied with this, then they're not satisfied with that . . . I know what it can be like, and I'm telling you the colonel has saved us a lot of shit."

"I know, I know." Van Rooyen's voice was impatient and self-excusing. "I only say he's going to find out his mistake with this kaffir."

The inside of the car was dark, the faces of the three policemen intermittently lit by the lights outside. Streetlamps, shop windows, colored illuminated signs, the headlamps of passing cars, all flashed their light across the three white faces, giving Bhengu varied flickering impressions of his keepers: Fourie's face drawn and blank, Van Rooyen's having gravitated to its usual sullen resentfulness, and Brown's alive and intent, having already put behind him all the unpleasantness of the immediate past.

The car was stopped by a traffic light and Brown turned

right around to look at the men in the back seat. "You blokes didn't do anything to him while I was away, did you?" Before either of the warrant officers could speak, Brown was already answering his own question. "Nah, of course not. I know you wouldn't."

"We did bugger-all," Van Rooyen said. "We just tapped him a bit. He knows we didn't do anything. He's just trying to drop us, that's all."

"Of course. I knew you didn't," Brown said, his mind somehow discarding Van Rooyen's partial confession. "I've always said this was just an act. But he'll find out it's not so easy to ruin my career."

On the pavements people were walking up and down, young men with girls, older men with their wives, apartment cleaners in a group talking, a man buying cigarettes at a café counter, doing the things they chose to be doing, free to pursue their own lives, and they were not just whites; Bhengu's people as well, coming and going in an illusion, a humiliating restricted parody of freedom. But tonight they were free to walk with their women and perhaps to take them home to bed. And they were alive, and tomorrow they would still be alive.

From somewhere in an apartment building next to the road Bhengu heard the sound of recorded piano music. He thought he recognized the piece. He had heard it before. The subtle melody rolled gently toward him, his mind's censoring faculties filtering out the traffic sound until he was aware only of the music. Somewhere inside the building a window or door closed and the music was gone. The traffic light changed and the car jerked slightly as Brown let in the clutch.

✠   ✠

"She plays it too fast," Humphrey Walters said. "Well, but much too fast. I tell her so, but she says it's good as a finger exercise that way. I always tell her that Beethoven is not a finger exercise."

"What's it called?"

"'Für Elise.' For Elise. She plays it over and over again. I must have heard her play it hundreds of times by now."

"I don't think I would grow tired of it easily," Bhengu said. "I'm not tired of it."

Bhengu looked up at the ceiling and then around at the rest of the room, the bay windows and the large stone fireplace. "It's a lovely house, Humphrey."

"Yes. I owe it to the kids in Soweto, of course." Reading the puzzlement on Bhengu's face, Walters continued, "Most of the houses in this bracket have come down by twenty thousand or more in the last six months."

"Are the whites that scared?"

"We are. We always have been, but doubly so since the riots."

"Twenty thousand rands is a lot of money. Convention could have put it to good use."

"With a lot of people it's a question of getting what they can out of the country. A loss on a house is nothing. They're scared that if they hang on they might lose everything. So they sell up and try to smuggle what they can out of the country."

"I don't think they need be concerned just yet."

"Don't tell me," Walters said. "I know."

The child in the next room finished the piece she had been playing and started again at the beginning, the full round notes of the piano tumbling easily into place, weaving a melody that filled the room and the air all around Bhengu, excluding all the harshness and brutality that was outside, soothing and easing everything that was tense and hard inside him. His senses seized the moment of beauty and held it. He was reluctant to speak or do anything that might disturb it. But Walters had got to his feet and was beckoning to him. "Let me show you my fortifications." He led Bhengu into the hall and pointed to the front door. "Do you see it?"

Bhengu had to go right up to the door to see that the inside consisted of a five-millimeter steel plate bolted against the wooden door. It had been painted white, the same as the door and door frame and, at a glance, looked like a slightly protruding wooden panel. "I felt I had to do something," Walters said. "I don't want what happened to Rod to happen to me. I'll show you the bedroom." The main bedroom had a deep bay window, like the one in the lounge, and running across the length of it was a rail, supporting a folding partition that cut off the window when extended. Walters closed it, shutting off the window from the rest of the room. Each section of the partition had a similar steel plate to the one on the front door, all painted white and looking as if they were an integral part of it. "For the rest we have heavy curtains on the windows so that they can't see into the house from outside and we keep the windows closed. I'm going to get air conditioning put in this summer."

They went back to the lounge and Walters poured them each a drink from the whisky bottle. "I believe they shot at Theo as well," Bhengu said.

"Yes."

"Fatima Meer, Woods. . . ."

"That's why I felt I had to take some sort of precaution. What does Beyers say?"

"He says that if someone wants to shoot him they will have plenty of opportunities, so taking precautions won't help much."

"Doesn't he do anything?"

"He keeps the blinds closed."

"Nothing else?"

"He plays his portable radio loud when he talks to you."

Walters smiled, a quiet private smile, connected perhaps to pleasant recollections. "Beyers is an innocent."

"Sure."

Walters' wife, Margaret, came slowly into the room. She was a small woman with rounded features that seemed to rumple when she was unhappy. Bhengu knew her well and as soon as he saw her face he knew that she was distressed. He got quickly to his feet and spoke her name. He wanted to go to her and put his arms around her, but all the years of his life prevented him from doing it. Despite his many liberal white friends there was always a measure of reserve in his dealings with them. It was a part of the South African legacy from which neither he nor they would ever be entirely free.

"Hello, Sam," Margaret said. "How are you keeping?" It was not an involuntary reaction, but a genuine inquiry. Bhengu could see that she was as careful not to look in her husband's direction as he was to avoid looking directly at her.

"I'm well. How are you?"

"So–so." She shrugged. "I'm just finishing dinner. I'll call you in a minute."

When she had gone and Bhengu had sat down again Walters started talking immediately, as if trying to dismiss his wife's presence. "We're receiving money from the Dutch churches and I'm grateful, of course. But that's not what I want. I want to work, but the bastards don't even answer my applications. Tell me what sort of job I can find where I'm only allowed to see one person at a time. I applied three months in advance to attend my kids' school concert, and two days before the concert is due it comes back, refused. The vindictive bastards."

"Maybe you should stop applying for permits. You give them the opportunity to refuse you."

"But how the hell am I going to live—just the simple things, like the school concert. It was the same with the school sports.

Brian ran in a couple of sprints . . . Jesus. If you can't even see your seven-year-old kid take part in the school sports . . ." Walters' voice was unsteady. It was the first time Bhengu had seen him since his restriction order had been gazetted, and he had never heard him sounding so bitter. "And my black friends—I'm the kiss of death to them. Mandela's been banned and he was involved in nothing. He was just a friend of mine. He's lost his job as a result. It was the same with Johnny Abrahamse."

"And Steve? How long before they took him in did you last see him?"

"A couple of months. You should have seen it, Sam. He'd taken over an old church right in the heart of white King William's Town. They'd partitioned it into separate offices and the place was really humming with all sorts of projects. And he had his own office where he saw people one at a time, in keeping with his banning order. The place was humming, really humming." The eagerness that had gradually been entering his voice, as he told about Steve, stopped suddenly, its source apparently shut off. "All destroyed by those bastards," he said.

Walters excused himself to go to the lavatory, and Bhengu went into the kitchen where Margaret was making a salad while dinner cooked. She looked up quickly as he came in, her pale face rumpling sadly at the sight of him. "It takes a bit of getting used to," he said.

She nodded without answering immediately. He could see that she had something particular she wanted to say to him, so he waited for her to speak rather than divert the conversation onto some other path. "I don't know what we're going to do," she said eventually. "We're like a couple of angel fish in a bowl. We fight with each other because there's no one else. There's just the two of us, alone with each other all the time. We used to have a busy social life, but it's all dried up now.

People can't stand it when they drop in on us, and Humphrey has to dash away every time there's a knock on the door. As a result we hardly see anyone these days, and when we do it's such a strain with Humphrey only supposed to talk to one person at a time. If he had a job it would be something. He sits around going to pieces. And lately he's been behaving the way he does when he has a girlfriend. The woman might even be in their pay, but he won't discuss it with me. I can't take any more of it, Sam."

"Shall I try to talk to him?"

"I don't think he'll talk to you about it."

"I'll try."

"You're a good friend, Sam."

Bhengu heard the lavatory flush and started back toward the lounge, but he stopped in the kitchen doorway. "This thing with the woman will pass," he said.

Margaret's face rumpled grotesquely, the features seeming to dissolve. "It'll kill me before it does. I've been through a lot with him, Sam."

"I'll try to speak to him about it."

The two men got back to the lounge at the same time, sitting down where they had been earlier. "You been chatting Margaret up?" Walters asked. There was a jeering note to the question.

"She's in trouble, Humphrey. She thinks you've got another woman."

"I don't want to discuss Margaret." The sound of his voice was so bitter that he might as easily have been talking about the authorities.

"This woman—are you sure she's not Special Branch?"

He dropped his voice low so that his wife would not hear. "I don't care. I'm getting what I want."

"And they're getting what they want."

"They're getting nothing out of me."

"What they want is the breakup of your family."

"What about your family?" The jeering note had returned to Walters' voice.

"My family's different," Bhengu said. "They can't be with me. You know that."

"And you want them with you?" Bhengu looked for an answer, knowing that he would not find one that would satisfy either himself or Walters. Before he could say anything Walters continued, "Don't talk to me about women, Sam. I know about yours and you know about mine. Don't talk to me about them."

"Okay," Bhengu said, "we won't talk about them."

The music from the next room was a smooth clear stream of sound, but now Bhengu wished it would stop. Whatever Walters' problems, he had his children under his own roof. With an effort of will Bhengu kept himself from thinking about his son. I can do nothing about it, he told himself. There's no point thinking about it.

❧ ❧

The uniformed guard took a long time examining Brown's identification before stepping through the small door in the steel-fronted motor gate. With the help of a second guard he swung it open from the inside to let them in. Brown drove the car down a short narrow passage between two buildings and into a small brightly lit courtyard, bringing it to a halt next to an office where the door was standing open. Bhengu watched him slip out of the driver's seat and go into the office, coming out a moment later with a middle-aged warder who looked as if he was either on the point of going to sleep or had just been awakened. He leaned forward to see into the car, his eyes stretched wide to make out the forms of the three men in the back seat.

"Why's he bare-ass?"

"It's orders," Brown said.

"You take him through the street like that?"

"He was in the car."

The warder looked carefully at Brown. He might have been searching for an explanation in the lieutenant's face. "What if somebody saw him like that? The newspapers?"

"It's night. Nobody could see him."

The warder shrugged and shook his head, relinquishing his search of Brown's face. "I've never had a prisoner brought in bare-ass before," he said.

"Nobody saw him."

"Do you people always move your prisoners like that?"

"He's a special case. I've got orders."

"Funny sort of orders. Maybe your officer's a nudist at heart." He snorted loudly in an uninspired attempt at laughter, glancing around the empty courtyard to see if there was anyone else present to appreciate his wit.

"Can we take him inside?" Brown asked.

"Everybody here wears prison dress," the warder said. "Even if he goes into the hospital he's got to have prison dress. The doctors will never allow bare-ass patients."

"He's got to be in isolation—Colonel Lategan's orders."

The warder went back into the office, still shaking his head. "I dunno why you blokes can't deliver your patients during the day like everybody else," Bhengu heard him say. "He can be in isolation, but he can't be bare-ass."

⌘   ⌘

The child had stopped playing. Bhengu heard Margaret in the next room, telling her that now homework had to be done and to get on with it. He was glad that he would not have to listen to the evidence of the well-structured life the other man's child led.

Humphrey Walters was frowning into his drink, his head turned slightly away. "I just don't want to see them get any satisfaction at your expense," Bhengu said. Walters nodded without saying anything, his eyes still fixed on the amber patterns in the whisky. Bhengu could see that nothing would be gained by pursuing the matter. "One other thing I want to say to you—don't ever break the terms of your banning order. Don't defy them. They can't stand that. If you fall into the hands of these people once, they never let you go."

"Do you think I don't know that? What about yourself?"

"It's too late for me to do anything about it. They've been spreading their net for me for a long time."

Walters looked up from his drink and straight at Bhengu at last. "How many times have they taken you in, Sam?"

"Seven times in the last three years. They are not going to give up now. It's become a question of pride by this time. They just have to break me."

"Why don't you leave?"

Bhengu ignored the question. Both of them knew that that was not even an alternative. "I want you to always be sure of this, Humphrey; that if I die in their custody it will not be suicide. No matter what the medical evidence is, I want you to be sure of that."

⌘   ⌘

This time there were clean sheets and a blanket on the bed and they had dressed Bhengu in a nightshirt made of coarse calico. Without lifting his head he could see the barred door of the cell and the white-painted wall on the other side of the passage. By the light coming in from the passage he could also see a large galvanized-iron bathtub up against the wall on the far side of the cell.

He was on his back, his arms at his sides, his hands palm-downward and enjoying the cool smooth surface of the sheets. He wondered if the water in the bathtub was warm. He had an uncertain image in his mind of two warders bringing in the bathtub and the water had been steaming then, but how long ago that had been he had no way of knowing. The image was so vague that he was not even sure that the memory was real. He tried to remember when last they had allowed him to bathe, but that was also uncertain—three or four days perhaps, possibly a week or even more. And in the city's tropical spring that was quite a long time. There were places where his back clung to the nightshirt with the residue of old sweat that had evaporated on his skin and had been replaced to evaporate again, leaving an even sticky layer.

From the passage he heard the soft shuffling footsteps of someone coming toward his cell door. A thin middle-aged warder, with hollow eyes and the untroubled serenity of a mind unafflicted by doubts and questionings, stopped in front of the iron bars of the door and looked steadily at him. The warder's uniform had been neatly pressed and the brass buckles polished, but something in his manner still contrived to make him appear untidy. He stared at Bhengu for a while, his placid face free of any expression, then without saying anything he moved away down the passage, the sound of his footsteps halting for a moment at each cell.

With the warder gone, Bhengu felt suddenly more isolated than he had been before. The fact that he did not want it all to be over yet, that he had left too much unfinished, bore in upon him. It was all circumstance, Bhengu told himself. If I had been allowed to live a normal life, everything would have been different. They were always pressing me. I was never able to organize things the way I wanted them. If it had not been for that, everything would have been fine.

The photograph of his son returned to his thoughts. It had been more than a year since he had last seen the boy, and then it had been for only a few hours. He remembered the child's suspicious face and the sullen answers he gave to questions. He could still see him, moving from one foot to the other, as he made an inattentive pretense of listening to what his father was saying, the distrust that he felt showing itself clearly on his face.

It's not just my fault, Bhengu thought. What about the child's mother? Where was she? Why couldn't she have done something? No. I don't want to think about her. I don't want to think about her at all. Why is it only my fault? Why not hers as well? Why couldn't she help the child? I won't think about her.

And that other one. He took us to Mama Mabaso's place, letting us think that we were going for a visit. Then he drove away with Winifred screaming at the side of the road and me wishing that I had died rather than live to see a day like that day. And he never came back once to find out what had happened to us. He was no sort of man. If he had come back just once, it would have been something.

It was different with me. The things I did, I did them for my people. I stayed as long as I could have. It was not that I wanted to leave. It was different with me, completely different. I would have stayed with them always if it had been possible.

✠   ✠

Mama Mabaso walked steadily down the long passage, as if she had been there many times before, turning in at the correct door and stopping before the open coffin. Bhengu stopped just behind her and looked down at the face of his father.

The undertakers had covered the body with a white silk sheet that was drawn into neat folds about the head so that only the face was visible. The features had been smoothed and removed of any expression that his dying might have given them. They wore a dignity that they had never possessed in life. Only the thick lower lip had not responded to the ministrations of the undertakers, still hanging open slightly. Bhengu remembered the way it had shaken when his father had been instructing the taxi driver to "Go on. Go on. Don't stop." The face had grown old in the intervening years. Unconsciously Bhengu had expected to see his father's face as it had been twenty years before. He had not expected the face to be as lean or as deeply furrowed, the cheeks sagging and empty.

Mama Mabaso leaned forward and kissed the forehead. Then she stepped back to make way for him. To Bhengu his father's face looked like a wax model, something of interest, but that held no special meaning for him. He ran the tips of the fingers of one hand across the forehead and he could feel the skin, like a thin plastic coating, ripple under his touch.

⌘ ⌘

He thought about the girl. There had been too many women; those he had known down the years, often trying to keep contact with them so that he would be able to use them again when they were needed: black women, undemanding, seeing him as a leader, perhaps feeling that it was the least they could do for the cause; liberal white women, voluntary Convention workers, eager for a new experience, excited by the idea of ignoring the Immorality Act . . .

The girl had stayed much longer than any of the others. In all the years she had never given a damn for Convention or her people's rights or even her own rights. Her politics were the politics of a man and a woman. She had wanted him because of some need within her, something that had to do with his being on the way up and that people were stopping to listen to him. And when Congress had finally been crushed and he had survived to become one of the leaders of the new generation to take the struggle further, she had wanted him for the stimulation of the danger and uncertainty of his life.

But the girl, by that time a woman, would not give him up when the time came. For her it was a matter of pride. No one had ever dealt with her that way before. She had always been the one that ended affairs. And, in bed, holding her narrow body in his arms, looking into her eyes, shadowed and dark, until he could see only them, Bhengu told her more than he ever should have.

✠ ✠

"I'll call her," the voice on the other end of the connection said.

"Hullo." Bhengu recognized her voice, immature-sounding and uncertain as always.

"It's Sam here."

"Oh, hullo." In the first moment she sounded surprised, but she regained control immediately. "Listen, Sam. I don't think you must phone me. I don't want you to try and contact me anymore."

"I understand," he said.

"I don't think I want you to try and contact me ever anymore."

"That's all right. I'm only calling to make sure that there's nothing wrong."

"Nothing is wrong. It was hard yesterday, but today it's all right."

"Okay, then. I won't phone you again."

"All right."

✠ ✠

Immediately he had been troubled by something in the hurried anxious way she had spoken. What he had heard in her voice may have been guilt or it may have been fear. It was likely that they would have picked her up for questioning. And she would have been frightened, probably badly enough frightened to have told them everything she knew. Bhengu was sure that she had not been sent to spy on him. It had all begun too far back for that. But eventually she had been rejected and it was possible that that had been too much. It might have been all a simple matter of pride.

He would not think about the girl either.

He could think about Mama Mabaso and Winifred. But when he thought about Winifred all he could see in his mind was the bloody crater that had been the lower part of her face. No. Not Winifred either.

There was only Mama Mabaso. To Jele and the others he was more a symbol than a man. Even surrounded by them he had always been alone. But all through the years he had been able to go to Mama Mabaso. She had always been strong and dependable. She and the women like her were what the Lategans and Engelbrechts truly had to fear because they could not be stopped. Their will to survive and their determination to see their children survive could not be destroyed. He had once asked her on what her faith was based. She had said, "On God, on life and on you, Sam."

Then Bhengu remembered the last time he had seen Mama Mabaso, and, after that, he did not want to think about her either.

It was consistent and strong, like the sound of a blacksmith's bellows, seeming to fill the cell and perhaps the passage beyond the barred door as well. Yet the air was still. Perhaps it was coming from outside. Could it be a wind, he wondered. But a wind would be even, not pulsing like bellows. Possibly it was some sort of machinery, especially designed to frighten him and all the others like him into confessing.

The water. There had been steam rising from it when they had brought it in. Perhaps it had not been too long ago, perhaps no more than an hour. Then it would still be warm. And he would be able to drink it. They had given him nothing to drink since they had forced him to drink the urine. If he could get to it, he would be able to drink from it and then get into it.

He tried to move and the sheet stuck to his arms where they protruded from the nightshirt. He wondered if he would be able to reach the water or even if he would be able to move at all. If I can move very slowly, he thought. How long I take to get there is of no importance. If I can move very slowly and keep on moving. If you keep on long enough you always get where you want to go in the end.

Bhengu moved his right arm until it slid off the bed and was pulled straight down by its own weight. He tried pressing down with the other arm and felt the answering pressure in his wrist and hand. Pushing down as hard as he could he found that he could move his buttocks slowly to the right, a little at a time. The sound of the bellows grew stronger, the draughts coming closer and closer together. Slowly the right side of Bhengu's buttocks moved out over the edge of the bed, further and further until he felt himself to be balancing like a seesaw. The rushing of the air from the bellows was everywhere, filling the cell, probably the whole prison, perhaps even the city, the machinery working furiously to multiply the sound.

He toppled slowly from the bed, sliding on his back, his legs folding helplessly under him and, finally, pitching face-forward but managing to get one of his arms in front to prevent his head from hitting the floor. He rested for a while on his knees with his arms tucked underneath his chest. His head was hanging forward and he could see his chest heaving, keeping time with the bellows.

He knelt very still, careful to make no effort, trying to slow his breathing. If it had only been quieter it would have been easier to handle, but the very intensity of the sound frightened him.

I don't want this. Bhengu finally made a conscious admission of it. I don't want it. I'm afraid and I've left too much unfinished. Let me go back. Please, Jesus, let me go back. Let me go back, if only to give the boy a decent life. I can't leave him the way he is. Please let me get out of here. I'll take the boy and leave the country. I'll take his mother too, if she will come. I'll devote my life to your work. I'll do anything. Perhaps I was wrong to live only for power. Perhaps I should have gone into the church. If that's what you want, I'll do it. For the boy's sake and for his mother and Mama Mabaso . . . Please, Lord Jesus, I want to get out of here. Give me a year to make everything good. After that I'll be able to do it. I'll be all right then. Just give me one more year and I'll be ready. I can't do it yet.

But it's too late, he told himself. The time for making deals is long past.

But you have all power. Do this one thing for me. I'll make it good for the boy. I'll do your work. I'll do anything . . .

The pumping of his breath was still fast and harsh, but now he knew that it was not prison machinery that caused it. He would wait a little longer, hope for it to subside, gain a little strength. Then he would try to reach the bathtub.

⌘   ⌘

The librarian, a lean-faced man in the latter part of a nervous middle-age, unclasped his hands long enough to gesticulate quickly in his direction. "I think he's the one," Bhengu heard him say.

The three men looked in the direction the librarian had indicated, their attention centering on Bhengu, and from that moment on did not allow it to be diverted for an instant. They came smoothly toward him, spreading out as they made their way between the desks, showing clearly that any thought of flight would be foolishness. Bhengu knew them immediately. He had met them many times before in different places and under other circumstances; not the same three individuals, but the same men nevertheless. They were unmistakable. The arrogant self-satisfied faces, secure in the knowledge that they were free from any possibility of prosecution and that their power over their quarry was absolute. It was impossible to confuse them with other men.

In dress and appearance they could have been three rising young executives. A few girls at another desk, attractive white girls, followed the three men with their eyes, probably thinking that they were exactly that. And yet the impression was only superficial. The power that executives carried with them was of a totally different nature and it imparted to the bearer a totally different manner.

They stopped at his desk, one directly in front and one on either side of him. "Mr. Sam Bhengu." It was the one in the center who spoke, the words quick and precise, somehow betraying the arrogance that Bhengu could see in their faces. Bhengu was already clearing the desk. He looked up at the speaker without answering. "Come with us, please."

A black Mercedes was waiting in front of the building with a fourth young executive at the steering wheel. One of the three who had come to fetch him sat in front next to the driver while Bhengu sat in the back between the other two. "Do you know where we are taking you?" the driver asked. He paused for a reply, and when there was none he answered the question himself. "Timol Heights. We are taking you to Timol Heights."

Bhengu found that he was able to crawl. For the first time in the last forty-eight hours his arms were obeying his commands, perhaps not precisely, but closely enough to get him across the cell. He reached the tub and touched the galvanized-iron side with the back of one of his hands. It was barely lukewarm. Concentrating hard now, he edged forward until his head was hanging over the water. Then he lifted one hand and put it down in the water to steady himself and to take his weight while he brought the other hand to join it.

The water was very shallow, only just covering his wrists with his hands palm-downward on the bottom of the tub. He reached down with his head, trying to get to it, but his chest caught on the sides of the tub and the sides were too high. To try to scoop up water in his cupped hands would have meant going down on his face, and if he was then not able to get up he would drown. Bhengu wriggled slowly back and forth, shuffling his hands further forward and working the top half of his body over the edge of the tub. Once it tipped toward him, but the other side, lifting up, struck hard against his forehead and he held it there. The water, real water, was just below him, eddying around his hands and casting faint reflections of the passage light up into his eyes. Reaching down with his face, he could almost touch it.

A little further. Just a little further. The tub lurched and he felt the hard edge pressing into his stomach. Very carefully he lowered himself onto his elbows and brought his face to the water. Then, forming his lips into a tube, he sucked it into his mouth.

✠ ✠

The illuminated G, indicating that they were on the ground level, went out as the elevator started moving, leaving the indicator panel in darkness. Bhengu knew that the way the elevator was designed it could only stop on the ground, the ninth and the tenth floors, and indicators were provided for just those three levels. The four young executives were leaning with their backs against the walls of the elevator, all facing him, all wearing the same artificial look of amusement and superiority. Bhengu turned to face the door. It was the only direction in which he would not have to look at his captors. "Timol Heights, Sam," he heard one of them say. "It's a long way down to the ground where you're going."

"You can't get out that way now," another added. "We had bars put on those windows."

He could not avoid hearing the voices. They were coming from behind him, impersonal, as yet not connected in his mind to the images of their owners. "That Timol," the first voice said, "he must have thought he could fly."

The elevator slowed suddenly, the indicator light for the ninth floor came on and a bell sounded briefly. The doors slid open, but no one in the elevator moved. Bhengu had traveled that route before, and he knew that the ninth floor was no more than a checkpoint. Immediately opposite the door of the elevator and facing them, a man in civilian clothes was sitting at a desk. By the time the doors of the elevator opened he was already looking straight at them. He looked at each face in turn before pressing a button mounted in the surface of the desk. The doors closed and the elevator was moving again. None of the members of Bhengu's escort had said anything to the man at the desk. The indicator light for the tenth floor blinked once, then came on brightly. Bhengu was careful to hold himself very square, keeping his neck straight. He had been in their hands before and he had come out of it. He would take it slowly, moment by moment. He knew that he was beyond the reach of any court's deliberations or the rantings of parliament. The few rights, no matter how limited, that he had taken for granted had now ceased to exist. There would be no way to make his stay there easy. It would only be possible to survive. They might tire of questioning you or eventually believe you. What was important was to hold out until that day came.

As he stepped out of the elevator on the tenth floor, two of Bhengu's escorts moved quickly in behind him, lifting his arms high behind his back and handcuffing his wrists together. Keeping his hands, now held close by the cuffs, high behind him and forcing his head down to the level of his knees, he was driven down a long passage. Close in front of his face the carpeted floor hurried quickly by, and his own feet and the feet of the two men behind him seemed to be marching briskly in step with each other. The upward pressure of his arms was uncomfortable, but not yet painful.

He saw the frame of a doorway on either side as he entered what he knew to be an interrogation room. He heard the sound of a chair move as someone got to his feet. And he heard the man's voice: "Ah, Mr. Samuel Bhengu, at last we've got you. We've been expecting you in Johannesburg for a long time. I've been looking forward to this. Welcome to John Vorster Square." Bhengu recognized the voice immediately and he could imagine the hands being rubbed eagerly and habitually together. He knew Captain Herman Bendall as a small man with sloping shoulders and an oblong bald patch that ran longitudinally across the top of his head. He had eyes that always seemed to be moist, adding to the impression of extreme pleasure whenever he rubbed his hands together. "What's wrong, Samuel Bhengu? Are you afraid? Only the guilty are afraid. You look worried. Are you worried?"

"No," Bhengu lied. He wondered vaguely how the back of his head could look worried.

"It's not no. It's no, Inkhosi."

"No."

"No, Inkhosi."

"No."

"No, Inkhosi."

Bhengu's hands were lifted still higher until it seemed that the muscles under his shoulder blades were tearing loose. "No," he grunted.

"No, Inkhosi," Bendall shouted, his voice thick with indignation. Bhengu's hands were forced right over, driving his head between his legs. He could feel the sinews of his right shoulder tearing. "No, Inkhosi," Bendall shouted again.

"No, Inkhosi." The Zulu word for king came out reluctantly. They had won the first skirmish and Bhengu knew that they had the ammunition to win all the other rounds as well. All that he had was his life, and the important thing was to come out alive. Take it easy, he told himself. You'll never be able to handle it this way. Take it easy. You've got a long time to get through.

"You are under my thumb. Do you understand that?" He waited for a reply, but Bhengu said nothing. They had dropped his hands to the point where he could lift his head enough to see Bendall's face, the bright damp eyes blinking angrily at him. "Do you understand?" His arms were again jerked upward and his head went down hard, striking one of his knees. "Do you understand?"

"Yes."

"Yes, Inkhosi."

"Yes, Inkhosi."

"That's better." The arms were allowed to fall again, not enough for the pain to stop, but enough so that it was not unbearable. "We are going to see plenty of you here, Samuel Bhengu, because you are guilty. Only the guilty come here." He turned his back on Bhengu and walked slowly to a far corner of the room. When he turned to face him again he had changed back to the smiling, superficially friendly manner of a few minutes before. "Let down his arms," he said magnanimously. It sounded like a king bestowing a special favor on one of his favorite subjects.

The men behind Bhengu let his arms go and he came painfully erect. "Thank you," he said.

"Thank you, Inkhosi," Bendall reminded him, the smile never for a moment leaving his face.

"Thank you, Inkhosi," Bhengu said.

"You people are unjust," Bendall said, still smiling, but his voice reproachful. "You are unjust to us. Do you know that? You want to take our country from us. That's not justice. This is our country and you want to take it. White people have also got rights, you know. We made this country and you want to take it. In 1652 when Jan van Riebeeck landed at the Cape there were no Bantu in South Africa. None. Did you know that?"

"There were no Bendalls either," Bhengu said.

The security policeman's moist eyes grew round with wonder. He ran around the desk and past Bhengu, stopping in the doorway. "Hear what this man is saying," Bhengu heard him shout. "Hear what he's saying. Come and hear what this man is saying." It must have been a regular performance on Bendall's part, because no one came to hear what Bhengu had been saying. Bendall came purposefully back into the office and took up his position behind the desk. The smile was gone and the look on his face appeared indicative of something like a child's impotent rage. "We know a lot about you, Samuel Bhengu. We've been watching your house twenty-four hours a day since August last year. And we have known that you were coming to visit us in Johannesburg for the last two months. We have our people in the location, Samuel Bhengu. We have our people everywhere." He paused to let Bhengu absorb what he had told him. "And tonight we are going to find out all the rest. Tonight you are going to tell us everything. We are going to know tonight, because you are going to tell us all you know. Do you understand?"

Of course I understand, you bastard, Bhengu thought. I understand all there is to know about you.

"I said, do you understand?"

"Yes, I understand."

"Yes, Inkhosi," Bendall screamed.

His arms were jerked upward again and the pain was more severe for the temporary relief. "Yes, Inkhosi." Bhengu struggled to get the words out.

"Take him away."

Bhengu measured the cell, walking quietly so that he would not wake the other prisoners. It measured eighteen strides by twelve and there were twenty-one others in with him. He sat down on one of the spare sleeping mats, resting his back against the wall. From all sides the sounds of the heavy regular breathing of sleeping men reached him, most of the men sleeping with an arm or an article of clothing across their faces to cut out the light from the electric-light bulb in the ceiling. In the corner furthest from the door was the lavatory pot, a large bucket that had to cater to the needs of all twenty-two men. Most of them had made use of it during the evening, and the loose, poorly fitting lid allowed the smell to reach every corner of the room and probably out into the passage as well. One of the men nearest to him was shivering violently. On the upper part of his body he was wearing only a shirt and had his arms wrapped around himself as protection against the cold air of the highveld night. No blankets had been provided.

Leaning back against the wall, Bhengu tried to relax. He knew that he needed to prepare himself for them, to be ready for anything they might have waiting for him. He would have to take whatever it was they had in mind for him, tell them nothing and still come through. If he tried to feed them harmless information to make things easier for himself, soon he would be telling them everything. Bhengu knew what they wanted more than anything else. They wanted names. Long lists of names: Convention members to be fed into the John Vorster Square processing machine, destined to come out meek and impotent, thankful only to be alive and determined never to return. If they broke one man, they could get a list of perhaps fifty names, perhaps even a hundred. Of all of those they only had to break one more to get another fifty names. And then another fifty . . . and another . . . And then there were the informers, the onetime laborers or messengers, some of whom had already bought trading stores in the homelands with the proceeds of their activities.

He could hear footsteps in the passage, the muffled sound of rubber-soled shoes. There were more than one man and they were walking quickly, the sound growing as they approached the cell. To Bhengu's imagination the speed at which they were walking was increasing too until they were rushing down the long passage, anxious to get to him.

They went quickly past the barred door of the cell, three blacks all wearing plain clothes and with the same purposeful expression on their faces. The footsteps retreated as quickly as they had approached. A door opened and closed and the sound was gone.

Tonight, Bendall had said. Tonight you are going to tell us everything. We are going to know tonight.

What method would they use? Would it be something old-fashioned, a well-tried universally respected method like cigarette ends applied to the tender parts of his skin? Something uncomplicated like keeping him awake for a week, a week during which a man discovers what a precarious commodity his sanity is? Shock treatment, with one electrode connected to his genitals, orgasm after painful orgasm wrenched out of his body till long after there was nothing left to emit? The box?

Was it possible that he might tell them what they wanted? Yes, it was possible. No man knew what he could endure until he was faced with it. And that he had been through it before without telling them anything was no guarantee that he could do it again. He might talk. It was certainly possible.

It was the head-shrinker that he feared most. He had often been told about it by others on whom it had been used. He had heard about the cold tingling sensation when the machine was switched on, the rushing sound in the victim's ears, the senses staggering as the brain struggled helplessly with the force of the electrical field. After Thompson Mzila had been through it he had hardly been able to hold his head upright. He had told Bhengu that it felt like a weight was dragging his head forward all the time. Joshua Mtimkulu had come out of it suffering from double vision. That had been nearly a year before and his vision was still affected.

They had taken his watch, so Bhengu had no way of knowing what the time was. He guessed that it must have been a little past midnight. The lesser questions retreated from his mind until only one remained. What time would they come for him? There were probably interrogation teams working all night, every night. They could come at any time. But at whatever time they came he was sure that it would be carefully chosen to serve their purpose well.

First they would keep him waiting, knowing that the longer he was kept wondering about what was going to happen to him the closer he would be to cracking before they even started. Probably three or four o'clock would be the time; when a human being's resources are at their lowest. He tried consciously to relax his neck and shoulders, the muscles in his face. I wish I could sleep, he thought. If I could sleep until they come, I'd be better able to face them. Even an hour's sleep would be something.

Tonight you are going to tell us everything, he had said, the weak eyes glaring, a petty bitchy sound to the voice. Tonight.

He asked himself how they had known he was coming to Johannesburg. He knew that there was only one possible answer. They had been informed. We have our men in the locations, Bendall had said. The circle of those who had known his plans had been very small. Could someone have told a friend? And could the friend have told a friend? And might that friend not have been a friend at all?

But had it necessarily been a man?

He thought about the girl. He did not want to think about her, but the memory of their last telephone conversation was clear in his mind. I don't want you to contact me, she had said. Had she been saying, You're dangerous, leave me alone? Or had she been saying, I've betrayed you and I can't face you, so leave me alone? There had been an anxiety to hang up, to cut the connection between them that seemed to Bhengu to have been rooted in more than just the ending of a long, often-painful affair.

He wondered about Robert and Mama Mabaso and Petronella. Might one of them have said something in an unguarded moment? Could Robert be the informer? No. Not Robert. Did I make a mistake somewhere? Did I somehow give something away? Who else will be incriminated? Are they going to pick up others? Mama Mabaso? Please, Jesus, not her. Robert? Petronella? Even the boy?

Tonight. Tonight is a long time if you are awake and waiting for it to pass, fearing what is to come before the night is over. If I could sleep at least, this part would be easier. Fearing, but not knowing what you are fearing, is the worst part, Bhengu told himself. What new tricks might they have learned? he wondered.

It was very cold in the cell. Bhengu had buttoned his shirt all the way to the collar and turned up the lapels of his jacket. The man who had been shivering had finally been wakened by the cold and was walking up and down the cell between the sleeping bodies, massaging his arms and legs. "Go, lie down," a voice growled at him. "The rest of us want to sleep." Bhengu watched him go back to the place where his mat was still spread on the floor, sit down on the cold cement and twist the mat around his shoulders, trying to use it as a blanket.

The first weak light of day had begun to enter the cell through the single window that opened into a well in the center of the building when Bhengu slept for the first time. The others were starting to wake up, so it was no more than a fitful rest, only just below the level of consciousness. Through the light shadows of his slumber he was aware that the night had passed and they had not come.

✠   ✠

The nightshirt floated around him like seaweed growing against a rock on a shore. Bhengu managed little movements with his hands, stirring the water into wavelets that reflected from the sides of the bathtub and splashed back toward him. It was perfect. He could not remember ever enjoying anything this much. The prison was quiet. There was no pain. And now everything was clear to him. All his priorities had changed. The only thing that was important was to be sitting here in the bathtub, making waves dance back and forth across the surface of the water. The feeling of the water against his skin, lapping cool up his stomach and back, the absence of pain and the clearness of his head; these were all very important. He thought about other things that were important. The feeling of a woman's breast; the taste of beer on a hot day; the figure of his son running down the road toward the car to meet him, his long limbs moving loose and free; the sound of rain on the thatched roof of a hut—these were important. All the rest was shit.

Please, Jesus. Please, Lord Jesus.

The bellows started up again, working faster and faster until the cell was again filled with the sound of them and his body was filled with the rushing of air. He had stopped using his hands to make ripples in the water, but the little waves continued, lapping furiously back and forth, driven by the heaving of his body.

Through the small window, high up in the wall of the cell, he could see nothing but darkness, the only light coming from the globe in the passage. The cell was peaceful, the air not wholly transparent but glowing gently with a soft luminescence. The water felt cool against his skin and the wavelets had stopped. Unbeckoned, the face of Nelson Mandela, as he had seen him many years before, addressing the crowd at Freedom Square in Sophiatown, returned to his conscious memory. He tried to drive it away. It was something he would rather have buried deep in the back of his mind, out of reach of his present awareness. He did not want it now.

But the memory was unavoidable, the face warm, the smile slow and knowing, the words thoughtful, sometimes even hesitant.

Bhengu remembered how, as a boy, he had wriggled his way to the front of the crowd to get as close as possible, sometimes working himself right next to the chair on which Mandela had stood while addressing the people. He had remembered many of the very phrases the great man had used, often quoting them word for word to his friends. Once on leaving the meeting Mandela had brushed right past him and had rested his hand momentarily on young Sam's head. For a few seconds he had not been able to speak at all. Then he left the square, dashing wildly through the thinning crowd, filled by a warm glow that penetrated to every part of his body, all the breathless way home to tell Mama Mabaso.

He wondered if Mandela had heard about him. And, if he had, what he thought. Bhengu was sure that he would approve. He would see what Bhengu had been doing as carrying on his own work. But had Mandela heard about him? Where he was it was possible that no news ever reached him. And yet newer prisoners arriving on the island would surely have mentioned the work of Convention, probably told him all about it. He might even have been awaiting the day when outside pressures would force the government to release him, allowing him to join forces with Bhengu. It was even possible that he had heard how they had broken Convention. To Mandela it would have been a familiar tale.

As long as he would have approved, Bhengu thought. I'm sure he would have approved.

There had been an afternoon in Cape Town with Humphrey Walters. It had been his first visit, so Walters had taken him for a drive along the slopes of the mountain above the city. Bhengu remembered him pointing out an old windmill, the university and Rhodes's memorial among the trees high up the slope. "This is the hospital on the right," Walters had said, "where Chris Barnard does all his transplants."

"Will we be able to see Robben Island?" Bhengu had asked him.

A few miles further on where the road wound around the seaward slope of Devil's Peak, Walters had stopped the car at the roadside. "There it is, out there in the middle of the bay," he had said. From the mountain slope high above it the city had been white and shining in the morning sun, filling the valley between the slope where they had stopped and Signal Hill on the far side. Beyond the city the deep-blue water of the bay

was calm and even, and in the center, seeming to float on it
like a brown autumn leaf, Bhengu could see the island.
Through the confusion in his mind he had heard Walters
speaking. "Sam, is something wrong?"

He had known immediately that not even Humphrey
Walters could have understood. If a man had not lived
through it, how could he have understood about the way the
M plan was going to save Sophiatown, or how anxiously he
had waited for Bloke to come to their house just to hear him
tell something new about Mandela, or what hope Congress
had given them, how at last they had a rallying point? How
could anyone else have understood how, after his father had
gone, when for a long time Sam had seen only darkness
ahead, there had been a man he could admire, even if at a distance? How could Walters have known just what magic the
name Mandela had held for all of them and how they had
heard with frantic excitement about the arms that were being
stored, hidden in a safe place, a place that turned out not to
be so safe after all, how Mandela had finally given up waiting?

Mandela's face was above him in the luminous air of the
cell. The restless desultory Freedom Square crowd was also
with him. For a moment he could feel the cold wind of a
Johannesburg winter day against his face. Then it was all replaced by the trucks and the ragged streams of people coming
out of the backyards. Bhengu would rather not have remembered.

⌘ ⌘

He had not expected the street names to be the same, but they
were all still there: Good Street, Gerty Street, Victoria Street,
Morris Street, and now Meyer Street. He looked up the road
toward the place where the big yellow rock used to block it
off, but the rock was gone, the road running on as if it had

never existed. One of the houses further up the hill on the right-hand side had been built on the spot where Mama Mabaso's house had stood, but it was impossible to judge which of them it was. Everything was so changed. Not one of the Sophiatown houses had been left standing after the removals. They had not wanted any vestige as a reminder of what had been there.

He walked slowly past the place where he imagined Mama Mabaso's house must have stood. The street was empty, just as all the others had been. The night itself was still and windless, the air crisp and dry with the autumn freshness he remembered from his youth. The streets were quiet with the quietness of white suburban streets at night in every part of the country, each isolated little family safe behind its own locked doors and bolted windows. Everything he remembered was gone: the cinema in Good Street, the swimming pool that was open to men and women on alternate days, the barbershop with the little wooden bench against the wall where you waited your turn, the shoemaker two blocks back down the road, the gym where K.K.K. Mohloi trained his fighters, the priory and Father Huddlestone, the thousands of little rooms where the tenants had lived, and all those people; they were all gone. And in place of Sophiatown with its noise and gaiety, its laughter and music, its drunkenness and its pain; in place of all that life and vitality there was this antiseptic place with its empty streets and locked doors, its rows of identical houses almost like those of a township. But here the houses were bigger than those Bhengu knew, carports provided for the family conveyance, the narrow strip of ground not quite as narrow . . .

The front door of one of the houses on his right opened and a broad-shouldered man in his early middle age, wearing only a vest on the top half of his body, hurried to his car, parked next to the house, his hands wrapped around his upper arms for warmth. He stopped at the car, noticing Bhengu for the first time, but the pause was only momentary. Then he unlocked the car door, took what looked like a roll of blankets from it and reentered the house, glancing curiously at Bhengu a second time as he closed the door.

From the crest of the hill Bhengu could see the lights of the Northcliff houses across the valley as clearly as if they had been in the next block. Below was Albertsville, which had been a colored area once and had lasted only a few years longer than Sophiatown. At least there they had not pulled down the houses.

He had to go. In a moment it had become impossible for him to stay any longer. He hurried back the way he had come, his hands deep in the pockets of his coat, looking straight ahead, not wanting to see either the houses or the people who lived in them. This was the first time he had returned. Now he had seen and that was enough.

Down at the main road where he would get the bus back into town a sign pointed up the hill. The name on it was Triomf. Triumph. The bastards had called it Triumph.

✠   ✠

It had been for nothing, then. He had done so much and suffered so greatly. Now he was dying and it had been for nothing. He had no home where he would be mourned. He had alienated his wife. His son was also suffering and he too might die. There had been no purpose to it at all.

He had got out of the bathtub and was lying down flat on the floor, his naked body shivering on the cold surface. His breath was coming normally and he could feel the slow rise and fall of his chest. The bed was out of his reach. He would have to cross the floor again to get to it and he doubted that that would be possible. It would be pleasant, though, to get back between the clean cool sheets. He remembered how they had felt against his skin. But they were too far away now, much too far.

Jele and the others—they would die too. They would all die, until the only people that remained would be the meek and humble and poor in spirit. There was a verse in the Gospel according to Saint Matthew that went, "Blessed are the poor in spirit, for they . . ." He could not remember the rest. For they shall live longest, most probably, he thought. Didn't it also say, Blessed are the meek? He could not remember.

After Convention and Community Programs had been broken, the way they had broken Congress, there would be a time of quiet as there had been after Congress, and then someone who was not poor in spirit, some new man who had not yet suffered and who thought, like a fool, that it was better for a man not to live than to live without dignity, some such man would start a new organization. And they would break that too and they would break him and all those that helped him. The camps and the prisons, the interrogation rooms and the tenth floor of John Vorster Square would again be filled to overflowing. The head-shrinker, the isolation cell, the boat rides, the sandbag would again have work to do. And after that man had also been broken and his organization torn to pieces and his child dying of malnutrition, still nothing would have been gained.

It had been for nothing. He could see it no other way. He was lying on the cement floor of a cell and he was dying. And it had been for nothing.

A sharp clear daylight was coming into the cell from the tiny window and also from the passage. Bhengu was back in the bed, the smooth coolness of the sheets as soothing as he had expected. He had a partial memory of being lifted from the floor, but nothing else. There was a new doctor. He was young and, like Sibul, he had features that were clearly Jewish, but whereas Sibul's face was broad, round and ineffective-looking, his was dark, discontented and arrogant. It was notable that he did not try to talk to Bhengu while examining him. Behind him, flitting back and forth, trying to be in the right place all the time, was a pretty, fair-haired nurse, probably still in her teens.

The doctor was doing it all again, probing Bhengu's body with his fingertips, testing the reflexes of knees and feet, inspecting his skin for damage, and he was doing it all more thoroughly than any of the others had. He paused at Bhengu's upper lip, rolling it over with the tip of a finger to look underneath, and again to look at the abrasions left on his feet and ankles. When he had finished he sat down on the edge of the bed and it seemed to Bhengu that he was looking straight into his eyes for the first time. "Can you hear me?" he asked. The nurse had moved to a position next to him and was leaning slightly forward, the better to see Bhengu's face. "Can you hear me?" the doctor repeated. There was nothing sympathetic in the sound of his voice. It was sharp and businesslike, almost hurried, but Bhengu could see that he was being very carefully watched. "Can you hear me?" Again the words were clear and precise, almost abrupt.

"Yes," Bhengu said. Once again his voice surprised him, sounding different from what he expected and seeming to function without his conscious direction.

"Good. How do you feel?"

". . . you feel," Bhengu's voice said.

"Let's have that again. How do you feel?"

". . . feel."

"Do you have any pain?"

This time his voice did not answer. Why do you not answer? Bhengu inquired of his voice. Why not answer him again? You were getting along fine without me. Why stop now?

"Do you have any pain?"

". . . any pain?" Bhengu's voice even put in the same questioning inflection that the doctor's voice had held. That's better, Bhengu told his voice. That's much better. Answer the man when he speaks to you.

"What is it, Dr. Rael?" the nurse asked.

"Say something," Dr. Rael said. He seemed not to have heard the nurse. "Say anything you like."

". . . you like," Bhengu's voice obliged.

"Say something of your own," Dr. Rael persisted.

But Bhengu's voice had grown tired of the conversation. "What is it, Doctor?" the nurse asked again. "Is it brain damage?"

Rael's answer to the girl's question was a slight raising of his eyebrows. "Help me turn him over," he said. The nurse removed the pillows so that Bhengu's body would be perfectly horizontal, then they rolled him over carefully onto his stomach and turned his head to face the wall. Behind him Bhengu could hear them moving around, preparing something that they were going to do to him.

Save yourself the trouble, Bhengu's mind told the doctor. They've already done everything they can. There's nothing left to do. Save me the trouble too.

The doctor was talking to the nurse, but he had taken her to the door of the cell and was keeping his voice too low for Bhengu to hear what they were saying. The doctor's monologue, for Bhengu had not heard the girl answer, had lasted for no more than a few seconds, then they were back at the bedside. "This is going to hurt," Rael said, but the way it was said was so businesslike and impersonal that he could not be sure that the doctor had been speaking to him. Perhaps he was telling the nurse, just for interest's sake. Perhaps she likes to know when it is going to hurt the patient. Or perhaps he was going to hurt the nurse. No, Bhengu thought. It's not the nurse who gets hurt.

The deep tingling started in the lower part of his body and spread slowly downward, like the steady seepage of a liquid, flowing down his legs and into his feet. It was the sharpest feeling he had experienced in any part of his body for the past three days, but it was not pain. Nothing hurts, his mind told the doctor. If you wanted to hurt me, you've come too late. Now nothing hurts.

Roberts came into the cell first, with Sibul following. "Look at that," he said. He was looking at the floor next to the bed. Bhengu tried to move to the edge of the bed to see down onto the floor, but the effort was too great.

"I wonder how the devil that happened," Sibul said.

The warder who had unlocked the cell came forward, also looking down at the floor. "I'll get a boy to clean it up," he said.

"But what I want to know is, how did it happen?" Sibul told him. "Did his food just get brought in and dumped down on the bed? Why didn't anyone try to feed him, is what I want to know."

"I don't know, Doctor. I'll get my senior."

Sibul advanced to near the bed, still looking down at the floor. "Obviously they just dumped his food down here and left him," he grumbled. His tone of voice was closer to that of petulance than threat. "They could have tried to feed him."

"I'll get my senior." The warder was backing toward the cell door.

"And you'd better get someone to clean up the mess."

"I'll get a boy."

As he was leaving, the warder bumped into Lategan coming in at the door, and made a hasty attempt at a salute. "Ex-

cuse me, Colonel." He looked worriedly into the security policeman's face to see if he had been the cause of offense.

"Yes, yes, all right." Lategan came into the cell, frowning
slightly in irritation.

"Look what happened here," Sibul said. "I told them to
feed him."

Lategan glanced at the plate of food that had fallen from
the bed, but said nothing. Bhengu saw him turn toward the
bed and they looked straight into each other's eyes. Bhengu
could again sense the nearness of contact between them. It
seemed to him that Lategan knew, as he knew, that what was
occupying them was futile. He was still frowning as he had
been when he entered the cell. The frown had nothing to do
with his having collided with the warder.

The cell door was standing open and the head warder, followed by the warder who had let the doctors in and a black
cleaner in prison uniform, carrying a bucket of soapy water
and a rag, entered, all looking worried. "Good afternoon,
gentlemen. Good afternoon, Colonel." It was the head warder
who had spoken. He looked down at the floor and turned
angrily to the cleaner. "Now yes, boy. Come on. Clean up.
Look at the mess on the floor. Make quick. Come on. Clean
up." By some strange twist of logic, that Bhengu's plate of
food was lying upturned on the floor had become the cleaner's
fault. The head warder shook his head in disgust, as if inwardly bemoaning the fact that he was saddled with cleaners
who were so stupid as to drop the patients' food on the floor.
He glanced quickly around at Lategan, who had only acknowledged his entry by a preoccupied nod. "We'll have this
cleaned up and be out of the way in a minute," he said.

"They should have fed him if he couldn't eat," Sibul said.

The head warder sighed and lifted his hands in a palms-up-
ward gesture. "Now yes, it is so that you haven't always got

the staff you need and the patients who can feed themselves must do it."

"They could have seen that he couldn't do it."

"Perhaps not." He turned his attention to the unfortunate cleaner who had so recently become guilty of causing the prison floors to be in such a disgusting state. "Hurry up, boy. Come on. Move your ass there."

"He should be in Addington," Sibul said, but the only reaction elicited was a helpless shrug from the head warder, who probably felt that that would at least relieve him of one unwelcome responsibility.

With the floor cleaned and the guilt-ridden cleaner dismissed, the two warders edged apologetically toward the door. "Shall I lock the door, Colonel?" the head warder asked.

By the expression or lack of expression on Lategan's face he might not have heard the question, but he shook his head briefly without turning around.

After they had left, leaving the door open, Sibul came to the side of the bed and looked into Bhengu's face. "How are we today, then?" The question was a reflex on Sibul's part when confronted by a patient and held no meaning at all. He was also trying by the very ordinariness of the question to make everything seem normal and as it should be, in fact as he would have wished it to be. Bhengu could see by his manner that he was trying to reassert a little of his lost authority. Bhengu had seen it before; the way Lategan's personality and status bent the will of others—prisoners, witnesses and fellow civil servants—to his. It was done effortlessly, using only a look, an inclination of the head, the smallest change of facial expression and, more than anything else, the other person's knowledge of who Lategan was and the nature of the power he commanded. It was a power that was rarely discussed, even in private, but it was present in the dealings of all security policemen with other men. And, in the case of some like Lategan, to whom the use of such authority and the yielding of other South Africans before its tacit but demonstrable potency, was accepted as natural by him and had established itself as an integral part of his personality; in the lives of such men it was an ever-present aura, surrounding them, isolating and separating them from both friends and enemies. No ordinary policeman was without a certain fear of them. No writer or artist could ever be sure just how far he would be allowed to go. Very few Opposition members of parliament or leaders of commerce ever felt entirely safe when confronted with the power of the political police and how they were answerable only to a very small clique of men, no different from themselves.

While Sibul was threshing around like a fish on a hook, Lategan was staring at the opposite wall, apparently deep in thought, and despite his complete immobility he was utterly master of the situation. "Should we examine him?" Sibul asked Roberts. The question reduced to nothing his pathetic attempt to take the initiative.

"Rael examined him this morning," Roberts said. He looked at his wristwatch. "I wonder where he is."

"He should have been here by now."

"He should be here at any time."

"Yes."

It was a pointless exchange of words, prompted by the difficult position both men felt themselves to be in. Neither could have analyzed his position to quite explain his difficulties, but as long as Lategan remained in the room, barely finding it necessary to acknowledge their presence, both men would have the need to excuse themselves.

Rael saved them by coming quickly into the cell, this time without his nurse. "Good morning. I hope I haven't kept you waiting." The tone of voice and manner contained no apology. He addressed himself to the two doctors. "I'll let you have a written report tomorrow, but the main fact is that his spinal fluid contains microscopic particles of blood. A cerebral hemorrhage is possible."

Lategan seemed to stir. "Minute particles?" His voice was unconsciously derisive.

Rael was standing with his back to the security policeman. He found no need to answer. His lean arrogant face was amused with a nasty bitchy sort of amusement. Its expression was closer to a sneer than a smile.

Sibul tried to use the moment to regain a little status. "You feel that he has a cerebral hemorrhage then?" He was still working at getting his voice to sound firm and earnest, still living the pretense of being in control.

"There's evidence of bleeding from the brain." The young physician was looking well pleased with himself. "He could be a very sick man."

Sibul looked around at Roberts. "I've said all along he should be in Addington."

"The security risks are too great," Lategan said. He was still not looking directly at the doctors.

"What do you say, Dr. Rael?" Sibul asked.

But Rael was not interested in Sibul's problems with the security police, or in Bhengu's well-being either. He was already looking at his watch. "He's your patient," he said. "I'm just telling you what's wrong with him."

"What's wrong with him or what you think is wrong with him?" It was Lategan's voice. He was still looking at the wall above Bhengu's head.

"For the purposes of the layman the two are identical," Rael said. He made a point of not turning at all, talking to Lategan while facing directly away from him. Rael was young and reckless, probably feeling that the world neither recognized nor rewarded his true worth and projecting the resulting hostilities at all of society. As he was not a civil servant, he had not grown into the habit of total obedience, but, in common with the other doctors he stood in awe of Lategan. It was an awe he could no more have admitted than he could have restrained his aggressive nature.

"Have I done something to upset you, Dr. Rael?" Lategan asked.

Rael ignored the question. He spoke to Sibul and Roberts. "He may have a cerebral hemorrhage. If he was my patient, I would have him in a place where he could be watched continually."

"Then he'll have to be in Addington?" Sibul asked hopefully.

Rael would not be drawn. "Also, you should visit him regularly yourselves. Either one of you should see him at least two or three times a day."

"Dr. Rael, have I done something to upset you?" Lategan asked again. His voice was quiet and uninterested, as if only the vaguest academic concern lay behind the question.

Bhengu was watching the face of the young physician. He saw the uneasy movement of his shoulders as he heard the question. The tendency to sneer returned to his face. Lategan's dominant personality and the nature of his position in the society Rael hated caused an upsurge of rebellion in the doctor. Whatever Rael was, he was not another of the yes-men with which Lategan was accustomed to dealing. "Not at all," Rael said. "I'm accustomed to having my work questioned by policemen. Good afternoon, gentlemen." In a moment he was gone, the sound of his leather-soled shoes quick on the cement floor of the passage. His last words and his contemptuous exit had been an obvious attempt to belittle the security policeman, but Bhengu knew that they were also a retreat. Rael was getting out of it while conspicuously disapproving and, equally conspicuously, keeping his own hands clean. But he was getting out of it.

Rael's sudden departure left a vacuum. For a few moments no one seemed anxious to fill it. Then Lategan spoke. "Addington is out of the question."

"You heard what he said, Colonel." Sibul was almost pleading. Roberts looked quickly from one to the other. He wanted only to do what would be least bother to everyone and safest for himself. Above all, he did not want to antagonize Lategan. It was all right for Rael. He was in private practice.

"He said there were microscopic particles of blood—microscopic particles. That doesn't sound so terrible to me."

"That can mean bleeding on the brain."

"Microscopic particles of blood. Can a man die from microscopic particles of blood?"

"It's hard to say."

"We could move him to the cells at Greenwood Park police station." The suggestion was Roberts'. His quick manner of speaking sounded even more agitated than usual. "I live near there. I'll look in on him occasionally."

Sibul's face was a reflection of the disgust he felt. "That's even worse. Who's going to watch him there? Rael said he should be watched continually."

Lategan looked at Bhengu again, his face thoughtful. "I can't see him going to another hospital," he said. "We can't afford the attention he'll attract, even in a police station. In any case, he may still be shamming. We can't dismiss that yet."

Bhengu was looking at the security policeman's face and he knew that Lategan did not believe what he was saying. Thinking logically, neither of the doctors would have either, but Roberts was ready to do whatever Lategan wanted and Sibul did not sccm to remember what his authority was or if he had any.

"I'm very unhappy about this," Sibul said. He had already yielded, but for his own sake he had to go through the motions of some sort of resistance. "I can't say I'm at all happy about this."

"What about you, Dr. Roberts?" Lategan's head was tilted to one side in feigned curiosity. Bhengu could not believe that he was really interested in the little doctor's opinion.

"He could be shamming, of course." Roberts looked defensively in the direction of Sibul.

"Good Lord, Frank," Sibul said. It was the first time Bhengu had heard him swear. "How do you feign blood in your spinal fluid?"

"Not that. Not that, of course. But he did say they were only microscopic particles." He was already looking toward Lategan for reassurance that he was doing the right thing.

The security policeman nodded sympathetically in his direction. Sibul threw up his hands in a short despairing gesture. "Colonel Lategan," he said, "I want your solemn promise that this man will be watched continually."

Lategan considered the promise that was required of him in silence. His eyes had found Bhengu's again and the two men looked straight at each other, each reading something of the other's consciousness in that remote contact. "Gentlemen," Lategan said. He paused. He was in no hurry to finish speaking. "I want this man back in my interrogation room." Bhengu's and Lategan's understanding of each other was absolute.

The magistrate was let into the cell by one of the warders. Bhengu recognized him from previous visits during other periods of detention. He was a middle-aged man, wearing his gray hair very short and a perpetually bored expression on his face. He came slowly across the cell, smothering a yawn with the back of his hand. In one hand he carried a notepad and pen. "Good morning, Mr. Bhengu," he said. "Any complaints?"

Any complaints, Bhengu wondered. I'm a dead man. Is that a cause for complaint? And if it is, what will you do about it? Complete a form? Four copies—one for the Justice Department, one for the security police, one for the district surgeon and one to file. But I'll still be a dead man. No complaints, Bhengu thought. No complaints at all. Thanks for coming.

"How do you feel?" The boredom on his face and the sleepy sound of his voice belied any interest the question might signify.

I feel fine, Bhengu thought. I'm attended by three doctors. I just have to feel fine. Never in my life have I been attended by three doctors. It would hardly be grateful of me if I felt any other way. I'm just fine. Thanks.

"If you don't answer me, I can't help you. For your own sake, you'd better answer me. I'm here to help you, you know. Don't ever forget that."

Oh, I won't forget it. I know about that sort of help. The last time I complained that I had been assaulted you wanted to know by whom. I told you that they had not introduced themselves. They just came into my cell and beat me up. So you said you'd see to it. That night they came back and they saw to it all right. No, thanks. I don't think I want your help. Nice of you to offer, though.

"You don't look too good." He started for the door where the warder was waiting for him. "Think things over, Mr. Bhengu. Your attitude is not going to help you. It will be in your own interest to cooperate next time I come."

It was night again. Had the rest of the day passed already? Had it been more than one day? What about Lategan? Bhengu remembered him saying that he wanted him back in the interrogation room, and he was not a man that normally got less than he asked for. The interrogation room? Lategan knew. He knew that his time to get what he was after was short. He knew that whatever the doctors did now it was already too late. He knew because by this time he knew what treatment his men had handed out. And he knew because he saw it in Bhengu. He had seen it in others.

There was a new warder on hospital duty, a young man, little more than a boy, looking shrunken in a uniform that was too big for him. Bhengu was surprised at the unguarded young face. Either you will not last in prison or your face will not, Bhengu thought. The warder had unlocked the cell door and was bringing a mug of something to him. As he came into the cell the passage light fell behind him and Bhengu could no longer see his face. He became a comical silhouette in his oversize uniform, his thin neck lost in a collar intended to cater for one twice its width. He stopped next to the bed and Bhengu could see his face again. He thought he saw real concern in it. "You awake now?" The voice too sounded concerned. "I've brought you something to drink. Amahewu. You know it?" He got one arm behind Bhengu and brought him into a sitting position. "Here. Drink it. It's good for you."

Bhengu felt the thick powdery liquid against the insides of his lips. He felt himself swallowing, his body eagerly taking hold of it. "That's it," the young warder said. "That's it."

He finished the drink and felt his tongue running along his lips making the best of it, not wanting to waste even the smallest part. The warder lowered his head to the pillow and stood, looking down at him. Bhengu wanted to say something to him. The words were in his brain and he was trying to bring them out, but somewhere in the chain of command a link was broken. In some part of his nervous system something was damaged and what Bhengu wanted to say got no further than the broken part, the little stream of words damming up there and lying stagnant. He wondered if in all of the interconnecting links you see on pictures of the brain there might not be some other way to get the message through. He was concentrating very hard to find such a way, some small detour that would serve his purpose. Bhengu could feel the pressure building up, like a pump forcing water down a pipe the end of which is sealed. ". . . have water," he said, and this time it was he that said it and not just his voice.

"You want water?" The warder leaned forward.

Oh sweet Jesus, don't tell me I have to repeat it, Bhengu thought. He tried again, directing his thoughts into a concentrated stream, forcing them hard against the sealed end of the pipe. ". . . water." Again the word was his. It was what he wished to say, not a meaningless echo of something else.

"I'll get you some," the warder said. He went quickly out of the cell, leaving the door open. Bhengu heard the soft falling of his feet clearly in the silence of the prison hospital as he went away to get the water, then he heard a tap running and the footsteps returning. The warder came back carrying an enameled jug in one hand and a mug in the other. Again he lifted Bhengu into a sitting position, steadied his head with one hand and held the water to his lips. It was cold and his body was even more eager for the water than it had been for the amahewu. When the first mug had been emptied the warder filled it again and brought it to his lips a second time. Again Bhengu drank it all, the cold liquid seeming to heal the raw places inside of him and to cool down the overheated places of which he had not been fully aware until he had felt the contrasting coolness of the water.

The warder laid him down on the pillow. "Okay?" he asked.

There was something else. Bhengu forced the pattern of his thoughts into a concentrated stream again. He knew now that it was possible for him to tell the warder what he wanted. The words came with as much difficulty as they had the first time. ". . . want . . . exercise . . ."

"You want to get up?"

Did he have to do it? Bhengu asked himself. Did he have to ask for confirmation each time? Bhengu concentrated again. "Yes," he said.

They had dressed him in a nightshirt again. The warder drew open the blankets and helped him to sit upright and then to get his legs off the bed. Bhengu felt his feet touch the floor, the same remote contact to which he was growing accustomed. Then he pressed down on the bed with his hands and got unsteadily to his feet, using his own strength. The way he had spoken, forcing the power of his thoughts into a narrow stream in order to get the words out, he now focused his attention on his legs.

Bhengu walked very slowly, leaning forward so that he could see his feet. It was important that he should see them. That way he could control their movements, see that the correct one moved each time, did what was required of it, but not too much, the stride not too long, each foot carefully positioned so that he would not overbalance. The bathtub had been taken away and he walked past the place where it had been and all the way to the open door of the cell. Turning to come back, he saw that the warder, still looking innocent and concerned in his shapeless uniform, had not moved from the side of the bed. He walked back to the bed, and then around the cell again, keeping close to the sides and turning carefully at the corners so as not to bump into the walls, his hands lifted just a little on either side in order to balance himself.

When he had finished and come back to the bed the warder helped him onto it and covered him with a sheet and blanket. Bhengu sat quietly for a while, working on a new word. "Time?" he asked at last.

"A little after seven o'clock," the warder said. "Where do you live?"

"Soweto." The answer came more quickly than before and

it surprised Bhengu. He had never lived in Soweto and had not intended to give that as an answer.

"They say you don't want to talk?" His eyes were examining Bhengu's face, perhaps trying to read his feelings there. "You better tell them something. If you don't they send you to solitary. I think it's terrible to be alone all the time. When they come out of solitary they all look terrible. I think you better tell them something. It's bad in solitary."

⌘ ⌘

If Bhengu sat on the floor he could sit upright without his head touching the roof of the cell. Now he moved to the bunk and lay down on his side. He could not bring himself to face upward. With the roof of the cell then only a handbreadth above his face, it was like being in a coffin. The cell was as long as the bunk and just wide enough for him to be able to sit down on the floor, fitting into the narrow space between the bunk and the wall. He wondered how long he had been there. It would have been wise for him to have marked the days on the wall or floor, but he had not thought of doing it at the beginning. At that stage he would never have thought that they might leave him there for more than a day or two. Lately he had been counting the days and he had marked off six so far. Before that there had been more than six, perhaps twice as many, perhaps three times. He did not know for sure. It would have been better if he could have had some certainty. But perhaps not; perhaps it would have made it worse.

The window was in the wall opposite the door. Through it he could see the dull reflected glow of daylight against a gray concrete wall. And that was all. He never saw a movement or heard a sound except the daily visit to bring food and change the latrine bucket. And then the door was only opened long enough for the dirty plate and the used bucket to be removed and replaced by others, the door swinging closed immediately, no word being spoken by either warder or prisoner, the whole operation taking perhaps four seconds, and that only once every twenty-four hours. Occasionally the observation hatch would slide open and for a few moments a pair of eyes would be visible in the opening. The eyes would stare at him as if to make sure that he was not up to some private mischief in there, then the hatch would close and again he would be alone with the dull gray light he could see through the tiny window.

Eighteen days. That was about it. More or less eighteen days. But it was not important. No. It was very important. But perhaps it had been longer. That would have been terrible. Longer than eighteen days would have been frightful.

Mama Mabaso was with him in the cell. She was sitting on the bunk and the low ceiling did not interfere with her head. That was very convenient, allowing her to sit up straight. It was perfect. "I want you to listen very carefully to what you must get from Johnson's mother, Sam. You must listen very carefully. I don't want you to bring the wrong things again. Do you understand?"

"Yes, Mama. I understand."

"But last time you also said that you understood, and then you forgot what you had to get."

"I won't forget, Mama."

"Are you sure, Sam?"

"Yes, Mama. I would never forget. I'm the best at remembering things."

"Oh, Sam." Mama Mabaso was laughing, her deep laughter, right out of her lungs, filling the cell. "Oh, Sam, you are the worst for remembering things."

He reached up to take her hand to assure her that he would never forget, but she was gone and the bunk was empty. He lay down on the floor, careful to get as far from the bunk as possible. Perhaps if he was not touching the bunk she would be able to come back.

To be able to make the turn at the end of the cell was very difficult. A man who could accomplish that was not doing too badly. Bhengu could do it. It had taken a lot of practice, but he could do it. He crawled to the end of the cell, then, tucking in his head, wriggled around till it went in underneath the bunk. With his shoulders against one wall and his buttocks against the other he worked his way slowly around the corner. The legs were the difficult part. He had long legs, so bringing them around the corner was not easy, but, drawing in his knees and dragging himself along by his hands, he could get around. After that he had to maneuver himself along under the bunk until he reached the door, make the turn at the door in the same way and come back. It was not everyone who could have accomplished it and Bhengu was very proud of it. I can do it, he told himself. I, Sam Bhengu, can do it. I can do the back-and-bum maneuver around the cell. I can do it.

He could see Winifred at the top of the steps. That was strange. He did not remember the steps. But Winifred was standing at the top of the steps, so there must be steps. "Come back here, Sam," she was shouting. "Come back here immediately."

"No. Mama said I can go."

"Mama did not. You come back here."

"Mama said I can go and you've got to stay."

"Mama did not say you can go. All right, I'm going to ask Mama."

"You can ask her. She said I can go." Sam was almost out of the yard. He only had to get around the corner and he would be away and Winifred would not be able to find him for the rest of the afternoon.

"You come back here, Sam. Now I have to do it all alone. I

have to put in the dog, feed the chickens, close the shed door—
all at the same time. You come back here."

"Too bad," Sam shouted back and he was around the
corner, out of sight of her.

She was gone and the steps were gone and Bhengu was
sorry he had run around the corner. He tried to go back, just
to see her for a little longer, but the corner around which he
had fled was also gone and there was no way that he could return.

What did I do wrong? Was there something terrible that I
did wrong? There must have been. My father told me that you
never got punished unless you did something wrong. It was
the law of things, he said. It was the way everything worked.
If you did nothing wrong, you prospered. My father? There's
something wrong about my father. Was he the man in the car
that went away and left me? No. That wouldn't have been my
father. Never. My father would never have done a thing like
that to me. Not my father. My father was a good man. That
was not my father.

The boy was holding a rock in both hands and standing
over the excrement. "Shall I put a rock on it, Papa? If I put a
rock on it, the smell from the soft part inside will come out."

"For heaven's sake, son, why did you do it there?"

"I didn't do it. It was there all the time. It's an old one;
that's why it's hard on the outside and soft on the inside, but I
want to hide it, and if I put a rock on it the smell from the soft
part will come out."

"Just leave it. We'll sit over here. Come."

"I didn't do it. I went to the lavatory. The lavatory is just a
plank with a hole in it."

"I know."

"It's dangerous, hey? A snake can just come up and bite
you in the bum."

"I don't think that will happen."

"But, if a snake comes up, what will it do?"

The struggle is for power. Freedom is only for those who have power. Power is everything. A walk with your child, a home for your wife, a school and a decent job, to be able to come and go like a man, to see your boy run with his dog, and live with dignity, to watch your own fruit grow on your own land; power is everything.

If I lie down on the bunk and expand my chest, I can crush the ceiling. I can expand it enough until the ceiling crashes around me. I, Sam Bhengu, can do it. I only have to lie still and breathe in slowly. I feel my chest rising and pressing against the concrete. I can feel the concrete, heavy and hard, resisting me . . .

Petronella was crying, the tears flowing out of her eyes and down her cheeks without interruption. She was not even trying to wipe them away with her hands. "I only want to live with you," she was saying. Her voice sounded as if some part of it hurt and was about to crack open. "Is that too much for a wife to ask?"

"It's impossible," he said.

"Why? Why is it impossible?"

"You know the life I lead. The organization demands it of me. It's better the way it is."

"I am your wife. Is it strange for a woman to want to live with her husband?"

"It's impossible. We are not important. Individuals are not important. The people are important. The people demand it." It was all lies. Bhengu knew it and he knew that Petronella knew it, but she would not be able to bring herself to accuse him of lying to her.

"I have demands too. I am your wife." But the tone of her voice was not demanding. "Surely I can have demands too?"

"The work is bigger than us," Bhengu said, and what he

said was a lie. He was thinking about the girl and he was thinking about other women.

"Is there not room for me and the work?"

"Each in its place," Bhengu said.

Where did I fall into the hands of the system? There must have been a time when I could have stopped, perhaps have followed a different route. There must somewhere have been a boundary where, had I not crossed it, I would have avoided them. Where was my mistake? Was I too challenging? Should I have held back, moved more slowly? Should I have examined each Convention worker more carefully, studied each face in more detail? There must be some trace of hypocrisy in the face of the informer. There must be some mark that gives him away. His face cannot be that of an honest man. Perhaps we were not ruthless enough. When we knew of informers we avoided them. Perhaps if we had killed them . . .

The girl was on the bunk. It was different from the way it had been when Mama Mabaso had been there. He could reach up and touch her. He could see the flickering uncertain smile that just touched the corners of her mouth, asking, do you still want me? Am I still the one? Anxious that it should be so. Is it I that you want?

He was on the bunk close to her, seeing her face close to his, timid and unsure. His hands were on her body, moving down the length of it until he found the place and heard the catching of her breath and the moaning sounds that she made, saw her eyes closed and her head thrown back, felt her legs encircling him; and the sounds that their lovemaking forced out of her, the little groans and cries filling the cell until the world was nothing but her body and the sounds she was making . . .

"Jesus Christ. Jesus Christ, you want to see this. Jesus Christ. Did you hear it? Did you hear those sounds? Fuck me." The little hatch in the door was open and the eyes of one of the warders, lively with amusement, were framed in it.

"It sounded like a woman was getting screwed in there. You sure there's no woman in there?"

"No, for fuck's sake. He's been doing it himself. For fuck's sake."

"I don't fuckin' believe it. Let me have a look."

"Well, I'm buggered."

"I've seen some funny things, but this . . ."

After they had left, Bhengu slid from the bunk and sat down on the floor, his back resting against the wall. He used his hand to wipe the semen from the blanket on the bunk.

⌘   ⌘

The light in the ceiling came on, scratching at Bhengu's unconscious state until he rose to the surface of awareness, resisted passing through it for a moment and, finally, drawn by the sound of voices, opened his eyes. The cell seemed full of people, a number of them talking at the same time. He closed his eyes again, opened them a second time and then looked carefully at the men in the room, examining each face individually.

Strydom, Brown and Fourie were on the far side of Dr. Roberts and the little warder who had given him the amahewu to drink and who now looked more concerned than ever. His mouth was hanging open in disbelief while Roberts looked agitated and defensive. The expression on Strydom's face was one of annoyance and boredom. He was looking past the doctor and warder in a way that suggested that they were being suffered but no more than that.

"Please, young man . . ." Roberts was saying, only to be interrupted by the warder.

"I'm not as clever as you, Doctor, but I know a sick man. And this man . . ."

"Please, young man, I think I know . . ."

"I've been with him a lot today and he's a sick man. He shouldn't even be here. He should be in a proper hospital, with people who know more than me." For a moment there seemed to be a possibility that he would stand between Bhengu and the others with his arms outstretched to stop them.

"Please, young man." Bhengu noticed how the electric light reflected from Roberts' head in two bright patches. He wondered, if Roberts moved, would the patches become one, like the reflections in a warped mirror? Was Roberts' head warped? Outside? "Please, young man, I think I know more about it than you do."

"I'm not saying I know more than Doctor. I know Doctor's much cleverer than me. I'm just saying I know a sick man when I see one and that's a sick man over there. That's all I'm saying."

"Yes, well I'll be the judge of that." Roberts' eyes blinked quickly as he spoke.

"The lumbar puncture finding was not conclusive. Was it, Doctor?" Strydom's voice contained a note that suggested that he was tired of dealing with fools. "The blood was only a few microscopic particles, I think."

"That's right. Quite right."

"You'll be making a note in the hospital logbook, I suppose?"

That was a new thought to Roberts and his eyes blinked even more quickly than before. Anything in writing was terribly binding and very difficult to dispute. When he spoke his words came out in rapid nervous succession. "Yes, yes, of course. I'll make a note in the log."

"What will you say?" Strydom's manner was that of a weary civil servant completing an irksome formality.

Roberts glanced quickly at Strydom, then at the warder. Finally he looked down at the floor. "I'll say there was no definite evidence of cerebral hemorrhage. The lumbar puncture finding was normal. I'll say there was no pathology."

"Are you satisfied now?" The way in which it was asked suggested to all in the cell that no sensible man could be other than satisfied. It also suggested that the warder's satisfaction or otherwise was academic in any event.

"I'm not saying I understand all that, but Captain must excuse me . . . I know a sick man when I see one."

Strydom had run out of patience. "Stand out of the way."

The warder remained where he was. Bhengu could see one of his knees shaking uncontrollably through the material of his trousers. Brown had also seen it and was nudging Fourie to draw his attention. "Captain must excuse me, but I have to look after this man and tomorrow I am going to report this to Head Warder Claasens." Despite the state of his nerves he managed to keep his voice steady.

Strydom could not believe what he was encountering. His pupils dilated wide with anger. "Are you out of your mind, man? Stand out of the way. Must we lock you up to get you out of the way?" Bhengu watched the strange encounter: on one side the security policeman, wearing a perfectly tailored 200-rand suit, and on the other side the young warder in his ugly khaki uniform, a size too large for him, his knee still shaking violently inside his trousers. "You are not responsible for this prisoner. The doctor is responsible and the doctor says he can go." Strydom nodded to Brown and Fourie and they moved toward the bed, Roberts backing away to make room for them. For the first time Bhengu noticed that Fourie was carrying a folded blanket over one arm.

Brown brushed past the warder and reached Bhengu first,

lifting him into a sitting position and swinging his legs off the bed. There was a small movement of the warder's right hand, as if he wanted to take hold of Brown to stop him, but Strydom's eyes were unwaveringly directed at him and the little gesture died before it was realized. "You hold him fast," Brown said to Fourie. He was holding Bhengu upright on the bed. Bhengu watched Fourie's face as the warrant officer drew close to him. He saw the withdrawal in the eyes and the aversion to even touching him. But Brown had given him an order and he forced himself to take Bhengu firmly by the arm, turning his face away. While Fourie held him upright Brown lifted the nightshirt, bunching it in his hands to get it over Bhengu's head and shoulders.

The warder came closer, his mouth hanging open in troubled amazement. "What are you doing now?" he asked. Strydom looked away, shaking his head in disgust. "What are you doing now? You can't undress him. The nightshirt can come back in the morning."

Brown looked around at Strydom, pausing for a moment in what he was doing. The warder had sounded sure of what he was saying. "Hurry up," Strydom said, now only vaguely irritated.

"But why must you take off the nightshirt?"

Brown had it off and threw it to the foot of the bed, ignoring the warder's question. Bhengu felt the relative coolness of the air against his skin, and was aware of his nakedness, the consciousness of his body, of one naked man in a group where all the others were clothed. Fourie opened the blanket and threw it around Bhengu's shoulders. Where the two ends met in front of him Bhengu felt his hands take hold of them and draw the ends tight. Brown helped him to his feet. "Can you walk?" Bhengu heard him say.

Bhengu started for the door without the help of any of them. He felt steadier than he had at any time during the last

three days. Holding tightly onto the ends of the blanket so that
it would not swing open in front, he went down the long passage to the courtyard.

⌘   ⌘

Mama Mabaso came slowly down the steps of the bus after
the other passengers had alighted. She had grown old. Coming
down the high stairs was difficult for her, and to manage them
at all she had to hold onto the passenger railing, carefully
negotiating each one separately, stopping for a moment on
each step before attempting the next. Bhengu held up a hand
to steady her and took her bag when she reached the ground.
It was an old shopping bag, bulging with all the oddments—an
old cardigan, pieces of material, a few balls of wool, a small
jar containing sugar and another with mealie meal—that went
with her everywhere now. She put her arms around Bhengu
and held him for a moment. Then together they moved away
from the bus stop and crossed the wide grassless common toward the little houses on the other side.

"Do you ever think about the old days in Sophiatown,
Sam?" she asked. She often spoke about the Sophiatown days
now. It seemed that in some way they had become more real
to her than the present.

"Not often, Mama."

"We were rich then, Sam."

"Yes, Mama."

"Do you remember the nice furniture we had in the house?
We had very nice furniture."

"I remember it."

"And Winifred? Do you ever think about her?"

"No. I never think about Winifred."

"Last night I was feeling so very lonely, Sam, and when I
woke up Winifred was in the room with me. I saw her bending

over me. She came to me. I think she saw I needed her. She was such a good girl. I was so glad when you and her came to me, Sam. It was nice, wasn't it?"

"It was fine."

"Things have turned out so badly, Sam." Bhengu could hear the thickness in her voice and, looking at her, he saw that she was crying. In recent years she had cried often and easily. He walked on next to her without saying anything. "Nothing is the way it used to be, Sam. Why didn't they leave us alone in Sophiatown?"

"Let's not talk about it, Mama."

"And you and Petronella are not happy. I wish you would treat her better, Sam." The words came out in erratic little bursts between her sobs. "Adultery is a sin, Sam. You shouldn't go with other women. The Lord will punish you."

"I don't want to talk about it, Mama. Please."

"I just want you to know how I feel, Sam."

"I know how you feel. You've told me many times."

"A man's life is not his own, Sam. A man's life is a link in a chain. You behave as if you think your life is your own."

"No, Mama. Whatever I'm guilty of, I'm not guilty of that."

"No, Sam, you're not. I'm sorry. But let Petronella and the boy come and stay with me. I'm lonely, Sam. I don't want to live alone now."

"I've spoken to her, Mama. She doesn't want to come. She feels you'll side with me against her."

"The silly child. I would never do that. I know how terrible it must be to be married to you, Sam. I would never side with you against your wife. Oh, Sam, I must have done something wrong when I brought you up. What did I do wrong, Sam?"

Bhengu put an arm around her shoulders. They were nearly at the long row of identical little houses. Already, with the sun not yet set, smoke was rising from chimneys all over the township, spreading into a gray blanket and changing the sun into a bright-red ball. "We'll get by," he said to her. "Don't worry about it."

❦   ❦

This time Strydom was driving the car and Bhengu sat in the back between Brown and Fourie. Again he was fascinated by the people on the pavements: a crowd of white people leaving a cinema; a woman squatting in the darkened doorway of a shop, covering herself with pieces of newspaper and cardboard as protection against the cold of the night; a man pressing a girl up against a wall in a quiet alley; a night watchman in the yard of a warehouse, warming his hands at a brazier, his face lit by the flickering red glow of the flames—they were all more vivid to him than they had ever been before. At the side of the road a gray-haired white man with the red lines of many years' heavy drinking in his face was unlocking the door of his car. Bhengu saw him from close by for an instant as they passed next to him. The eyes appeared angry and startled and he grabbed hold of the car's door handle as if for support. When they stopped for a traffic light at the end of the block Bhengu found that he had turned around. The man had the door of his car open and was pulling himself into the front seat, his arms and legs not seeming to obey his brain's instructions accurately. Bhengu knew him. He had never seen him before, but he knew him as well as he knew himself. He knew him and he knew why he was drunk. The man was throwing a blanket over the failures of the past, the regrets about things he had done and others that he had never done. He had found himself to be a victim of his life and now he was drunk. Bhengu knew him well.

Strydom was turning his head to speak to one of the men in the back. The light from a neon sign formed a red glow along the line of his profile. The one eye that Bhengu could see also

flashed with reflected light. His mouth opened a little and
Bhengu could see the insides of his lips before they curled
over into his mouth, and the movement of his tongue. "How
long have we kept him like this?" The words were of no importance. What he was seeing was more than just the image of
a man. He had the realization that he was seeing beyond that,
deep into the soul of the man, the core that made him an indi-
vidual. Strydom too was a victim of his life, covering the pain
of consciousness with the unmitigating drive to destroy those
he saw as enemies of himself and his people. It was a different
kind of drug.

"You mean naked and in solitary?" Brown had spoken. He
was leaning forward a little, the dark curl of hair that he always positioned so carefully hanging down over his forehead.
His mouth was held open a little way in anticipation of need-
ing to speak again, anxious to please Strydom. The senior
officer kept his face turned slightly toward them, but he said
nothing. "About twenty days," Brown said. "Something like
that."

"He could walk all right tonight."

Bhengu was watching Brown's face and he saw it turn in
his direction, their eyes meeting for a moment, then Brown
was looking to the front again. "He can if he wants to."

"Yes, he can if he wants to."

Fourie's hands were hanging loosely in his lap. Bhengu
remembered times in the past few days when his hands had
been so tightly clenched together that the blood seemed to
have been driven from them entirely. He was looking straight
ahead and his face was leaner than before, but completely
relaxed, neutral of any emotion. He had found his own way to
handle the difficulties of human awareness. He had learned to
remove himself from them. From now on he would go
through the day, each day, doing exactly what they told him
to do and he would never question anything again. Whatever

else he did all his life, never again would he be able to examine his own thoughts or feelings.

Strydom brought the car to a halt at a traffic light on the embankment. Away to the right, beyond the lawns with the tall palms growing in them, Bhengu could see the small-craft harbor, the boats lying still in the quiet water, their masts a little forest of naked stalks, and beyond them the main harbor with the reflections of the bright lights in the shipyards streaming in yellow trails across the water. On the grass nearby a young man, wearing only a white shirt, denim trousers and tennis shoes, was sitting with his back to one of the palms eating a curry mixture out of a hollowed-out loaf of bread. Across the front of them a long line of cars, their headlight beams dipped onto the road, came rushing down from the freeway or from the night's entertainment in the city. It was all as if he had never seen it before and would never see it again.

⌘   ⌘

"It won't be long," Bhengu said. "I just want to say good-bye to them. Come in with me."

"I'm not even supposed to be here." Smith had been driving. He started opening the door on his side. "For Christ's sake don't be long, Sam."

"I said I won't." Bhengu was already out of the car and opening the front gate. "In any event, for the next week or so we'll be in places continuously where we aren't supposed to be."

"That's different. It's necessary."

"I won't be long, Willie."

Robert and his wife, a fat woman Bhengu had once made love to in the days before her obesity, were in the tiny lounge. Robert got quickly to his feet as they came in. "Where are you going?" he asked.

By the light from the oil lamp in the room, Robert's face looked more intense than he had ever seen it before. The woman looked only slightly troubled, her broad placid features covering whatever was inside. He remembered her face during their one unsatisfactory copulation, turned to the side with both eyes tightly closed, an entirely passive partner, suffering it for reasons of her own. "What's wrong?" Bhengu asked.

"Where are you going?" Robert repeated. "Tell me, where are you going?" Robert had always been a man to do the best with whatever life dished up to him. He was not one to try to change things or to expect explanations from life. Bhengu had never known him to sound so determined before.

"To Johannesburg," Bhengu said.

"Again? Are you mad?"

It was a fair question. He had spent sixty-seven days between John Vorster Square and the camp the previous time he had gone to Johannesburg. "We'll be careful."

"You were careful last time. What about your wife and child? Don't you ever think about them?"

Smith had come in and was standing just behind Bhengu. He could feel the little mulatto behind him and he could hear his uneasy shuffling from one foot to the other. "Take it easy, Robert. We'll be all right."

"You won't be. They'll get you."

"We've got other people's passes, permits, everything. The cops will never know the difference if we get picked up. One black face is the same as the next to any white cop."

"And if they're waiting for you? What if they're waiting for you?"

"They won't be waiting for us."

"They're going to get you this time, Sam."

Robert's voice was a warning. It carried absolute conviction, but Bhengu could not afford to listen to it. "Where's Mama?" he asked.

"In her bedroom. You mustn't go in."

"Why not?"

"She said she doesn't want anyone to come in. She's praying and she doesn't want anyone to come in."

Bhengu looked past Robert to the closed bedroom door. He could not remember a previous occasion when anyone had tried to stop him from seeing Mama Mabaso or when she had wanted to avoid him. "I want to say good-bye to her. It'll be a while before I see her again," he said softly.

The intensity was fading from Robert's face and being replaced by a look of resignation. For all their differences in personality and approach to life they had always been friends, ever since the day Bhengu had chased the taxi that had his father inside and Robert had come down the road after him. Bhengu could see now that what was in Robert's face was worry, not anger. "She doesn't want to see you, Sam."

"I don't believe it." Bhengu had difficulty speaking.

"She doesn't want to be disturbed."

"She didn't mean me, Robert."

"She said you. She mentioned your name. She doesn't want to see you." Bhengu stepped aside to get past his stepbrother. "Don't, Sam. Don't go in there." Robert's voice was weary and it held within it both a warning and a plea, but Bhengu could no more have left with the memory of that closed door in his mind than he could have avoided going to Johannesburg. He started toward the door. It seemed to him that only by an exercise of will did Robert prevent himself from grabbing hold of him. "Don't go in, Sam. Please."

Bhengu opened the door, leaving it slightly ajar, and stepped into the room. In the light that came in through the narrow opening he saw the old woman kneeling at the side of her bed. It was an attitude in which he had seen her many times before. As a child he had often knelt next to her. She remained in the same position for some time, her head resting on the back of her hands. When she did move it was very slowly, her head lifting off her hands and turning to face him. She was dry-eyed and did not look as if she had been weeping at all, but her face was numb with grief, devastated by the shock of what she was feeling. It was not the expression of her face that held his attention, though. He saw the thin black line, running straight from the top of her forehead to the point of her nose. The question formed itself within his mind: "Who is it?" But Bhengu could not have asked it and she could not have answered him.

For a while they looked at each other in silence, the old woman's eyes not pleading with him to stay, knowing that it was already too late, and he unable to approach her. Eventually she turned her face from him and allowed it to sink back onto her hands.

Willie Smith was in the doorway when Bhengu came out. "We've got to go. We've been here too long."

"Yes."

Bhengu felt Robert take his hand in the two consecutive grips of an African handshake. "We'll be all right," he heard himself mumble.

At the car he got in behind the wheel, Smith getting back into the passenger seat. He pushed the car hard through the township streets wherever he could, being careful to avoid the children. In a few minutes they were on the main highway to Pietermaritzburg. Glancing at the other man, Bhengu could see that the incident at Mama Mabaso's house was troubling him. When Smith finally spoke he asked, "What was that mark on the old lady's face?"

It was a little while before Bhengu replied. "Nothing. Just an old woman's fantasy."

☒ ☒

His breathing was becoming like a bellows again. It had been normal since the night. Now it built up quickly, the steady pulsation of his chest growing deeper and faster, the sound louder and harsher, a raw abrasive noise that he was sure his guards must hear.

Brown was at the desk, leaning back in the chair, his chin resting on his chest, and sleeping deeply. Fourie was the only other one on duty and he was at the window, looking down into a street that was just starting to take on its early-morning mist-gray color.

Not again, Bhengu thought, not this again. Let me go quietly now. Not this. I don't want any more struggling. Just let me go quietly. Let me not have this. Please let me not have this.

But it continued for longer than it had during the night, his chest rising and falling like that of an athlete at the end of a hard race, until a portion of the ceiling directly above him seemed to be throbbing to the rhythm of his breathing. Across his stomach his hands, hanging limply, held together by the short stainless-steel chain of the cuffs, moved with the movement of his body. He tried to change position slightly, to move partially onto his side, but his legs were without strength again and he got no reaction from them.

It's the shackles doing it, he told himself. My legs were all right until they were shackled again. They were getting better until they put these bastard things on.

Please, Jesus. Please, Lord Jesus. Let it stop. Please, let it stop. The other thing doesn't matter. I can manage it now. If I must I can manage it. But let this stop. The rest doesn't matter at all.

Fourie came away from the window, either the movement

of Bhengu's chest or the sound of his breathing having drawn his attention. Bhengu watched him coming, and Fourie was also throbbing, rippling evenly back and forth. The warrant officer got only as far as the desk, stopping behind Brown and shaking him gently by the shoulder. Brown woke up, startled, lifting up his hands from the desk as if in readiness to ward off an attack. He turned quickly, only relaxing when he saw that the hand on his shoulder belonged to no one more hostile than his subordinate officer. Fourie nodded in Bhengu's direction. Brown got quickly to his feet, his face still a little wild at being wakened from his sleep, possibly with the memory of Lategan's threatening instructions about the care of the prisoner haunting him. He came and stood over Bhengu, pressing a hand down on his naked chest. Bhengu felt his chest straining upward at each breath against the weight of the security policeman. "You aren't doing this on purpose, are you, Sam?" There was no sign in his voice that he might believe his suggestion. Brown leaned more heavily on his hand, as if by constricting Bhengu's breathing he might restore it to normal. "Shit. If this man dies, I'm going to be in trouble." It was said dispassionately. As far as Brown was concerned, Bhengu's presence did not seem to be a factor that required consideration. "I'm bloody going to be in the shit."

Bhengu had been watching Fourie's face and he had seen the warrant officer withdraw still further from them. Bhengu's death was a possibility that had to be excluded from his conscious thinking. It could not be considered under any circumstances. In a moment he had slipped so far from the reality of all that was happening and had happened that he was no longer even capable of suggesting who they might call on.

"What do you think, Len?" Brown asked. He got no reply, so he turned to look at the warrant officer. "Len, what do you think?" Through the protective layers the essence of the question penetrated and Fourie shrugged. "I think I'll phone Colonel Lategan," Brown said. "What do you think?"

Phoning Lategan was a way of avoiding any sort of responsibility, and the idea was seized upon by the warrant officer's dulled senses. "Yes," he said.

"I'll phone him. He'll be getting up by this time already."

Brown used the telephone on the desk to dial the colonel's number. Through the rushing sound of his breathing Bhengu could hear him speaking. "Can I speak to the colonel, please? . . . Colonel? Brown here, sir. He's breathing very funny . . . It's like he's out of breath . . . It just started a moment ago, just a few minutes . . . I wondered if I should call Dr. Roberts. That's why I phoned . . . Yes, Colonel . . . Yes, Colonel." He hung up. "He says we must just leave him. He'll come straight in and have a look himself."

"What must we do with him now?"

"Nothing. Just wait for the colonel to come in." Brown settled himself back in the chair and frowned at Bhengu, his carefully arranged hair having become unsettled and hanging over his forehead in disorder. "The colonel can also be damned unreasonable at times," Brown said. He paused a moment, as if expecting Fourie to affirm his statement. When he said nothing, Brown went on: "Sometimes he behaves like we've got no rights in this country. Sometimes you'd think we're kaffirs the way he treats us. Look at this thing of the other night. He said he'd break me down to sergeant if it happened again. Jesus. Just one little slip and he treats you like that. I told him nothing happened while I was away. But he wouldn't even listen to me. I tried to tell him twice, and he just said I don't know what I'm talking about." He nodded once toward Bhengu. "That's why I still think this bugger is shamming. Because when I left that night he was okay, and ever since then he's been putting on this act." Fourie was leaning forward in his chair, his elbows on his knees, looking down at the floor in front of him. The look on his face was worried, but the absent expression was also there, as if he was concerned but perhaps could not remember the cause of his concern. "You blokes just sat and watched him that night when I was away, didn't you?"

"Yes." The word came out hoarsely.

"You didn't try to interrogate him or anything, did you?" The tone of Brown's voice was complaining, answering the questions for Fourie; telling him, I know you didn't, so just confirm it for me, old man.

"No, we didn't," Fourie said.

"I know it. I never doubted it, but do you think the colonel will listen to me when I tell him? Has he spoken to you about it yet?" Brown was facing the warrant officer and saw the quick shake of his head. "Well, I got shit about it. I don't know why I get all the flak." Brown was silent for a moment as he considered the many injustices of the world that seemed to have found a target in himself lately. "I really paid for screwing that kid," he said. "My sins really caught up with me this time. The colonel kept on and on about Van Rooyen, asking me all sorts of questions about him. He's really got it in for him and me. You're lucky—he didn't ask much about you. Old Van Rooyen's not so bad. I don't know why he's got it in for him and me like that."

The glow from the window was growing slowly, gradually overpowering the light from the fluorescent tube in the ceiling and throwing a shadow across Fourie's face, making of it no more than a blank silhouette.

Bhengu's breathing had become painful, the unaccustomedly harsh passage of air tearing at his throat and starting bouts of coughing. There was also a pain above his heart that had not been there before. For days now he had felt no pain and it took him by surprise. He had thought that that was something of the past for him. Bhengu remembered being told that pain was the warning system of the body. If you felt it, you knew that something was wrong. It's all right, he told the pain. You can go. I know damn well that something is wrong. You don't have to tell me. You can go along now. Just leave me as I am. I'll make out without your help. I don't need a warning system. Just run along now.

"Van Rooyen's a bit of a stupid bugger," Brown told Fourie. "He's stupid, like the way he told us about his wife, but he's not so bad. He's just the way he is, but his heart's all right. He's not a bad chap—old Van Rooyen."

Coming from down below, Bhengu heard the humming of the elevator, the first time he had heard it that morning. He wondered if it was Lategan already. Both of the security policemen had heard it as well and both had the same thought. Fourie was sitting upright, almost at attention, and Brown seemed ready to rise to his feet. The elevator doors opened and Brown heard Lategan's sharp decisive stride in the passage, his leather-soled shoes clicking clearly on the tiled surface.

The colonel came quickly into the room and walked straight to Bhengu. He stopped above him looking down without tilting his head forward at all, only his eyes directed downward, his back held straight as if to emphasize his height above Bhengu. His face was critical and severe, but no longer skeptical. He had known for some time and now he was acknowledging the truth to himself. Both Fourie and Brown had risen, Brown coming to stand behind Lategan and Fourie remaining at the table in front of the window. Lategan turned suddenly and looked directly at Fourie. "Where's Van Rooyen?"

To the warrant officer Lategan's question was an accusation, cutting through the self-protective layers with which he tried to insulate himself. Bhengu could see the sudden alarm in his face. It was Brown who answered. "Major Engelbrecht took him off night shift. He'll be coming on in half an hour, Colonel."

Lategan was still looking straight at Fourie. "I'll see you and him in my office as soon as he comes in."

For Fourie to have answered would have been an impossibility. He was saved the embarrassment of trying by the sound of the elevator moving again. "I hope that's Major Engelbrecht," Lategan said.

"It's a bit early for . . ." Brown bit the sentence short. Seeing the look on Lategan's face, it was safest to say nothing at all.

"I asked him to come in."

Engelbrecht came in, wearing his sunglasses despite the fact that it was not yet full daylight outside. "Good morning, Colonel. Good morning." He came to a stop next to Lategan, whose only acknowledgment of his presence was to gesture toward Bhengu by an inclination of his head. "Have you seen Van Rooyen and Fourie yet?" Engelbrecht asked him.

Bhengu could see on Fourie's face the growing dread struggling with the need to smother it all utterly. "I'll see them this morning," Lategan said.

"He'll have to be banned for the rest of his days."

"He'll never be quoted again in this country—that's for bloody sure."

The breathing eased off more quickly than it had started; a few deep breaths separated by longer pauses and Bhengu was breathing normally again. The pain over his heart dulled and was gone, and the irritation of the raw place in his throat disappeared almost completely. "You don't think he's hyperventilating on purpose?' Engelbrecht asked.

"Ask Fourie."

Fourie was still in front of the window and Engelbrecht had to move a step to see his face and the fear in it. He found no need to ask the question. "When did it start?"

"About an hour ago." Brown's voice was weak, revealing
the awareness that he was not yet out of it. "Plus, minus an
hour ago." He looked quickly at Fourie, his face showing that
there was something he did not yet understand, something
they had hidden from him.

Bhengu had seen the look. To him it was a game they
played, each man examining the faces of the others—read the
faces and know the truth, win the big prize. The members of
the night shift examined the faces of their seniors to sense
their moods, possibly to discover just how serious their sins
were, whether there was need for fear. Their faces in turn
were studied for traces of guilt or the lies behind which they
were sheltering. Lategan and Engelbrecht looked at each
other, silently asking the same question—What would you do?
Do you believe him? How far should we cover? The doctors
too, when they were present, searched the faces of the officers,
Roberts looking for a sign of approval, Sibul for assurance
that he had not gone too far, that he had not tried to exercise
rights that did not exist. And all of them stared at Bhengu's
face, trying to read it all there. Is it an act? Is this another one
of your dirty commie kaffir terrorist tricks? Or is it real? And
those that knew the answers also watched him. They had
questions of their own that needed answering as badly as any
of the others did. How long have you got? Are you going to
be able to tell them anything? Or are you going to make it? Is
the day going to come when you walk out of here, knowing all
that you do? Are we going to see such a day? It was a game, a
game of read-the-signs-in-the-faces and for the winners there
might be prizes: promotions, increasingly important assign-
ments, the grateful thanks of the community to its protectors.
For the losers there would be forfeits that had to be paid: a
departmental inquiry to be faced, a transfer back to the ordinary police, perhaps even a prosecution. No, not a prosecution. That would never be allowed. It would be an admission.

"We better call Roberts." It was Engelbrecht who had spoken, his voice holding almost a question.

"He's all right now. Call Roberts if it starts again."

"We could move him to Pretoria Central. They've got a proper hospital."

"You're mad." Lategan turned suddenly away from Bhengu. "We'll leave Pretoria out of this."

"He got sick." Engelbrecht sounded patient and reasonable. "We don't know how he got sick. There was a struggle. He may have hit his head. We don't know if he did or if he didn't. Nobody can say for sure. Nobody's to blame."

Lategan started for the door. Before he went out he spoke to Fourie. "As soon as Van Rooyen gets here—be in my office."

⌘   ⌘

The roadblock was above Pietermaritzburg where the road to Mooi River climbs out of the long wooded gorge coming up from the Natal capital and appears for the first time on the highveld. Well before they reached him Bhengu could see the red-and-white-striped reflector tunic of the policeman positioned in the middle of the road to stop the traffic.

Immediately his attention was drawn to the island separating their half of the highway from the other direction of traffic. But the place had been carefully chosen. An unbroken steel-mesh fence and a dense hedge made it impossible to turn back. He heard Willie Smith voicing the same thought. "We can't turn around here."

"It'll be all right," Bhengu said.

The headlights were picking out the figure in the road now, not just the reflections from his tunic. The policeman was waving an arm to show them to slow down. The car immediately ahead, a red coupé, had come to a halt at the side of the

road. Two policemen in khaki uniforms went up to the
driver's window, shone their flashlights into the car and waved
it on. Bhengu saw the car accelerate up the slight incline, then
he was opposite the policeman in the road himself. The policeman was waving Bhengu to the side of the road where his colleagues were waiting. Bhengu brought the car to a halt at the
edge of the tarmac. Ahead he could now see a line of cars
parked on the gravel shoulder of the road, the drivers of
which had not been as lucky as the man in the red coupé.
"Look at the brothers waiting," Smith said. "Isn't it bloody
typical?"

The two young uniformed policemen that had inspected the
red coupé came to the window on Bhengu's side. One flashed
a flashlight onto Bhengu's face. "Pull up over there," he said.

Bhengu stopped the car at the back of the row of cars of
other black drivers. Opening his window and looking out, he
could see a larger group of policemen at the head of the queue
of cars, but they seemed to be making no effort to examine the
cars or the drivers' documents. On the road another car was
stopped. The two young policemen approached the car and
one of them shone a flashlight into the driver's window. From
where he was sitting Bhengu saw the light fall on the white
faces of the occupants and saw the policeman wave them on,
then the taillights were fading into the distance until they
topped the rise and were gone.

"What do you think?" Smith asked.

"It'll be all right," Bhengu said. "A kaffir's a kaffir to them.
The papers will get us through."

"I hope so."

"Just relax. You just relax and it'll be all right."

On the road more cars were allowed to pass. Another car
with a black driver was directed to the back of the queue and
he pulled in behind them, brightly lighting them with his
headlights for a moment until he switched them off, leaving

them in darkness again and everything as it had been before: the policeman with the reflector tunic stopping the cars, the other two with the flashlights making their cursory check, and the drivers and passengers of the cars at the side of the road wondering what was going to happen to them before the night was through.

They did not have long to wait. A uniformed police officer, flicking a swagger stick back and forth in his right hand, and a short man wearing a suit had come away from the group at the head of the queue and were walking slowly from car to car. The policeman had a flashlight in his free hand, which he shone into each car in turn. They were stopping a short while at each car, not hurrying, but Bhengu could see that they were not inspecting the travelers' documents, as might have been expected. They seemed to be doing no more than looking at the people inside the cars.

"There's one coming down this side, looking in the trunks," Smith said. "What are they doing on your side?"

"Just looking inside the cars."

"Examining papers?"

"No. Just looking." The front car in the queue switched on its lights and drove off. Bhengu could hear the exhaust note through his open window. "They're letting them go when they've had a look."

"What the hell's going on, Sam?"

"Only one possible thing. They've got a man there who'll recognize the one he's looking for." Almost as he spoke Bhengu learned who the man was. The headlights of a car that had been allowed to proceed lit up the policeman and the man in the suit. And Bhengu recognized the man wearing the suit immediately. "It's Lategan," he told Smith.

"Good Christ. What now?"

"We may as well save the other brothers the trouble," Bhengu said. Lategan and the other policeman were still six or seven cars away, working their unhurried way along the queue. Bhengu got out of the car and stood next to the open door. "Colonel Lategan," he called. "Are you looking for me?"

✠ ✠

Would it never stop? Dear Christ, would it never, never stop? His breath was driving through his throat like a steam engine and the pain over his heart had started again. Dr. Sibul was bending over him, wiping something off his lips. He could see the roll of fat at the back of Sibul's neck move up and down as the doctor changed position. Behind Sibul he could see Lategan and some of the other security policemen as no more than an ill-defined blur. "Must he be shackled?" It was Sibul who had spoken, and even through the roar of racing breath that filled Bhengu's head he could hear the anger in the doctor's voice. He saw Lategan turn his head, and Strydom emerged out of the blur that made up the security policemen to unlock the shackles. First he felt the anklets click open one by one, his feet falling free onto the foam mattress, then the cuffs came off his hands and they slid off his stomach to fall at his sides, one hand slipping off the bed, the knuckles making gentle remote contact with the floor. Sibul had straightened up and was facing Lategan. "Now are you satisfied?"

"You people didn't stop us from bringing him back."

"Well, now I'm telling you that he can't stay here." Bhengu was surprised at the resoluteness in the doctor's voice.

Lategan's face seemed calm, clearly unimpressed by the other man's display of temper. His voice too was calm. "We'll send him to Pretoria."

It took a moment for Lategan's words to register in the doctor's mind, but when they did his face relaxed immediately, the resolute expression disappearing as if it had never existed.

Sending Bhengu to Pretoria would free Sibul of responsibility. What happened to Bhengu after that would not be his business. "Where's Dr. Roberts?" he asked. He was trying to restore a little gruffness of tone to his voice.

"I haven't seen him here," Lategan said.

"He should have come to visit this man. I told him he should have come. Dr. Rael told him."

"Isn't he a member of your staff?" Lategan sounded bored. They both knew that this was Sibul's final gesture in the direction of concern for his patient before he pulled himself out of it.

"Not exactly."

"I thought he was a member of your staff."

"No. He's not a member of my staff. He's . . ." But Sibul was talking to himself. His voice trailed off ineffectually. Bhengu watched Lategan turning away, his outline blurred like an unfocused image on the lens of a camera.

The breathing was easing again, the process slower than before this time, but definitely easing. The irritation it had caused in his throat started him coughing, a long succession of painful blasts, each aggravating his throat enough to cause the next. At last the coughing stopped and the breathing also returned to normal. Sibul was getting ready to leave, putting on his jacket and picking up his bag from the desk. He moved away in the direction of the door and faded into the haze around the security policemen. Bhengu heard his voice from out of the haze. "When will he go?"

"I'll try to get an aircraft."

The figures of the other men in the room were vague shadows in the haze. Bhengu could see them moving back and forth, their features and even their clothing indistinguishable from each other. The haze became denser and the figures too disappeared. All that remained was the sense of something alive, like shadows flitting across a dimly lit window, which

Bhengu knew must have been the movements of the other men in the room. The haze grew still denser and moved right up to the edge of the bed until it filled the room and there was nothing else.

The air was shimmering like the heat waves off a road on a very hot day. The voices were filtering through the waves, sometimes reaching him clearly, then drifting away again. He recognized the voices of Van Rooyen and the warrant officer called André de Jager. Van Rooyen was speaking and Bhengu could hear the uncertainty in his voice under the bravado with which he tried to cover it. "The colonel will never drop us," he was saying. "I know the colonel."

"You took a helluva chance."

"He looked for it. Nobody can tell me he didn't look for it. That kaffir takes us for fools."

"Yes, but you took a helluva chance."

"I told him he's going to talk or I'm going to fuck him up so he never forgets it."

"What did the colonel say?"

"He crapped me and Fourie out. He said we disobeyed orders and we mustn't think we'll get promotion soon. He was fuckin' cross, I'm telling you."

"He's a white man."

"He's a white man, all right. He was fuckin' cross, but he won't drop us."

"Did he say that?"

"No, he didn't say it, but I know him."

"All I can say is you took a helluva chance."

"Yes, we surely took a chance, but I wasn't going to let that kaffir take us for a fool any longer."

The haze was clearing and Bhengu could see the figures of the two men dimly against the lighted window. They were seated on either side of the table. The door opened and he saw

Engelbrecht as he entered the room. "André," the major said, his voice soft, sounding almost thoughtful, without any clear emphasis, expecting instant attention from the warrant officer and getting it as De Jager got quickly to his feet. "Colonel Lategan can't get an aircraft. I want you to go to Smith Street and pick up a van. I want mattresses in the back for him," he inclined his head toward Bhengu, "and for two officers who are going to ride in the back with him. See Sergeant Van Zyl at Smith Street."

"Yes, Major." He started for the door. "Am I going with him to Pretoria?"

"No."

After he had left, Engelbrecht directed his attention at Van Rooyen. The haze had retreated completely, melting out of the window and into the distance until Bhengu could see the tops of the buildings on the far side of one of the main arteries coming down from the city center, their east-facing walls bright in the morning sunlight. Van Rooyen was still seated, his bloated shapeless face like that of a disgruntled schoolboy who could not understand why the teacher was angry with him. Slowly the warrant officer became conscious of the major's attention. With Engelbrecht it was something you could never be entirely sure of because of the sunglasses. Bhengu saw the feeling of uneasiness growing in Van Rooyen until he got out of the chair uncertainly and stood next to the table, making little fidgeting movements with his hands. "Phone your wife," Engelbrecht said eventually, after he had his man in the desired condition. "Tell her you're going to Pretoria. You should be back tomorrow."

"Yes, Major." There was nothing informal in the tone of Van Rooyen's voice. He started toward the telephone on the desk.

"Not from here," Engelbrecht said.

The warrant officer had already been reaching for the telephone. He withdrew his hand and made for the door. Engelbrecht watched him go, then sat down at the desk. Bhengu could see his face clearly, lean except for the fleshy nose, his mouth a thin straight line seemingly without lips at all, and the sunglasses in which Bhengu could see the reflection of the fluorescent light in the ceiling hiding his eyes and whatever was behind them. He remembered a previous occasion when he had seen the reflection of the fluorescent light in Engelbrecht's sunglasses. It seemed to have been a long time before. He tried to remember when it could have been, but time had had little significance lately.

Lategan came into the room. Engelbrecht started getting to his feet, but the other man waved a hand at him to indicate that he should remain seated. "Sit, George, sit." He sat down on the edge of the desk himself.

"Army wouldn't let you have a plane?"

"No. They said they haven't got one to spare at the moment."

"And Pretoria? What did the brigadier say?"

"He agrees. We must send him up."

"What did you tell him?"

"The truth." Lategan stopped speaking and Engelbrecht waited for him to expand on his answer, curious to hear what was currently being described in that way. "We had a struggle with him."

Engelbrecht took a deep breath. "It's a fuckup."

Lategan's eyes and face were hard as he answered. "Those little bastards disobeying orders. If this bugger dies now, we'll learn nothing. And you know what sort of shit is going to be flying?"

"We should get rid of them."

"Not yet. We'll have to get past this first."

"After that they should go."

"For sure. I'm sending Gerrit with Brown, Van Rooyen

and Fourie to take him there. I can't afford any more fuckups.
And you can start working on Jele in the meantime."

His friend's name drove straight at him out of the conversation that had been little more than a meaningless jumble of
words, but he brought his mind under control immediately.
From what Lategan had said they might have Jele, it was true,
but it might also be just another way of testing him, a device
to break down his act, if it was an act. And even now they
would prefer to believe that it was an act. Bhengu had experience of their working methods. But they dropped the subject
immediately, going on to talk about other things, their voices
no more than a mumbled backdrop to his thoughts. Perhaps
they did have Jele. If it had been a stunt and they did not have
him, they would have belabored the point. That was their
style. And yet you could not be sure with Lategan. He was far
more subtle than the others. If they did have Jele, Bhengu did
not want to think about it. Jele had been a good friend, and if
he was in their hands there was nothing Bhengu could do to
help him. There was nothing Bhengu could do to help himself.
Christ knows, he thought, there's no one who can help either
of us.

Engelbrecht was leaving, stopping a moment in the door.
"I'll send Kleynhans in to watch him," he said.

Engelbrecht left and Lategan remained, still sitting on the
edge of the desk. He had his eyes directed at the wall above
Bhengu's head, his chin drawn in. It was the characteristic attitude in which Bhengu had so often seen him. It always
reminded Bhengu of a boxer with a suspect jaw, tucking it in
under his shoulder where it would be out of harm's way. He
could feel the other man's need to make contact, but also his
reluctance to do so. The expression of his face was determined, but then Bhengu could hardly remember an occasion
when Lategan's face had been anything but determined. The
eyes were different, not the cold hooded eyes, the soul buried

deep, that political policemen in all dictatorships turned toward their victims. Now they seemed introspective. Bhengu knew that it might be no more than a trick of the light. He had never before seen such an expression on the face of a security policeman, but if he had been told that he would one day see that expression on the face of one of them, he would have expected to find that Lategan was the one. Both men knew that under other circumstances the relationship between them might have been quite different, but as things were they were both victims of the illimitable sovereignty that the group, to which each belonged, exercised over his life. There could be no escape for either.

The policeman's eyes flicked toward him, looking into his eyes for a moment, then away again. When he spoke it was still without looking at Bhengu. "You've been at it a long time, Sam. You're one of the few that went through Congress and is still fighting." The tone of his voice was not friendly, but neither was it hostile. It was thoughtful and possibly even regretful. Bhengu was aware that this might be yet another device. He had learned through many detentions and interrogations that with his captors nothing could ever be assumed to be as it appeared. "You were one of the toughest. Maybe you were the toughest. We never got much out of you." Bhengu wished he could answer him. He wanted to say, You never got a damned thing out of me and we both know it. "It's all been for nothing, though, hasn't it?" Yes, Bhengu thought, it's all been for nothing—what I've done and what you've done. Everything. "All for nothing. You didn't really think we'd let you go on with your plans, did you? Did you think we'd let you do what you like with our country? We've got nowhere else to go, Sam. It's the only place we've got and we aren't going to give it to you." Why? Bhengu asked himself. Was it possible that the colonel actually needed to talk to him? Did even he have a conscience that troubled him from time to time? Or was this just another futile exercise in self-justification? Come on, Colonel, Bhengu thought, I thought the Special Branch was supposed to be tougher than that. I thought nothing ever touches you guys.

Suddenly Lategan got to his feet and came right up to him. He leaned over him, bringing his face close to Bhengu's, and now he was looking straight into his prisoner's eyes. "Can you hear me, Sam?" He waited a moment as if half-expecting a reply. "I wonder if you can hear me. You're dying, aren't you? You're dying and you're blaming us. But we didn't kill you. You killed yourself. Where did you think this would all end? Did you think we'd allow it indefinitely? You've been at it for nearly twenty years. Did you think you could go on forever? It wasn't Van Rooyen and Fourie who killed you, Sam. You did it yourself. Anytime in those twenty years you could have stopped and you would have saved yourself. That was enough time, wasn't it? Wasn't twenty years enough? You made your own choice. Don't blame us, Sam. It was your choice. You killed yourself as surely as if you'd taken a knife and slit your own throat." The words had come out quickly, almost convulsively, and they stopped as suddenly as they had started.

Now Bhengu understood. Lategan was saying good-bye. For some mental reason of his own he had to explain himself to Bhengu, even to clear himself. Bhengu had to speak. He had to talk to Lategan. What he had to say had suddenly become the only important thing left to him. He channeled the forces of his mind as he had with the young prison warder, forcing the words to find new routes in his brain. What he wanted to say forced itself along the tunnels of his thinking, the pressure building where its path was blocked to pour its floodwaters into new ways. The immobility of his vocal system yielded for only a moment. "You also," he said.

Lategan withdrew suddenly from Bhengu. Standing erect

he looked down at the dying man. Bhengu could see that he understood and he could see the fear in his face. Again, as at the hospital when he had wanted Bhengu's return to the interrogation room, their understanding of each other was absolute.

✠ ✠

Brown combed his hair, arranging the curl on his forehead without the assistance of a mirror. At the table Fourie was reading his novel. Van Rooyen was on the other side, rocking back on his chair, his head and shoulders resting against the wall. "How long are you going to be away?" he asked Brown.

Brown grinned at him. "Twenty minutes there, five minutes on the job, twenty minutes back again. Forty-five minutes." He slipped the comb ostentatiously into an inside pocket of his jacket. In his mind he might have been a musketeer sheathing his sword. "No. I won't be more than two hours."

"You can screw a lot in two hours," Van Rooyen said. The expression of his face was balanced between vicarious pleasure at how Brown was going to spend the next two hours and chagrined envy that it was not going to be him.

"Don't wait up for me, Mama," Brown said as he stopped in the door. He waited until Fourie also looked up from his book. "Just keep old Sam quiet. I'll see you two later."

After he had gone Van Rooyen stretched himself in his chair. "The bugger," he said. "The bugger. He also takes his chances." Now there was clearly more of envy than pleasure in his voice.

"He's a fool," Fourie said. "He risks his family life, everything, just for that."

"His wife will never find out. How will she find out?"

"You never know."

"She won't find out." Fourie went back to his reading and

Van Rooyen looked around for someone else to support his view. "What about you, Sam? What do you say? Is Lieutenant Brown a fool or not?"

"My opinion of all of you is exactly the same," Bhengu said.

Van Rooyen's eyes narrowed. His lips curved up at the corners in a nervous little smile to hide the insult that he felt. "You're going to come unstuck, kaffir."

"So are you. I might get mine first, but you'll get yours too. You can take that as a prophecy."

Van Rooyen waved a broad finger at him. "You'll come unstuck, kaffir. You don't go home from here until we say you can. You better remember that."

Bhengu looked up at the ceiling. The shackles on his feet decreed that that or the wall next to him were the only directions he could face if he was not looking straight at the two security policemen. He had no desire to start an argument with the most limited of his guards. He also did not want to be goaded into saying anything foolish.

But Van Rooyen was not going to let the exchange end on such an unsatisfactory note. In common with any brutal and unintelligent man in a position of power who has just lost a verbal battle, he would have to reassert his dominance by using that power. "What were you going to do with us if the revolution was a success?" he asked. Bhengu did not answer him. He could think of a few things he would have liked to do to Van Rooyen in particular, but there would be no dividends in explaining them to him. "What were you going to do? Slit our throats?"

The idea appeals to me, Bhengu thought, yours especially.

"Convention," Van Rooyen said, "Convention. What a balls-up. If we hadn't closed it, you would all have killed each other in the end anyway."

Bhengu was still looking up at the ceiling. He heard Fourie

joining the conversation. "Leave him alone, Charl. I want to read."

"Wait first. Wait first. I'm not doing anything to him. I just want to hear what he has to say."

"Yes, but I want to read. How the hell can I read with you arguing all the time?"

"Wait first. There'll be plenty of time for reading. I want to hear what he has to say." Bhengu could hear the playful brutality in the policeman's voice that would not let go of a victim until he was satisfied. And Bhengu knew that ultimately the man in the position of power was the victor in any argument. "I want to hear what he has to say about Convention." He lingered over the word "Convention," trying to let the sneering tone of his voice get to Bhengu. "What was Convention trying to do, kaffir? Probably just organizing fucking parties where you could get hold of the maids." Bhengu closed his eyes, regretting that he was unable to close his ears to the sound of Van Rooyen's voice. "Convention," the security policeman sneered. "Convention. Nothing run by a kaffir can be worth a fuck. And where is Convention now? Tell me, where is Convention now?"

"Please, Charl. In God's name leave him alone."

"Wait first. He hasn't answered me yet."

"He isn't going to answer you."

"He'll have to."

"We're not supposed to question him. They told us to guard him, nothing else. Major Engelbrecht said so. And Lieutenant Brown should never have gone away like he did."

"This is not serious questioning." Van Rooyen's voice was overly conciliatory. "This is just friendly questioning. I just want him to tell me where is Convention now? Come on, kaffir, tell me where is Convention now? Where is Convention? Come on, tell me."

"Jesus, Charl."

"Where is Convention now, kaffir?" Van Rooyen ignored the other policeman. "I want to know what happened to Convention. You know what happened to Convention—now I want you to tell me." Fourie was worriedly watching both Van Rooyen and Bhengu, his eyes flicking back and forth between the two. He was not a man to go looking for trouble. And what Van Rooyen was doing was going to mean trouble. They had an order to leave Bhengu alone and Van Rooyen was disobeying the order. "You know what happened to Convention, kaffir—now why won't you tell me? I want to know." Van Rooyen was enjoying himself, leaning his elbows on the table, his features fixed into the nasty little grin Bhengu had got to know well. His derisory superiority, as he perceived it to be, was a blanket over his own insecurities, reinforcing a troubled and faltering self-esteem. "Come on, kaffir, why won't you talk? I'm sure you know what happened to Convention. It was your little baby, wasn't it? So why won't you tell me?"

"Jesus, Charl, we mustn't question him."

"He has to tell me. Tonight he has to tell me what happened to Convention. Come on, kaffir, talk. Tell the white boss what happened to Convention. I'm sure you remember what happened to that fuckup of yours."

Bhengu tried to shut his mind to them, but the words were a whirling carousel within his senses, one of them repeating itself with growing insistence—Convention . . . Convention . . . Convention . . . Bhengu knew what had happened to Convention. He remembered it too clearly for his own peace of mind. He would rather have forgotten. It was something he normally shut out of his thinking, not wanting to reexamine it or keep it alive. It was better out of the way where it could not reach him or hurt him anymore.

Now it was all returning, the memories piling upon each other, unbidden, thronging past the reluctant censoring equipment of his brain, overwhelming his power to withstand them.

He would have given what remained of his life to have been able to close his mind to it all. But it was impossible. Already the disjointed images of meetings, faces, rooms were with him. He remembered the gatherings where they had planned it all, deciding that they would do everything out in the open to show the world that they had nothing to hide. He remembered how the money had come in, more than they had hoped for or had ever thought possible. "It's going to be an empire," Jele had said, his voice no more than a whisper. Perhaps he had not dared to say it out loud for fear that it might disappear, turning out to be only another illusion. Bhengu's memory fastened onto a series of smiling faces, one replacing another in quick succession, the faces of friends whose lives had been changed by Convention: a man born in a mud hut who had become a manager, a washerwoman who had become an operator, the unemployed who had found the opportunity for labor and the dignity that was a part of it . . .

The start had been a simple trading store, a mud-and-wattle structure deep in the Natal hills. The directorate had originally not been in favor, but the man who would be a proprietor had persuaded them. On opening day his stock had been an assortment of cheap groceries and blankets. But a year later the stock had been a lot less ragged and, along with the blankets, there had been shorts, Tee shirts that cost less than a rand, skirts, ropes, oil lamps that could give light to huts where there was no electricity, belts, canvas kit bags, spades, balaclavas to shield your face against the cold on winter mornings before the sun was up, axes, saddles, a single-shear plough an ox could pull, storm lanterns, in fact almost everything a human being could reasonably need.

The shack was empty now, the stock gone. The manager had gone back to being an errand boy. The windows were broken and the dirt road leading to it was overgrown with weeds. At the back a shed made of corrugated iron, the sheets still shining new in the sun, was the only clue that a man had worked and hoped and failed.

"Wait first." Van Rooyen's voice reached him dimly through the stream of his recollections. "Wait first. I want him to tell me . . ."

The overall factory had been their special pride, a mighty steel barn filled with the machinery to provide overalls for an army of mechanics, and school shirts for the children of the people at a price that they would be able to pay. They had built it in the area where the dumpings had been worst, where the people who the government said had no right in the cities had been brought and told, this is your home. The people who had no right in the cities had settled upon the open grass flats, hoping that father or brother or son, living alone in the the men's hostel in the city, would be able to send enough to help them through; each hoping that something would happen that he or she would also get a pass that would allow them to go where there was work; hoping until there was no more hope left in them, only the knowledge that this was their life and always would be. The old people and the children who were not strong enough for a winter in the tents with too little food died before the houses came. And some died because of the hope that was lost and the future that was empty.

A bitterness descended upon the people of the settlement, drifting among the new little houses like a mist from the swamp near the road. It entered through open doors and windows and moved through the apathetic groups that gathered in the streets to pass the time of which they had so much. It filled the minds and distorted the will of the people, dominating everyone. No one escaped it.

It had been there that Convention had decided that the overall factory had to be built. The people had stood in queues at the doors, waiting for the chance to work. For a short time the bitterness had receded and been replaced by the beginnings of a new hope. In the minds of the people there had suddenly been more than just the pain of their anger.

Bhengu had seen it all and he knew that there was strength in bitterness; strength to try, to fight, to kill if necessary, to live by any means at all, but to live. Bitterness could keep a man alive after he should long since have died. It could keep food in the mouths of the young under circumstances when otherwise there would have been no food at all. There was strength in bitterness because it grew out of anger and because it knew no morality. And when the bitterness had retreated so also had the strength withered.

The great steel barn had been situated in plain view of the main road, so it had been left standing. But now the looms and sewing machines stood silent. A watchman and his pack of dogs were stationed inside the security fence to see that no one came close. The bitterness of the people had again become a tangible reality, hanging over the settlement and polluting its air, leaving no passing traveler untouched by it. Bhengu could see it in the eyes and hear it in the voices of the people, and now it was stronger than ever before. And the evil that it worked in the hearts of the people had become the legacy of the young.

"Where's Convention now? I want to know. He has to tell me . . ." The words were muted, distant, repeating themselves again and again like a far-off insistent echo of Van Rooyen's voice. "I want to know what happened . . ."

The little hamlet where the leather works had stood was an irregular scattering of mud huts and houses with unplastered brick walls. It was a rocky hillside place where nothing but the tough grass of the veld could grow. The people—old men, women and children—had formed a bewildered hopeful gathering in the grounds of the church as the priest had pointed to the site. "You can build it here," he had said.

"What?" the people had asked. "What are you going to build?"

"A leather works," Bhengu had told them.

"A leather works?" They had looked at each other in wonder. "There is going to be a leather works? Who will work in it?" It had been too much to expect that it could be their own leather works.

"You will work there," he had said, "but first you are going to build it."

"We are going to build a leather works?" They had looked at each other and smiled, suspecting that some strange joke was being played on them. But they had come every day. Old men, women, children and the few young men, some of them in tattered scraps of clothing, mixed the concrete and sank the foundations, planted the pillars, laid the bricks, fastening the iron sheets of the roof, made mistakes and fixed them up again. Every day while the sun was up the houses, shacks and huts had been deserted as everyone had come to help. Those that had not been given something to do sat on the ground waiting for the chance to relieve someone. Once a job had been given to anyone it became almost impossible to take it away and give it to another. Everyone had wanted to be part of it. And together, to their continuing amazement, they had built a leather works.

Here there had never been bitterness; only the confusion of not understanding and the patience that had come with eventual acceptance. So they had worked like people who could not believe that what they were doing was real; as if each morning when they came from their homes they expected to see that what they had done so far might have disappeared during the night, leaving the space next to the church vacant again, and life would have returned to what it had been before.

Bhengu knew how the police had encamped around the

leather works, pitching a forest of tents in the churchyard, and had torn it down. The young white men in their riot suits had swarmed over the building, pulling off the roofing, smashing down the brick walls and sawing off the wooden pillars that had supported the roof. When it was over the trucks had come and they had loaded the rubble onto them, until finally all that was left was the concrete slab that had been the floor and the wooden stumps where the pillars had been sawn off. Next to it the little room where the power plant had been housed had been left a skeleton, the roof, doors and windows gone, the plant itself removed, perhaps to provide power for a resort where white kids could spend their summer holidays.

Bhengu had come back once after it was all over. He and Jele had stood in the dusty road, looking at the place where the factory had been, trying to adjust their minds to what they were seeing, perhaps to find some way into the future. It had been a month since the leather works had been broken down, but the people who had built it and worked in it during its short life were gathered around its remains. Now that it was gone the ruin where it had once stood still somehow formed the center of the little community. They came slowly up to Bhengu and Jele, their faces seeking an explanation, and yct embarrassed, perhaps suspecting that they had no right to one. "What are you doing here?" Bhengu had asked.

"We come here every day," one of the old men had said.

"Why?" Bhengu had asked the question as a reflex. He had not really wanted to know.

"There is nothing else. We come here every day."

Bhengu had looked past the gathering to the flat empty cement slab that had been the leather works. "The materials?" he asked. He was as bewildered as they were. "Why did they take the materials?"

"They know if they don't take it we build it again," the old man had said.

Another voice was superimposed on the voice of the old man, searching Bhengu out, drawing him back to the interrogation room, driving back the other world he had once known. "Are you going to tell me, kaffir? I want to know . . ."

The clinics had been the most doubtful project of all. They would take a lot of money to build, far too much to run, and precious little would be coming in. For a long time Bhengu had felt that they were an impossible undertaking. But the money had come and the first of the clinics had started functioning. The other had been ready to start. The building had been completed and the furniture and equipment had arrived. Two nursing sisters were sleeping inside the building and the doctor's baggage was standing in the waiting room . . .

Bhengu had heard the story from the sisters afterward; how they had been wakened in the early-morning hours by the engine of their light delivery van being started. They had come outside into the blinding light from a spot lamp. Squinting past the light, they had seen an unbroken ring of policemen in riot uniform, carbines and rifles at the ready, encircling the complex.

Bhengu remembered Convention and he knew what had happened to it all, to the dozens of small people who had been given the chance for dignity and a decent living, people who had previously never had either. Now it was all gone, the stock and equipment sold, the money going to government-approved charities, dust gathering in patches of old grease where machinery had once stood, the clinic on the hilltop closed, a simple-minded watchman entertaining curious visitors with a little dance and then going back to sleep in the sun. It was all gone and Bhengu would never see it rise up again. The clerks, operators, maintenance men and managers had gone back to being laborers or messengers or delivery boys or cleaners. The people who had stood in long queues at the clinics, waiting their turn for attention, would stay up in the hills in their huts and wait for the pain to pass and perhaps die, waiting. Bhengu knew what had happened to Convention. He knew and with an effort he tried again to shut it out of his thinking.

"Where is Convention? Tell me where is Convention? Come on, kaffir, I want to know what happened to Convention." The security policeman's sadistically playful voice went on, breaking through the chain of Bhengu's memories.

Come over here, Bhengu thought. Just come over here.

"Come on, kaffir, where is Convention now?"

Come over here, so that I can get these cuffs around your neck and I'll show you where Convention is. I'll send you there. Just do me one favor—come over here.

"Where is Convention, kaffir? Are you going to tell me?"

"In God's name, Charl . . ."

"Wait first. He has to tell me what happened to Convention."

"We all know what happened to Convention."

Forget Convention, Bhengu told himself. It belongs in the past. You've got no use for it now. Look to the future. But there is no future. But forget Convention. I can't. But try. I can't forget it. I won't be able to. But forget it. You have to.

"You have to tell me, kaffir. I'm not letting you off."

Forget Van Rooyen. He's a nothing. Don't let him get to you. Forget him and forget Convention.

"You going to have to tell me, kaffir."

I can't forget, Bhengu thought. I can't.

"Come on, kaffir, I'm sure you remember."

Come over here, Bhengu thought. Come over to me. Come and make me tell you.

"I'm waiting, kaffir. I want to know."

Bhengu started to snore, the rhythm slow, long-drawn and deliberate. For the first moment Van Rooyen was silent, his brain taking a little while to adjust to this new development.

Then he shouted and Bhengu could hear the sound of his chair going over, banging against the wall and landing on the floor, its steel framework clattering on the tiled surface. "I'll make you talk, kaffir. For me you'll fuckin' talk." Through eyes that were open only a fraction to make it appear that he was still asleep and snoring, Bhengu watched him come quickly across the room, a wild uncontrollable rage on his face, his hands outstretched as if to strangle Bhengu. But Bhengu never discovered his intention. He waited until the last possible moment, then swung his cuffed hands up hard, the chain wrapping tight around Van Rooyen's wrists. The policeman's hands were driven up past Bhengu's head. He was thrown off balance and fell headlong, his shoulder hard into Bhengu's stomach.

Bhengu's hands swung down now, the cuffs taking Van Rooyen around the back of the neck. He pulled as hard as the muscles in his arms allowed, drawing his elbows in tight next to his sides and clamping Van Rooyen's head against his chest, the chin pressed upward and the head twisted to one side. The policeman struggled wildly. Bhengu could feel the punches he was throwing landing against his rib cage and kidneys. But the security policeman was clamped at a bad angle. The movement of his arms was restricted and there was no leverage in the blows. Bhengu could also feel that some of the punches were off target, striking into the wall on one side and the frame of the bed on the other.

Suddenly Van Rooyen's efforts turned to extricating himself rather than attacking Bhengu. He tried to work his hands in under the other man's forearms to prise open Bhengu's hold. But a shackled man is more vulnerable in a fight than a man with his hands free, and he fights with greater desperation. When he has won an advantage he does not yield it easily.

Bhengu was a big man and he had his elbows locked into his sides. He could feel the way Van Rooyen's head was bent back and the way his neck was twisted. He could also hear the grunting sounds the warrant officer was making and could feel the growing paucity of his efforts.

Fourie came across the room at a run. He dug his fingers under Bhengu's wrists and threw his whole weight backward to lift them. Van Rooyen was barely struggling at all. For a few more seconds Bhengu's grip held.

Finally the weight became too much and his arms gave, Fourie falling backward onto the floor. He was up immediately to help Van Rooyen. The fleshy body of the security policeman remained stationary for a few seconds after Bhengu's grip was released. Then he slid slowly to the floor and knelt there, holding the back of his neck with both hands. He moved his neck slowly from side to side, seeming to test whether it was still functional. "You're going to shit, kaffir," he said.

☒ ☒

Strydom was waiting at the elevator. Bhengu could see him in the light from the fitting on the landing. The ripple-glass window behind him showed that it was night again. He wondered if it had taken so long because they were not able to find a suitable vehicle, or if it was again just a matter of traveling at night so that they would not be seen. Fourie and Van Rooyen on either side of him had his arms over their shoulders. This time he was not able to walk on his own. They were having to support him while he contributed only a few stumbling steps from time to time. Behind him he heard Brown's footsteps, the lieutenant following close on their heels. The blanket they had wrapped around him was secured at the neck by a safety pin, and as he was dragged along he could feel it swinging open and closed in front.

The building was quiet, the other offices in darkness and

the elevator stationary until they summoned it. Once inside, he stood close to Strydom, the hard steel-colored eyes not directed at him, the face unsmiling. You're the one, Bhengu thought. You'll take over from Lategan in time. You might be Engelbrecht's junior now, but you'll be the one. I pity you, you poor bastard.

On either side of him Van Rooyen and Fourie were rigid with discipline and care that they should do the right thing. Both of them knew that they were being watched and would be watched for a long time to come. It was not that they had killed a man. Death was an active partner in their profession. It was that they had disobeyed an order. They could no longer be trusted.

The truck had been brought into the basement. Strydom unlocked the back. Bhengu could see that they had covered the floor area with plastic foam mattresses. Brown got in first, ducking to avoid hitting his head against the roof of the canopy. Then they were turning Bhengu around and passing him backward into the truck, Brown's fingers digging in under his armpits, the hands of the others holding him tight around the legs and waist.

The plastic foam mattresses were soft, a relief after having been made to walk. At the back of the truck he could hear Strydom's voice as he gave orders to the other policemen. He heard the doors of the cab open and close. Fourie came crawling into the back with them, pulling closed the doors after him. The starter motor whined briefly and the engine started. Bhengu felt his body jerk as the truck pulled away, followed by the slight unsteadiness of being inside a moving vehicle. Through the small window in the side he could see the passing streetlights.

✠ ✠

"You're going to shit, kaffir." The desperate drive for power that Bhengu had resisted was reflected in the hatred in Van Rooyen's narrow eyes. Bhengu knew the culture that had spawned Van Rooyen and he knew that the security policeman's desperation had probably grown out of a childhood in which every need to assert himself had been trampled upon. It was a state of mind that knew no reason. "Help me here, Len. I want him over on his stomach."

"What for?" Fourie was standing next to him.

"Just help me. I'm going to let him shit."

"You've got to fuckin' leave him alone now. We've had enough shit already. We're supposed to just guard him."

"I'm going to let the bastard shit. Do you think I'm going to let him get away with this?" Bhengu could see fear in Van Rooyen's eyes. It was a fear that Bhengu might successfully resist him. The security policeman was not able to compromise with his need to dominate his prisoner. Any resistance by Bhengu threatened the shaky basis upon which his personality functioned. "You saw what he did. Do you think I'm going to let him get away with that?"

"Leave him alone, man. In God's name leave him alone."

"I'll see him right by myself." Van Rooyen turned and went quickly out of the interrogation room, leaving the door open.

Fourie looked worriedly at Bhengu. "Was it necessary to do that?"

"No, but I enjoyed it," Bhengu said. He was afraid of what Van Rooyen was going to do, but he was not going to show his fear to either of them.

"That Van Rooyen's a mad bastard," Fourie said. "I'm just telling you that you shouldn't have done that."

"You're here, aren't you?" Bhengu said.

Fourie shook his head, took up his book and went back to the table. He sat down and concentrated his attention on the page with the air of a man who is determined to have nothing further to do with the night's activities. Van Rooyen came back carrying a second pair of handcuffs. He closed the door behind him and locked it. Bhengu saw Fourie look up and he saw a moment of alarm in his eyes. "Leave him alone, please."

"You're off your head if you think I'm going to let him get away with this."

Bhengu watched Van Rooyen as he approached the bed, unlocking one side of the cuffs and dropping the key into a pocket. He moved slowly, apparently relaxed, his arms hanging at his sides, the cuffs dangling from his left hand. Without hurrying he covered the distance from the door to the head of the bed, keeping just out of Bhengu's reach. He crossed the room again going to the foot of the bed, then, without pausing, back to its head, all the time taking it slowly, forcing Bhengu to follow his movements, making him wait for the moment of attack. Van Rooyen was wearing the grin he employed in facing every difficult situation. It was no more than a grimace now, made more ridiculous by a spasmodic twitching of his cheek just below the left eye. But whatever his inner uncertainties, Van Rooyen was the one who had his hands and feet free. And he was the one who was armed with the second pair of cuffs. Bhengu knew that a pair of cuffs, swung as a club, could be a deadly weapon under such circumstances. It was he who was bound, his feet immovable and his hands shackled together, waiting helplessly for the policeman to strike. And it was Van Rooyen who could decide when to stay clear and at which moment to attack.

When Van Rooyen did attack it was with a quickness surprising in a hefty man and Bhengu was too late to stop the blow. It was a low-swinging left-hand punch, coming up from the area of Bhengu's knees and landing in his testicles. With his feet anchored at the foot of the bed, his body jerked upward in reaction to the pain. Almost immediately Van Rooyen had the second pair of cuffs locked shut around the short connecting link of the cuffs Bhengu was wearing and had thrown himself onto the floor at the head of the bed, using his full weight to jerk Bhengu's arms upward over his head. The second cuffs clicked closed around the steel leg of the bed and Bhengu's hands were fastened above his head while his body was still numb with the pain in his testicles. Van Rooyen got to his feet. The look of pleasure and the confidence of regained power in his face were unmistakable. "Now, kaffir, we'll see who's the boss. You're going to tell me who's the boss." He glanced over his shoulder at Fourie, who was still seated at the table. "Help me get him onto his stomach."

"You're mad, man."

"If you don't help me I'll do it alone."

"You're going to get us both in the shit, Charl. Do you realize that?"

To Van Rooyen the protestations of a lightweight like Fourie were not worthy of an answer. His attention was with his prisoner. Bhengu's feet were shackled side by side to the rigid steel bar attached to the foot of the bed. To turn him onto his stomach both feet would have to be released, he would have to be rolled over and then both feet secured in the opposite anklets.

Van Rooyen released Bhengu's feet one by one. He pretended to be straightening up and turning away from the bed, when he made a grab for Bhengu's testicles. This time Bhengu was ready for him. His left knee, coming up hard, took the security policeman in the chest and sent him staggering backward. Fourie was on his feet again. "Leave him alone now," he shouted. He started toward the bed. "I'm going to take the cuffs off his hands. This is just going to bring us in the shit."

Van Rooyen came forward, massaging his chest with both hands. "Leave him," he said. He intercepted Fourie before he reached Bhengu, pressed his hand palm-forward against the smaller man's chest and shoved him hard, throwing his shoulder into the movement. Fourie was sent stumbling backward to come to a stop against the edge of the table.

"In God's name, Charl, are you off your head?"

"He's going to have to learn. I'm going to teach him something." Van Rooyen advanced slowly on Bhengu, both hands raised in readiness for the prisoner's legs, which were free now. He did not need to look around at Fourie. He knew his man. The little warrant officer remained against the edge of the table where Van Rooyen's shove had sent him. "Now, kaffir, we are going to see who's boss in this country."

"You're off your head," Fourie complained. Neither Bhengu nor Van Rooyen heard him.

Lifting the knee nearest to Van Rooyen to protect his genitals, Bhengu awaited his approach. The security policeman moved in even more slowly than before, circling up toward the head of the bed. Come on, you bastard, Bhengu thought. I'll be able to reach you anywhere. Just come close enough.

Van Rooyen feinted forward, pulling away just in time to avoid Bhengu's foot, which shot out to meet him, then moved slowly around toward the bottom of the bed, staying out of range of Bhengu's legs. He feinted again, and again pulled back just in time. All the time his face wore the same little grin, only the corners of his mouth turned up, the purpose of which was to show Bhengu how inevitable it all was, that it could not be avoided. He circled up toward the head of the bed again. Then he feinted a third time, darting in closer than before, barely an arm's length from the other man. Bhengu's kick was a reflex and one that Van Rooyen had been expecting. He ducked low to avoid the kick and as Bhengu's leg reached full stretch he threw himself forward, locking his arms in a clamp around the black man's left thigh.

Bhengu lifted his free leg as high as he could and brought his heel down hard on Van Rooyen's head, then again and again, the blows landing on the policeman's shoulders and upper arms. Bhengu was straining to lift his leg high with each kick so that he could drive it home hard. There was a tingling in the leg Van Rooyen was holding as his grip cut off the flow of blood. The constriction around Bhengu's thigh was growing tighter as Van Rooyen locked his arms together, each hand clamped tightly onto the opposite arm. He had managed to work his head around to Bhengu's side where the kicks no longer reached it, most of them striking only glancing blows against his shoulder and upper arm. "Come help me, Len. In God's name come help me," Bhengu heard him shout.

Good. So the bastard is having a hard time of it. Let me just land one kick in the right place . . . Let me just land one.

But Bhengu was tiring. The strain of lifting his leg so high with each kick was wearing down his resistance. The three weeks in solitary were also counting against him. "Come on, Len. What's wrong with you?" Fourie had taken a few steps toward them, but had stopped. Even through the effort he was making Bhengu could see the indecision on his face. There was an element in his consciousness that said that what Van Rooyen was doing was wrong, but all of his training and experience had conditioned him to help a fellow policeman against a prisoner always and under any circumstances. There could never be any exceptions to that rule. "Help me, Len. What the hell's wrong with you? Help me." Van Rooyen's voice held a demand in it. He was asking no more than he would willingly give.

The conditioning won. Fourie ran the last few steps and fell onto Bhengu's free leg. The effort he had been making, the combined weight of the two men and the lack of exercise during the last three weeks were together too much for Bhengu. He heard Van Rooyen say, "Now, kaffir, we'll see something."

Although he struggled and resisted them, the weight was too great and he could not maintain the effort. His legs became leaden with weariness until slowly they were pressed flat and pinned down on the bed. Then, with his hands above his head, he was totally without any way to defend himself. He felt Van Rooyen's fingers wrapping themselves around his testicles. "Roll over, kaffir, or there'll be nothing left of them."

✠ ✠

Turning his head, Bhengu could see into the cab. Van Rooyen was still there, but Strydom had left the truck. The Special Branch captain's voice was coming from somewhere at the back. Brown and Fourie had also got out and the door at the back was open. Through the open door he could see dark figures moving. "We've got Sam Bhengu here," he heard Strydom say. "We're taking him to Pretoria."

"Who do you say you've got?"

"Sam Bhengu, the agitator. We're taking him to the hospital in Pretoria Central."

The figure of a policeman, his cap outlined against the night sky, appeared in the door. The beam of an electric flashlight fell on Bhengu's face, the unexpected brightness causing him to shut his eyes. "Such a kaffir, hey. Yes, lock up the agitator."

"I also want to see." It was a new voice. The flashlight changed hands and the beam again fell on Bhengu's face. "He looks reasonably fucked up," the new voice said. "You've had him nicely in hand, it looks like."

"No," Strydom said. "I think he's bullshitting us."

"He looks to me reasonably fucked up, I must say."

"Well, it's not something we did. There must be something wrong with him. Where do we get gas? We must make tracks. I want to be in Pretoria for breakfast."

"Bring the van around the back. Wait. Here's Herman. Herman, come here. Have you heard of Sam Bhengu? Come have a look here."

Bhengu turned his face to the front before the flashlight beam found him again. He saw the light fall around him on the back of the cab. "No. He doesn't want to look at us now."

"Who is Sam Bhengu, now, actually?"

"He's an agitator, man. You must know him." It was the man who had invited Herman who answered.

"No what. None of my friends are agitators." The remark was very funny and all the policemen at the back of the truck laughed. Herman was not a man to disappoint an audience if he could help it, so he tried again. "I must say an agitator looks just the same as any other kaffir," he said. The second remark was even funnier than the first and the laughter was still more prolonged.

A voice said, "Yes, old Herman, you're also a different character."

♂ ♂

Bhengu had heard of the sandbag. Van Rooyen was crouching next to his face and holding it up for him to see. It was small, a little bigger than a man's fist and filled with coarse white sand. Van Rooyen had taken a little out of the bag and let Bhengu watch it run through his fingers. The neck of the bag was narrower and was empty of sand to provide a grip for its manipulator. With the side of his face pressed down against the plastic foam mattress Bhengu heard Van Rooyen say, "You're going to sing for me now. I want to hear you sing."

"We may not." Fourie's voice was afraid. He stayed at the table, well out of Van Rooyen's way.

"I'll give you ten seconds to start singing."

"We may not interrogate him," Fourie said. "We may not. Captain Strydom said we must watch him, nothing else."

"Rubbish, man. I'm going to make him talk. And if he talks they aren't going to worry about anything. I'll tell them you didn't want to and I'll get all the credit."

"I'm against it," Fourie said.

"Your ten seconds are finished, kaffir. Are you going to talk?"

I can handle anything you can dish out, Bhengu thought. Whatever you do there'll be some way I can handle it.

He saw in the corner of his field of vision Van Rooyen raising his arm to shoulder level. The security policeman remained, poised, apparently aiming the blow, possibly just extending the moment for his victim's benefit. Bhengu waited for it. He could feel the muscles in his neck and shoulders draw tight to take the weight when it struck. Would it be better to relax, Bhengu wondered. Or to have your muscles tensed? No. There was no good way. You just have to take it, he told himself. Take it and try to give the bastard no satisfaction.

The first blow fell just below the base of Bhengu's skull, a few centimeters lower than Van Rooyen had intended. It was a jarring shock that seemed to travel the length of his spinal column, shuddering into his brain. It's all right, Bhengu thought. I can handle this. I'll be all right. Brown said he'd be away for two hours. I'll be able to hold out till then.

He could just see the wall clock above the door. It was almost eleven. That meant that Brown should be back in an hour. It would be all right. An hour of this would be no problem. The bastard would gain nothing.

Van Rooyen paused before the second blow, again allowing Bhengu time to consider. The pause told Bhengu that that was the first one. Consider what ten such will do to you. Consider what a hundred will do. A thousand.

When the second blow fell its effect was identical to the first, a jarring numbing sensation that traveled the length of his nervous system. It was unlike the methods of torture where cigarette ends burned holes in the tender parts of your skin or punches were thrown at your kidneys. To Bhengu it seemed that the assault was directed at every part of him. The blows had not yet become painful but each one vibrated through the length of his body, carried on a stunned and tingling nervous system. There was only a moment's hesitation now when the next one fell, then the next and the next and the next . . .

I can do it. He'll have to come up with something more than this. I can do it. And when I get out of here I'll get across the border and . . . I've just got to get through this. And I will. I know I can do it.

Unconsciously he was pressing his head hard down on the plastic foam mattress, as if to get as far from the sandbag as possible. His head was turned slightly to the side and he could see Fourie out of one eye. The warrant officer was standing in front of the table, his fists held tightly at his sides. Every time a blow fell his image blurred, like a motion-picture projector going momentarily out of focus.

"You'll leave bruises." Fourie's voice had risen a few notes higher.

"You've just got to know how. You mustn't hit too hard. Just let the bag fall under its own weight. And you've got to hit the right place. You can scramble a man's brains without leaving a single mark."

"How do you know? You'll leave bruises."

"I've done it before. Gerrit Strydom showed me. There won't be a single bruise—that I promise you."

"Captain Strydom did not mean you must use it now. We're not allowed to." There was panic in Fourie's voice. Between the blows Bhengu saw him move a step closer.

"You stop there." Van Rooyen's tone of voice held a warning in it that stopped the other policeman immediately. "If you won't help me, then just stay out of my way."

"You're still going to bring us in the shit."

"You wait and see. This kaffir's going to talk. You just wait and see."

"Captain Strydom said we may not . . ."

"You just shut up now, Len. I'm going to let this kaffir sing for me."

"I just hope there aren't any bruises."

"There won't be."

The blows fell in steady repetition, one following the other, each followed by a pause of perhaps a second, giving Bhengu a moment in which to contemplate the next one, a moment to steel himself against it, resist it so that the impact would be more severe. There would be a moment before each blow fell in which Bhengu would have time to hope that it had been the last one, that Van Rooyen had seen the foolishness of what he was doing and had relented.

Bhengu had been through many forms of interrogation in the twenty years since he had first joined Congress, and one particular style had always been the worst. There was nothing worse than having them working on you but asking no questions, inflicting the pain but giving you no way by which to relieve it. With no questions asked you could give no answers. You could only endure. You were not even granted the pleasure of resisting something. There was only the pain. And Bhengu knew that Van Rooyen understood this. The security policeman guided the blows onto the target at the base of Bhengu's skull one after the other, seemingly untiringly, and he asked no questions. The time for questions would come.

I can do it. If this is all there is, then I can do it. Brown will be back and he'll stop them. In the meantime I can hold out. I've managed with worse than this. I can handle it.

"Lieutenant Brown is going to come back anytime. You're going to see your ass."

"Malcolm Brown has got nothing to say." The act of brutality was reinforcing the illusion of power in his mind. And the illusion was adding to his confidence. With Bhengu in his power and suffering, Van Rooyen was afraid of no one. "I'm in charge now," he told Fourie.

"Oh yes?" The question was a fearful hesitant challenge.

"Yes. Malcolm Brown has got nothing to say."

"We'll see when he comes back."

"I'm in charge now. I know it and this kaffir knows it. Hey, kaffir? You know who's in charge here."

Slowly the sense of vibration grew, working up into his brain and down along his spine, eventually reaching every nerve end of his body. A heavy pain was spreading, slow-moving, first filling his head in the back of his skull and seeping gradually upward and forward, each blow helping it on, moving it a little further. Bhengu tried to look at the wall clock. He thought the hands read after twelve, in which case Brown should be back, but the hands of the clock were indistinct and he could not be sure. Fourie was still standing in front of the table, but now his outline was blurred, not only with each blow, but also during the periods between. A few times Van Rooyen crouched next to him bringing his face close, but it was no more than the undefined pink-white shape of a man's head. Bhengu was not sorry that he could not see the other man's grin of triumph. Something he could see was the gleam of sweat along the smooth edges of the policeman's face, a silver outline in the light from the fluorescent fitting.

As the blows fell Bhengu could feel his wrists and ankles where they jerked against the cuffs holding them. With each convulsive movement of his body they strained at the restraining steel, ineffectually trying to break free. He could feel the skin of one of his ankles tear, the tissue rumpling like paper. Compared to the pain in his head and now flooding his body, it was only an annoyance, a minor irritation.

As long as you can keep it up I can hold out. I'll stay with it all night if I have to. I can manage. Don't worry about me.

I've been through worse than this, much worse. I can handle it.

Van Rooyen was working hard, swinging the bag with a steady rhythm, his head moving back and forth with it. In the corner of his field of vision Bhengu could see the policeman's head bobbing with each blow, an occasional spray of sweat gleaming brightly in the white light in the room. Bhengu was fascinated by the spray of sweat and he found himself watching for it. He was retreating from the pain into a private place where he could do nothing but wait for the flash of sweat as it detached itself from the policeman's face. Was it with every sixth blow that it happened? Or was it every seventh? He would count them. It was important to know. Then suddenly Bhengu was not sure whether it was the sweat he saw or something within his own head.

The mumbling started when the pain was filling the whole case of his skull so that there was no room for thoughts, only the thoughts that the pain itself forced on him. It was low in tone, the words indistinct, starting hesitantly in small bursts, but the bursts growing in frequency until the mumbling was not wavering for a moment, running on like a long murmured prayer. Bhengu listened to his own voice carefully, trying to catch the words.

I agree, Mama. I agree with what you're saying. It's fine. It's really fine, Mama. Yes, I agree. It's fine with me.

If only the mumbling would stop it would be much better. I could stand it if I just did not have the mumbling. I know I could. I've been through worse than this. I'm sure I could stand it. It's only the mumbling that's a problem.

"You're off your head. Do you know that?" Bhengu heard Fourie's voice above the mumbling.

"This kaffir is going to know who is the boss in this country."

"You're fuckin' mad. Lieutenant Brown should have been back long ago. He can come in here anytime."

"I say this kaffir is going to know who he must call boss."

"Do you know what they'll do to you for disobeying orders?"

"Keep quiet, you. We'll see what they say when this canary sings for me."

"Lieutenant Brown can walk in here anytime."

"Malcolm Brown has got nothing to say." Van Rooyen brought his face close to Bhengu's. His voice was a seductive whisper. "We know who's in charge here, hey, boy? You and me—we know who's in charge here."

The mumbling was filling the whole room. Bhengu wondered if they could hear it or if it was something only he could hear. The pain was everywhere now, not just in his head. The pain and the mumbling were all one, running into each other. The pain had become the mumbling and the mumbling had become the pain.

"Listen how he talks to himself." Van Rooyen's voice reached him through the pain. "Soon he'll be ready to talk to me."

They could hear it. That was a pity. He would rather have kept it to himself. It was like being naked in the presence of the clothed policemen. He did not want them to hear the mumbling. He wished there was some way he could stop it, but his voice was operating independently of his will, the sound running on freely.

"Listen how nicely he talks."

"You're off your head. You're breaking him. Colonel Lategan doesn't want that."

"Listen how he talks. Soon he'll be singing a song to me."

You're wrong there, friend. You're terribly wrong there. I can make it. Your friend is wrong too. You aren't going to break me. I can handle this. Even with the mumbling I can handle it. It's not me. It's my voice. Someone else is using my voice. If only I could find a way to stop them . . . But I can handle it. With or without the mumbling I can handle it. I wish it would stop, though. I can manage except for the mumbling. Only that makes it impossible. No. I can do it anyway.

There was no hesitation in the pattern of the blows. They still followed each other in steady repetition, the timing between them exactly the same, working their inevitable destruction on the cells of his brain. And the mumbling ran through it all as persistent as the blows themselves.

"Now you're going to sing for me, boy." Van Rooyen's voice was far away, heard distantly against the thunder of his own voice. "Now you're going to sing. I want to know what you were doing in Johannesburg and I want to know . . ."

I can hold out. I can last as long as I have to. I know I can. Soon Brown must come back. I can hold out until he does. I know what to expect now . . .

Bhengu did not expect the scream. It was a single long-drawn hoarse note. It was worse than the mumbling, very much worse.

Something gave inside his head, stopping the pain immediately. It was then that Sam Bhengu knew he was dying.

☒ ☒

The hum of the engine was soothing, lulling his senses and easing the few remaining tensions. Brown had moved to the front and Fourie and Van Rooyen were in the back with him. Before Brown had gone he had put a pillow under Bhengu's head so that now he could see out of the small window in the door, watching the taillights of the cars traveling in the other direction whip past and drop away quickly into the distance, two small red spots in the darkness. The close-set headlights of a small car had remained some distance behind them, occasionally drawing a little closer and then dropping back again.

Van Rooyen was sprawled backward, his head and shoulders against the side of the truck. In the momentary flashes of light from outside Bhengu could see the sullen discontent and growing apprehension on the broad fleshy face. Opposite him Fourie was sitting up, hunched slightly forward, his hands folded tightly together in his lap, his face preoccupied as it always was now.

It was all right. Before it had been very bad, but now it was all right. He would be able to do it now. All he wanted to do was lie quietly until the time came. He knew that he was ready. It had taken a time to get there, but he had done it and he was ready.

He tried consciously to turn his mind back to the people he had known, the names and faces who had filled his life, but some part of his consciousness withheld its cooperation, holding him in the back of the truck with the even hum of the engine and the slight plastic and body smell of the mattresses. The part that held him back was telling him that it was over now. Only one thing remained and he was able to do it.

Forget it all, Bhengu told himself. Everything is going to be fine. There are no problems.

The tips of his fingers, resting on the mattress on either side of him, picked up the vibrations of the truck. In the light from the car behind he could see the quick involuntary muscular twitch in Van Rooyen's fear-filled face. His ears picked up a brief crackle of static from the VHF receiver in the cab. He knew he could do it now. It was going to be all right.